RECKLESS HARMONY

HARMONY FALLS
BOOK SIX

ELIZABETH KELLY

EK PUBLISHING INC.

RECKLESS HARMONY

Is it still sleeping with the enemy if you're falling in love?

Local plumber and animal rescuer Rayna Abrams has a problem.

A rich, arrogant, annoyingly sexy problem. A problem who happens to be her millionaire neighbour, Isaac Stark. He wants her property.

And will stop at nothing to get it.

But after a life of uncertainty, the only thing more important to Rayna than the animals is her home. She'll be damned if she sells it and lets Stark tear it down to build his McMansion.

It's a war Rayna fully intends to win until she sees a side of Stark that she never suspected existed. A side that threatens her resolve.

Isaac Stark wants Rayna's property, and what he wants, he gets. Always.

But when his usual tactics don't work, he pivots to a new battle plan... play nice.

The new plan works perfectly until he develops pesky feelings for the stubborn, kind-hearted, sexy Rayna.

Now, they're falling into bed together every night and giving a whole new meaning to 'keep your enemies closer.'

Can they learn to trust each other *and* their growing feelings, or are they destined to remain divided?

CHAPTER 1

If Rayna had known her Friday night would end with her sworn enemy's face planted firmly between her tits, she would have worn a bra.

It had started normally enough. She'd worked later than usual unclogging a toilet because of a hysterical client and a boss who couldn't say no, then spent nearly two hours coaxing a stray dog out from under a parked car in the Walmart parking lot with chicken nuggets and a prayer. Once the dog had been assessed and safely dropped off at a foster home, she'd delivered food and supplies to three other fosters before finally parking in her driveway.

By that time, it was almost nine, and despite her growling stomach, she didn't have the energy to cook anything. She'd stripped off her work clothes, had a hot shower, pulled on a pair of yoga pants and her rattiest, most comfortable sweatshirt and grabbed the box of Cheerios. She'd stuffed a few handfuls of cereal into her mouth while checking the Little Whiskers Rescue emails. There'd been the usual number of emails asking for help with animals that she had neither the resources nor the budget to help. There were also emails from both the cat and dog team foster coordinators, as well as one from Zuri, her events coordinator volunteer, about the upcoming bachelor/bachelorette auction fundraiser.

Rayna heavily regretted agreeing to the fundraiser, especially now that the date was getting closer and they were still looking for an MC and at least five more bachelorettes, but it was too late to back out now.

She hesitated before closing the email, shoving a final handful of Cheerios into her mouth, and closing the lid of her ancient laptop. It made a decidedly disturbing whirring noise that grew louder and louder, and she crunched down the cereal, waiting for the laptop to decide if it would continue gasping for existence or blow up and kill them all.

The whirring stopped, and she gave the laptop a thumbs up. "Decided to fight another day, huh?"

She stood with a soft grunt and muttered a curse when she nearly tripped over her ancient beagle, Bea, who was sound asleep on the floor beside her feet. There was no point in scolding the dog. Bea was mostly blind and nearly completely deaf, and she was living out her golden years in a state of permanent bliss, not affected in the least by the many foster cats and dogs that came in and out of her life like a revolving door.

Rayna reached down and patted Bea's side. The dog's tail thumped happily on the floor before she lifted it, and a long, low, *braaaap* filled the air. It was followed immediately by a smell that Rayna's bestie Emma referred to as Bea's death smell.

As Rayna escaped the kitchen, waving her hand in front of her face in a vain attempt to dispel the noxious fumes, she had to admit that Emma wasn't exaggerating. Bea's farts did usually smell like she was dying.

Happily, despite the blindness, deafness, and her advanced age, Bea was surprisingly healthy. At this point, if

Rayna didn't do something about her stress level, the beagle would probably outlive her.

Shrill barking erupted from the living room, and she sighed, veered away from the stairs, and headed toward the living room. She clapped her hands sharply as she entered. "Ladies, what is the issue in here?"

The two tiny black chihuahuas, completely identical and impossible to tell apart unless you lifted one and checked for the white blotch on her belly, ignored her as they continued to bark at the bookshelf in the corner of the room.

"Ghosts?" she said as she joined them.

Their tiny bodies quivering and their oversized ears on high alert, they let out another volley of high-pitched barks that made Rayna's fillings vibrate.

"Coco! Lola! Enough, please!"

She scooped up a dog in each hand. At three pounds each, they weren't even as heavy as the hand weights Rayna had in her home gym. Still, she hadn't done a workout Wednesday or Thursday night, and it wouldn't hurt to get some exercise in. Holding the dogs securely, she did a few bicep curls as she examined the bookshelf.

"Freddie, get out of there, buddy," she said when she caught a glimpse of black and white fur.

Still pumping the chihuahuas like they were dumbbells, she made a psp, psp, psp sound. There was an answering hiss from the bookcase before the long-haired tuxedo cat emerged from behind a battered copy of The Call of the Wild and a dust-covered vase with equally dusty fake flowers in it.

She sighed and made a mental note to dust tomorrow as the cat jumped gracefully to the ground and strutted toward her. The chihuahuas growled in unison and she shushed them as she lifted them up and down toward her shoulders.

"Freddie's been here a lot longer than you have, and he's been known to cut a bitch," she told the dogs as Freddie sniffed at her yoga pants before, tail up and flicking back and forth delicately, he left the living room.

"I told you when you arrived last week to steer clear of him, and I meant it," she said as she carried them upstairs, still lifting them rhythmically. "He's lived a hard life and will mess you up if you give him attitude."

She set the dogs down in the hallway, smiling a little when, their tails wagging eagerly, they followed her into her bedroom and then into the attached bathroom.

"He doesn't want to be a jerk," she said as, her stomach still growling, she reached for her toothbrush, "but he also likes his personal space. If you want to make a new friend, stick with Bea or even Molly. She's desperate for some attention. I don't know if it's pregnancy hormones or what, but that cat is..."

She trailed off, staring at herself in the bathroom mirror. She hadn't seen Molly once since she'd gotten home forty minutes ago, and that was weird. Really weird. Usually, she couldn't keep the friendly calico cat from climbing in her lap or twining around her legs the minute she walked through the door.

She stared at the two chihuahuas, who stared back. "Where's Molly?"

Their tails wagged, and Lola, or maybe it was Coco, sat down and gave her a hopeful look.

"I don't have a c-o-o-k-i-e for you," she said. "I need to find Molly."

She left the bathroom and called for the cat, making every cat enticing sound in her arsenal as she walked the upstairs hallway and checked every room before going downstairs. Coco and Lola followed her dutifully, more out of the hope they'd get a cookie than any sense of loyalty, as she checked each room on the main floor.

Her stomach starting to churn, she rechecked the laundry

room, a favourite place for both Molly and Freddie. Freddie was in there, scratching around in the litter box, and he stopped what he was doing to give her a haughty glare.

"Freddie, baby, where's Molly?" she asked. "Where is she?"

Freddie jumped out of the litter box and leaped onto the washing machine before taking another leap onto the wall shelf that held the laundry supplies. He curled up between the soap and the basket of odd socks before cocking one leg and licking his butt hole.

"Shit," she said as she left the laundry room and headed back into the kitchen. She studied the room as Coco and Lola joined Bea, who had moved to a dog bed in the corner of the room. They climbed in beside her, curling up between her front legs as she snored loudly.

Her heart thumping, she walked out of the kitchen and down the hallway. "What the hell?" she said as she stared at the basement door. She always kept the basement door closed but it was currently open. Just a bit, but big enough for even a very pregnant cat to get through.

She ran to the door and flicked the light switch. She walked down the wooden steps, squinting in the dim light from the bulbs hanging from the ceiling. The basement was unfinished, and while she had plans to finish it someday, those plans hinged on both money and time - neither of which she currently had very much of.

"Molly, here, kitty, kitty," she said. The basement was even colder than usual, and her heart clanked to a stop when she heard the tell-tale whistle of wind.

"No, no, no," she repeated as she jogged across the basement in the direction of the whistling. The basement had three small windows, none big enough to egress. She stared in mute horror at the middle one and the broken glass that littered the floor below it. A large rock sat among the shattered glass, and she muttered a curse. Who the hell would try to break in through the basement window? And why? It's not like she had anything of value in the place.

She froze as she stared at the hole in the glass. The window might have been too small for a human to crawl through, but it was more than big enough for a cat determined to get outside. And Molly was forever making a break for the outdoors. She'd spent at least a year outside before being taken in by the rescue, and despite being heavily pregnant and the cold weather, she was convinced her destiny waited for her beyond the house.

Using her phone's flashlight, Rayna studied the glass, whispering, "Oh shit" under her breath when she saw the bit of orange fur clinging to the broken glass. Molly had escaped.

CHAPTER 2

R ayna ran back upstairs, dropping her phone on the
counter and snatching the high-powered flashlight
from under the sink. She shoved her feet into her boots and
grabbed the plastic container of cat treats before clattering
out the back door. The basement window faced the backyard, and the brief hope that Molly might be in the fenced-in
yard died as she swept the yard with her flashlight.

"Molly," she called, "here, kitty, kitty. Come to Mama."
She shook the container hard, then waited, holding her
breath and trying to hear over the pounding beat of her heart
for Molly's distinctive meow.

She shook the container again and again as she walked
the yard, searching every inch of it, her flashlight piercing
the darkness. Her nose and ears started to burn from the
cold, and her teeth chattered, but she kept grimly calling.
Beyond the yard was nothing but woods filled with animals
more than happy to devour a cat-sized snack.

"Molly," she called, making her voice the high-pitched
wheedle that cats loved. "Here, kitty, kitty."

She listened intently, relief washing over her when she heard Molly's meow. "Molly! Here, kitty, kitty!"

Molly meowed and then kept meowing as the moonlight made the snow gleam. Shivering wildly, Rayna followed the sound across the yard to the fence. She could hear Molly meowing, but she couldn't see her anywhere, and she swept the flashlight along the top of the fence, wondering if the cat wasn't balancing on it like a furry tightrope walker.

It was empty and feeling panicky, she called for Molly again. Molly responded with a loud meow that sounded like it was right above Rayna's head. Her stomach landed in the snow at her feet as she shone the flashlight at the big elm tree in the yard beside hers.

"Oh, Molly," she said.

The cat meowed at her from her perch on one of the branches. Rayna shook the container again, "C'mon, sweetheart, come down from the tree."

Molly stood and stretched in the circle of light, her pregnant belly lightly swaying as she walked back and forth on the narrow branch before making a plaintive meow.

"Oh honey, come on, please," Rayna said as her teeth chattered loudly. "You got up there. You can get down. Please?"

Molly meowed again before settling on her haunches on the branch and staring directly at Rayna. She could practically see the 'help me, Mama' look in the cat's green eyes.

"Well, fuck," she muttered before glancing at the house beside hers. A few months ago, she would have just walked into the backyard without any hesitation, but that was when Josie Walters owned it.

Now, the house and the land were owned by resident millionaire, cocky asshole, and her sworn enemy, Isaac Stark. A man with more money than God and an attitude to match. He'd bought Josie's property, along with Sean Barr's property to the left of Josie's. Now, he wanted Rayna's property, as well.

He'd spent the last few months offering increasingly higher offers through his real estate agent until he'd finally shown up in person on her doorstep. They'd hated each other on sight, and after calling him out on his less-than-subtle threats to make noise complaints and/or get her rescue shut down, he'd given her his final offer for the property. Although way above the value of her property, it still hadn't been enough to sway her. She'd told him to get the hell out of her house and she hadn't seen or spoken to him since. Thank God.

Oh, please. You wish you could see him. He's hot as fucking hell, and you know it.

Fine. Maybe she could appreciate how aesthetically pleasing he was to the eye, but he was also an arrogant asshole who thought Rayna would say how high just because he said jump. She'd garnered an immense amount of satisfaction from refusing to give him what he wanted like everyone else in his life apparently did.

She sighed and studied the cat in the tree. Not selling him her house was a stupid decision. With the money he'd offered, she could get a better house and have plenty of money left over to not just keep her animal rescue going but also improve it.

Despite that, she couldn't sell the house. She loved her home, and after growing up in poverty and moving from rental to rental every few months, her ability to not only stay above the poverty line but also do something as incredible as buy a house on her own meant something to her. This *house* meant something to her, and despite its flaws and how many things needed to be fixed - and there were *so many things* - she couldn't see herself living anywhere else.

Molly meowed again, and Rayna stopped hesitating. She

shut the flashlight off, tossed it and the cat treats over the fence and said, "I'm coming, sweetheart."

Like everything else on her property, the fence had seen better days, and she hoped like hell the wooden planks wouldn't simply disintegrate as she grabbed the top and boosted herself up. The fence creaked alarmingly but held her weight as she hauled herself over the top of it and dropped with a gentle thud to the other side.

She picked up the flashlight and treats and brushed off the snow from her yoga pants as she stared furtively at the house. The blinds were all drawn, but muted light shone out from behind them. The asshole was home, and she had no doubt he'd call the cops on her for trespassing if he caught her in his backyard.

She stood at the tree's base, softly calling Molly's name and shaking the treat container. The cat meowed and paced on the branch but made no effort to climb down.

"Fuck," she muttered. With another look at the house, she shut off the flashlight and set it and the treat container beside the tree. She snagged one of the hair bands from her wrist and used it to tuck her hair into a messy bun on top of her head as she studied the tree. The moonlight reflecting off the snow made it plenty bright enough to climb the tree, and she grabbed one of the lower branches and, grunting loudly, boosted herself up. She climbed carefully from branch to branch, the cold bark turning her fingers numb almost immediately.

"You are the worst, Molly," she called as she inched closer to the calico. "I can't believe you'd even put your unborn children in danger like this. You have a warm bed, a clean litter box, food, and friends at my house, and you pull this happy horseshit? You're lucky you're cute."

Molly meowed at her, and Rayna studied the branches above her. They were getting thinner, and she needed to be very careful to choose ones that would hold her weight. She glanced down, her stomach churning at how high up she was. She wasn't afraid of heights, but she didn't fancy falling from a tree and breaking her leg... or her neck.

She held her hand out toward Molly. "C'mon, sweetheart. Jump down a couple of branches. What do you say? Just a couple, sweetie."

Molly stood, and Rayna watched in disbelief as she jumped to the branch above her.

"What the fuck, Molly?" she snapped. "Are you being a dick on purpose tonight?"

Molly meowed plaintively, rubbing her face against the tree trunk before peering at Rayna.

With another sigh, Rayna boosted herself up onto the branch above her. It was thinner than she liked, but it felt sturdy enough and -

The crack of the branch as it broke and the immediate sickening drop as she plunged toward the ground was enough to bring a truly epic horror movie girl scream from her throat.

She was going to die. She was going to die in Isaac fucking Stark's backyard, and her only solace in that knowledge was that he'd never get all of her splattered brains hosed out of his goddamn backyard.

She let out a strangled yelp as a fire burned across her back, and she was pulled up short, her sweatshirt snagging around her neck and rucking halfway up her stomach.

She dangled and swayed, her feet nowhere close to the ground, and for some reason, she could feel the bite of a cold, hard branch against her back. Craning her neck, she stared at the thick branch that had somehow slid under the bottom of her sweatshirt as she fell and now poked out from the neckline of her sweater and pressed against the back of her head. She'd been hooked as neatly as a fish.

"Holy fuck," she breathed as she twisted and swayed midair. "It's a friggin' miracle."

It really *was* a miracle, and while she was incredibly grateful not to have her skull smashed open like an overripe pumpkin in her enemy's backyard, she was still in a bit of a pickle.

Actually - she stared down at the ground below her swaying feet - it was a significant pickle.

She was still at least eight feet from the ground, maybe more, and her back hurt like a motherfucker and based on the liquid dripping down her back, it was entirely possible the branch had scraped off a layer of skin right to the damn bone.

Also, she had no fucking idea how she would get down. If she lifted her arms and wriggled, she could probably slither right out of her sweatshirt, but did she want to fall eight feet? Nope, she fucking didn't. That was still break your neck height.

The light above the back door of Mr. Dickhead Millionaire's house flicked on, and she groaned loudly, tempted to just wiggle out of her sweatshirt and risk broken limbs.

Instead, she continued to dangle limply as Isaac Stark, his feet shoved into boots and his stupid perfect body clad in sweatpants and a thick hoodie, walked out of his house.

CHAPTER 3

R ayna's hope that maybe Stark wouldn't notice her dangling from his tree like the world's worst Christmas ornament died a quick death when his gaze zeroed in on her immediately. It was too dark to tell, but she had no doubt his much too pretty blue eyes were full of annoyance.

She half expected him to turn around and go back into the house. Call the police on her for trespassing and leave her to dangle while he waited for Sheriff Walker to show up. Christ, she hoped it wasn't the sheriff. She'd recently become friends with his fiancée, Grace, and she really didn't want Grace to know about this.

To her surprise, Stark walked toward her, wading through the thick, untouched snow of his backyard until he stood wordlessly beneath her dangling body.

The moonlight highlighted his narrow nose and high cheekbones and illuminated the short beard that covered his jaw. Huh, that was new. The last time she'd seen him, he'd only had stubble.

Oh, Jesus, she was not suddenly picturing what that beard might feel like against her inner thigh. Nope, she was not because, one, Stark was her mortal enemy, and two, she was dangling from a goddamn tree.

He studied her, the seconds quietly ticking away before he said. "Ms. Abrams."

"Stark," she said.

"Is there a reason you're trespassing on my property at ten fifty-seven at night?" He checked the watch adorning his wrist, which definitely cost more than Rayna's car.

"There's a cat in the tree," she said.

He bent and picked up the flashlight she left at the bottom of the tree, flicking it on before shining it up into the tree.

"Is it your cat?" he asked as Molly made her 'Hello, new friend' meow.

"No, it's the Pope's," she said.

His jaw tightened, a muscle tick tick ticking before he shined the flashlight on her, examining how she'd been snagged so thoroughly by the branch before sighing loudly. "Do you have any idea how lucky you are?"

"Do you think you could just call the sheriff to report me for trespassing rather than lecturing me? I'd like to get the fuck out of this tree sometime in the next century," she said.

With another harsh sigh, he shut off the flashlight and left it beside the cat treat container before trudging back toward the house. Rayna could no longer feel her feet, and fuck, did her back hurt, but she would rather freeze to death or bleed out before pleading with that asshole Stark to help her. Nope, she would dangle like a fly in a spider's web with patience and dignity while she waited for the police to arrive and get her ass out of this fucking tree.

Her entire body was trembling from the cold, and her exposed stomach was covered with goosebumps. She stared up into the tree, squinting to see Molly, who looked like she might have moved down a few branches.

"You little jerk," Rayna said. "You better come down from there yourself. Otherwise, you'll be living in that tree permanently. Do you hear me? I am never climbing this tree again, so -"

The squeak of the back door had her whipping her head back toward the house, groaning at the bright shard of pain it sent through her back. To her utter shock, Stark, carrying a kitchen chair, was headed back toward her.

She watched silently as he set the chair on the ground below her and hopped up on it. His face was about waist level with her, and her stomach erupted with even more goosebumps when she felt his breath on her skin.

If her nipples weren't already hard as glass from the frigid temperatures, they sure as shit would be diamonds right now. All because of a man's breath on her stomach. Even worse, the breath of a guy she hated even more than her childhood bully, Phoebe, and she loathed that stuck-up snot of a witch.

"What are you doing?" she snapped when he put his hands on her hips.

"Helping you out of the tree?" He raised one perfectly groomed eyebrow at her. "Please tell me you're not so stubborn that you'll insist you don't need my help."

"You can't lift me off the branch," she said. "I don't care how strong you think you are."

"I'm not lifting you," he said, his tone suggesting she was as dumb as a piece of toast. "Wrap your legs around my body and raise your arms. With a bit of luck and some pulling on my part, we should be able to slide you out of your sweatshirt."

"No," she said immediately. "We're not doing that."

"Do you have a better idea?" he asked.

God, she wished he'd let go of her hips. His touch, combined with how fucking cold she was and the pain in her back, made it nearly impossible to think clearly.

He gave her an impatient shake that sent agony racing up her back. "Ms. Abrams? Give me another suggestion then."

The whimper of pain escaped her lips before she could stop it, and his hands tightened on her hips. "What's wrong?"

"Nothing," she said. "Look, I'm not wearing anything under the sweatshirt, okay?"

"Okay," he said.

"I'm not wearing a bra," she clarified. "The ladies are swinging wild and free tonight."

"How delightful for you," he said dryly. "I've seen breasts before, Ms. Abrams."

"I don't want you seeing *my* breasts," she said.

"That makes two of us," Stark said, "but if you want out of this tree, neither of us are getting what we want."

Okay, so she was not hurt by Stark's disinterest in her tits. Not one tiny bit.

His hands still on her hips, he said, "Do you want my help or not, Ms. Abrams?"

"Yes," she said, trying hard to remember that despite their mutual hatred, Stark *was* trying to help her instead of leaving her to freeze to death in his tree.

"Wrap your legs around me," he said.

She wrapped her legs just under his arms, hooking her feet together against his back as he slid his arms around her waist. His face rested against her bare stomach for a second or two, and that unexpected beard made her thoughts go somewhere that was incredibly poorly timed and inappropriate.

"Ready?" He tipped his head back to stare up at her.

She nodded, and he said, "On three, lift your arms straight up in the air, and I'll pull, all right?"

"Yes," she said.

"One, two, three."

She lifted her arms as Stark pulled hard on her waist. She gritted her teeth against the pain as the branch slid across her scraped and bleeding back and twisted her head to the right when her sweatshirt got caught on her chin. It slid neatly past her face, and her free-wheelin' breasts popped out into the cold night air as the inside of her sweatshirt suddenly covered her face. Stark gave her another big yank, and she let her legs slide down a bit to hook around his ribcage. Holy fuck, this was working. This was actually working. She would slide right out of this damn shirt and -

She squealed in pain when she was pulled to an abrupt stop by her hair. Her messy bun had tangled on the end of the branch, and pain danced across her scalp when Stark gave her another hard tug.

"Stop!" she shouted, her thick sweatshirt muffling her voice. "Wait, just…"

Oh, fuck her sideways, Stark gave her another brisk pull, and she dropped a few inches before pulling up tight again. Christ, her scalp was on fucking fire.

"What the hell?" Stark grunted, his hands sliding up her back as she dropped, and oh Jesus Christ and a baby lamb, she could feel his warm breath directly between her breasts which meant he was face first in her tits, and was it possible for someone to die of humiliation?

"My hair!" she hollered. "My hair is caught!"

She twisted her head and body wildly, ignoring the pain in her scalp and her fear that she was about to give herself a giant bald spot. She'd rather have a bald spot than have Stark's face in her tits for one moment longer.

"Whoa," he shouted like she was a scared horse. "Stop twisting!"

"Ignoring him, she twisted even more violently, and oh fucking hell, did Stark's mouth just graze her nipple?

"Stop!" Now Stark's voice was muffled, and yup, that was definitely his goddamn tongue she felt on her nipple.

Panic and, God fucking help her, just a touch of horniness infusing her body, she made one final twist of her head. She was abruptly and gloriously free, her upper body sliding the rest of the way out of the sweatshirt and leaving behind what she was sure would be a significant chunk of hair, bloody skin, and possibly spinal fluid on the branch.

Stark made a muffled yell as she dropped like a stone out of the sweatshirt. Her momentum knocked him off balance, and his face still pressed up against her left breast, they fell off the chair and into the snow.

She landed on top of him with a hard 'oof' and pancakes on a hot fucking griddle, now her nipple was *entirely inside* of his mouth, and she scrambled off him, ignoring his grunt of pain when one flailing knee slammed into his ribs.

She slapped her arms over her naked breasts, her chest heaving, her breath steaming out in the cold air as Stark climbed nimbly to his feet, and they stared silently at each other.

Rayna didn't know whether to laugh or cry when Molly landed with a soft thud on the chair between them, making an inquisitive meow as she rubbed up against the back of the chair. Rayna snatched up the pregnant cat, pressing her against her boobs like a living, breathing fur-covered bikini. Molly purred loudly, lounging contently against Rayna's naked chest.

Rayna glanced at her sweatshirt, still hanging from the tree, but decided she'd never liked that particular shirt anyway. She straightened her back, hissing air between her teeth at how that little movement made it sting and burn and gave Stark a painfully formal nod.

"Thank you."

"You're welcome." He glanced at his hands, a scowl marring his perfect face. "Is this blood?"

She stared at the smears of her blood on his hands, but before she could say anything, he had pushed past the chair between them and turned her around roughly.

"Fuck," he said. "Your back is scraped to shit."

"It's fine," Rayna said.

"It isn't."

She shivered when he traced one finger down her back. She pulled away and turned to face him. "Stop that."

He scowled at her. "You need medical attention."

"The last I heard, you're not a doctor," she said. "It's not that bad. Look, I need to go. I'm freezing, and Molly is pregnant and shouldn't be out in the cold like this. Thank you for your help."

She turned and marched toward the gate, hoping like hell Stark hadn't added a lock to it. She half expected Stark to follow her, maybe even offer to help clean her back, and she wasn't entirely sure how she felt about that. But when she reached the gate and unlatched it, she glanced back to discover nothing but an empty yard and bright moonlight.

She closed the gate behind her and jogged to her yard, letting herself into the backyard and then into the house. She made sure the basement door was closed before she set Molly on the floor.

The cat stretched and purred, following Rayna and rubbing against her legs as she trudged upstairs to her bedroom to inspect the damage to her back. She stood with her back to the full-length mirror and twisted her head to stare at her reflection.

"Ugh," she muttered, staring at the enormous scrape

down the center of her back. Already, her skin was beginning to swell and bruise, and with another muttered curse, she grabbed her phone and called Emma.

"Hey, Rayna, what's up?" Emma answered on the second ring.

"Are you busy? I need your help."

CHAPTER 4

S weat dripping down his forehead, Stark pressed a button on the treadmill, his run slowing down to a jog to match the decrease in the treadmill's speed. He jogged another few minutes, continuing to decrease the speed until he was walking normally before he turned off the treadmill.

He stepped off of it and took a swig of water from his water bottle. He was alone in the gym, which, while unusual, was a welcome change. He had no qualms about his employees using the gym he'd built behind the office building, and the gym was for them as much as it was for him, but after a mostly sleepless night, he wasn't up to small talk.

He glanced out the window, stretching his quads and grimacing at the burn as he stared at the snow falling in big, thick flakes. His preference was to run the trails of Harmony Falls Park, and even in the colder weather, he often went for a run on one of the flatter trails, the only sound his thudding footsteps and the cold, fresh air invigorating him.

But he'd woken this morning to a snowstorm and subzero temperatures, and even he wasn't ridiculous enough to run outside in that weather. Instead, he'd settled for a run on the treadmill, pushing himself harder than he usually did in an effort to escape the thoughts that had kept him awake most of the night.

Was it your thoughts that kept you awake or your hard-on from remembering how pretty Rayna Abrams's breasts are? Pretty and perfect, right?

His upper lip curled, and he wiped angrily at the back of his neck with a towel before stomping toward the locker room. Discovering his next door neighbour stuck in his tree trying to rescue a stupid cat had not been on his weekend Bingo card.

True, but it happened, and now you know exactly what her breasts look like and how soft her skin is. Tell me again, how many times did you practically suck on her goddamn nipple?

It wasn't his fault! She was the one not wearing a bra. She was the one who'd started twisting and screaming and losing her damn mind while her tits were in his face. He would have preferred not to know what her nipples tasted like, thank you very much.

Liar.

His neighbour was not his type. A plumber and the owner of a local animal rescue, the woman's outfits made her look like she got dressed in the dark. He'd never seen her hair in anything but a ponytail, and she didn't wear makeup. His attraction had always skewed toward women who wore makeup, had perfect hair, and wore flattering clothes that weren't covered in animal hair, and God knows what else.

She might not have a fashion sense, but does she need one with breasts like that?

His scowl deepened. He didn't care how goddamn perfect her tits were. He hated Rayna Abrams and her stupid refusal to sell her property. If it weren't for her, he would be halfway to having his new house built. Instead, he was stuck living in a bungalow with horrifying wallpaper, linoleum flooring, and furniture that was popular sometime in the eighties. It was a far cry from his penthouse in the city.

So then stay in the city. You can work remotely, and the New Cassel office struggles more than the Harmony Falls office. It would be better for the company if you returned to the city.

He stripped off his gym clothes, grabbed his towel, and walked naked to the showers. He turned on the water, stepping back and letting the water heat as he stared moodily at the tile his interior designer had convinced him he'd absolutely needed despite the hefty price tag.

He *should* return to the city, return to his penthouse with its marble flooring and Italian furnishings and the best of the best when it came to decor. It was a far cry from the crappy house he lived in now, but despite how much he loved his penthouse, he hadn't been happy in the city. Not like he was here in Harmony Falls.

Harmony Falls was small with mediocre restaurants, he could only get a decent cup of coffee at the coffee shop on Main Street, and the town was overrun entirely by obnoxious tourists in the summer, but he could breathe here. Harmony Falls held nothing but good memories for him. Away from his father's barely hidden contempt and disapproval, he could be who he really was.

No, what he needed to do was convince Ms. Rayna Abrams, she of the perfect breasts, to sell him her property. Then he could tear down that eyesore she called a house, along with the bungalow he was in, and build his perfect home.

You don't need all three properties, you know. You could build your perfect house on the two properties you own now.

Sure, but he wanted the privacy that owning the third property would give him, and what he wanted, he got. Always. What was the point of having as much money and power as he did if it couldn't give him what he wanted?

She's not going to sell it to you.

He stepped under the hot water and let it beat down on him, then quickly washed his hair and body.

Rayna Abrams would eventually sell her property. It was simply a matter of finding the right price or, in her case, the right motivation to make her sell.

He thought again about filing a noise complaint about the barking that almost always emanated from her house before dismissing the idea. Despite how much he personally hated her, discreet inquiries had revealed that Rayna was well-liked in the town, and any attempt on his part to smear her reputation would undoubtedly backfire.

Besides, his earlier threat to put in a noise complaint had been met with scorn from Rayna and not even a hint of fear. She wasn't easily intimidated, and his usual tactics of getting what he wanted from his enemies would obviously not work. No, he needed to figure out a different way to deal with his annoying next door neighbour, one that wouldn't have the entire town at his throat for bullying the local animal rescuer.

He muttered a curse when the water pressure noticeably decreased, and he ducked under the spray and rinsed clear of shampoo and soap before shutting off the water and toweling dry.

He wrapped the towel around his waist and headed back to the locker room. A few weeks ago, he and the other employees noticed that the water pressure was decreasing intermittently. His assistant brought in a local plumber who diagnosed the problem as a partially closed shut-off valve and a flow restrictor on the shower head. He'd spent ten minutes in the gym, pronounced the problem fixed, and billed a ridiculously high fee.

Stark dressed quickly and, steeling himself against the cold, walked from the gym to his office building. It was only about twenty feet away, but his fingers were numb by the time he used his keycard to open the back door and stepped into the building.

He'd bought the town's old firehouse that had sat empty for years for a damn good price and, with some heavy construction and renovations, had converted it into office space for Stark Entertainment. The lower floor housed offices and cubicles, and the upper floor had a freshly remodeled kitchen and a large living area filled with couches, two foosball tables, a pool table, and a large screen television. The kitchen was outfitted with all the latest and best gadgets, including a cappuccino maker, popcorn maker, and panini press. He'd wanted only the best for his employees - happy employees were productive employees - and he'd spared no expense in the new office.

He walked down the long hallway and into the bright and open space of the lower floor, studying the area with a satisfied smile. He had started Stark Entertainment a decade ago, leaving the safety of his father's company along with his father's derision and scorn. He'd developed the first six video games for Stark Entertainment himself. While they'd done well and brought in enough profit for him to rent a small office and employ a receptionist and second developer, it was the creation and subsequent explosion in popularity of the Shadow Series video games that had put his company on the map.

Two years after the release of Shadow Dragons, the games his company developed were the hottest commodities in the gaming world. Over the last decade, Stark Entertainment had only increased in value. He became a millionaire by the age of twenty-seven and a multimillionaire by thirty. And not a single dollar of it was because of his father's wealth. Stark had turned down his mother's generous offer to help fund the start-up costs for his business. His father had cut Stark off both personally and monetarily the minute he'd decided to start his own company.

The middle of the lower-level office space housed the bullpen, where he could see various employees working at their computers or conversing quietly with one another. The massive bay doors at the front of the converted fire station had been replaced with two giant windows that allowed in plenty of natural light. The reception desk was placed strategically near the front door, and their receptionist, Aditi, chatted with a courier as she signed for a package.

Large offices ran along the far right wall. The office walls were made of frosted glass to help maintain an open and airy feel. One sat empty, but the others housed his head developer, Lucas, the controller, James, his assistant/office manager, Hollis, and lastly, his own office.

He started across the space, stopping when a body came sliding down from the upper level on the metal pole Stark had left in place during renovations. The dark-haired man landed lightly on his feet and smiled cheerfully. "Morning, Boss."

"Hello, Rupert. How was your weekend?"

"Kick-ass," Rupert said as he joined him in walking. "Me and Darius went on that two-day wilderness retreat in the Park. We saw a pack of wolves… it was epic. Yours?"

"Good, thanks," Stark said.

"Nice." Rupert held out his fist, and Stark bumped it before the junior developer veered off toward the bullpen.

Stark stopped in front of Hollis's office and knocked lightly on the door.

His assistant glanced up from her laptop and immediately stood. "Good morning, sir."

"Hollis," he said. "Seriously with the 'sir' shit again?"

She just shrugged and tugged on her suit jacket before

straightening her already straight notepad on her freakishly neat desk. "How was your weekend, Mr. Stark?"

Hollis had been his assistant and office manager in the New Cassel office for six years, and she had never once referred to him by anything other than Sir or Mr. Stark. Only a few people in his life called him Isaac, and while Hollis wasn't on that list, he had mentioned once that she could call him Stark like most people did.

Her withering look of disapproval had made it very clear he'd crossed some invisible line he didn't know existed, and it had taken nearly two months for her to stop calling him Sir and return to using Mr. Stark again.

When he'd decided to open the second office here in Harmony Falls, there had been two people he was determined to bring with him - one of his best and brightest developers, Lucas Wright and Hollis.

He'd been confident of his ability to convince Lucas to work here in Harmony Falls but less sure of Hollis. He was pleasantly surprised when she'd agreed to move to Harmony Falls and manage the office.

She was a type A personality who ran the office with iron efficiency, and he knew that one of the reasons the New Cassel office was struggling was because Hollis was no longer there to keep things moving smoothly.

He realized she was staring at him with one slightly arched eyebrow as she waited for his answer.

"My weekend was good. Yours?"

"Fine," she said briskly. Despite how many years they'd worked together, she never engaged in small talk with him, keeping their relationship strictly professional. He knew she was single and didn't have children, and that was the extent of his knowledge of her personal life.

If he was being honest, it was what he preferred, and her standoffish and sometimes cold personality didn't bother him in the least. He valued efficiency and discretion, and he and Hollis had worked well together since the moment he'd hired her.

"The gym shower's water pressure is low again," he said.

She frowned. "I knew that plumber was useless. I'll find another one right away, sir. My apologies."

"Nothing to apologize for," he said.

She returned to her seat and glanced at her laptop. "Your coffee is on your desk. You have a noon call with Jian to discuss overseas sales and a meeting with James at three this afternoon. Otherwise, your schedule is open."

"Thank you, Hollis," he said. "Have I told you lately that the office would fall apart without you?"

"Untrue," she said, but a faint look of pleasure crossed her face. "Your coffee is getting cold."

He grinned and headed toward his office.

CHAPTER 5

"Are you sure I can't get you something to drink? We have tea and coffee, or if you prefer something cold, there's iced tea or soda."

Rayna used the wrench to make one final turn on the pipe before sliding out from under the sink. She climbed to her feet and dropped the wrench in her toolkit as she smiled at the pretty church secretary. "I'm finished, actually."

"Oh, really? That didn't take long at all." The secretary gave her a pleased look.

"Just a small leak that replacing a section of the pipe solved the issue," Rayna said.

"Great, well, thank you so much. If you want to give me your invoice, I'll get it to our accountant for payment."

"Sure." Rayna studied the secretary, her gaze dropping to the woman's bare left hand before deciding to go for it. They needed more bachelorettes, and Zuri had been handling the lion's share of the work to find them. It was time for Rayna to do her part.

"Hey, uh, Nora, was it?" Rayna asked.

"Nola," the receptionist said.

"Right. Nola. Sorry. Weird question, but are you single?"

Nola blinked at her, one hand reaching up to clutch the neckline of her cardigan together. She looked to be about Rayna's age and was very pretty, but she certainly dressed the part of a church secretary with her dowdy cardigan, ankle-length skirt, and a shirt that buttoned up to her neck.

Oh, please, like you're any fashion expert, girl.

Her inner voice made a good point, but while Rayna didn't have a clue what the latest fashions were, she also didn't dress like she was sixty-five years old.

Unkind.

Seriously unkind, and Rayna inwardly scolded herself fiercely as Nola said, "Um, why?"

"I run an animal rescue called Little Whiskers Rescue," Rayna said.

"I know," Nola said. "You helped one of our parishioners, Mrs. Garrety, find a new home for her cat when she had to go into assisted living last year."

"Ah, okay. Well, anyway, we do fundraisers throughout the year, and one of the fundraisers we're doing this year is a bachelor/bachelorette auction, and we're looking for a few more bachelorettes."

Nola's hand tightened on her cardigan. "You want me to be a bachelorette?"

"Yes," Rayna said.

"But why?" Nola looked herself up and down. "I look... bad. No one would bid on me."

More guilt rushed through Rayna, and she said, "You're gorgeous, and you'd have so many bids."

"What...uh, what happens if someone bids on you?" Nola asked.

"They win a date with you. What you do on the date is up to you. If you decide to do this, I'll get you in touch with Zuri, who's running the auction. She'll get all of your pertinent information, and you can let her know what you're offering as a date activity."

"Date activity," Nola repeated.

"That's right. For example, one of our bachelorettes is offering a dinner at The Gilded Fork."

Nola's eyes widened. "That place is, um, kind of expensive."

"It doesn't have to be expensive or fancy," Rayna said hurriedly. "Another bachelorette is offering a homemade dinner and a beginner lesson in whittling."

"Whittling," Nola said.

"I know, right? Wild. Anyway, your date can be anything you want it to be," Rayna said. "When it's your turn, Zuri will announce your date night plan and if a guy or... girl?"

"Uh... I'm into guys," Nola said, her face turning pink.

"Okay. If a guy is interested, he'll bid on you."

"I don't really have anything to offer," Nola said. "I'm a very boring person."

"I'm sure that's not true," Rayna said. "Why don't I give you my card, and if you're interested in participating in the auction fundraiser, you can text me and -"

"That won't be necessary."

Nola's face paled, and she took a step back from Rayna as a man with silver hair and a fat belly stepped into the kitchen. He wore a navy blue shirt that had to work hard to stretch across his stomach, and a white strip of paper was tucked into his collar. He stared furiously at Rayna. "I am paying you to fix the pipes, not to encourage my daughter to model your whorish ways."

"Daddy!" Nola gasped.

Rayna stared steadily at him. "It's actually the church who's paying me, not you, isn't that right, Reverend?"

The pastor's face turned bright red, and he huffed out a

snort. "Expect me to be speaking to your supervisor about your attitude, Miss...?"

"Abrams," Rayna said. "Rayna Abrams. That's Rayna with a y. I'll write my boss's number on the invoice so you can call him."

His nostrils flaring, the pastor gripped Nola's arm. "See that you do, Miss Abrams."

He stared at his daughter. "What will Abraham say when he finds out you offered yourself up like a common whore?"

Nola looked like she was about to cry. "I wasn't going to participate in the bachelorette auction, Daddy. I swear. Please don't mention this to Abraham."

"Actions have consequences, and Abraham deserves to know how easily his future wife was tempted by sin. Come to my office once you've escorted Miss Abrams from the building, and we will pray for God's forgiveness for your sins."

"I took the afternoon off today. Remember?" Nola said timidly. "I'm meeting Sarah for lunch and then helping her paint the nursery. I won't be home until dinner."

Her father made a loud snort. "If you would rather spend your afternoon in leisure rather than hard work, that's your choice, I suppose."

"Painting a nursery isn't exactly an afternoon of leisure," Rayna said.

The pastor looked like his head might pop off the top of his neck like an overripe tomato. "Mind your business! Nola, pay Miss Abrams and make sure she leaves her boss's number with you."

Nola cringed as her father stormed out of the kitchen. There was a moment of awkward silence before Nola, looking like she was about three seconds from crying, said, "I'm so sorry."

"You have nothing to apologize for," Rayna said.

"I should have told you right away that I had a boyfriend," Nola said.

"No big deal," Rayna said. "So, you're engaged?"

"No," Nola said quickly. "I mean, we will be, eventually... we're very committed to each other, but Abraham hasn't proposed yet."

"Okay," Rayna said.

"There was another moment of awkwardness before Rayna said, "I'll get you that invoice and clean up my tools so you can get out of here. Sound good?"

"Yes," Nola said. "Thank you, Miss Abrams."

"Call me Rayna."

RAYNA STOPPED THE VAN AT THE END OF THE CHURCH'S LONG driveway and blew on her hands as she waited for the traffic to clear. Christ, her work van's heater was on its last legs, and if Doug didn't approve the work order to get it fixed soon, Rayna would go on damn strike.

You'll be lucky you don't get fired once that asshole pastor talks to Doug.

Rayna snorted and cranked the useless heater up another few degrees. Despite his inability to approve a work order in a timely manner, Doug was a damn good boss who wouldn't give one shit about the pastor's little temper tantrum. Of course, it also helped that Doug was an animal lover and his wife, Judy, was one of Rayna's most dedicated volunteers at the rescue. Finding out Rayna was trying to recruit people to her auction for the rescue during working hours wouldn't even be a blip on Doug's no bullshit at work policy.

She blew on her hands again before her gaze landed on Nola standing on the sidewalk in front of the church. She stood next to a bus stop sign, and despite being dressed warmly in a thick winter jacket with a knitted hat and mittens, Rayna could see her shivering wildly. The snow had finally stopped, but a bitterly cold wind blew.

Not surprised at all that the asshole pastor wouldn't give his daughter a ride, Rayna pulled out onto the street and stopped in front of Nola. She buzzed down the passenger window and leaned over. "Hey, you want a ride?"

Nola blinked at her. "What?"

"Where are you going for lunch?" Rayna asked.

"Nan's Diner," Nola said, before looking away.

"Well, hop in. I'm driving right past it."

"Oh no, that's okay," Nola said. "I don't want to trouble you."

"It's no trouble," Rayna said. "C'mon, it's better than freezing your ass... uh, I mean butt off waiting for the bus, right?"

Nola hesitated a moment longer before suddenly yanking open the door and climbing into the passenger seat.

Rayna rolled up the window as Nola clicked her seatbelt into place and smiled at her. "Thank you so much, Miss Abrams."

"It's Rayna, and you're welcome. Although, to be honest, I'm not sure my work van is that much warmer than outside. The heater is on its last legs."

She pulled back out onto the street as Nola gave her a smile that lit up her face and turned her pretty features into something strikingly beautiful. "This is much better than waiting for the bus. Thank you."

CHAPTER 6

Nola waved at Rayna and walked slowly toward Nan Diner's front door. When Rayna's work van turned left off of Main Street and disappeared, Nola turned abruptly and hurried down the sidewalk to the Walgreens. She stepped into the warm store and walked down the first aisle, staring blankly at the shelves.

While she was grateful for the plumber's kindness in giving her a ride downtown, it did mean she was nearly forty-five minutes early for her appointment. She supposed she could grab a quick bite at the diner, but it seemed like a pointless waste of her limited funds when she'd quickly eaten a sandwich at her desk just an hour earlier.

She'd had to eat it while keeping one eye on her father's office. If he'd seen her eating a sandwich, her whole cover story about lunch and helping Sarah paint the nursery would have been blown.

Her nerves, already frayed to begin with, tightened another notch at being reminded of her blatant lie to her father. It was a dangerous lie, one easily discoverable by her father if he happened to mention it to Sarah at church on

Sunday. But she'd had no choice. There were a limited number of people her father approved of her spending time with, and she'd chosen to involve Sarah in her lie because she was just as timid, if not more timid, than Nola. If her father did happen to mention Nola painting the nursery with her, Sarah was so intimidated by the Reverend Norwood that the odds of her just meekly agreeing to whatever he said were high.

Still, Nola couldn't just wander the Walgreens or any of the shops along Main Street for the next forty-five minutes. What if someone from the church saw her and happened to mention it to her father?

Her stomach clenched tight, the sandwich she'd eaten churning unpleasantly in her guts. She glanced furtively around the store, suddenly convinced that one of the church members would come marching into the aisle at any moment, demanding to know why Nola wasn't at her desk at the church and did her father know she was here?

Her stomach still churning, she hurried out of the store. Her breath catching in her throat at the cold wind, she walked purposefully across the street and stopped in front of the bright red door. She looked to her left and to her right, saw no one she knew, and, her hand trembling, pulled open the door and stepped inside.

The tattoo shop was not at all what she expected. She'd expected something small and dark and maybe even a little grungy. Instead, it was an ample bright space with gleaming floors, and the air smelled of disinfectant. To the left of the door was a reception counter with a glass display of jewelry. A spinning rack of Crimson Door Tattoo keychains sat on top of the counter, along with a small laptop and a tablet. A pile of Crimson Door Tattoo t-shirts sat in a box on the floor just in front of the counter.

She stared at the big sign taped to the front of the counter that said, "Please remove wet footwear!" and took off her winter boots, leaving them on the big mat by the door and slipping her feet into a pair of the cheap rubber slippers provided.

To the right was a seating area with a large leather couch and a coffee table with a few black binders displayed. A mini-fridge and a small table with a Keurig coffee machine, mugs, and sugar sat against the wall near the couch.

The shop was empty of people, and she drummed her fingers on the gleaming surface of the counter, unsure of what to do. She studied the three tattooing stations, chewing anxiously at her bottom lip. They were completely open to anyone who walked into the shop. What if someone from the church came in and saw her being tattooed?

She would have to take the chance, she decided. It had taken her forever even to work up the nerve to book the appointment, and then she'd had to wait over three months for it. If she cancelled now, she knew in her heart that she would never have the courage to rebook the appointment. It would be a waste of the money she'd spent at the silent auction way back in the spring.

There were three doors at the back of the shop, all of them closed, and she studied them for a few seconds before loudly clearing her throat. The doors didn't magically open, and she finally decided to sit on the couch and wait.

She hung her coat on the coat tree near the door, stuffing her hat and mittens into the pockets before sinking grace-fully onto the couch. She tugged at her cardigan and then her long skirt before readjusting her thick tights. She was reaching for the closest black binder when one of the three doors opened, and a giant of a man with thick dark hair stepped out. She recognized him, of course. They might not have traveled in the same social circles, but she didn't think there was anyone in town who didn't know the owner of Crimson Door Tattoo.

Preacher.

She had no idea what his real name was or even his last name. She suspected that not many people did. But it didn't matter. Everyone knew who he was. Even someone like her, sheltered from the town gossip and unaware of almost everything that went on, knew who he was.

If his size, tattoos, and intimidating manner weren't enough to make a name for himself in town, his incredible tattooing talent - a talent that, according to Nola's Googling, had him on more than one top ten list of best tattooists in the country - was more than enough.

She knew damn well how lucky she'd been to win the silent auction bid for a tattoo by Preacher.

She stood up, her nervous smile fading when Preacher stared silently at her. "Hi, I'm, um, Nola. I have an appointment with you."

"You're early," Preacher said.

"Yes, I thought I had to take the bus, but then I was given a ride, so I didn't... that is... sorry." She knew her cheeks were bright red, and Preacher was staring at her like she was a fool, and she really wished she wasn't so awkward and inept around people.

She tensed when Preacher walked over, her anxiety nearly getting the best of her when she realized how big he really was. He reminded her of another man, that one just as broad shouldered and covered in tattoos as well.

Nix.

His image was flash-fried into her brain despite her best efforts to forget all about him. Only an inch or two shorter than Preacher, with dark hair and the most gorgeous blue eyes surrounded by thick lashes. A broad chest and muscular arms covered entirely in tattoos from his wrists up to where his t-shirt sleeves had started mid-bicep. The tattoos would go all the way up to his shoulders. She was sure of it. Heck, Nix's entire body was probably covered in ink.

The muscles in her lower belly tightened, and her core ached with an unfamiliar pulse. She took a deep breath. She might have been on the naive side about sex, but she knew what she was feeling. Lust. One of the seven deadly sins her father was always going on and on about from his pulpit.

She lusted after a man she'd only met for a few minutes, and how terrible did that make her? She was in a relationship with a good, solid Christian man, but it was a tattooed atheist who occupied her fantasies.

But could God really blame her? Nix was basically a hero. He'd not only given her his jacket when she was ministering to the less fortunate in the cold, but he'd saved her from some very unsavoury characters not even twenty minutes later. If he hadn't been there…

She shivered at the memory. If he hadn't been there, she would have been kidnapped and raped. She could try to sugarcoat what happened that day, try to pretend that her father hadn't put her in terrible danger by forcing her to minister alone in a dangerous section of the south side, but she was only lying to herself. If it hadn't been for Nix, she…

"Lady? Hello? Are you even listening to me?"

Preacher's exasperated tone jerked her neatly from her memories. She stared at him, her cheeks flaming red again before another apology tumbled from her mouth. "I'm so sorry. I was, um… sorry."

"Right," Preacher said. "So, you understand that the silent auction prize is for one of my flash designs, yes? Not a custom design?"

"Yes," Nola said.

"And that the auction prize is for a two-hour tattoo maxi-

39

mum? I won't be doing a full sleeve tattoo or anything super elaborate."

"I understand," Nola said.

"Then we're good to go." Preacher pointed to the closest black binder on the coffee table. "Look through the binder and choose a tattoo."

"Right, okay," she said.

Preacher walked away, stepping behind the counter and picking up the tablet next to the laptop. Nola grabbed the binder and sank onto the couch, flipping through it page by page as she studied each tattoo. She had already decided she wanted a bird, and when she turned to a page that had various bird designs, she studied them with excitement.

The excitement dimmed when she couldn't imagine any of them on her body for the rest of her life. She turned the last page in the binder and, with a glance at Preacher who was still absorbed with the tablet, set it down and reached for a second binder. She wondered if maybe she needed to re-evaluate what kind of tattoo she was getting. She had her heart set on a bird, but the tattoo was permanent, and she wanted to love the bird she chose. Because she *was* getting a tattoo even if her father would lose his mind over it. And, yeah, maybe this was a sad act of rebellion for a twenty-five-year-old, but she'd wanted one since she was eighteen.

Besides, her father would never know because he would never see it.

She flipped idly through the pages, scanning each tattoo. She needed to stay open to a tattoo other than a dove. She couldn't afford a custom tattoo, at least not from someone of Preacher's talents. She'd lucked out in winning the silent auction bid, but it had cost her a ridiculous amount of money, and it had been silly for her to think that she would find her perfect tattoo from a book of pre-drawn...

Her breath caught in her throat, and she leaned forward

eagerly, her nose nearly touching the page as she studied the dove tattoo at the bottom of the page. It was a fairly simplistic tattoo, she supposed. Just a black and white drawing of a dove with its wings stretched out in flight. But it was its simplicity that drew her in, and she studied each carefully drawn line, tracing the wings with the tip of her finger.

"You're the one," she murmured, smiling a little at the sheer delight she could hear in her voice. "You're perfect."

The bell above the door jingled, and a blast of cold air swept through the shop. She glanced toward the door as Nix - the very man who occupied way too many of her thoughts - walked into the shop.

He carried a Nan's Diner bag in one tattooed hand, and his nose and the tips of his ears were red from the cold.

"Christ, it's colder than a fucking -"

He abruptly stopped when he caught sight of Nola, and for absolutely no reason at all, she turned scarlet. There were nearly thirty seconds of silence before Nola, her brain screaming at her to say something, stood and said, "Oh, um, hello. It's nice to see you again. Nix, right?"

He nodded, glancing at Preacher, before turning back to her. "What are you doing here?"

"I'm getting a tattoo," she said.

"You're getting a tattoo," he said.

"That's right. A bird. Back in the spring, Preacher offered a tattoo for a silent auction prize, and I, um, won the bid. So, here I am. Are you here to get a tattoo also?" Her gaze flickered to his arms. They were covered by a leather jacket - the same one she'd worn for a brief, glorious half hour that night he'd saved her life. The coat had smelled so good - like sandalwood and amber. Later that night, in her bedroom, she had pressed her cardigan to her face and, like a teenager in the throes of her first crush, repeatedly inhaled the faint scent of his cologne that lingered on the fabric.

"I work here," he said.

"Oh, uh, right, I knew that. You mentioned that... before... when we first met," she said.

How could she have forgotten that?

Because you're too busy wondering what it would be like to have his face buried between -

She cut that thought off quickly, but it was too late. She could practically feel the heat burning her face to a crisp.

Preacher joined her in the seating area as Nix continued to stand by the door with a look she couldn't decipher.

"You find one you like?" Preacher asked.

"I did," she said and showed him the dove. "I'd like this one, please."

Annoyance flickered across his face. "That's not my binder."

"I'm sorry?" she said.

"That binder isn't mine. I told you to look through that one." He pointed to the other one.

"Oh, I did, but I didn't see one I liked, so I thought..."

"That's Nix's book," Preacher said. "His tattoos."

"Oh... um," her gaze flickered to Nix and then back to Preacher. "Could you still tattoo this one, though?"

"I never tattoo another artist's work," Preacher said, his tone suggesting she had just insulted him in the worst way. "Pick one from the book I showed you."

She stared at the dove tattoo before taking a deep breath. "Could I book with Nix instead?"

"You paid money for Preacher to tattoo you. He's a better artist than I am, and you should get what you paid for," Nix said quickly.

"I want this tattoo, and I want you," she said.

There was an awkward silence, and oh God, why did she

say that? She studied the door, wondering if there was any way she could gracefully run by Nix in her rubber slippers and out the door, never to think or speak of this humiliating moment again.

Her cheeks were back to a bright, fiery red, and she realized with confusion that Nix's cheeks were a bit red, too.

Amusement tinged the annoyance in Preacher's voice. "Don't listen to him. He's just as good of an artist as I am, so if you want Nix to do the tattoo, I'm fine with it."

"I do," she said firmly, even though a part of her still wanted to flee the shop and never look back.

"You'll have to book for a different day. Nix is just starting his lunch break, and he has another tattoo this afternoon," Preacher said.

Disappointment washed over her, along with trepidation at having to come up with another lie to tell her father, but it was worth the risk to get the perfect tattoo. "Okay, I can rebook."

Nix studied her for a few seconds. "I can do the tattoo now."

"Really?" She sounded like an excited little kid.

A small grin crossed Nix's face, and Nola's heart went into overdrive. She'd thought him handsome before, but now... now, she could barely breathe in his presence.

"Just give me five minutes," he said.

CHAPTER 7

Rayna parked her truck on the quiet side street and grabbed her lunch bag. Typically, she would return to the Sneaky Leaks office space for her lunch break, but her next client wasn't far from downtown.

She unwrapped her sandwich and took a bite while checking her emails. There were over a dozen emails requesting help for animals, but thankfully, her dog and cat foster coordinators were handling them. Her phone dinged with an incoming text, and she responded to Reba, their cat and dog medical volunteer, confirming that she could do further testing at the vet for a cat that had been vomiting off and on for two days.

In between bites of her sandwich, she answered various messages from different volunteers, assured Zuri she hadn't forgotten about their meeting regarding the bachelor/bachelorette auction, and called Brandt Vet Clinic to book an appointment to spay the cat of a senior with limited funds who couldn't afford it.

Out of all the programs she'd set up within Little Whiskers Rescue, she was most proud of their Helping

Hands program. The program utilized rescue funds to support low-income families in Harmony Falls with veterinary care for their animals.

Speaking of funds, she really needed to rebook her meeting with the rescue's accountant. Mack had cancelled twice now, and with year end rapidly approaching, she needed to know the exact numbers in order to allocate funds for the various rescue programs for the following year.

She sighed and rubbed at her forehead. Dealing with the money side was her least favourite part of the rescue work, and she knew how lucky she was to have Mack. He'd been with the rescue since the start, volunteering his time to handle donations and bank accounts and doing all the book-keeping. Still, she was sometimes uneasy at how little she paid attention to the money side, but she was already stretched thin as it was. She couldn't be a control freak over *every* aspect of the rescue. She'd go into complete burnout if she tried.

Her work phone rang, and she hit the answer button. "Go for Abrams."

Her boss laughed. "God, you're such a dork."

"Takes one to know one, Douglas."

He laughed again, and she grinned before biting into her apple and chewing noisily. "What's up?"

"Where you at?"

"Just outside of downtown."

"Perfect. I need you to handle an emergency call."

"Sure. Where?"

"Stark Entertainment. Their office is the old fire station."

She froze with the apple halfway to her mouth. The sandwich she'd eaten now sat like a rock in her stomach.

"Rayna, you still there?"

"Yeah," she said. "Can you ask Jimmy instead?"

"He's way over on the south side. You're closest."

"What's the emergency?" Rayna asked.

Doug hesitated, and Rayna said, "Doug? What's the emergency?"

"Low water pressure in the gym showers."

She scowled. "That isn't an emergency."

"It is when it's the gym shower of the richest guy in town."

She didn't reply, and Doug said, "Head over there now, please, Rayna."

"One, I'm on my lunch break, and I still have thirty minutes left. Two, I already have a client appointment booked for after lunch."

"You'll be paid overtime for your lunch hour, and I've already asked Ranjit to cover your one o'clock."

"What? Why? Just send Ranjit to Stark's."

"I want you to do it."

She tossed her half-eaten apple into her lunch bag. "I'm not doing it, Doug."

"Yes, you are."

"No, I'm not."

Doug huffed in annoyance. "I don't have time for your bullshit today, Rayna."

"I have never once refused to work a job, Doug. I take all the messy jobs without complaint, don't I? The exploding toilet? The broken sewage pipe under the trailer in the middle of July when the weather was over a hundred degrees? Who took care of those monstrosities without a single complaint? Me, that's who."

"You did, which means this one will be a piece of cake for you," Doug said.

She tossed her half-eaten apple into her lunch bag. "Why can't Ranjit do it?"

"Because you're my best, Rayna, and the guy is a multi-millionaire."

"What does that have to do with anything?"

"You do a good job like you always do, and we've got a new client. One with bottomless pockets. We all know he'll be building a new house on that property he bought sooner or later, and it'll probably be a goddamn mansion with seven fucking bathrooms. I want Sneaky Leaks to be the plumber he calls to install those seven fucking bathrooms."

"He won't be building any home until I sell him my property, and I'm never selling it to him, so this is a moot point," Rayna said.

Doug sighed. "Rayna, I get that he isn't your favourite guy, but I am asking you as your boss to do your goddamn job. Getting on Stark's good side will only help the company, which in turn will help you. You want a raise next year, play nice with the multimillionaire."

"I really hate you, Douglas," Rayna said morosely.

"No, you fucking love me," Doug said. "Get your ass over to Stark's gym and be nice, Rayna. I don't care how much you hate his guts. Got it?"

"Got it," Rayna said.

"Thanks, kid." Doug ended the call.

Rayna stared at her phone before letting loose with a very loud and very satisfying "Fuck!".

"THANK YOU FOR COMING SO QUICKLY, MS. ABRAMS."

Rayna didn't want to be intimidated by the woman standing in front of her, but she couldn't help it. The receptionist had asked her to wait a moment while she called Stark's assistant, Hollis, and the woman had arrived at the reception desk roughly thirty seconds later. Hollis's expensive suit, her perfect hair and makeup, and how she practically oozed sophistication made Rayna even more self-conscious of her make-up-free face, her hair pulled back in its usual ponytail, and the ill-fitting cut of her Sneaky Leaks golf shirt.

She wondered idly if Stark and the woman were sleeping together. She seemed like Stark's type of woman. He certainly didn't find Rayna's look appealing, that was for sure.

You have no idea what his type of woman is. And hey, why exactly do you care that he doesn't find you or your tits attractive? You hate him, remember?

She pulled at her shirt before studying the bright and open space they stood in. Whoever had been in charge of renovating the fire station into a working office had done an incredible job. The big bullpen in the middle was bustling with activity, and she glanced up when she heard a burst of loud laughter from the open upper floor. Was Stark in the office right now, just waiting to cast his judgmental gaze on her? Probably not. He would disapprove of laughter in the workplace. She could feel the tension oozing out of her shoulders.

Hollis was still waiting for her reply, and Rayna forced herself to focus. "You're welcome. So, the problem is in the gym?"

"Yes. We've been noticing a decrease in water pressure for a few weeks now. I brought in a plumber to address the issue, and he said it was a partially closed shut-off valve and a shower head restrictor. He said he'd fixed the problem. Obviously, he was mistaken."

"Well, I'm happy to take a look and solve the problem," Rayna said.

"Good. The gym is located behind the main building. Let me grab my jacket and -"

"Hi! You're a plumber, right?"

Rayna's shirt was tugged on, and she looked down to see

a small dark-haired girl, who couldn't have been more than six years old, standing beside her.

"I am," she said, glancing at Hollis. The woman had a strange look on her face, one part annoyance to two parts... shit, was that anxiety? Did the pixie-size girl actually make her nervous?

"That's so cool," the little girl said.

"How did you know that?" Rayna asked. She hadn't brought any of her work tools in with her.

"It says on your shirt." The little girl stared at the embroidered patch on Rayna's shirt. "Sneaky Leaks Plumbing. That's a funny name."

"Aren't you a little young to work here?" Rayna grinned at the girl.

She giggled and took Rayna's hand, hanging off of it as she swung her small body back and forth with enthusiasm. "I don't work here, silly. My daddy works here. I'm only here because I have a dentist's appointment in half an hour, but he had to stop by the office because he forgot something. He always forgets things. He has a very chaotic and disorganized personality, but he means well."

Rayna blinked in surprise. "You know a lot of big words for a six-year-old."

"I'm seven!" the little girl said indignantly. "My Aunt Nora says I'm probably a genius, but Daddy won't get me tested because he wants me to have a normal childhood without any pressure to live up to certain expectations. Hey, what's your name?"

"I'm Rayna," Rayna said.

"I'm Eva," she said.

"Nice to meet you."

"You too. Do you like being a plumber?"

"I do," Rayna said.

"I'm going to be a race car driver when I grow up. Or a

doctor. Or maybe an accountant like Daddy. I'm not sure yet. I might be a mechanic like my Uncle Shepherd. I'm gonna have a fast car when I grow up. My favourite car is the Ford Mustang Shelby GT500. What's your favourite car?"

"Oh, um... I..."

Before Rayna could think of an answer, Eva turned her attention to Hollis. "Hi, Hollis."

"Hello, Eva." Hollis gave the little girl a stiff smile.

"I like your hair today. Do you ever braid it? My daddy braids my hair, and he knows how to do French braids and Dutch braids because Emma taught him how to do Dutch braids," Eva said.

She let go of Rayna's hand and ran her hand over Hollis's suit jacket. "I like your suit, too."

Looking visibly uncomfortable, Hollis stepped back. Eva grimaced. "Sorry, I shouldn't touch you."

She turned back to Rayna. "Daddy says I shouldn't bother Hollis when I'm here because she isn't a person who enjoys being around little kids, and also, I like to give hugs and be touchy-feely like my Aunt Nora, and Hollis hates that. She doesn't like hugs. Do you like hugs, Rayna?"

"Yeah, I like -"

"Eva! Hey, I asked you to come straight back to my office when you were finished in the bathroom." A dark-haired man with blue eyes and a killer body scooped Eva into his arms.

"Sorry, Daddy," Eva said cheerfully. "I was distracted by Rayna. She's a plumber."

The man smiled at her. "Hi. I know you."

"You do?"

"Well, sort of," he laughed. "I'm James, and I'm one of your bachelors for the upcoming fundraiser."

"Oh, awesome. It's great to meet you." She shook James's

hand. "Thank you so much for participating. We really appreciate it."

"You're welcome."

"How did you hear about it?" Rayna asked.

"Emma," James said. "She popped into my office one day and convinced/bribed me to participate."

Rayna laughed. "Bribery with chocolate chip cookies or banana bread? Both are crowd favourites."

"The cookies," James said. "I can't resist cookies."

"It's true," Eva said. "I have to hide them at home, or he eats them all after I go to bed."

"Hey, no sharing family secrets with strangers, remember, Eva?" James said with a good-natured grin. His grin faltered a little when he glanced at Hollis. "Hi, Hollis."

"Hello, James," Hollis said.

There were a few seconds of silence before Eva frowned. "Why is it weird?"

"It's not weird. You're weird." James tickled her, and Eva laughed before kissing his cheek.

"C'mon, Daddy, we gotta go, or I'll miss my cleaning."

"Right as always, Bunnykins." James smiled at Rayna. "Good to formally meet you, Rayna. I'll see you at the fundraiser."

"See you then," Rayna said.

James turned and walked away, and Rayna glanced at Hollis just in time to see the woman's gaze slip to James's admittedly very tight ass. She looked away, giving Rayna a bit of a flustered smile.

"I don't suppose you'd be interested in participating in the fundraiser if you're single? I run Little Whiskers Rescue, and we're looking for a few more bachelorettes," Rayna said.

"Absolutely not," Hollis said and then grimaced. "Sorry, that was rude. I'm single, but I'm not interested in participating in the fundraiser as a bachelorette. I'm happy to donate separately, though."

"That's very kind. Thank you. Or," Rayna glanced at James's retreating back, "you could come to the fundraiser and bid on one of the bachelors. It's for a great cause, and you'll get a fun night out with your bachelor if you win the bid."

Hollis cleared her throat, her gaze slipping to James a final time before she smiled her stiff smile. "Give me a moment to get my jacket, and I'll take you to the gym. All right?"

"Sounds good," Rayna said.

CHAPTER 8

"Take off my underwear?" Nola stared at Nix, real panic curling at her edges.

"Yes," Nix said patiently. "If you want the tattoo on the front of your hip, you'll need to remove everything from the waist down."

Nola perched on the side of the tattoo bed, staring wide-eyed at Nix. She'd been prepared to remove her skirt and tights, but she hadn't expected to remove her underwear.

She sucked in a breath, giving Nix a shaky smile. "I, um, I thought maybe I could just hold them out of the way."

Nix shook his head. "I need space to tattoo, and I can't have your hand or clothing in the way."

"But," she glanced around the shop, "anyone could come in and see me half…"

She trailed off, mortified that she couldn't even say the word naked in front of Nix.

Nix pointed to the curtain hanging from a track in the ceiling. "I'll pull the curtain around us, and you'll have a paper sheet covering the area that I'm not tattooing."

Her face was so red that she was sure people walking by the store would see it beckoning to them like a beacon.

"You could put the tattoo somewhere else." Nix picked up the stencil he'd created. "This is a good size for your calf or forearm."

That was an impossible solution, but before she could say anything, Nix said, "But I'm guessing you want the tattoo to be easily hidden."

"Yes," she said, wishing she didn't sound quite so pathetic.

Nix didn't reply, staring silently at her as she warred internally with the decision about whether she could strip half-naked in front of a man.

In front of a man or in front of this *man? Because you're conveniently forgetting that you've been naked in front of Abraham multiple times.*

Sure, but that was different. Abraham was her boyfriend and not….

Not nearly as handsome as Nix?

No, no, that wasn't at all what she was thinking. Abraham was… cute. What she'd been thinking was that he wasn't as intimidating as Nix. Abraham was gentle and calm and would never punch someone in the face.

Nix punched the guy because he was trying to kidnap you, Nola. Have you forgotten that?

She'd been lost in her thoughts for nearly two minutes, and she needed to make a damn decision. Nix was kind enough to tattoo her last minute, and here she was, being a big baby about nothing. Nix saw plenty of bodies when he was tattooing, she was sure of it, and her nakedness wouldn't even be a blip on his radar.

She wanted a tattoo, and, more importantly, she wanted that dove tattoo. It was exactly what she had pictured in her head, and she knew how lucky she was to find the perfect tattoo from flash art.

She could do this. She hoped.

"Okay," she said before she could chicken out.

Nix stood up from the rolling stool and pulled the curtain around the tattoo station. He placed a folded paper cover on the bed beside her and pointed to a second rolling stool next to the bed. "You can place your clothes and purse on that stool. Just say my name when you're ready. Okay?"

She nodded, her throat too tight for her to speak. Nix left, and her hands shaking, she quickly stripped off her thick tights and long skirt, folded them neatly and placed them on the stool with her purse. With another glance at the curtain, she removed her underwear and hid it under her skirt before lying on the bed and covering her lower half with the crinkly paper sheet.

Her heart pounding, she said, "I'm ready, Nix."

He pulled open the curtain and joined her, drawing it closed behind him. Nola tried not to think about how intimate it felt to be with Nix here in the small, hidden space as she stared at the ceiling.

She listened to the sounds of Nix preparing his station, nodded when he showed her the brand new needle in its wrapping and tried to keep her breath more 'perfectly calm cat' and less 'panting buffalo.'

"Tattoo on your left hip, correct?" Nix asked as he sat on the stool and rolled it close to the bed.

"Yes," she said, her fingers tightening on the paper sheet.

"I need you to move the sheet so it exposes your left hip," Nix said, his voice brisk and professional. "If you're comfortable with exposing your left leg, that will make it a little easier for me, but it's not necessary to move it from your leg."

"Uh, no, that's fine," she said.

She took another deep breath and carefully shifted the sheet over until her left leg was clear of the paper. Then, hoping Nix didn't see how badly her hands shook, she moved the top half of the sheet until her hip was exposed. She kept her right hand pressed firmly against her crotch, keeping the sheet tight against it. She didn't think her hand would be in the way, but even if it were, Nix would have to work around it. She wasn't risking the sheet pulling up or falling off and exposing her to Nix.

"Perfect," Nix said. "Can you put your left arm above your waist?"

"Yes." She tucked her left arm under her head, staring at Nix as he carefully placed the stencil on her skin. He peeled it away and studied her hip for a moment before grabbing a hand mirror and angling it so she could see it.

"What do you think of placement?"

"Perfect," she said.

"Do you want to stand up so you can see how it looks?" he asked.

"No," she said hurriedly before he could roll his stool back.

"Are you sure?" he asked.

"Yes, I think it looks great," she said. She couldn't imagine trying to stand and keep the stiff paper sheet covering all her bits while Nix watched. Nope, that was asking too much of her frayed nerves.

Nix picked up the tattoo gun. "Let me know if you need me to stop, all right? If it hurts to the point that you need a break, it's fine to ask for one."

"Okay," she said.

"The tattoo won't take long, but if you need to reposition, let me know first," he said. "It's important that you hold completely still while I'm tattooing."

"I won't move," she said.

"Good. Here we go," he said. He pressed a button on his phone, and music drifted from a small speaker on a rolling cart that also held a sharps container and a package of gauze.

A smile crossed her face, and Nix said, "What?"

"You're a Taylor Swift fan?" she asked.

"I like all sorts of different music," he said. "I can change it if you prefer."

"No, I… I love Taylor Swift. I just didn't think you would be a Swiftie," she said.

That got her another one of those oh-so-pretty smiles, and her pulse thudded in her ears as a not entirely unpleasant tingling began in her lower pelvis.

He snapped on some gloves and bent over her hip. She stared at the top of his dark head as the buzz of the tattoo gun started. He touched it to her skin and did a few seconds of tattooing before stopping and staring at her. "You good?"

"Yes," she said. "It doesn't hurt as much as I thought."

He nodded and bent over her hip again. She watched him work, fascinated by the look of concentration on his face and the steady, confident movement of his hand as he tattooed her.

Forty minutes later, she'd been lulled into a state of relaxation by the music, the sound of the tattoo gun, and Nix's rhythmic motion of tattooing and wiping her skin clear.

When he shut off the gun and gave her skin one final wipe, she was almost disappointed. For the first time in months, she'd been entirely at ease and not plagued by any of her usual anxiety. She could have sat there for hours, studying Nix and feeling the sharp bite against her skin as he moved the tattoo gun over her flesh.

Nix set down the tattoo gun, turned off the music, and picked up the hand mirror. He angled it over her hip again, and her breath caught in her throat when she saw the tattoo.

"It's so beautiful." Her voice was barely above a whisper. "I love it."

"Yeah?" Nix gave her a pleased look before wiping the

tattoo again. "It's red right now, and your skin is a bit swollen, but it'll look even better once it's healed."

"I think it's perfect," she said.

"Good. I'm glad you like it."

"Not just like. Love," she said happily.

When Nix set down the mirror, she sat up a little, staring again at the tattoo, not ready to stop looking at it. "It's exactly what I wanted."

He cleaned it again before placing a sticky clear bandage over it. "This is called SecondSkin. It'll help protect the tattoo as it heals. Keep it on for the next seven days. You can shower or bathe with it on. All right?"

She nodded, still staring happily at the tattoo as Nix threw the needle into the sharps container. He paused a beat before saying, "What made you decide to choose a dove?"

"Well, it's the most beautiful dove I've ever seen," she said, "and to me it symbolizes..."

"What?" he asked.

"Freedom," she said. "How she can fly away and go wherever she wants, be whoever she wants to be, without anyone judging her or making her feel bad or..."

She stopped, feeling the traitorous blush rising in her skin as she smiled uncomfortably at Nix. "It really is so beautiful, and you're a very talented artist."

"Thanks," he said.

"Thank you," she said. "I love it so much, I really do, and I can't believe I finally have a tattoo. I've wanted one for so long. And I was surprised at how... relaxing it was. It didn't hurt nearly as much as I thought it might. I already want another one."

"Careful," he said with a slight grin, "or you'll end up as tattooed as me."

She laughed, studying the tattoos on his arms. "I'm not sure I could pull off the sleeve tattoos as well as you do."

"How will you know if you don't try?" he said with another one of those - oh god, parts of her were definitely tingling now - grin.

Before she could reply, the bell jingled over the door, and Nix glanced at his watch. "That's my next appointment."

"Right," she said. "Thank you for tattooing me on such short notice."

"You're welcome," he said.

He stared at her like maybe he was going to say something else before he stood abruptly. "Just pull the curtain back when you're dressed."

"Okay," she said, clutching the paper sheet against her body as Nix ducked behind the curtain.

She could hear him greeting his next client, and she stared at her tattoo again before sliding off the bed. Nix hadn't looked once at her bare leg or even acted like he knew she was half-naked under the thin paper sheet.

Why would he? You're not his type, Nola. Just because he's nice to you doesn't mean he's attracted to you.

She knew that. So, why was she feeling so disappointed?

CHAPTER 9

"Aditi, can you scan this and email it to me? Hollis isn't at her desk, and it's a bit of a rush." Stark handed the receptionist the package of papers.

"Of course," Aditi said. "I'll do it right now."

"Thank you. Where is Hollis?" Stark asked.

"She's with the plumber in the gym," Aditi said. "Rayna's figured out the problem and asked her to -"

"Rayna?" Stark's body went stiff. "Did you say Rayna?"

"Yes." Aditi was already starting to scan the papers. "Rayna Abrams. She's a plumber. I went to school with her. She's super nice despite her tragic background."

"What do you mean tragic background?" Stark asked.

"Oh, well," Aditi glanced around, "I'm not really one to gossip, but everyone in the town knows about Rayna's childhood, so I guess it's not gossiping, right?"

Stark could barely keep a straight face. He liked the receptionist, and she was excellent at her job, but she was the biggest gossip in the office. Normally, he didn't participate in office gossip ever, but he couldn't resist his sudden urge to know exactly what made Rayna's childhood so tragic.

Aditi pushed the scan button on the printer. "Honestly, I'm surprised you haven't heard about it already. You go to Grind My Beans nearly every day and Seo-Jun is the biggest gossip in town. I swear she only works at the coffee shop so she can collect gossip on everyone and spread -"

"Aditi," Stark said impatiently, "what's Rayna's tragic background?"

"She had a really terrible childhood. Like, awful," Aditi said. "She grew up on the south side in severe poverty. Both her parents were horrible alcoholics and couldn't keep jobs. They lived in the grossest places and moved around a lot. I think they were even homeless a few times. Once, near the end of high school, Rayna was coming to school in dirty clothes, and it was apparent she wasn't showering every day because they were living in her dad's car. She got really skinny because I think her parents weren't even, like, feeding her."

"Jesus," Stark said.

"Yeah, it was pretty bad. She was bullied terribly for her clothes and not showering, and I don't even know how she dealt with it. A group of girls led by Phoebe Edwards were so mean to her. Phoebe was the worst of them, and she nearly got Rayna expelled from school once because Rayna punched her in the face."

"Rayna punched another girl?" Stark said.

"Totally, but I mean, Phoebe kind of deserved it. She was so awful to Rayna. Anyway, Phoebe's dad threatened to, like, sue the school if they didn't kick Rayna out, but the principal and the guidance counselor smoothed it over somehow."

Aditi's face turned solemn. "But, then, two months before graduation, Rayna missed school for nearly two weeks. We were sure she'd dropped out because of being homeless and stuff. But then she came back to school and was, like, showered and had clean clothes, and she graduated with the rest of us."

"What happened?" Stark asked.

Aditi shrugged. "No one knows. Well, Emma over at Twisted Stitches probably does - she's been Rayna's best friend since they were kids - but the rest of us don't have a clue."

"Where are her parents now?" Stark asked.

"Oh, they died in a car accident six months after we graduated high school," Aditi said. "Her mom was driving while drunk, and she was speeding and lost control. They hit a tree, and both of them were killed instantly. I was dating a guy whose dad was a paramedic, and his dad said neither of them was wearing a seatbelt, and they had to scrape Rayna's parents off the pavement. Rayna had to go in and identify the bodies even though they were all gooey and stuff. Isn't that awful?"

"Yes," Stark said. His skin had gone prickly and tight, and the protein bar he'd eaten half an hour earlier was like a stone in his stomach.

"Anyway," Aditi gave Stark a cheerful smile, "despite her awful childhood, Rayna is so nice, and she does so much for animals. She runs an animal rescue right here in Harmony Falls."

She turned to her computer and typed rapidly before grabbing the papers and handing them to him. "The documents have been emailed to you."

"Thank you." Stark took the documents back to his office. He sat in his chair, stared blankly at his computer, then stood and headed toward the back exit. He stepped outside, regretting his decision not to grab his jacket when the cold air hit his skin, and stared at the white van with "Sneaky Leaks Plumbing" emblazoned on the side of it in bold purple letters parked next to the gym.

He didn't need to go to the gym. Hollis was perfectly capable of handling the plumbing issue. Nope, what he needed to do was go back to his office and not think about Rayna Abrams and her crappy childhood. What did he care if she'd had a tough start to life? It didn't change the fact that she had something he wanted.

Perfect breasts with gorgeous pink nipples and satin soft skin.

He muttered a curse and reached for the door handle. He wanted Rayna's land, nothing else. His sudden obsession with her breasts was just a by-product of not being laid since he moved to Harmony Falls. He would spend this weekend in New Cassel, enjoying his penthouse and the company of a beautiful woman who wanted the same thing he wanted - easy, simple, no commitment sex.

He yanked open the door, hesitated, and then let it go, walking toward the gym. He stepped inside the warm building, letting the door close quietly behind him as he stared at Rayna and Hollis.

They stood at the far end near the entrance to the locker room. Rayna studied one of the weight machines, reaching out to trace her fingers along it as she said, "This is state of the art gym equipment."

"Is it?" Hollis asked. "I've never used it."

"Yes," Rayna said. "His equipment is much better than either of our local gyms, and Iron Fitness just renovated last year and brought in all new equipment."

"You're one of them," Hollis said.

Rayna glanced at her. "Them?"

"Gym fanatic," Hollis said.

"That obvious?" Rayna asked with a grin.

"You're drooling a little," Hollis said.

Rayna laughed. "I do enjoy a good workout."

Stark's brain immediately went to a vision of Rayna

straddling his hips, her firm, naked body riding him hard, both of them panting and sweating and -

Enough!

"Is this place for Stark only, or does he offer memberships?" Rayna asked.

"The gym is for Mr. Stark and employees of Stark Entertainment only," Hollis said. "Sorry."

"No worries," Rayna said.

"Which gym do you use?" Hollis asked politely.

"Oh, I don't have a gym membership," Rayna said. "I used to, but this year, I needed to use my gym fee to pay for a couple of cat spays."

"You use your money for the rescue?" Hollis asked.

"I try not to, but when donations are low, sometimes it's a necessity." Rayna shrugged. "It's all good, though. I got some equipment from a Facebook local free group and use it at home."

Rayna touched the equipment again, and Stark could practically see the yearning on her face from across the room. He walked toward them as she smiled at Hollis. "So, if you give me ten minutes, I'll write up the estimate, and you can discuss it with your boss."

"We can discuss it now." Stark joined them, pretending not to notice how Rayna's body stiffened or the irritation that flickered across her face before a mask of polite professionalism settled onto her features.

"Mr. Stark, this is Rayna Abrams," Hollis said. "She works for -"

"We've met," Rayna said.

"Ms. Abrams," Stark said.

"Stark," Rayna said.

Hollis studied them both, her dark brown eyes unreadable as thick tension filled the room. "I'll leave the two of you to discuss the issue."

She left the gym, and Rayna gave Stark a thin smile. "I believe the water pressure issue is from a leaking pipe."

"You believe, or you know?" he asked.

Her nostrils flared, but she kept that thin smile on her face. "I know. I used a listening disc to detect and pinpoint the water leak."

"This building is brand new, less than six months old. Why would the pipes be leaking?" He could hear the exasperation in his voice.

"Most likely, it happened during installation," Rayna said. "In order to fix the leak, I'll need to remove some of the shower tiles and cut an access hole in the backer board."

Fresh irritation washed over him. "The tile is very expensive, Ms. Abrams."

"I can assure you that if you leave the leak, the resulting water damage will be more expensive," she said.

"You're certain it's behind the shower wall," he said.

"Yes."

"How certain?"

She gave him a withering look. "I am very confident in my diagnosis."

"Maybe we should have a more experienced member of your team consult on the issue."

Jesus, he couldn't stop needling her which did him no favours in getting what he wanted from her, but how her pretty brown eyes lit up with fire whenever he did fascinated him.

Those eyes were flashing fire and brimstone at him right now. He was pretty sure he'd be a smoking pile of flesh and bone on the floor if Rayna glared any harder at him.

"I have more than enough experience for this job," she snapped.

"You're young," he said.

"What does that have to do with anything?" she said.

"You're old, but I'm not holding that against you. Your shitty attitude, however…"

"I'm only thirty-two," he said, "and wanting to ensure that I have the best person for the job is not a shitty attitude."

"I am excellent at my job, but I have neither the time nor the interest in convincing you of that. I'll give my estimate to Hollis, and you can contact our office if you'd like to hire us for the job."

She pushed past him and stalked toward the door. He stared at her ass in her cheap polyester pants, his face flushing when she suddenly turned and caught him staring.

"Sneaky Leaks Plumbing is the best plumbing company in town, and you'd be an idiot if you didn't hire us for this job just because I won't sell you my land."

"That has nothing to do with it," he said.

"Bullshit," she snapped. "It has everything to do with it. You've already insulted me enough today. Don't insult me further by pretending it doesn't."

She left the gym, and Stark muttered a curse. Christ, what was it about Rayna Abrams that got under his skin and made him act so fucking childish?

CHAPTER 10

"R ay-Ray, are you even listening to me?"

Rayna turned and smiled at the woman standing in her kitchen. "Of course I am."

"She isn't," Arianna said to Emma. "Right?"

"She's a little zoned out." Emma studied a notepad in front of her, her fingers absently tracing the port wine birthmark on her left cheek.

"She's in, like, another universe tonight," Arianna said.

Rayna wanted to argue, but Arianna was right - she was distracted. She gave the pretty woman a faint smile. "Sorry, Arianna."

While she and Emma had been best friends since they were kids, her friendship with Arianna was relatively new and, Rayna supposed, a little unconventional. She'd met the twenty-year-old influencer and makeup artist at a volunteer event, and despite their differences, they had become friends.

Or, as Emma liked to say, Arianna had imprinted on Rayna like a baby duck.

Either way, she genuinely liked Arianna and enjoyed her company. And while Arianna was occasionally self-absorbed, she never hesitated to help Rayna with volunteer events for the rescue.

"It's, like, fine," Arianna said. "But I really thought Zuri was going to strangle you tonight."

Rayna grimaced as Emma made a sound of agreement. She would have to apologize to her events coordinator asap. Zuri went above and beyond when it came to fundraisers, and this bachelor/bachelorette fundraiser was a huge undertaking.

Zuri had left about ten minutes ago, and while Rayna hadn't gotten the sense that she was frustrated with her, she wasn't risking the chance. She would apologize on her knees if necessary.

You know who else would like you on your knees?

She gritted her teeth, cursing her inner thoughts and her vivid imagination. Stark was not attracted to her, and just because she caught him checking out her ass earlier today didn't mean he wanted a damn blow job from her. Besides, the polyester pants she wore to work didn't do a thing for her ass, so even if he was checking it out, it didn't -

"Rayna!" Arianna's voice was full of exasperation, and Rayna tossed every single Stark thought out of her head with a concentrated effort. "What is going on with you tonight?"

"Nothing, just a weird day at work," Rayna said.

Arianna shuddered. "How many toilets did you have to plunge?"

"None," Rayna said. "But it was busy and..."

"And what?" Arianna sat down beside Emma.

When Rayna didn't reply, Emma said, "And she had to go to a call at her mortal enemy's workplace."

"Ooh!" Arianna immediately perked up. "You saw Isaac Stark? He's so dreamy. I saw him at the coffee shop the other day, and he was totally checking me out."

"He's way too old for you," Rayna said. "If he was checking you out, then that makes him a pervert."

Arianna gave her a pout. "Okay, fine, he didn't even glance at me, but why do you have to ruin my hot guy fantasy, Ray-Ray?"

"Because he's an asshole, and I don't want you in his orbit," Rayna said. "Stay away from him, honey."

"Sure," Arianna said. "So, are you grumpy because you had to plunge his toilet, and it was super gross?"

"My job isn't just plunging toilets," Rayna said.

"Right." Arianna didn't look like she believed her.

"She's grumpy and distracted because he gave her a super hard time about knowing her own damn job," Emma said. "Which, despite how much I love his video games and admire his talent, really is an asshole move on his part."

"Exactly!" Rayna said, sinking into a chair across from them. "And then, and then - he had the audacity to hire us for the job."

Emma blinked at her as Arianna said, "I don't get it. Why is that a bad thing?"

"Because he basically said right to my face that he didn't think I could do the job, and then later called my boss and not only agreed to the estimate, but insisted that I be the one who does the work."

"Maybe he felt bad for being so rude," Arianna said.

"He doesn't have the emotional capacity to feel bad," Rayna said. "All he cares about is himself and his money. Other people are just pawns to him. He is incapable of feeling emotion."

Emma laughed. "Okay, do you think you're exaggerating just a little? He did save you from the tree the other night. How is your back, by the way?"

"Sore and spectacularly bruised," Rayna said.

"What tree?" Arianna asked. She petted Molly, who was weaving around her feet and purring loudly.

Not one to miss out on pets, Bea immediately heaved herself out of her bed and headed toward Arianna, nudging Molly out of the way and pressing her head against Arianna's leg.

"It's a long story," Rayna said.

"Bea, you'd better not fart," Arianna said.

Immediately, there was a long, low braaap, and Arianna made a disgusted face. "Bea!"

"You practically dared her to do it," Rayna said.

Arianna waved her hand in front of her face before standing. "Okay, I'm leaving before the smell, like, permeates my clothing. Ray-Ray, you want me at the hall at six for the fundraiser, right?"

"That's right," Rayna said. "Thank you again for volunteering to do the bachelorettes' makeup. I know a lot of them appreciate it."

"Oh, like, of course," Arianna said. "I'm happy to help the ladies and the animals. And, like, you're still okay with me doing a live stream video of some of it for my followers, right?"

"Yes," Rayna said with a grin. "That's fine with me."

"Okay, good." Arianna grimaced. "Oh God, Bea, you smell so bad." She blew a kiss to Rayna and headed toward the door. "Oh, Em-Em - I almost forgot! Your foundation will be in by then, so I'll bring it with me, okay?"

"Thanks, Arianna," Emma said.

"Of course!" Arianna blew another kiss and left.

Emma waited until she heard the front door close before saying, "Em-Em?"

"Welcome to the Arianna nickname club," Rayna said with a laugh.

Emma rolled her eyes before studying the notepad again.

"Okay, so Lucas, Connor, Wyatt, and Nathan will start setting up tables and chairs at five thirty."

"Man, I wish we could have gotten Wyatt to be a bachelor," Rayna said. "Women love a hot cowboy."

"I know, but Wyatt hasn't dated a single person since Lydia left him. He's still not over her."

"It's been years," Rayna said.

Emma shrugged. "I feel for the guy but honestly think he's better off without her. We have Addison Moore and Grace Larkin at the ticket table, Doug overseeing the PA system, and his wife Judy, Wanda Taber, and Savina Ras in charge of the appetizers and wine. Wren is backstage with you and me, organizing the bachelor and bachelorettes for when they go on stage, and Solomon Whitaker agreed to be the MC. How did you make that happen?"

"Savina," Rayna said. "She's been friends with him and his wife for years. Hey, thanks for getting that James guy at Stark Entertainment to volunteer to be a bachelor. I met him today at the Stark offices, and he's super cute."

"Isn't he?" Emma grinned at her. "Total sweetheart, as well. You think you might bid on him at the auction?"

"No," Rayna said.

"Why not?" Emma asked.

Rayna just shrugged. "I'm broke and have no money to bid, and I'm busy with house renovations and the rescue. No time for a relationship."

"Or you're not interested because you want to bang Isaac Stark."

Rayna glared at her. "That was told to you with the expectation of it being a secret, Emma."

Emma looked around the kitchen, her gaze landing on Bea, who had headed back to her bed in the corner and Molly, who was sitting on top of Bea and kneading the beagle's back with her claws while she purred away. "You think Bea or Molly are going to say something? Hey, where are those cute but yappy Chihuahuas you had running around here?"

"Diane is fostering them," Rayna said. "She picked them up last night."

"So, are you not interested in James because of Stark?" Emma asked.

Rayna shook her head. "It has nothing to do with him. And I hate that I'm attracted to Stark. Hate it."

"I know," Emma said sympathetically.

"He's trying to bully me out of my own home, and all I can think about is how much I want his dick in my cooch," Rayna said with a sigh. "I'm so mad at myself."

"He's hot, smart, and talented," Emma said. "I get it."

"He's also a rich asshole who thinks he's better than everyone else in this town. I don't even get why he's living here. You just know he has some mansion in New Cassel. Why did he move here?"

"I don't know," Emma said. "Lucas has worked with Stark for years but knows barely anything about him. Stark isn't much for sharing personal stuff. Lucas knows he spent time here as a child with his grandparents, but that's all. Oh, and it's a penthouse."

"What?" Rayna asked.

"Stark has a penthouse in New Cassel, not a mansion. Lucas has been to it - says it's huge and has an incredible view of the city."

"Of course it does," Rayna said, rolling her eyes.

"Speaking of Lucas." Emma checked her phone. "He's on his way home from his parents, and I told him I'd be at home waiting for him."

"Dressed in slutty lingerie and ready to rock his world?" Rayna asked.

A red flush flooded Emma's cheeks. "Maybe."

Rayna grinned at her. "You know how happy I am for you, right, Emmy? Lucas is so lucky to have you as his girlfriend."

"He really is," Emma said with a cheeky laugh as she closed the notebook and grabbed her stuff. "Seriously, though, I know Lucas and I haven't been dating that long, but I love him so much, Rayna. I'm going to marry that boy."

"Pfft, tell me something I don't know," Rayna said.

Emma cupped her shoulders and said, "Listen, I know you're super stressed about the upcoming fundraiser, but we still have nearly two weeks to iron out all the kinks and issues. It'll be great, sweetie."

"Okay, thanks, Emma." She followed Emma to the front door and opened it as Emma slid her jacket and boots on. "Shit!"

"What's wrong?" Emma peered around her. "Oh no."

Rayna stepped onto the front porch and studied the cardboard box sitting near the door, then squatted and carefully opened it. With Emma hovering over her shoulder, she parted the blanket and stared with dismay at the three tiny kittens curled up together.

"They're so little," Emma said.

Rayna sighed and picked up the box, carrying it into the kitchen. She touched the kittens, relieved when they meowed and squirmed, and their little bodies were still relatively warm.

"How old do you think they are?" Emma asked.

"Four weeks, maybe?" Rayna said.

"They couldn't have been out there that long," Emma frowned. "Arianna's only been gone twenty minutes, and she would have told you there was a box on the porch."

Her frown deepened as Rayna reached for her phone. "Wait, I thought you were getting a doorbell cam?"

"I used the money to help a low-income senior buy food for her dog," Rayna said.

"Honey, you need a camera," Emma said. "With the number of sketchy people who drop animals off at your house, you shouldn't be opening the door without knowing who it is first."

"Yeah, I know," Rayna said, texting rapidly. "But there's always something else that feels more important to buy, and right now, cash is super low for the rescue."

"Promise me when you get some funds from the auction, you'll get a new one," Emma said.

"I'll try, but our vet bills are crazy high, and our Helping Hands fund is almost empty," Rayna said.

Her phone dinged, and she read it, relief washing over her. "Thank God. Catelyn can take the babies."

"Who's Catelyn?"

"A new volunteer with neonate experience," Rayna said. "These babies need bottle feeding, and our only other neonate foster is in Jamaica right now."

She rubbed at her forehead, trying to think past the sudden exhaustion. She'd been looking forward to a hot shower and her warm bed after Emma left, but that wasn't happening now. "Okay, I gotta get these babies and some supplies to Catelyn asap. Who knows when they ate last."

"Do you want me to go with you?" Emma asked.

"Nah, you go home to your man and get your freak on," Rayna said. "Love you, Emmy."

"Love you too, Rayna."

CHAPTER 11

"You sound tired, love."

"I'm fine." Stark switched his phone to his other ear, and one finger typed at his keyboard. "Did you talk to your doctor about the heart palpitations?"

"I did." His mother sounded as carefree as she always did. "They did some tests and said it's nothing to worry about."

"Nothing to worry about?" Stark stopped typing. "There is absolutely something to worry about. I want you to get a second opinion from Dr. Moren. I'll call and book you an appointment."

"You mean you'll have Hollis call and book an appointment," his mother said with a laugh. "I'm perfectly capable of booking my own doctor's appointment, darling."

"You are, but I know you, and it'll slip your mind the moment we get off the phone. Hollis will call you and coordinate a time that works, okay?"

"Sure," his mother said. "How are things going, dearest? You really do sound quite tired."

"Just a long day," he said.

"Any luck getting the third property from your neighbour?" she asked.

He grimaced. "No, but I did have to rescue her from my tree a few days ago."

"That sounds like a fun story," his mother said. "Do tell."

He relayed the entire story, skipping the part where he had Rayna's tits in his face, and was amused by his mother's reactions despite how tired he was.

"Oh my goodness," his mother said when he was finished. "I think I might love your neighbour."

"Don't, Mom," he said. "She's the enemy, remember?"

"Isaac, how can someone so dedicated to saving innocent animals be the enemy?"

"She's deliberately not selling me her property because she hates me," he said.

"You don't know that for certain," his mother said.

"I do. The property is great, but the house is falling apart. The amount I offered her is way above the value of her property. I'm being nice, and she has no reason not to sell it to me."

His mother laughed. "No one has ever accused you of being nice, sweetheart."

He ignored the little jab of hurt he felt. His mother wasn't being malicious, and besides, she was right. He wasn't a nice guy and never would be.

"Have you tried asking her why she wants to keep the property so much? Maybe if you can find common ground, you can -"

"We have nothing in common, Mom. She's a plumber who runs an animal rescue, and I'm... me. She has a million animals at her house, and all of her clothes come from Walmart."

"Don't be a snob, Isaac." His mother's tone lost its playfulness. "I didn't raise you to be judgmental about others."

"Sorry, ma'am," he said.

He knew why she was so pissed. He had sounded scarily similar to his father, and he hated that there was even a part of him that was anything like his old man.

"It won't happen again," he said.

"See that it doesn't," she said, her voice still sharp.

There was silence before she sighed. "Sorry, dearest. I shouldn't take my trauma over your father out on you."

"You didn't. I was being a judgmental asshole and deserved to be called out on it," he said. "I'm sure Rayna Abrams is a perfectly nice person, but she has something I want and -"

"And you're not used to being denied what you want," his mother said.

"Pretty much," he said.

She laughed. "Oh, my love, I do adore you. Try not to be the big bad wolf to the poor girl, though, would you? Take it down a notch and maybe be her friend, or at the very least, be civil with her."

"She'll probably feed me to a dog if I show any sign of weakness around her."

His mother laughed again. "Well, I do hope she doesn't turn you into dog chow, dearest. Listen, I must run. I'm having my usual Thursday night dinner with Sandra Wilkinson, and you know how she abhors tardiness. Love you, my boy."

"I love you too."

Stark ended the call and stared blankly at his computer screen before leaning back and spinning his chair around to stare out his office window. Snow fell softly, and he studied the flakes for nearly five minutes before rubbing one hand against his jaw.

He was tired and in a bad mood. Work had been nothing but putting out fires all week, and he was seriously considering leaving tonight for New Cassel instead of tomorrow night. Lucas, James, and Hollis could handle anything that came up at the office, and it had been forever since he'd had a three-day weekend. Hell, it'd been forever since he'd had a weekend. As much as he wanted to deny it, he was a workaholic and didn't see that changing anytime soon. Not when he had nothing else in his life.

Whoa, where did that come from?

He muttered a curse and shut down his computer. He liked his life. No, he fucking *loved* his life, and just because he'd had a bad week and was feeling rattled and out of sorts didn't mean he was suddenly questioning every decision he'd ever made.

Besides, everyone felt lonely occasionally, even assholes like him.

He stuck his laptop in his bag, grabbed his phone and shut off the office light. He would go to New Cassel tonight. He'd relax in the luxuriousness of his penthouse, drink five hundred dollar scotch, and enjoy the company of a beautiful woman.

His mind immediately conjured an image of Rayna, with her fiery brown eyes and how her lips looked soft and lush, even when thinned with anger. He pictured those lips wrapped around his dick and said appendage immediately hardened.

He grunted with annoyance and banished Rayna's image from his head. He adjusted his dick, waiting impatiently for his erection to subside before leaving his office. He popped his head into Hollis's office. "Hey, I'm taking the day off tomorrow."

She blinked at him, and he took more than a bit of pleasure in shocking his normally unflappable assistant.

"Okay," she said. "Not available day off, or working from home day off."

"Only available for emergencies day off," he said.

"All right. Enjoy your weekend, Mr. Stark," she said.

"You as well, Hollis." He hesitated. "Do you, uh, have any plans for the weekend?"

She arched one perfect eyebrow at him. "Nothing in particular."

"Right. Well, have a good one."

She nodded. "Before you go, James is in a meeting and isn't available. Can you sign off on paying the Sneaky Leak's invoice?"

He dropped his computer bag on the chair and scrawled his signature on the paper Hollis held out to him. Trying to sound casual, he said, "She finished it quickly."

"Yes, she did," Hollis said. "And she only had to remove two tiles to do it."

"Seriously?" he asked.

Hollis nodded. "Yes. I've arranged to have the backer board and tile replaced next week, and because Rayna fixed the leaking pipe without cutting a huge hole, she's saved you money on both materials and labour. I sent you an email about this."

"Right," he said. "It's been busy this week, and I haven't had the chance to read it."

That was complete bullshit. He had avoided all things Rayna related because anytime he thought of her, it typically led to some very lucid and dirty fantasies of how she might sound when he went down on her.

Christ. He really needed to get laid this weekend.

Hollis was staring at him like she knew he was full of bullshit, and he decided to make his damn escape. "See you Monday, Hollis."

"Enjoy your weekend, Mr. Stark."

STARK SET HIS COMPUTER BAG ON THE SIDE TABLE IN THE hallway before walking to the kitchen. He didn't bother to turn on the light as he grabbed a bottle of water from the fridge and checked the weather app on his phone.

It was supposed to snow off and on all night, but there were no weather advisories regarding travel. He would pack an overnight bag and leave before -

"What the hell?"

He stared out the window over the sink. It faced the backyard, and he could see a light bobbing along the fence line. It stopped in front of the tree before shining up into the branches.

"Shit," he said. "Not again."

He whipped open the back door and stepped out into the yard, stalking silently through the snow until he stood behind Rayna.

She was staring up into the tree as she scanned the branches with the flashlight. "Molly," she said in a soft voice. "Molly, honey, are you up there? Come to Mama."

"Planning on climbing my tree again, Ms. Abrams?"

She shrieked and whirled around. Stark winced and held his hand up to block the light shining directly into his eyes. "Can you lower that?"

She pointed the flashlight at the ground. "You scared the crap out of me! Why are you sneaking up on me in…"

"In my own backyard?" he asked.

She flushed, and he crossed his arms over his chest, giving her a pointed look. "You're trespassing again."

She turned around, ignoring him completely, and scanned the tree again.

Immediately annoyed by being ignored, he said, "Is there a reason you're in my yard, Ms. Abrams?"

"Molly got out again," she said. "Have you seen her? She's the pregnant calico cat - orange and black and white."

"I haven't seen her," he said.

"Are you sure?"

"Positive," he said.

She turned to face him, snowflakes catching on her lashes as she chewed at her bottom lip. Even in the dim light of the flashlight, he could see the worry on her face. She swept the flashlight around his yard before pushing past him. "Okay, thanks."

He watched in astonishment as she grabbed the top of the fence separating their properties and nimbly pulled herself up and over it. She dropped into her yard with a soft grunt, and he marched over to the fence.

"What are you doing?"

She was studying the dark forest behind their yards. "I'm getting warmer clothes and a better flashlight and searching the woods for Molly."

"There are wolves in the woods, Ms. Abrams."

"I'm aware," she said.

Before he could say anything else, she headed across her yard and toward her house.

Thrown off by his immediate anxiety over her going into the woods, he shouted, "It's just a cat! You're going to get eaten by wolves over a damn cat?"

Without turning around, she held her hand out and popped her middle finger at him.

"Real mature," he snapped, his anxiety for her disappearing in an instant.

He stalked back into his house, slamming the back door before walking toward his bedroom. "She's crazy," he said. "Certifiably insane. She'll get herself killed, and then I'll never get her damn property."

You can't let her go out there alone. It's too dangerous.

"Fuck!" he shouted before stalking toward the closet. If he was about to be tromping through the fucking woods as a potential snack for wolves, he wasn't wearing a goddamn suit for the festivities.

He paused in front of the closet. He'd left the door half open this morning, and he cocked his head at the soft meow coming from inside of it. He opened it fully, his eyes widening in disbelief. "Are you fucking kidding me?"

CHAPTER 12

Rayna ignored the pounding on her front door as she searched through the kitchen junk drawer for batteries for the good flashlight.

"C'mon," she snarled, yanking the drawer open further as a flurry of pencils, receipts, and tape dispensers fell to the ground. She pawed through the contents, her heart thudding and her stomach churning. Where the fuck were the batteries?

The pounding grew louder, and she shouted, "Fuck!" before stomping down the hallway to the front door. She yanked it open. "Can I help... what do you want?"

She glared at Stark, who glared right back. "I found your stupid cat."

"What?" She went still, relief washing over her. "You found Molly?"

"Yes. She's in my goddamn house."

"You let her into your house?" she said, confused.

"I didn't *let* her into my house," he snapped. "I have no fucking idea how she got into my house, but you need to come get her immediately."

"Fine," she said. "Christ, you don't have to be such a dick about it."

He didn't answer, just turned around and stomped down the porch stairs. She shut the door behind her and followed him silently into his house. She didn't say a word when he led her past the kitchen and living room and down a narrow hallway papered in horrible wallpaper that featured oversized shiny pink roses and... were those sparkles?

He opened a door, and she paused on the threshold. "Is this your bedroom?"

"Yes, why?" He gave her an impatient look.

"I'm not going into your bedroom," she said. Butterflies were flapping around in her stomach, and she couldn't seem to stop staring at his bed. Stark slept there. He slept there, maybe naked, and it was way too easy to picture herself in that bed, definitely naked and riding Stark's face to the best orgasm of her life.

Rayna!

"If you want your damn cat, you're coming into my bedroom," he growled.

Her stomach still quivering, she stepped into the room, following him toward a closed door near the far end of the room. He opened it, and she blinked in surprise.

"Holy shit."

"You need to take your cat home immediately," Stark said.

Ignoring him, she sat cross-legged in front of the closet and reached out to pet Molly. "Hello, sweet girl."

Molly purred loudly before bending her head to groom one of the three tiny kittens sleeping against her belly.

"Look at your sweet babies. What a good girl," she said.

"No," Stark said. "Not a good girl. There is blood and... *goo*... all over my favourite cashmere sweater, Ms. Abrams."

She studied the dark grey sweater that Molly was nesting

on. Feeling nearly giddy with relief over Molly being safe, she said, "Maybe you should learn to put your clothes away."

"I did," he snarled. "It was on that shelf, and your dumb cat must have pulled it down to give birth. Do you have any idea how much that sweater cost? It's ruined."

She laughed. "Yeah, go ahead and bill the rescue for it. I'll get my accountant on it asap."

Stark sighed before squatting beside her. He watched silently as she carefully picked up each baby and examined them. They looked perfect, with bellies already round with milk, and Molly had cleaned them well. She placed them back against Molly, smiling when they started meowing and squirming. Molly meowed back, and Rayna gently rearranged the babies until they were each at a nipple.

They began to nurse, and she petted Molly again. Stark made another sigh of impatience. "How exactly did your cat escape your house and get into mine?"

"I have no idea," she said. "Did you leave a window open?"

"In the middle of winter?" he asked. "You shouldn't be letting your cats roam like this."

"Obviously, I wasn't," she said. "Molly is an escape artist."

"Maybe you should have been watching her better," he said.

Anger washed over her. How dare he judge her when he had no idea what it was like to keep a cat determined to be outdoors inside. He was such an asshole.

"You need to get them out of here, Ms. Abrams," Stark said.

She stared at the purring Molly, scratching lightly at her chin as a truly diabolical plan took hold in her head. She hesitated for only a few seconds before deciding that fuck it, Stark deserved to be messed with.

"Sorry," she said briskly. "I can't move Molly or the babies."

"What do you mean?"

"If I move them from the area Molly chose as her nest, the babies will die," she lied.

He blinked at her. "They'll die?"

"Yes," she said. "Molly will abandon them if we try to put the babies in a different nesting area."

"Are you serious?"

"Completely serious," she said. "The most we can do is change out the birthing bedding. Any more than that and Molly will leave her babies to die."

"Christ, this is why I like dogs and not cats," he snapped.

Feeling bad only that she was besmirching Molly's good name, she shrugged. "It's biology. I'm afraid you're stuck with them for now."

"For how long?" he asked.

"Not that long. Just eight weeks," she said.

His eyes nearly bugged out of his head, and she had to fight hard not to start laughing. "Two months? I have to have this cat and her babies in my closet for two months?"

"Afraid so," she said. "Unless you want to be a kitten murderer?"

He muttered another curse. "I am not set up to take care of a cat."

She grinned at him. "It's no problem. I have everything at my house that you'll need to be a foster."

"I am not a cat foster," he snapped.

"You're not *not* a cat foster," she said.

His face suggested he wanted to murder her, and Rayna couldn't remember the last time she'd been so happy.

She stood and gave him another megawatt smile. "Come back to my house, and we'll get all the supplies you need for Molly and her babies."

"Ms. Abrams, I cannot…"

She stared silently at him as his gaze dropped to Molly

and her babies. He raked his hand through his hair. "I was supposed to go away this weekend."

"Oh, I can check in on Molly and the babies while you're gone," she said.

"I am not leaving you alone in my house," he said.

"Do you think I'm going to booby-trap it?" she asked before rolling her eyes.

"I don't know how to look after kittens," he said.

"You don't have to. Molly will do all the work," she said. "You just have to feed her, give her fresh water, and clean her litter box."

His face turned green. "Her litter box?"

"Yes, she shits in a box," she said cheerfully.

"Fuck," he whispered before he stared at the kittens again, and his body slumped. "Fine. Let's get the damn supplies."

ACUTELY AWARE OF STARK AND HIS ANNOYED SIGHS BEHIND her, Rayna stepped inside her house. Bea waited at the door, tail wagging happily and her nose sniffing the new scent in the house. She nosed past Rayna and made a soft, welcoming woof before bumping her face against Stark's legs.

Stark bent and stroked her head and long, silky ears, studying her white muzzle. "Hello, old girl."

"Her name is Bea," Rayna said. "Follow me, and we'll get the supplies."

She led him to the back of the house, past the kitchen and the laundry room. Freddie was sitting in the doorway, and he gave Stark a suspicious look, his tail lashing back and forth.

Always unhappy about new people in the house, the cat turned and disappeared into the laundry room as Stark made a loud grunt and a muttered curse. She turned to see him bracing his hand against the wall, frowning at Bea, who, now that he had stopped, immediately plopped her ass onto his feet, panting happily and grinning up at him.

"Your dog just tried to trip me."

"It wasn't on purpose," Rayna said. "She's mostly blind."

"Off my feet, Bea," Stark said.

Bea didn't move, just continued to pant happily and Rayna said, "She didn't hear you. She's almost completely deaf."

"Christ, how old is she?" Stark said. Despite the annoyance she could hear in his voice, he was infinitely gentle when he reached down and nudged Bea's shoulder. "Move, Bea."

She stood obligingly, letting out a loud fart as she did so.

"Oh my God," Stark said as the smell washed over both of them. "There is something seriously wrong with your dog, Ms. Abrams. Nothing healthy can make that smell."

Despite herself, Rayna laughed. "She's actually very healthy."

"I don't believe it," Stark muttered. "Can we please get out of this hallway before your dog's flatulence kills us both?"

"Such a drama queen," she said but started walking again. She opened the door to her home gym/storage room and headed to the far side of the room. Large metal shelves were braced along one wall. Plastic bins filled with various dog and cat supplies, cans and small bags of both dog and cat food, toys, and empty litter boxes filled the shelves.

Larger bags of food and boxes of kitty litter were piled neatly on the floor, and she reached for a bin labeled 'neonate' supplies and pulled it from the shelf with a loud grunt.

She set it on the ground and searched past the cans of kitten milk replacement, bottles, and nipples for a small kitchen scale, half a dozen towels, and a few small soft blankets. She added food and water dishes, a flat of wet food and a bag of dry food to the pile before grabbing an empty litter box, a litter scoop, and a big box of kitty litter.

"Okay, this should get you started. I'll also need you to fill out our foster form application and submit it. It's on the website, but if you give me your phone number, I'll text the link to you. I'll be your point of contact for Molly and the babies. If there are any issues with Molly or her babies, text me immediately, it doesn't matter what time it is."

There was no reply, and she turned around to see Stark on the other side of the room, examining her gym equipment with a look of disgust on his face.

"Stark, are you listening to me?"

He reached out and poked at the single stack home gym she'd picked up for free. "Christ, was this thing made in the seventies?"

"It's not that old," she said defensively.

"It's falling apart," he said.

"It's fine."

He gave the machine a shake. The home gym rattled wildly, and when a screw fell off and rolled on the ground to hit Stark's foot, he gave her a 'told you so' look that set her teeth on edge.

"It's a death trap," he said.

"You're being a drama queen again."

He studied the small rack of hand weights against the wall before examining her stationary bike. "This was definitely made in the seventies."

"It still works," she said.

"Does it?" He pushed at one pedal with his foot.

It snapped off and hit the floor with a thud. Bea wandered over and examined the pedal with interest as Stark stared at Rayna.

"You're paying to fix that," she said.

"Bill me," he said. "I'll have my accountant get right on it."

93

He moved on to her ancient treadmill before she could think of a snarky reply. He turned it on and grimaced when the motor started with a loud squeal. The belt moved at a turtle's pace, and when smoke started to seep from beneath it, Stark shut off the treadmill.

"It's fine," she said before he could say anything.

"The belt is smoking," he said.

"It only does that for the first couple of minutes," she said.

"Do you have a death wish when you're working out, Ms. Abrams? Is that why you use this crap?"

She sighed and said, "Not all of us can afford the fancy-ass equipment at your personal fancy-ass gym, Stark. Some of us make do with what we have. Now, if you're finished judging me on my home gym, do you think you can use those fancy gym equipment muscles of yours to carry the litter?"

She loaded the other supplies into a reusable bag as Stark picked up the box of litter. She snagged a cardboard box from the laundry room, and without speaking, they carried the supplies back to his house. She got to work setting up the litter box and filling the dishes with food and water.

"C'mon, Molly," she coaxed softly. "Come have a bite to eat so I can change your nest."

Stark had disappeared, and she made some psp, psp, psp, sounds until, with a soft meow, Molly left the babies and joined Rayna. She petted the cat a few times, and when Molly started to eat, she moved to the closet.

Stark returned holding a black garbage bag, and she picked up the kittens, placing them on a towel before picking up Stark's ruined sweater. Without speaking, he opened the garbage bag, and she put the sweater inside it.

Working quickly, she placed the box on the closet floor and set up another nest of towels and soft blankets inside of it. By the time Molly finished eating and returned to the closet, the babies were in their new nest. Molly jumped into the box and inspected each of them, grooming them lightly before settling in next to them so they could nurse again.

"Good girl, Molly," Rayna crooned, petting the calico cat gently. "You're being such a good mama."

She closed the closet door halfway and climbed to her feet. "The box will keep the babies contained but allow Molly to come and go from the nest. Molly should be fed three times a day with the wet food. She needs more calories now that she's nursing."

Looking uncharacteristically uncertain, Stark said, "Will it upset her if I reach into the closet to get my clothes every day."

"No," she said. "She's very friendly, and while she seems protective of the babies, she's not crazy psycho mama protective."

She pulled out her phone. "Can I get your phone number?"

He hesitated, and she rolled her eyes. "Trust me, I won't text you unless necessary. But I need you to fill out the foster form, and you need to be able to reach me in case of emergencies. Things can go wrong with babies this small."

He tensed. "How am I supposed to know if something's wrong?"

"The best way is by weighing the babies daily." She pointed to the scale. "Use that to weigh the babies every day at the same time. They should gain seven to ten grams a day, and if they don't, text me. If you're not sure if there's something wrong, text me. It's better to be safe than sorry, and it'll be easy enough for me to pop over and check the babies."

"This would be much easier if you would just take them to your house, Ms. Abrams," he said.

"Wouldn't it?" she said breezily. "But unfortunately, unless you want to be known as the town kitten murderer, the babies and Molly need to stay here."

God, she really should feel guilty about lying, but she didn't. Not one bit. She needed a foster for Molly and the babies anyway, and it wouldn't kill Stark to have a few cats in his house for eight weeks.

He grimaced before reciting his phone number. She added it to her phone. "Perfect. I'll send you the foster form. Are you still planning on going away this weekend? If so, I'll need a key to your house so I can feed Molly and check on her and the babies."

"I'll be staying home this weekend," he said.

Enjoying herself way too much, she gave him a cheeky grin and a wave. "Have a great weekend. I'll show myself out."

CHAPTER 13

Stark paused the video game and tossed the controller on the bed before cracking his neck lightly. He reached for his beer, grimaced at the warm taste and set the bottle back on the nightstand.

He grabbed his phone and checked messages, staring at the zero new texts before dropping his phone beside the controller. He stared blankly at the television screen on the wall across from the bed. It was Saturday night, and he was sitting alone in his bedroom, playing video games. Christ, it was as if he was living his teenage years all over again.

He studied his phone again. He had only a few friends in New Cassel, and here in Harmony Falls, he had precisely zero. Introverted and obsessed with gaming as a teenager, he'd never found it easy to make friends. As an adult, he'd been more focused on building his company than making friends.

It had never bothered him before. He enjoyed his solitude, but lately... lately, he'd been craving friendship and connection. Hell, a couple of weeks ago, he'd almost asked James if he wanted to go for a beer after work despite his strict rule of never sharing personal information with coworkers.

He picked up the game controller and restarted the game. He played mostly on autopilot, his thoughts returning again and again to his sudden desire for more connection with others.

When the small calico cat jumped onto the bed and butted her head against his hand, he said, "You just got me killed by a zombie, you know."

Molly purred loudly in response, and he glanced at her. "Aren't you supposed to be taking care of some babies?"

She butted his hand again, chirping at him.

"Look, let's get something straight. I don't like cats, and I don't want you living in my house. I especially am not enjoying scooping your shit out of the box every day. But here we are, so let's make the best of the situation. You keep your babies alive, and I'll feed you and keep your litter box clean, but otherwise, there are no interactions. Clear?"

Molly meowed, a plaintive little sound that made him pause the game to stare at her. "What?"

She bumped his hand, and he sighed before running his hand along her back. "There, I petted you. Happy?"

Purring loudly, she immediately flopped onto her side, her front paws kneading the air as she stared at him. When he didn't pet her, she rolled to her back and exposed her belly, making another of those sad meows.

"No way," he said. "I once dated a woman who had a cat. I know the belly is a trap."

She meowed again before rolling back to her side. He stroked along her ribs and down her tail before scratching under her chin. Her purring turned deafening, and she jumped up and climbed onto his lap.

"Whoa," he said, "no. Go on, cat. I don't want you in my lap."

Molly flopped down in his lap, her claws kneading his thigh through his sweatpants. He winced and gave her a gentle poke in the haunch. "No means no, lady."

She rubbed the side of her face against his knee, and he petted around her head again. "We need to have a serious discussion about consent, cat."

Still purring, she rubbed against his knee again, and he scratched under her chin and petted her soft body for nearly five minutes before she sat up and, with one final nudge to his hand, left his lap and jumped off the bed. She disappeared into the closet, and he heard her jump into the cardboard box.

"That's it?" he called. "You were just using me, is that right?"

She meowed, the sound muffled, and he rolled his eyes before picking up the controller. He stared at the buttons, another weird wave of loneliness washing over him.

"Fuck it," he said and shut off the game. It was nearly eleven, but he couldn't stand to sit here alone any longer. He'd go for a beer at the Thirsty Beaver. It was the most popular pub in Harmony Falls, and even if he sat at the bar and drank a beer alone, maybe he wouldn't *feel* so lonely surrounded by others.

He was dressed and out the door five minutes later. He glanced at Rayna's house. It was dark, and her battered old SUV wasn't parked in the driveway. He climbed into his car and turned the heat to high, blowing on his hands as he waited for the car to warm up. Christ, when he finally had all three properties and could start building, he'd make sure the three-car garage he planned to have was heated. This winter weather was bullshit.

With another glance at Rayna's, he pulled out of his driveway and headed toward the pub. He'd chosen to buy in this area specifically because of its privacy. It was close enough to town not to feel isolated but far enough to provide peace and quiet, especially during the summer when tourists flooded the town.

He hadn't driven more than five minutes before his headlights illuminated the vehicle parked on the side of the road. He slowed his car as his pulse picked up. He recognized the vehicle. The ancient SUV belonged to Rayna.

The stretch of road was dark and empty, without a house in at least a five-mile vicinity, and he scowled. "What the hell is she doing out here?"

With a muttered curse, he pulled over and parked behind her SUV. No doubt the piece of shit vehicle had broken down. He might have an intense dislike for his next door neighbour, but not even he would leave her stranded alone on the side of the road.

He shut off his vehicle and climbed out, grunting in surprise when he approached the driver's side and it was empty.

"Where the hell is she?" he said, his voice loud in the silence. Christ, he hoped she hadn't started walking into town or some bullshit like that. She was a woman on the smaller side, and while Harmony Falls was a reasonably safe place to live, walking into town would put her squarely on the south side, and some bad shit went down on that side of town.

A flash of light in his peripheral vision made him turn. He squinted at the beam of light that was about thirty feet from the side of the road.

A bad feeling in his stomach, he shouted, "Ms. Abrams!"

"What?" Her voice was faint but clear.

"What are you doing out here?"

"Working on my tan," she shouted.

"For fuck's sake," he said and waded across the snow-filled ditch toward the light. As he grew closer, he could hear Rayna speaking softly.

"It's okay, sweetheart. You're okay. Please hold still for a few minutes. I know it hurts, sweet girl."

He could see her on her knees beside a barbed wire fence, and he pushed through the last few feet of snow to crouch beside her. "What are you doing… oh, shit."

"Shh, sweet girl. It's okay." Rayna petted the shaking, whining dog, pressing hard on the dog's side when the lab cross tried to lurch to her feet. "No, girl. Stay. Don't move."

He grabbed the flashlight from where it was stuck in the snow and shone it on the dog. She was lying on her side in the snow in front of the fence, and he winced when he saw the barbed wire around her left back leg. It was wrapped around the meaty part of the dog's upper leg, and the dog's fur and the snow around it were soaked with blood.

"Jesus, what happened?" he asked.

"She's a stray in the area who I've been trying to catch for a few weeks now. Someone saw her tangled in the fence and called me."

"Who?" he asked.

"I don't know," she said impatiently. "Some guy. He didn't stick around. He just told me approximately where he'd seen her."

"He left her here to suffer?"

She gave him another impatient look. "Welcome to the world of animal rescue. People are both great and awful. What are you doing here?"

"I was headed into town. How will you get her free?"

"If I can get her to stay still without me having to hold her down, I'll cut the wire with these." She waved her free hand at him, and he studied the small bolt cutters she held.

He held his hand out. "You hold the dog. I'll cut the wire."

He expected her to argue, but she handed him the cutters

without speaking before holding the dog down with both hands. Working quickly, he cut the wire from the dog's leg, grimacing as he peeled it away, and she made a sharp yelp of pain.

"I know, sweetheart," Rayna said softly. "We'll get you feeling better soon, I promise. You're a good girl."

He unwound the last of the bloody barbed wire from the dog. "She's free."

"Thank you," Rayna said.

She stood, keeping one hand on the dog's ribs. "Can you stand, sweet girl?"

The dog stayed where she was, whining softly and continuously, and Rayna stroked her light coloured fur. "Okay, girl. I'll carry you."

She squatted, but before she could slide her hands under the dog's body, Stark nudged her out of the way. "I'll do it."

"You'll get blood on your clothes," Rayna warned.

He ignored her and lifted the dog. She hung limply in his arms, and he gave Rayna a worried look. "Now what?"

Rayna was already pulling out her phone. "Bring her to my SUV, please."

He followed her through the deep snow, the dog's whines making his chest tight.

"Hey, Nathan, it's Rayna. Yeah, sorry to call, but I have a badly injured dog. Her hind left leg was caught up in some barbed wire. It looks like she was trapped for quite a while and thrashed a lot. The leg is pretty bad... might need to be amputated bad."

Stark's stomach clenched as he stared at the dog in his arms. They crossed the ditch as Rayna said, "Okay, I'm on my way. Should be there in about fifteen minutes. Thanks, Nathan."

She opened the back of the SUV. There were already thick blankets laid out, and he gently set the dog down. Still whining and panting, she laid her head on the blankets and closed her eyes.

"Thank you," Rayna said again as she closed the door.

"What now?" he asked.

"Now I'm hauling ass to Brandt Vet Clinic." She brushed past him and yanked open the driver's door. "Thank you again. I appreciate your help."

She climbed into her SUV and drove off. He slid behind the wheel of his vehicle, watching the dwindling lights of Rayna's vehicle before muttering a curse and following her. She'd need help carrying the dog into the vet clinic, right?

CHAPTER 14

I t took nearly twenty minutes to get to the clinic, and Stark drove slowly down the long, bumpy driveway to the vet clinic and parked next to Rayna's SUV. Lights burned in the clinic building as he joined Rayna at the back of her SUV.

"What are you doing here?" she asked as she opened up the back.

"You need me to carry the dog into the clinic," he said.

"I'm stronger than I look," she said.

He ignored her and carefully picked up the dog. As they walked toward the clinic, the door opened, and a dark-haired man wearing just a t-shirt and jeans stepped out into the cold.

"Hey, Rayna."

"Hi, Nathan. Sorry, it's so late."

"It's not a problem," he said. "Bring her inside."

Stark carried the dog inside, following Rayna and Nathan through the front lobby to the swinging door that separated the treatment area from the rest of the clinic.

"Set her down here, please." Nathan pointed to a metal treatment table covered with a blanket.

Stark set the dog down, and Nathan glanced at him. "I'm Nathan Henshaw."

"Isaac Stark," he said.

Nathan petted the dog with a gentle hand. "Hey, girl. Looks like you got yourself into some trouble." He glanced at Rayna. "Is this the stray you've been trying to catch?"

"Yes," Rayna said.

"Okay. Can you hold her upper half, please?"

Rayna nodded, and Stark stepped back to give them both room, silently watching as Nathan assessed the dog's leg, prodding and manipulating it lightly, making soft noises of comfort when the dog cried out in pain.

Nathan stepped back, and Rayna said, "Do we need to amputate?"

"No, I think it looks worse than it is because there's so much torn skin," he said.

"Thank God," Rayna said.

"For now, I'll sedate, give pain meds, and clean and suture the wounds. I don't think her leg is broken, but radiographs would confirm that."

Stark watched as Rayna chewed viciously at her bottom lip. She studied the dog before taking a deep breath. "Are the x-rays necessary?"

"There are definitely no major breaks, but there could be a slight fracture." Nathan glanced at the dog. "That being said, we can save costs by not doing the radiographs."

"Yeah, okay, let's hold off on doing them," Rayna said, a tired defeat in her voice that made Stark's chest tighten again. "I wish we could do the x-rays, but you know…"

"I do," Nathan said sympathetically. He squeezed Rayna's shoulder. "Is it better to do them? Sure, but sometimes you can only do what you can do."

Rayna's phone rang, and she glanced at it and pinched the bridge of her nose. "Sorry, I need to take this."

She took a few steps away. "Hey, Nicole. What's up?"

She listened for a few minutes before saying, "He's not putting any weight on it? When did he fall down the stairs? Okay, I'm actually at Brandt's Vet Clinic right now. Can you meet me here with -"

She stopped, listening quietly and pinching the bridge of her nose again. "Yeah, no, I get it. I'll be there soon to grab him. Sure, no problem."

She ended the call and turned to Nathan. "Mr. Magoo fell down the stairs."

"Again?" Nathan said. "I told Nicole the last time that she needed to carry him down the stairs from now on. He's too old and unsteady to use the stairs."

"Yeah, I told her the same thing, and she promised me she would, but..." Rayna took another deep breath. "She thinks his leg might actually be broken this time but can't bring him to the clinic because her husband is on nights and the kids are in bed. Do you think he should be seen tonight, or do you think I can save on the emergency fee and keep him quiet until the morning and bring him in then?"

"Bring him now," Nathan said. "I'll give you the two-for-one emergency fee deal."

"Thanks, Nathan." Rayna gave him a grateful smile. "Nicole's deep on the south side, so I'll be at least thirty minutes."

"I'll be here," Nathan said cheerfully.

Stark followed Rayna into the lobby, lightly taking hold of her arm and bringing her to a stop at the front door. "Hey, you're driving over to the south side right now?"

"Yes," she said, glancing pointedly at his hand on her arm.

He didn't loosen his grip. "That's too dangerous, Ms. Abrams."

"I'll be fine. Let go of me, please."

He released her, irritation washing over him as she walked out of the clinic without saying another word. He followed her. "You shouldn't go alone to the south side at this time of night. You'll be kidnapped or murdered."

"Okay, drama queen," she said as she opened the SUV's driver door and slid inside.

She gaped at him when he opened the passenger door and climbed into the seat. "What are you doing?"

"Going with you," he said.

"No," she said.

"Yes," he said.

"Get out of my car, Stark."

"Make me," he said.

"Jesus, I do not have fucking time for this," she snapped before starting the SUV. He buckled his seat belt as she drove down the driveway. He winced and braced his hand against the roof as they flew over the bumps. "Christ, does this thing have any shocks?"

She didn't answer, and he glanced at her. "Do you own anything that isn't thirty years old?"

"No one asked you to get in the car," she said.

"Like I'm going to let you die on the south side tonight," he said.

"Only because you know if I die, you'll never get my property," she said.

"Precisely," he snapped.

"Yeah, well, the joke's on you because you're not getting it as long as I'm alive either," she snipped.

"Why aren't you doing x-rays for that dog?" he asked.

She blinked at the sudden change in subject. "Nathan said they weren't necessary."

"No, that isn't what he said," Stark said. "What if that dog's leg is broken?"

She stared stonily at the road. "It's a chance we'll have to take."

"You're a rescue. Aren't you supposed to be helping the animals? Why aren't you doing the x-rays when it's obvious the poor dog needs them?"

"Because x-rays cost money," she snarled, her brown eyes spitting sparks. "If I do the x-rays for this dog, then I can't do the x-rays for Mr. Magoo, who may need them more. Or tomorrow, I might get a call with a dog who definitely has a broken leg, and not doing the x-rays isn't an option. When you rely solely on donations, you don't get the luxury of giving every animal the best treatment available. Sometimes you have to make difficult decisions, and unless you'd like to put your money where your goddamn mouth is and foot the bill tonight, maybe you could do me a favour and quit berating me for the hard fucking choices I have to make."

She stopped, dragging in a ragged breath, her hands clenched tight around the steering wheel. Feeling like the biggest dickhead in the universe, Stark said, "I apologize for what I said."

She just nodded, and he looked away from what he was pretty sure was the shine of tears in her eyes. Christ, he really was an asshole.

———

STARK PARKED HIS CAR IN THE DRIVEWAY AND CLIMBED OUT. Rayna was parking her SUV in her driveway. She glanced at him before she disappeared into her house, holding a cat carrier. He walked to his house, stepping into the warmth and kicking off his boots.

He went into the kitchen and studied the blood on his jacket before taking it off and draping it over a chair. He'd drop it off for dry cleaning later today, though he didn't hold out much hope they'd actually get it clean.

He brewed himself a cup of coffee, checking the time on the microwave. It was just after five in the morning, and despite having been awake all night, he felt jumpy and restless. He'd never quite had a night like last night before.

On the way to the south side, Rayna had gotten another call, this one from a new foster who'd been fostering two kittens for two weeks. One of the kittens had scratched her kid, and she was demanding that Rayna pick up both kittens immediately.

After picking up Mr. Magoo, Rayna stopped at the kitten foster home and grabbed the two kittens before heading back toward the clinic. They hadn't been at the clinic for more than ten minutes before she'd gotten another call. This one was about a stray cat that had been caught in a trap, and the people wanted it off their property, or they'd leave it in the trap overnight in the cold. They'd left Mr. Magoo and the kittens at the clinic and gone to get the cat before returning to the clinic.

By that time, it was almost three in the morning, and Stark could have left, but he'd stayed instead. Mr. Magoo, an ancient shih-tzu with cataracts and a cheerful attitude despite having what turned out to be a broken leg, was x-rayed and given pain meds and a kennel to rest in. Nathan would cast his leg in the morning with the help of his staff. The stray dog had been put in a larger kennel, her wounds sutured, and her body relaxed after being given sedatives and pain medication.

After examining the stray cat, they discovered that he was friendly but intact. Rayna had arranged to leave him at the clinic to be neutered the following morning while she looked for a foster home for him. Finally, at around four-thirty, with the two kittens in tow, Rayna had dropped him off at his car, and they'd both driven home.

He walked into the den and looked out the window. It was the only one in the house that faced Rayna's house. He could see the lights on in the kitchen. She apparently wasn't headed to bed either. Maybe she was as amped up as he was.

I know a way you could help her relax. Help you both relax.

He headed toward his bedroom. Fucking Rayna was not the answer to his restlessness. He flopped down on the bed and stared at the ceiling before standing and checking on Molly. The kittens were sleeping against her, and Molly made a soft chirp to him. He reached into the box and scratched her cheeks before returning to his bed. He sat down and stared at the television, then turned on his gaming system. He would game for a while until his jittery energy was gone.

Two hours later, he was back in the kitchen, yawning hugely and grabbing a glass of water to drink before going to bed. He rubbed his gritty eyes and yawned again. Christ, he was finally feeling the effects of being up all night.

He left the kitchen and hesitated before walking to the den to check out the window again. Rayna was leaving her house. Her hair was in its usual ponytail, but she had changed her clothes. Even from where he stood, he could see the weariness on her face as she climbed into the SUV and started it.

"Christ, does she never sleep?" he said as she backed out of her driveway and drove away.

He closed the blinds and headed back to his room, falling on the bed with a soft groan and closing his eyes.

CHAPTER 15

"I'm so sorry." Rayna hurried into Brandt Vet Clinic, giving Fatima an apologetic smile. "I meant to be here this morning but got caught up in helping another stray dog."

"It's fine." One of the clinic's receptionists, Fatima, gave her a bright smile. "I heard you had quite the night last night."

"It was a bit insane." Rayna leaned against the counter, hoping she didn't look as exhausted as she felt.

"You look exhausted," Fatima said sympathetically, inadvertently crushing Rayna's hope.

Rayna made a face. "As soon as I'm finished here, I'm going home and straight to my bed."

The phone rang, and Fatima reached for it. "Head to the treatment area. Dr. Nathan is expecting you."

"Thanks, Fatima." Rayna pushed through the swinging doors, stopping short when a giant St. Bernard barked loudly.

"He's friendly." Hal, one of the vet techs and the epitome of a silver-haired fox, was holding the dog while another tech clipped its nails. "He just has a lot to say."

Rayna laughed. "How are you, Hal?"

"Can't complain. Savina picked up the lab mix half an hour ago. She named her Maeve and texted Reba with her name and suspected age, and we emailed the medical records."

"She did?" Rayna gave Hal a grateful look. "You two are peaches for taking her on such short notice."

"Eh, what my girl wants, my girl gets," Hal said with a grin. "And as soon as you texted a picture of her face to Savina, I knew she'd say yes. She can't resist labs."

"That's why I did it," Rayna said. "I'm evil like that."

Hal's grin widened. "That's the rumour. I'm just glad the leg didn't have a fracture. I wasn't looking forward to carrying Maeve in and out of the house while it healed."

Rayna grimaced. "So, we're not entirely certain she doesn't have a fracture, so it's probably best if she's on crate rest and has limited yard time."

"Nails are done. I'll take him up front," the tech said.

"Thanks, Allie." Hal released the St. Bernard and stood, joining Rayna by the lab counter. "Maeve doesn't have a fracture. Radiographs this morning confirmed it."

"What? I didn't authorize x-rays for Maeve," Rayna said as panic flooded her. The rescue absolutely did not have money in the budget to do x-rays on both Maeve and Mr. Magoo. "You did x-rays?"

"We did," Hal confirmed.

"I need to speak to Nathan," Rayna said. Shit, she'd have to apologize and explain there was a mix-up and hope like hell that he was good with adding the cost to the balance already owed by the rescue.

"I know he's just finishing up a meeting with Warren," Hal said. "Maybe talk to Laila? She was the one who told us to do the x-rays."

As if he'd summoned her, Laila came in from the side

yard, her cheeks rosy from the cold and holding Mr. Magoo. The curvy blonde was the clinic's office manager, and she gave Rayna a cheerful smile. "Hey, Rayna. How are you?"

"Good," Rayna said. "Do you have a minute to talk?"

"Sure." Still carrying Mr. Magoo, Laila led her to the far end of the treatment area. She'd turned an unused storage space into a tiny office, and Rayna squeezed in past the bookshelf and sat in the folding chair in front of Laila's minuscule desk.

Laila plopped down in her chair and stroked Mr. Magoo's fuzzy head. The dog lounged contentedly against her chest, its left hind leg in a cast. The cast was wrapped in lime green bandaging, and someone had cut out hearts from pink bandaging and stuck them all over the cast.

Laila kissed Mr. Magoo's head. "I just took him out for a pee, and considering how ancient he is, he's doing really well. Of course, we have him on all the good pain meds."

Rayna smiled. "He's a good boy."

"He's the best boy," Laila declared before kissing his head again. "Nathan said you weren't sending him back to his original foster home. Is that right?"

"Yes." Rayna could hear the discouragement in her voice. "I don't have another foster home for him currently, which means he'll be coming back to my house for now. Nicole is a good person, and she means well, but she's too busy with her kids to give Mr. Magoo the proper care he needs. He shouldn't be allowed to do stairs."

"What if I took him?" Laila said. "I know it's been a while since I fostered for Little Whiskers, but life isn't as busy now, and I have more time for a dog. Plus, I can bring Mr. Magoo to work with me, so he'll never be alone."

"Are you serious?" A little of Rayna's discouragement lifted. "You'd foster him?"

"Yes," Laila said. "I love this little dude."

"Oh my God, that would be amazing. I can bring you some supplies later tonight if that works."

"You have enough on your plate, and I know you were up all night," Laila said. "Is Myrna still a supply location for fosters?"

"Yes," Rayna said.

"Perfect. I'll text her and arrange to swing by after work and pick up the supplies I need for Mr. Magoo," Laila said.

"You're a lifesaver," Rayna said. "Thank you, Laila."

"My pleasure. What was it you wanted to chat to me about?"

"That stray lab mix I brought in last night with the injured leg."

"Maeve," Laila said. "I think Savina Ras picked her up a while ago."

"She did," Rayna said. "But Hal said you told them to do x-rays on her, and last night, I specifically told Nathan not to do them. As you know, the rescue's bill with the clinic is high, and we didn't have it in the budget to x-ray her and Mr. Magoo."

"Oh, it was paid for by a private donation," Laila said.

"What? Who?" Rayna asked.

"Isaac Stark."

Rayna's mouth dropped open, and she stared silently at Laila. Laila raised an eyebrow. "Why do you look like that?"

"I'm sorry, did you say Isaac Stark paid for it?"

"Yes." Laila smooched Mr. Magoo again, who licked her face happily.

"Isaac Stark, the millionaire?"

"Well, I heard he's a multimillionaire, but yes. He called around eleven this morning and asked to speak to the office manager. He has the deepest voice, doesn't he?" Laila's gaze went distant. "I've only seen him once at Grind My Beans, but I was not prepared for how handsome he is. Those eyes of his are something else. Anyway, he said he'd helped you last night with the dog, and he wanted to pay for her to have x-rays."

Rayna continued to stare at her. "I can't believe it."

"It's true," Laila said. "He also paid Mr. Magoo's bill in its entirety and paid to have the stray cat you brought in neutered and vaccinated."

Rayna hadn't thought her shock could go any deeper, but holy fucking shit, she was wrong.

"He paid for everything last night?" she asked.

"Yes." Laila studied her. "Was it wrong to accept the donation?"

"No, no." Rayna slumped against her chair, shock and lack of sleep making her feel slow and stupid. "I don't know why he did it. He hates me."

"I'm sure he doesn't hate you," Laila said. "Nathan said he stayed and helped you all night. Why would he do that if he hated you?"

"I... I don't know," Rayna said. She was too tired to think straight, and her shock over Stark paying for the treatment was draining what little battery she had left.

She sat up straight and smiled at Laila. "Okay, well, thank you. I appreciate you letting me know, and I'll get one of our volunteers to send him a thank you card."

"You bet." Laila stood, and she and Rayna squeezed out of her office. As they headed toward the main treatment area, Rayna said, "So, you're still good for the fundraiser on Friday?"

"Sure am," Laila said. "Although I'm a little nervous that no one is going to bid on me."

"Just do what I'm doing." Dr. Warren Brandt, the original owner of the clinic before he sold it to Nathan and one of the nicest people Rayna had ever met, had left Nathan's office to examine a poodle that Hal held on one of the exam tables.

"What's that?" Laila asked.

"Make someone promise to bid on you if the room goes awkwardly silent when you're standing on stage," Warren said.

Hal laughed as Laila said, "Who did you ask?"

"Wanda Taber," Warren said. "I made her swear she would bid on me if no one else did."

"That's kind of brilliant," Laila said.

"Not bad for an old man, am I right?" Warren grinned at them both. "But honestly, Laila, it isn't something you'll need to worry about."

"Thanks, Warren." Laila squeezed his shoulder before heading toward reception with Mr. Magoo. "See you Friday night, Rayna."

Nathan stuck his head out of his office. "Rayna, hey. You have a few minutes to talk about treatment plans for Maeve and Mr. Magoo?"

"I do," Rayna said. With a wave to Warren and Hal, she followed Nathan into his office.

STARK DIPPED HIS HEAD UNDER THE SHOWER SPRAY AND RINSED away the shampoo. He adjusted the temperature, grumbling about the lack of hot water under his breath. His penthouse had a never-ending supply of hot water and a walk-in shower with multiple shower heads that wasn't the size of a damn linen closet.

He soaped his body and rinsed clean. If it weren't for Rayna Abrams and her refusal to sell her property, he would be well on his way to having a perfect shower built in his new house.

"Do you mind if I join you?"

He jerked wildly, nearly slipping and falling on the slick

shower floor before he whipped around and stared wide-eyed at Rayna through the foggy glass door. "What the fuck?"

"Hey. I don't have any hot water at my place. Can I use your shower?" She grinned at him. She wore a long t-shirt, and he studied her bare legs and how her nipples pressed against the thin fabric.

"How did you get in my house?" he asked.

"Does it matter? Can I join you or not?"

He stared at her for long seconds, the hot water drumming against his ribcage before he opened the shower door. Her smile widened, and he sucked in a harsh breath when she whipped off her t-shirt and dropped it on the floor.

She was naked under the shirt, and he studied her tight body, his gaze lingering on her breasts before dropping to her pussy. His cock hardened, and he resisted the urge to fist it as Rayna stepped into the shower with him and closed the door.

Her body pressed against his, and he made a low moan as she said, "Tight fit in here, huh?"

"Yeah," he said hoarsely.

"Turn around, please," she said.

He turned to face her, his cock brushing against her flat abdomen. She reached out and gripped him in her hand. He groaned, his hips jutting forward as she stroked him with a long, slow motion of her hand. "Do you like that?"

"Yes," he muttered, slapping one hand against the tile wall as he rocked his hips into her.

"It's so nice of you to let me use your shower," she murmured as she leaned forward and brushed her nipples against his chest. "A thank you isn't really enough, is it?"

"What did you have in mind?" he gritted out before cupping one firm breast and toying with her nipple. Her back arched, and her soft moan made him want to come all over her damn hand.

"I don't know," she said, giving him a bold smile. "What do you want?"

"Your mouth," he said without hesitating.

She sank to her knees immediately, and he wound his hand into her hair. She stared up at him, and he used his free hand to rub his thumb over her lips. "Open for me, Rayna."

She opened, and he slid his cock deep into her mouth, gasping when she sucked hard, and he was immediately on the verge of coming. "Oh fuck, baby, wait. Just wait... or I'll come in your ... fuuuuck!"

Stark leaned against the shower wall, one hand stroking his cock hard and furious, his body shaking as he came hard. His entire body shuddering, he stared at his cum swirling down the drain before straightening. He glanced behind him, a fucked up part of him half expecting to see Rayna standing behind him in the shower.

"Fuck," he said, staring at his softening cock. Having a sex fantasy in the shower about his goddamn enemy was not how he'd planned to start his Tuesday morning. His body still shaking, he quickly rinsed off in the now cool water and turned off the shower.

What the hell was wrong with him? Wanting to fuck the woman who was making his life hell and thwarting his plans was bullshit. He wasn't some adolescent school boy for fuck's sake.

He dried off, wrapped the towel around his waist, and stepped into the bedroom. He needed to get his thoughts and his fucking dick under control before...

He stopped, staring blankly at Molly's food dish. He'd given her wet food before getting into the shower, just like he did every morning, but she hadn't eaten it. She usually had licked the damn bowl clean by the time he got out of the shower. He turned around to stare at the bed, unease rippling through him. After eating breakfast, Molly would always lounge on the bed waiting for him.

Over the past five days, he and the cat had fallen into a routine. Molly spent most of her time with the kittens, but after every meal, she'd seek him out to demand petting. His initial refusal had proved futile since Molly just followed him around and bumped into him or climbed into his lap or wound around his legs, meowing and purring until he gave in and petted her. And while he would never admit this, he was starting to enjoy the little cat's soft chirps and purrs and even the feel of her scratchy tongue when she licked his hand affectionately.

"Cat?" he said in the direction of the closet. "Why are you being weird?"

There was no answering meow, and now the unease turned to worry. Molly always chirped, purred, or meowed when she heard his voice. Always. Christ, had she gotten outside somehow?

His stomach a tight knot, he hurried over to the closet and opened the door wide. Relief swept through him when he saw Molly lying in the box with her babies. "Jesus Christ, cat, you scared the shit out of me. I thought you'd gotten out and... cat?"

He frowned when Molly continued to lie quietly, and he crouched in front of the box. "Molly?"

He touched her soft fur, and she opened her eyes to stare at him before closing them. She didn't purr, and she didn't open her eyes again when he scratched her cheek. "What's wrong, sweetie?"

She abruptly stood and jumped out of the box, but his relief was short lived when she made a hwucking sound and threw up on the floor. She gave him a look of pure misery before jumping onto his bed and lying down. He petted her a few times, and when she rolled to her side, he stared at her belly. One of her nipples looked bright red, and he touched the skin around it lightly with his finger. It was hot and hard to the touch, and he could have sworn pain crossed Molly's face.

"It's okay, Molly," he said, his worry deepening. "Hold on, I'll get you some help. It's okay, sweetie."

He grabbed his phone from the bedside table and scrolled to Rayna's number before hitting the call button.

CHAPTER 16

"Sorry, sweet girl, I know that hurts." Rayna pressed gently on Molly's nipple again as Stark hovered behind her.

Molly hissed lightly, and Rayna stared at Stark when he grabbed her wrist and pulled her hand away from Molly's belly.

"You're hurting her," he said.

She shook her hand free and petted Molly gently under the chin. She didn't purr, and Rayna's worry grew when the cat laid her head on Stark's bed and closed her eyes.

"Something's wrong," Stark said. "I know it."

She glanced at him, a little surprised to see the worry on his face. She opened her mouth to say something snarky like, "What do you care? You don't even like her," but closed it with a snap when Stark stroked Molly's side lightly. "You'll be okay, sweetie."

Holy shit? Was Stark sincerely worried about the cat?

She swallowed her surprise and said, "I think she has mastitis."

"That's an infection, right?"

"Yes." She stood and pulled her phone from her pocket, checking the time. It was just after eight and she called the vet clinic, quickly explaining the situation to Fatima. She ended the call, and Stark gave her an expectant look.

"If I can get her to the clinic in the next fifteen minutes, Nathan can look at her before his first appointment at nine."

"We can't move her from the nest," he said, looking like he might throw up. "The babies will die."

Guilt rushed through her. She swallowed hard and said, "Yeah, about that... I kind of, maybe, fibbed a little because I needed a foster home for Molly and the babies. She won't abandon the babies if we move her or them to a new spot or house or whatever."

She waited for the familiar muscle tick in his jaw, the one that said he was doing everything in his power not to murder her. To her shock, he grabbed his phone and shoved it into his pocket, giving Molly another worried look.

"I'll drive."

"HAVE THE KITTENS LOST WEIGHT?" NATHAN KEPT ONE HAND on Molly to prevent her from jumping off the exam table as he studied the kittens in the crate.

Rayna glanced at Stark, who was standing on the other side of the table and gently petting Molly's face and throat.

He shook his head. "They gained less than normal yesterday but still gained. I haven't weighed them yet today."

"Okay, that's a good sign." Nathan examined each of the kittens. "The babies look good. She's keeping them clean and well-fed."

"She's very attentive to them." Stark continued to pet Molly. "She only leaves them for a few minutes at a time."

He leaned down, and Rayna nearly fell over when he

scratched Molly's cheeks and said in a low voice, "You're a good mama. Yes, you are."

Molly chirped at him before butting her head against his chin, and Stark gave Nathan an excited look. "That's a good sign, right? Her chirping like that? Normally, she does it all the time, and she wasn't this morning."

"It's a good sign," Nathan said before turning to Rayna. "So, I suspect mastitis, but the good news is only two nipples seem to be affected, and I think we've caught it pretty early."

"You suspect mastitis, or you know that's what it is," Stark said.

"I'm confident," Nathan said. "Rayna, the most cost-effective plan is to send her home with some antibiotics and pain meds. The babies are still nursing, so I'll go with a safe antibiotic, but even still, it might cause some diarrhea for the babies, so you'll need to keep a close eye on them. If they do get diarrhea, you may have to bottle feed them for a few days."

"Okay," Rayna said. She'd taken this week off to finish last-minute details for the fundraiser on Friday, and bottle-feeding kittens every two hours didn't exactly fit into her plan. But she had no other neonate fosters available. She would have to hope that the antibiotics didn't wreak havoc with the babies' stomachs.

"If you do have to bottle feed, you'll need to express Molly's milk manually, so her milk supply doesn't dry up," Nathan said.

Rayna made a face. "I didn't have 'milking a cat' on my Bingo card for this week."

Nathan grinned. "Well, hopefully, you won't have to."

"Do you really just diagnose this by looking at her?" Stark frowned at Nathan. "That doesn't seem safe. What if it's something else?"

"Stark," Rayna said, giving him a look. She didn't care

how worried Stark was. She wasn't about to let him piss off her favourite vet in Harmony Falls. Nathan went above and beyond for the rescue, and she fiercely protected their relationship.

Nathan gave Stark a thoughtful look. "Molly shows all the classic symptoms of mastitis. However, if you want to be completely sure, we could take a blood sample to check for infection and perform a bacterial culture to identify the bacterial strain, ensuring we use the correct antibiotic. We could also do a milk cytology to check for bacteria and white blood cells. But the testing is expensive, and the rescue -"

"Do all of those tests," Stark said. "I'll cover the expense."

Nathan glanced at Rayna, who said, "I appreciate the gesture, but -"

"I have a work meeting at the office that I can't miss," Stark said to Nathan, ignoring Rayna's protest. "But it should only last a couple of hours. Can I leave Molly and the babies here at the clinic while you do the testing? I'll take them home after my meeting is over."

"Molly and the babies will need extra care and attention," Rayna said.

"I'm aware, Ms. Abrams," he said before turning back to Nathan. "I'm happy to pay a boarding fee to keep Molly here while I'm at the office."

"That won't be necessary," Nathan said, glancing at Rayna. "We'll run the tests and then keep Molly and the babies until you're available. I'll draw up an estimate for the procedure cost, and you can sign it before you leave."

"It won't be more than a couple of hours," Stark said. Rayna's mouth dropped when he bent and kissed the cat's head. "I won't be gone long, sweetie, and then I'll be back to take you home."

He straightened and held out his hand to Nathan. "Thank

you. I'll leave my number with the receptionist. If Molly worsens or anything changes, call me immediately."

Nathan shook his hand with a bemused look. "Okay."

Stark bent and kissed Molly's head again. "Be a good girl, sweetie. I'll see you soon."

He reached into the crate and gently petted each of the kittens before striding toward the foyer. Rayna stared at Nathan, and he said, "That was… unexpected."

"You have no idea," she said and chased after Stark.

She found him at the front desk, where he was giving Fatima his phone number.

"Molly's staying at the clinic for a bit to do some more testing," Rayna said to Fatima. "Nathan is just doing an estimate for us to sign."

They waited in silence for a few minutes. Stark was texting rapidly on his phone, and Fatima looked him up and down before giving Rayna a look that she had no problem interpreting. Fatima was married, but Rayna couldn't blame her for eyeing Stark like a tasty steak. Rayna might hate him, but he was objectively hot. And even hotter when he was paying the vet bill for a foster cat.

Fatima checked her computer and then printed off a piece of paper. "Okay, Nathan finished the estimate. You know the drill, Rayna."

She held it out, but Stark took the paper before Rayna could. He scanned it and then picked up a pen and started filling it out.

Rayna leaned a little closer as, alarm in his voice, Stark said, "Why is this here? Molly isn't dying."

"That's a standard section we have you fill out whenever you're leaving an animal in our care. Obviously, the risk is very low that Molly will go into cardiac arrest or crash on us. Still, there's always a risk, so we ask that you let us know if you want life saving measures taken as we're trying to contact you, or if you want us to wait until we've spoken to you," Fatima said.

Stark gave her a withering look. "Obviously, I want you to save her life."

"Okay, well, um, just initial there," Fatima said.

Stark initialed as Fatima said, "We also need an amount you're willing to spend on life-saving measures until we can speak with you."

"Put five hundred dollars," Rayna said to Stark. It was her typical number for this sort of thing. She hated having to put a price on an animal's life, and such a low one at that, but she had to be practical. She couldn't spend all of the rescue's funds on one animal.

Stark glared at her before writing 'No Limit" in big letters next to the dollar amount. He turned his gaze to Fatima, and she returned his look nervously as he said, "There is no dollar limit for the life-saving measures for Molly. Is that clear? I don't care what the final cost is. You don't stop helping her."

"Okay," Fatima said.

"Stark," Rayna said. "Are you -"

"Do not argue with me, Ms. Abrams," he snapped. "Molly's life is not up for debate."

She rolled her eyes. "All right. Christ, don't get your underpants in a twist over it."

Fatima stared at her with wide eyes as Stark signed and dated the form and handed it back to her. He texted again on his phone before shoving it into his pocket. "I need to get to the office, but I've arranged for an Uber to pick you up here and take you home."

"Oh, uh… thanks," Rayna said.

He nodded and left the clinic.

CHAPTER 17

Rayna rapped on Stark's front door before shoving her hands deep into her coat pockets. There was a bitterly cold wind blowing, and she glanced behind her at Stark's car. After leaving the clinic, she'd spent most of the day with Zuri, going over details for the fundraiser. She'd arrived home just after two, and after dropping her ancient laptop at the house, she headed over to Stark's.

She rapped again and was considering texting him when the door opened. Stark raised one eyebrow. "What can I do for you, Ms. Abrams?"

"I'm here to check on Molly and to discuss her care with you," she said.

He scowled. "What is there to discuss?"

"Can I come in? I'm freezing my ass off out here," she said.

He hesitated, and she said, "She's not your cat, Stark. She belongs to the rescue."

He moved back, and she stepped inside, shutting the door behind her. "How is she doing?"

"She's good," Stark said as he led her down the hallway

with the horrific wallpaper. "She had her first dose of antibiotics, and Dr. Henshaw gave her some fluids before we left the clinic. They've helped her to feel better."

He opened his bedroom door, and Rayna followed him into the room. "That's good. I'm glad she's… what in the nut waffle is this?"

Stark cleared his throat, his cheeks already a little red. "I picked her up a few things before I went back to the clinic."

"A few things?" Rayna studied the large and elaborate cat trees stuffed into the tiny room. "You bought her two cat trees?"

"I didn't know which one she would like better," he said defensively.

"Is that a self-cleaning litter box?" Rayna asked.

He glanced at the state-of-the-art litter box. "Yes."

"And a water fountain?"

"The pet store employee said most cats like to drink from a fountain," Stark said.

"Right," Rayna said. "Did they also convince you to buy every cat toy in the store?"

"I didn't buy that many," he snapped.

She pointed to the floor that was covered with cat toys. "There has to be at least a hundred toys in here, Stark."

"An exaggeration on your part, Ms. Abrams," he said.

"Yeah, but only slightly." Her eyes widened when she heard Molly's squeaky meow coming from the bed. She stared at the large, clear plastic container that sat on Stark's bed next to a slim laptop and Stark's phone. She could see Molly inside on a nest of fluffy blankets, the three kittens sleeping in a pile against her chest.

"What is this?" she asked as she approached the bed. She reached inside and petted Molly's cheeks, smiling a little when Molly made a soft chirp. "You look like you feel better, sweet girl."

She turned to Stark. "Why are they in a container on your bed?"

"Molly didn't like being stuck in the closet all the time," Stark said.

"So, is your plan to let Molly and the babies sleep on the bed with you?" She gave him an amused look.

"Of course not," he snapped. "You've seen that Molly is feeling better, so if you'll excuse me, I have some work to do."

She glanced at the television on the wall across from the bed. "Is that Cat TV?"

Stark gave her another defensive look. "Molly likes to watch the birds while she's feeding her babies."

"You know, if I didn't know your heart was cold and black, I'd almost be thinking you like having a cat in the house," she said.

"Hardly," he said with a disdainful look. "You led me to believe I had no choice by lying to me about the babies dying. Or have you forgotten that, Ms. Abrams?"

"Nope," she said cheerfully. "I lied like a boss that day."

She held up her hand for a high-five, lowering it when he scowled at her.

"Do you think tricking me into keeping a cat and her kittens in my home is amusing?"

"A little?" she said.

His scowl deepened, and she sighed. "Look, I'm sorry I lied, okay? But I was desperate for a foster home for Molly and her babies. The rescue has a shortage of fosters right now."

He didn't reply, and she said, "But the good news is - Molly isn't your problem anymore. I had a foster who was on a break message me this afternoon. She's ready to foster again, and she said she'd be happy to take Molly and the babies. She can take them anytime."

She could have sworn anxiety flickered across his face

before that familiar scowl stamped back into it. "Has she fostered a mother and babies before?"

"Yes," Rayna said. "Plenty of times."

He cleared his throat. "A cat with mastitis?"

"Yes," Rayna said. "She knows what to do for Molly, and if necessary, she can bottle feed the babies."

He stared silently at her, and confusion rocketing through her, she said, "It's what's best for Molly."

He studied Molly and the babies before shaking his head. "No. What's best for Molly is staying in a familiar place. She's not feeling well, and moving her now could be detrimental to her health and the babies' health. She'll stay here with me."

Rayna stared at the guy pretending to be Stark and, frankly, doing a *terrible* job at it. "I...what?"

"Molly will stay here with me," Stark said. "I know her likes and dislikes, and she's comfortable here. Who knows what that other foster will do to her."

Rayna blinked. "Jami is one of my best fosters. Molly will be perfectly safe with her."

"Does she know that Molly is an escape artist?" Stark challenged. "Or that she likes her wet food heated up for precisely thirty seconds in the microwave? Or that she likes to have her paws massaged?"

"Um... no. But you can tell her that."

"Molly is staying with me."

"She needs medicine twice a day," Rayna said. "Assuming she heals quickly, that's the least amount of work you'll need to do. If the babies get diarrhea, they'll need to be bottle-fed every few hours, and Molly will need her milk expressed manually. Do you understand that?"

"I do," he said stiffly. "It won't be a problem."

"Why? Because you'll hire someone to come in and do it for you?" she asked.

He glared at her, and she sighed. "Stark, look, I

appreciate how much you care for Molly and the babies, but if you bail on me after only a few days, it'll be more work for me to find her a foster home then. I have three other cats I can give Jami to foster. So, I can't leave her open while I wait for you to realize playing nurse to a cat isn't nearly as fun as you think it is. Do you understand?"

"I understand perfectly, Ms. Abrams," he said. "And I can assure you I am not going to bail on you after a few days."

She studied him. "Molly belongs to the rescue. I could make you give her to Jami."

He stepped closer to the bed, and Molly jumped out of the container, rubbing up against his hip and meowing softly. He put a possessive hand on Molly's side and gave Rayna an icy look. "Molly and the babies stay with me."

"Fine!" She threw her hands up. "But when you come to me in a few days, I get to tell you I told you so, and you have to keep playing nursemaid to Molly until I find a new foster for her."

"I assure you that won't be necessary," he said.

"You really like her, don't you?" Rayna said.

He refused to meet her gaze. "Are we done here, Ms. Abrams? Because I have work to do."

She drifted closer to him, her urge to tease and torment him impossible to resist. "Isaac 'I hate cats' Stark is smitten with one."

"I never said I hated cats."

"It was implied."

He sighed, staring down at her when she stopped in front of him. Molly butted her head against Rayna's hand, and she petted her gently before grinning at Stark. "Admit it. You think Molly's great."

"She's fine," he said.

"Fine," she said. "You demanded she get all the tests at the

133

vet, which you paid for in full, then spent another thousand dollars on her this afternoon because she's... fine."

"It wasn't a thousand," he said.

She raised her eyebrows at him and was both delighted and floored when he blushed and mumbled, "It was eight hundred."

"Huh," she said. "So, I guess this means your heart isn't completely dead and cold."

His nostrils flared angrily. "You know nothing about me, Ms. Abrams, and your belief that I am a monster is entirely unfounded."

"That's fair." God, he smelled good. Did he always smell this good? She inhaled deeply, her body lighting up in all the right ways at his good, clean scent. She studied his mouth, those firm lips she'd spent way too many hours thinking about how they might feel on her mouth, her breasts... her pussy.

Hot and heavy lust flooded her body, and her pussy began to ache with a dull throb. It wanted to be filled, stretched, teased. She leaned closer until her chest nearly brushed his.

"Ms. Abrams?" There was confusion in Stark's gaze, but there was something else, too, wasn't there? Something that suggested he felt the same damn pull she did.

You hate him, Rayna! Stop this!

She did hate him. He was an entitled asshole trying to bully her into selling her property. But he'd also paid for Molly's care and Maeve's and Mr. Magoo's and the stray cat. And God, he was so fucking pretty, and it'd been so damn long since she'd gotten laid.

"I never said thank you for what you did on Saturday night," she said. "Not just for helping me all night but for paying for Maeve and the others' treatment, too."

"You're welcome." Now, he was staring at *her* mouth.

Her nipples had turned to hard pebbles against her bra, and the deep throb in her pussy was impossible to ignore.

"Saying thank you doesn't seem like enough," she said.

His whole body twitched wildly, but his voice was steady enough when he said, "What did you have in mind?"

"What do you want?" She could hear the need in her voice.

Hot desire flooded his face. Holy shit... did he want her as much as she wanted him?

His big hand cupped her head, and she parted her lips when he rubbed his thumb across her mouth.

"Fuck," he muttered, his fingers tightening against her skull. She licked his thumb with a quick, light stroke, stupidly desperate for a part of him, *any* part of him, inside of her.

His nostrils flared, and he pulled her toward him until her breasts touched his chest, and she could feel the hard bulge of his erection against her midsection. He bent his head, and she tilted her head to give him better access to her mouth as her pulse quickened in anticipation.

"Why the fuck haven't you done something about that sparkle wallpaper? It's a fucking eyesore. Also, why are you working from home? I stopped at the office, and they said you'd be working from home all week. Since when do you work from... what the hell?"

Stark pushed away from her so quickly that Rayna nearly fell on her face. He caught her upper arm in a hard grip and kept her upright before backing away to stand next to the bed. She turned, staring wide-eyed at the blond man standing in the doorway.

"What the fuck are you doing here, Jasper?" Stark rasped.

Jasper raised an eyebrow. "Is that any way to talk to family, Isaac?"

He walked toward Rayna, his hand extended. "Jasper Stark."

She shook his hand. "Rayna Abrams."

"Nice to meet you." His dark eyes gave her a quick once over before he smiled cheerfully at her. "Isaac didn't mention he was dating someone."

"We're not dating," Stark said quickly.

The look on Stark's face suggested he would rather eat dirt than date her, and any lingering lust Rayna might have felt disappeared faster than Freddie when a stranger came to the house. She gave him a frosty look as he said, "What are you doing here, Jasper? And how did you get into my house?"

"The door was unlocked," Jasper said breezily. "I guess now that you live in the country, you don't lock your doors? Not a good idea, buddy."

Stark huffed out an angry breath. "An unlocked door doesn't mean you can just waltz right the fuck in."

Jasper grinned at Rayna. "Do your cousins treat you so rudely, Rayna?"

"I don't have any cousins," she said.

"Well, trust me when I say that... what the fuck? Is that a... cat?" Jasper stared in disbelief as Molly, purring loudly, walked back and forth on the bed, rubbing against Stark's hip. "Why do you have a cat?"

"It's cats. Multiple," Rayna said.

Jasper laughed. "Are you kidding me?"

"Nope," Rayna said and pointed to the clear container on Stark's bed.

Jasper's jaw dropped. "Kittens? You have a cat and kittens in your house?"

"It wasn't my idea," Stark said through gritted teeth. "She's forcing me to keep them."

"He's straight-up lying," Rayna said to Jasper. "I just gave him the option of moving them to a different foster home, and he refused."

Jasper laughed again. "Who are you, and what have you done to my cousin?"

"I'm his number one enemy, actually," Rayna said.

"Are you?" Jasper gave her an admiring look. "That's intriguing. What have you done to piss him off? And how have you survived against Isaac 'tremble before me, mere mortals,' Stark?"

"I'm tougher than I look," Rayna said.

"Gorgeous and tough… a lethal combination." Jasper let his gaze linger on her mouth.

Ignoring the fact that Jasper's gaze didn't send even one tiny tingle to her crotch, Rayna smiled at him. "You're pretty gorgeous yourself."

Another angry huff behind her, this one so hard she felt the end of her ponytail flutter.

"Ms. Abrams, isn't it time you left?" Stark said pointedly.

"No need to be rude, Isaac," Jasper said.

"Ms. Abrams has a busy schedule. I'm sure there is a plumbing emergency somewhere in town," Stark said.

"You're a plumber?" Jasper asked

"I am," Rayna said. "But I'm on vacation this week. I run a local animal rescue, and we're having a big fundraiser this weekend, so I took the week off to organize the final details."

"What kind of fundraiser?" Jasper asked.

"Jasper," Stark ground out.

"A bachelor/bachelorette fundraiser," Rayna said. "It's this Friday at the Harmony Falls Community Hall. You should attend. Tickets are only twenty dollars, and you'll get appetizers and wine and the chance to bid on a bachelorette or," she cocked her head, "bachelor?"

"Bachelorette for me. Will you be one of those bachelorettes?" Jasper asked with a cute smile.

"No, but we have some really amazing women participating in the fundraiser," Rayna said. "You should check it out. Especially if you're as rich as your cousin."

Jasper's grin widened. "Oh, I do like you, Rayna Abrams."

"You're the only Stark who does," she said cheekily.

"Ms. Abrams, it's time for you to leave," Stark snapped.

"See what I mean?" she said to Jasper. "It was nice to meet you, Jasper. I hope to see you Friday night."

He took her hand and pressed a kiss against her knuckles. "Likewise, Rayna."

CHAPTER 18

"What are you doing here, Jasper?" Stark poured them both cups of coffee and slid Jasper's across the table to him.

"It's good to see you too, Isaac," Jasper said.

Stark bit back his retort. His cousin might not be his favourite person, but he hadn't done anything to piss him off today. Yet.

Oh yeah? So interrupting you when you were about to fuck Rayna didn't piss you off?

He ignored his inner voice. Nothing would have happened between him and Rayna. One of them would have come to their senses even if Jasper hadn't interrupted.

You sure about that? She wanted you to fuck her. Don't pretend she didn't.

"Isaac?"

"What?" he scowled at his cousin.

"What the fuck is going on with you? First, you're not at your office on a Tuesday afternoon, then I find you in your bedroom about to fuck a plumber, and you have goddamn cats now."

"They're not my cats," he said. "The cat broke into my damn house and had babies, and it's too dangerous to move her while the babies are this young."

"Right. And you were about to fuck the plumber because why?"

"The plumber has a name, and I wasn't about to fuck her," Stark snapped.

"Well, that's some bullshit right there," Jasper said. He gave him that look, the one that always set Stark's teeth on edge. "Never thought I'd see you slumming like that for a bit of pussy."

"Shut up, Jasper," Stark said. "Besides, you were practically trying to dry hump her in my bedroom."

Jasper laughed. "Sure, but can you blame me? With a body like that, I don't care if she cleans toilets all day. I'll just make sure she showers before I fuck her."

Stark immediately tamped down his anger. He knew his cousin, and if he even suspected that he was pissing him off, Jasper would use it to his advantage. Still, he couldn't help but growl out, "Stay away from Rayna, Jasper."

"So, you do like her." Jasper pounced like a particularly vicious feline.

"I hate her," Stark said, "but she has something I want, and I don't need you fucking her or fucking *with* her. Got it?"

The genuine Jasper appeared, quick as a striking snake, the jovial, benevolent look on his face disappearing. "The days of you telling me what to do ended the minute you abandoned our company."

"I didn't abandon the company, and it's my father's company, not yours," Stark said. "What's with this 'our' shit?"

He was deliberately provoking his cousin, and he fucking knew better, but he couldn't help it. Jasper's interest in Rayna was eating away at him.

Jasper gave him a thin smile. "Your father relies heavily

on me now. The company may not be legally mine, but it's technically mine just as much as it's his. It would fall apart without me."

"There's that inflated sense of self-worth I don't miss," Stark said.

"Fuck you, Isaac." The mask Jasper had put on the moment he saw Rayna had disappeared entirely. "You've acted like you're better than the rest of us for years, and I am fucking over it. You're an entitled prick who doesn't deserve everything that's fallen into your lap."

"Fallen into my lap?" Stark snarled. "I built my company from the ground up, unlike you, who just 'kissed my father's ass' your way up the ladder. You want to talk about entitlement, but I'd rather talk about how you're running my father's company into the ground because you don't have a fucking clue about gaming."

Jasper froze, his hand tightening on the coffee mug in front of him until Stark expected it to simply shatter under the pressure. His face grim, Jasper said, "I don't know what the fuck you're talking about. And I plan on finding who it is in the company feeding you false information and suing their ass into the fucking stratosphere."

Stark barked harsh laughter. "Are you kidding me? No one is feeding me information, Jasper. Everyone in the gaming community knows that Stark Gaming is in the fucking tank. Your last seven games have all been shit because you have no goddamn idea how to hire a developer who knows what they're doing. You've convinced my father that you know the gaming market, but just because my father refuses to see through your bullshit doesn't mean the rest of us are in the dark."

"The changes I've made have saved the company," Jasper said. "Your father would have been out of business years ago if it wasn't for me. You think because you're the big fucking name in gaming now that you can just bulldoze over us smaller companies, even when they're family."

"Why are you here, Jasper?" Stark asked. He was suddenly exhausted, and he didn't have it in him to fight with his cousin. Not when it was the same fucking argument they'd had repeatedly over the years.

"Your father wants to meet with you."

"He sent you to Harmony Falls to tell me that?"

"He's busy," Jasper said dismissively.

"And I'm not?"

"It's a Tuesday afternoon, and you're babysitting a fucking cat," Jasper said.

"If my father wants to meet with me, have his assistant set up a phone meeting with Hollis."

"He wants to see you," Jasper said.

Dread filled Stark's stomach. He tried to ignore it and pretend he wasn't turning into that scared little kid he always was around his father, but just the thought of being in the same room with his father made him feel small and insignificant.

"No," he said harshly. "Phone meeting only."

"Not good enough," Jasper said. "Your father wants to speak to you in person."

"Too fucking bad," Stark said. "I'm not a little kid he can order around anymore."

Jasper sighed. "Get the fuck over yourself, Isaac. Your dad isn't a young guy anymore, and it won't kill you to do what he asks for once."

"For once?" Stark barked bitter laughter. "For fucking once, Jasper?"

Jasper waved his hand dismissively. "Stop clinging to the past, Isaac."

Stark stood. "Time for you to go."

"Will you meet with your father or not?" Jasper asked.

"Not in person," Stark said. "Those are my conditions. He can take them or leave them."

"You're such an asshole." Jasper stood and stalked out of the kitchen toward the front door. "You need to grow the fuck up, Isaac."

He slammed the door behind him, and Stark sucked in a deep breath before slumping against the wall. There was a soft chirp, and he stared at Molly, who weaved around his feet. She hadn't left the bedroom once since she'd had her kittens, and he squatted and picked her up.

She purred loudly, headbutting his chin repeatedly until he stroked her soft fur. He glanced around almost guiltily before resting his ear against her side, listening to the rumble of her purr as she kneaded his chest.

After only a few minutes, his anxiety had lessened, and he pressed a kiss against the cat's forehead. "Thanks, sweetie. Let's get you back to your babies now, okay?"

She made her distinctive squeaky meow, and he smiled before carrying her back to the bedroom.

"SO, YOU HAVE NO IDEA WHY YOUR FATHER WANTS TO MEET with you?" His mother asked.

"What's on your head, Mom?" Stark asked.

She touched the multi-coloured wrap that was wound around her head. "Oh, this is a healing wrap that Janelle brought me. You soak it in this scented liquid that is full of healing herbs and it's supposed to draw out any illnesses or negative energy you carry in your body."

"Wait, are you feeling sick?" he asked.

"Not at all," she said cheerfully. "But Janelle is completely caught up in this MLM pyramid scheme and is desperate to offload some stock."

He rolled his eyes. "So, it's a bunch of bullshit."

"Utter bullshit," she said, "but the healing liquid smells lovely and really softens my hair."

"Mom, I know Janelle is your friend, but you have to stop spending your money on this crap."

"Darling boy, we both know I have more money than God, and I'll never be able to spend it all before I die," his mother said. "You certainly don't need it as an inheritance, Mr. Moneybags, so why shouldn't I spend it on frivolous things."

He couldn't help but laugh. "That's a fair point."

"You're avoiding my question about your father," she said.

He sighed. "I don't know why he wants to meet, but since he refuses to meet under my terms, it doesn't really matter."

She smiled at him. "Good for you, Isaac. I'm proud of you for standing up to him."

He shrugged. "It's just refusing to meet with him. That's hardly an act of rebellion."

"When it comes to your father, it is," she said. "Now, tell me again the story of how you're working at home all this week because of a cat and her kittens."

He gave her a look that would wither anyone else, but she just laughed and waved her hand at him. "Show me those darling babies again, please."

He flipped the camera on his phone and pointed it at the container. Molly was grooming the babies, and his mother made a quiet squeal. "Oh, they really are just the sweetest things."

He flipped the camera back to himself, grinning at the delight on her face. "I love that you have a pet now, Isaac. I worry about my boy being all alone."

"I don't have a pet, Mom. I'm just fostering Molly and the babies until Molly is feeling better and the babies are older. Then they'll go to a new foster home," he said.

"Will they, though?" She grinned at him.

"It's your fault I'm fostering them," he said.

She readjusted the wrap on her head and sat back. "Oh, I do need to hear how this is my fault, dearest."

"You suggested I be nice to Ms. Abrams to get what I want. I'm being nice."

"Ah," she said, "and is it working? Has she agreed to sell you her property?"

"No," he said. "But I did help her with a stray dog the other night, and I paid some vet bills for the rescue, so that'll win me points, right?"

"Oh, absolutely," his mother said.

"I know you're mocking me," he said, "but I don't care."

She laughed. "I'm your mother, Isaac. I would never mock. Now, be honest with me. Are you only doing these things in order to convince her to sell her property?"

"Yes," he said. "Why else would I do them?"

She shrugged. "I think you like this Rayna Abrams."

"I don't," he said quickly. "I hate her, Mom."

"There is a thin line between hate and lust," she said.

"And this conversation is over. Goodbye, Mom. I love you."

"I love you too, my boy. Tell that sweet cat and her adorable kittens that grandma also loves them."

She laughed at how he rolled his eyes before blowing him a kiss and ending the call.

He tossed his phone on the bed and petted Molly absent-mindedly when she jumped out of the container and sat on his chest, purring loudly. Despite what he'd told Rayna, he was, in fact, keeping Molly and the kittens on the bed in their container at night.

It was no big deal. The bed was plenty big enough for him and the container, and this way, if Molly needed him at night, he was right there. She spent most of the night with her babies, but he'd woken up more than once to find her curled into his armpit or sleeping between his legs. It was kind of nice to have her there if he was being honest. He would never admit this to anyone, but having Molly in the house made him feel less lonely.

He rubbed his chin against Molly's forehead, smiling at how her purring grew louder. His phone rang, and he glanced at it before answering it. "Hey, Hollis. What's up?"

"Hi. Are you still planning to come into the office tomorrow for the staff meeting?"

"I am," he said.

"Can I reschedule it for two instead of four? A few of our employees are helping out with the Little Whiskers fundraiser and are hoping to leave a bit early."

"Two o'clock works. Are you attending the fundraiser?"

"I've decided to buy a ticket," Hollis said. "It's for a good cause."

"It is," he said. When you purchase yours, could you also buy one for me? Put both of them on my card."

"Thank you, Mr. Stark," Hollis said. "I'll have your ticket here at the office tomorrow."

"Perfect. Oh, one more thing. Can you arrange for Rayna Abrams to receive an access card to the gym? Let her know she can use it whenever she'd like."

Always the professional, Hollis didn't pause. "Of course, Mr. Stark. I'll set it up this afternoon."

"Thank you, Hollis."

He ended the call and kissed Molly's forehead when she chirped at him. "I know what you're thinking, but I'm not doing this because I'm worried about her injuring herself with that shit she calls gym equipment at her house."

Molly stared at him unblinkingly, and he cleared his throat before looking away. "It's just another way of convincing her to sell her property. That's it, cat."

Molly chirped at him before jumping into the nest with the babies. With a loud sigh, Stark grabbed his laptop. He was behind on work because the memory of Rayna licking his thumb kept popping into his head, and the knowledge that if they hadn't been interrupted by his goddamn cousin, he might now know exactly how it felt to have his cock buried deep inside of Rayna's perfect body.

His dick was already starting to harden, and he adjusted it with a grimace. Christ, he really needed to get laid.

CHAPTER 19

"So, Stark not only stopped and helped you with a stray dog in the dark and the cold, but he also drove to the south side with you, paid for a bunch of the rescue's vet bills, and is continuing to foster Molly and her babies even though you have another foster home for them?" Emma said.

"When you say it like that, Emmy, he almost sounds like a nice guy." Rayna flopped onto the couch, wincing when a spring in the worn out piece of furniture poked into her butt. She shifted further to the right, watching with amusement as the black and white cat sitting in the middle of the living room snagged a kitten as she raced by him, pinned her down with one paw and roughly groomed her. "Can you believe how much Freddie loves these babies? Normally, he is either indifferent or actively hates any other cats that come through here."

"Yes, yes, it's very cute," Emma said. "Let's get back to how nice Isaac Stark is being to you."

"He's only doing it because he thinks it'll convince me to sell my property to him. It's why he bought a ticket to the fundraiser and gave me an access card to his personal gym."

"Wait... what?" Emma stopped with her mug halfway to her mouth. "He's letting you use his gym? Are you serious right now?"

Rayna nodded. "Yeah. His assistant, Hollis, contacted me about purchasing tickets for the fundraiser. Then she asked if I could come by the office because she had an access card for me for the gym. I picked it up earlier this afternoon."

Emma stared at her like she had two heads. "Lucas told me the gym was only for Stark and employees."

"That's what Hollis told me earlier, as well. I asked her why Stark was giving me this, but -"

Emma laughed. "She just stared you down, right?"

"Basically," Rayna said. "Hollis seems very stern."

"She is," Emma said. "Surprisingly, she and Lucas get along well even though she is severely type A and Lucas is... Lucas."

"Do you think she and Stark are sleeping together?" Rayna asked casually.

Either it wasn't casual enough, or, more likely, Emma could see right through her because she immediately said, "Why do you care?"

"I don't," Rayna said. "I was just curious."

"So, you're lying to your best friend now?" Emma asked as Bea ambled into the room. She ignored Frankie's annoyed hiss and leaned against Emma's legs. Emma reached down to pet her, glancing at Rayna. "Well?"

"Ugh. Fine. I might have, maybe, licked Stark's thumb the other day."

Emma ignored Bea nosing at her hand, her mouth dropping open as she stared at Rayna. "You did what?"

"It was just something that happened."

"Licking someone's thumb is not something that just *happens*, Rayna Abrams," Emma said. "Give me every detail."

Ten minutes later, Emma studied her thoughtfully. "So, he's into you as much as you're into him."

"Not necessarily," Rayna said.

"You just told me he had an erection because you licked his thumb," Emma said.

"He's a guy. They get random erections all the time," Rayna said.

"Girl, please," Emma said.

Rayna sighed. "Fine. Yeah, it seems like he's into me. But it's a terrible idea to sleep together because we also hate each other. I'm sure he regrets the moment as much as I do."

"Does he? He just gave you free access to his state-of-the-art gym."

"Because he thinks if he's nice to me, I'll sell my property to him," Rayna said.

Emma paused. "Shit, you might be right."

"I *am* right," Rayna said. "Trust me, Emma, he only wants one thing from me - my property."

"Eh, pretty sure he wants to know what your o-face looks like, too," Emma said.

"Emma!" Rayna couldn't help but laugh. "Since when did you get so... unprudish about sex?"

"Since having Lucas in my bed every night. That man is shameless. Also, he's amazing in bed."

"Good for you, honey," Rayna said with a grin. "You deserve amazing sex."

"To answer your earlier question, no, I don't think Hollis and Stark are sleeping together. Lucas says Stark has firm boundaries at work, and Hollis does too. She's worked for Stark for years and still calls him Mr. Stark."

"Maybe she's so formal because they're secretly sleeping together," Rayna said.

"You sound jealous."

"I'm not," she said. "Just curious."

Emma stared her down, and Rayna sighed. "Maybe a little jealous. But only because I haven't been laid in so long, and Stark is stupidly good looking, and, Em, I honestly don't know why he's even attracted to me. I am so not his type."

Emma hesitated, and Rayna said, "Just say it, Emmy."

"This isn't a dig against you because you are stunningly gorgeous, but it's true that you're not his usual type. Again, Stark doesn't share anything personal at the office, but he has brought dates to office functions on occasion, and Lucas says they're…"

"They're what?" Rayna asked.

"Basically models with perfect hair and makeup and expensive clothes, and they're always lawyers or doctors or executive types."

Rayna glanced at her stained leggings and ripped t-shirt. "Colour me surprised. He has expensive taste in everything else. Why wouldn't that include his girlfriends? Hell, just one of his suits probably costs more than my entire wardrobe. I sincerely doubt Stark has even stepped foot in a Walmart his entire life."

"Probably not," Emma agreed before checking her phone. "I better go. I have some errands to run before I head home, and I want to be at the store early tomorrow since I'm leaving early to help with the fundraiser."

"Thanks, Emmy. I really appreciate everything you've done to help with this."

"Anytime." Emma winced when the second kitten barreled into the room and climbed her leg to perch on her knee. "Haven't found a foster home for these kittens yet, huh?"

"No," Rayna sighed. "Foster homes are in short supply right now. But we'll have information about fostering at the fundraiser tomorrow, and I'm hoping we get some interest."

"Before I go…" Emma made a face.

"Uh oh," Rayna said.

"Do you know who Paula Plink and Denise Macklin are?"

Rayna nodded. "Retired nurses and two of the biggest gossips in town."

"They're also members of Harmony Falls Evangelical Church."

Rayna grimaced. "The one led by that asshole, the Reverend Newood or something?"

"Norwood," Emma said, "and yeah, that's the one. They were in the store the other day, and I overheard them talking about the good reverend planning a protest."

"Okay," Rayna said. "What does that have to do with me?"

"He's planning on protesting the fundraiser," Emma said.

"Are you fucking kidding me?" Rayna groaned.

"I wish I were," Emma said. "It might not happen. You know what gossips they are. It could just be a rumour."

"Yeah, but if they attend that church, then they probably have first-hand knowledge of it, right?" Rayna said.

"Yeah," Emma said. "Sorry, honey."

"It's fine," Rayna said with a sigh. "It's a free country, and people are allowed to protest whatever they want. I don't get why they are, though. It's just people bidding for a date with someone they find attractive. It's not a live sex show, for God's sake."

She rubbed Bea's stomach when the beagle lay at her feet and rolled to her back. "I shouldn't be surprised, though. I was called to a job at his church, and I tried to convince the secretary, Nola, to be a bachelorette. I didn't know she was the pastor's daughter. He overheard me and blew a gasket. Went on and on about how I was trying to whore out his daughter."

"What an asshole. If Paula and Denise are to be believed, he's also upset about the," Emma made finger quotes, "rampant homosexuality you're promoting at the fundraiser."

"Of course he is," Rayna said in annoyance. "Never mind that out of sixteen bachelors and bachelorettes, we have two bachelors and one bachelorette who are gay. I wouldn't really call that rampant."

"He's a terrible person," Emma said. "Everyone knows it. You know my grandma is the most devout Christian ever, right?"

"Yep," Rayna said.

"She was over the moon thrilled when my cousin got engaged to his boyfriend. She couldn't have been happier for them because she actually understands what it means to be a Christian."

Rayna sighed. "Well, we'll just have to hope that they aren't over-the-top obnoxious with the protesting."

"Ian and Lennox are bachelors at the fundraiser, right?" Emma said.

"Yes," Rayna said. "Why?"

"They're deputies. They might be willing to speak with him if there is a protest. Maybe they could even ask other deputies to show up and do crowd control or something."

"I don't think it'll get that crazy. Do you?" Rayna gave Emma a worried look.

"Probably not, but it wouldn't hurt to give them the heads up. I know Wanda's on dispatch at the station tomorrow morning. I'll call and mention it to her."

"Thank you, Emmy. I appreciate it."

"You're welcome. Okay, I really do need to go." With one last pat to Bea, Emma stood and gave Rayna a quick kiss on the cheek. "I'll see you at the community center at two tomorrow."

"You bet." She walked Emma to the door and waved goodbye before returning to the couch. She flopped down on it and stared moodily at the two kittens who were climbing all over Freddie. The black and white cat's tail flicked rapidly, but he made no effort to discipline the babies who were now biting at his tail.

"You'll regret spoiling them when they're twice that size, Freddie," Rayna said.

He ignored her, and she grabbed her phone and scrolled to Stark's name in her text messages. She typed rapidly and, before she could chicken out, hit the send button.

RAYNA

Thank you for the gym access card.

She tossed her phone onto the couch and considered opening her laptop to check the rescue emails before grabbing her phone again. Her pulse fluttered when she saw the dots indicating Stark was replying, and she was annoyed with herself at her excitement.

"Who cares what he has to say," she said to Bea, who had heaved herself onto the couch beside her. She stroked Bea's ears, her fingers pausing when Stark's reply came through.

STARK

You're welcome.

"You're welcome? That's it?" she said to Bea. She sat and stewed for a moment before typing and hitting send.

RAYNA

I appreciate the gesture, but I'm still not selling my property to you.

STARK

I gave you access to my gym, Ms. Abrams because using your gym equipment will get you killed. It's called being nice. You should consider trying it sometime.

RAYNA

Ha, ha. Why do you care if my gym
equipment kills me?

STARK

I don't like bad smells.

RAYNA

Unlike you, I am a nice person with friends.
My dead body would be discovered long
before it started to smell.

STARK

Or Bea would eat your body before it could
smell.

She laughed out loud, glancing down at Bea. "He's got me on that one. You would totally eat my dead body, wouldn't you, sweet girl?"

RAYNA

You're not wrong.

STARK

I rarely am.

She rolled her eyes and stuck her tongue out at her phone screen, but her pulse did that weird fluttering thing again when she saw the three dots.

STARK

Just promise me you'll use my gym rather
than the death trap equipment from the
seventies.

RAYNA

It's from the eighties, but, yes, I'll use your
gym instead. And I'm still not selling my
property to you.

STARK

I heard you the first time, Ms. Abrams. Enjoy your evening.

She tossed her phone on the couch, a little weirded out by how disappointed she was that Stark had ended the conversation.

"Whatever, Bea. I hate him, and he hates me, and I don't care what he says. He's only doing this to try to convince me to sell. But I'm happy to let him have his delusions while I use his kick-ass gym. In fact, I'm treating myself to something nice this evening and trying out the fancy new gym right now. Be good while I'm gone, sweetie."

She leaned down and kissed the dog's forehead before heading to her bedroom to change into her workout clothes.

CHAPTER 20

"Excuse us, please. You're in our way."

Nola took a step back, her friendly smile faltering when the two women gave her and her sign a frosty look before continuing into the community center.

Not that she could blame them. She stared at the sign she held. She had chosen one that said, "Repent, sinners!" in big red letters. In her mind, it was the least offensive choice of the signs her father had piled in the back of his SUV for the protesters to choose from. She couldn't force herself to pick up the signs reading 'homosexuality is a sin' or 'whores burn in hell.' Not when she didn't believe either to be true.

"You okay, Nola?" Josephine asked. She was around Nola's age, with short blonde hair and a passion for God and diamond painting kits.

"Fine," Nola said. She glanced around for her father or Abraham, but they were both at the far end of the protest group. She and Josephine had drifted away from their fellow protesters, but she still lowered her voice. "I don't want to be here. Protesting against people trying to help innocent animals isn't right, Josephine."

"I understand, but how they're helping animals is a sin, Nola," Josephine said earnestly. "They're promoting sex before marriage and encouraging the sin of homosexuality."

"Going on a date doesn't mean it ends in sex," Nola said.

"That isn't what our fathers say," Josephine said. "Sinners who don't know God's love and how important it is to stay pure before marriage are having sex on dates all the time."

Nola didn't reply. Familiar guilt crept into her, and she didn't dare look toward Abraham again for fear the truth of what she did with him on a regular basis would be written all over her face for Josephine to see.

Not so regular anymore, Nola. Abraham no longer finds you attractive. He doesn't even know you have a tattoo yet because he's avoiding being intimate with you.

That wasn't true. Abraham was just very busy lately. She hardly saw him at all anymore. He was either working, helping her father with church matters, or spending his free time with the men's prayer group. She missed him, but she understood the importance of his faith to him.

Do you miss him, though?

"Nola, what are you doing?"

She turned and smiled at Abraham, who had left her father to join them. "Hi!"

"What are you doing?" he repeated. "You've been standing here like a lump for the last five minutes, and I saw you let those two women pass you without saying anything to them."

"What was I supposed to say?" she asked.

He sighed, impatience creeping into his voice. "I don't have time for your nonsense today, Nola. This protest is important to both me and your father."

She kept the smile on her face with sheer willpower. "Sorry. I'll do better."

"Thank you," he said.

She hesitated before setting down her sign and sliding her arms around his waist. He stiffened and glanced behind him before breaking her hold and stepping back. "You know how I feel about public displays of affection, Nola. It's especially inappropriate here."

"I haven't seen you for two days, and I've missed you." She gave him a teasing smile. "Plus, I'm cold, and you're a pretty handsome heater."

The compliment didn't mollify him. "You knew it would be cold tonight. Why aren't you wearing a hat and scarf?"

"I forgot them," she said.

He tucked his scarf a little closer to his throat. "Well, consider this God's punishment for being forgetful."

"Right," she said.

He looked pointedly at her sign, and she picked it up again, earning her a strained smile of satisfaction. When he turned to leave, she caught his hand. "Stay here with me?"

"I can't," he said. "Your father needs me."

He walked away, and Nola turned to face Josephine. The young woman smiled at her. "You're so lucky to have Abraham as a boyfriend."

"I am," Nola said, hoping her smile didn't look as unnatural as it felt. More cars were pulling into the community center parking lot, and she studied the nearly two dozen church members holding signs at the edge of the parking lot, staring with blatant hostility at the people trying to enter the community hall.

Was this really God's love? It didn't feel like it to her, although lately, nothing at the church she'd grown up in felt like God's love. And if it was, then she didn't want anything to do with that God.

"I hope I find someone as godly and perfect as Abraham someday," Josephine said with a soft sigh.

Nola hunched her shoulders, trying to warm both her

neck and her ears. It was a dismal way to spend a Friday evening, and she really wished she hadn't forgotten her hat and scarf. It was just getting colder and darker, and she'd probably have frostbite by the time her father let them leave.

"Come on, Josephine," Nola said. "We should join the others."

She took a step back and made a startled yelp when her foot slipped on some ice beneath the snow. She dropped her sign and tried to catch her balance, but her foot was still sliding, and she was definitely about to fall on her ass. Her body tensed, preparing itself for a hard impact that never arrived.

Instead, two leather-clad arms slid around her and caught her neatly. Her back pressed against a hard chest, and she made an embarrassing grunt of surprise before staring up at the man who'd caught her.

Her eyes widened, her pulse went into overdrive, and her cold body immediately set itself on fire.

"You okay?" Nix's deep voice sounded as tasty as honey to her.

She breathed deeply of his now familiar scent as she nodded dumbly. His big hands were clasped loosely around her hips, and she stared at the tattoos on them before staring up at his face again.

"I slipped on the ice," she finally said.

She ignored her disappointment when he let go of her hips and stepped away. She turned to face him, her smile jittery and nervous. "Thank you."

"You're welcome."

"It seems like you're always, um, saving me."

He just shrugged, and her pulse still thumping and bumping, she said, "What are you doing here?"

He glanced at the community center. "I'm participating in the fundraiser."

"Oh. You're um… you're one of the bachelors?"

He nodded, and a gleeful little voice inside her said, *"He's single!"*

So what? She wasn't.

"That's nice," she said inanely. Why did she lose all of her brain cells when she was around Nix?

"Do you actually think so?" He glanced at her fallen sign, and she turned bright red as he studied the other protesters.

"Oh, I, uh..." She trailed off. What was she supposed to say? She was obviously here protesting the fundraiser, and nothing she said would change that.

Josephine joined them, smiling timidly at Nix. "Hello. I'm Josephine, and I'd love to talk to you about the healing grace of God's love."

"I'm an atheist," Nix said, his gaze returning to Nola. "You look like you're freezing."

She smiled faintly. "At least I'm wearing a coat this time, right?"

His disapproving look did something to her insides that wasn't exactly unpleasant. In fact, she was feeling a little tingly in the most inappropriate place.

"I forgot my hat and scarf, but I'm actually not that cold," she lied.

"Your lips are blue," he said. He unwound the scarf from his neck, and she stood in silent surprise as he wrapped it around hers. It was thick, delightfully soft, and warm.

"There," he said gruffly. "You can keep the scarf."

"You can't keep giving me your clothes," she said and then blushed at how incredibly improper her comment was. "I mean, your, uh, winter clothes, not your *clothes*, clothes."

He grinned, and there went her stupid heart again, thumping away like she'd run a marathon and her crotch... well, she absolutely did not want to talk about what it was currently doing.

"Nola?" Abraham pushed past Nix and stood beside her, sliding a possessive arm around her shoulders.

Oh, now he was fine with public displays of affection?

She ignored her immediate urge to push Abraham's arm away as he glared at Nix. "I saw you touching my girlfriend. You're lucky I don't have you arrested for assault."

"Abraham!" Anger, an unfamiliar emotion at best, washed over Nola, and she gave into her urge and pushed away his arm. "Stop it. I slipped on the ice, and he caught me. He saved me from smashing my head on the pavement."

Before Abraham could reply - oh, this was just *perfect* - her father arrived. His face was red, and he was already beginning to bleat like an angry goat.

Unkind, Nola!

"Get away from my daughter, you..." Her father's eyes widened as recognition washed over his face. "You. I remember you. You were harassing my daughter while she ministered to the poor."

"No, he wasn't, Daddy," Nola said. "He saved me from -"

"Nola, hush," Abraham said.

She glared at Abraham as her father sneered at Nix. "Of course you would be here with the rest of the sinners. A man like you, covered in the devil's marks, wouldn't hesitate to participate in a whorish gathering like this."

Her father studied the tattoos visible on Nix's hands. "Do you think the devil will show mercy on you when you join him in hell? Do you believe defiling your body with tattoos will gain you his favour? Because I assure you, you will burn just like all the other sinners who mark their bodies as you have done."

Nix's gaze flickered to Nola's hip. Just for a moment, but it was enough to make the blood drain from her face and her lips go numb. Oh God. He would tell her father about her tattoo, and she couldn't blame him for it. Her father was being so rude, and finding out his daughter had a tattoo would be the only way to shut him up.

Of course, it would also cost her everything, but that wasn't Nix's problem, was it?

She stared wide-eyed at Nix and waited for him to destroy her life.

Instead of telling her father he'd tattooed her, Nix eyed the three of them a final time before giving her father a stiff smile. "Always a pleasure talking with you, Reverend."

He walked away as every muscle in Nola's body went limp with relief.

CHAPTER 21

"**B**achelorettes and bachelors! Can I have your attention, please?" Zuri whistled piercingly, and the chatter of voices quieted.

Rayna squeezed past Jesse, a local fireman and one of their bachelors, and joined Zuri as she smiled at the crowd.

They were standing backstage in what the community center called its studio - a large room with a small stage that local theatre groups often rented out. A heavy burgundy curtain was pulled across the stage, but Rayna could still hear the faint murmur of voices from the guests at the fundraiser.

Zuri, holding a clipboard and wearing a stunning turquoise dress that gleamed against her dark skin, took a deep breath. "I just got the news that tickets for the fundraiser are completely sold out."

There was a smattering of applause and cheers, and Zuri grinned at everyone. "I appreciate each and every one of you and can't thank you enough for helping to make this night a success. And it *will* be a success, I know it. Now, I have a few last-minute instructions for our bachelors and bachelorettes, so if you can join me, that would be great."

As the eight men and eight women crowded around Zuri, Arianna joined Rayna. "Ray-Ray! Did you see how, like, sexy and beautiful the bachelorettes are?"

"I did," Rayna said. "You did an amazing job on their makeup, Arianna."

"I totally did," Arianna said proudly. "Edna Bakersfield looks seventy instead of ninety."

"Edna is eighty-one, not ninety," Rayna said as she glanced at the elderly woman sitting on a chair with her cane planted firmly between her legs, staring at Zuri as she talked animatedly to her and the others.

"What happens when no one bids on her?" Arianna asked.

"Shh," Rayna said with another glance at Edna.

"She can't hear me," Arianna said. "She turned her hearing aids off earlier. She said all the noise was giving her a headache. But seriously, what will you do when it's crickets in the audience?"

"Someone will bid on her," Rayna said.

"Sure, Ray-Ray. Cheri Ladd was the only bachelorette who wouldn't let me do her makeup." Arianna gave the white woman who managed The Gemstone Gallery an annoyed look. "She was, like, super rude about it too."

"Sorry, sweetie," Rayna said. "I appreciate you volunteering your time tonight."

"Oh, it's, like, no problem. You know I'd do anything for you." Arianna grabbed her phone. "I'm going to go take some video of the crowd for my Instagram post. I'll be right back."

She headed toward the side stairs as Emma walked up and slung her arm around Rayna's shoulders. "I have some good news for you."

"Oh yeah?" Rayna said.

"The protesters are gone," Emma said.

"What?" Rayna said. "How?"

"Grace Larken," Emma said. "Or rather, her fiancé, Sheriff

Walker. Lennox and Ian spoke with the protesters and asked them to stop, but they were ignored. So Grace called the sheriff, and he agreed to come by."

"Oh my God, I could kiss her right now," Rayna said. "How did the sheriff convince them to leave?"

Emma shrugged. "I don't know the details, but the sheriff has a way with people, right? Even supreme assholes like the Reverend Norwood. It's what makes him so good at his job."

"I am definitely buying Grace dinner for this," Rayna said.

"In not-so-good news," Emma said, "Phoebe Edwards is here."

"For fuck's sake," Rayna snapped. She walked toward the curtain and pulled aside one end, peeking out at the crowd of people who were starting to settle at their tables in the large space.

"On the left, near the front of the stage," Emma pointed over Rayna's shoulder.

Rayna followed Emma's finger, her upper lip curling when she saw the pretty, dark-haired engineer. "Ugh. What is she doing here? She hates me, animals, and doing nice things for others."

Emma snorted. "Isn't that the truth. She's probably here because it's the only way she can get a date."

"I wish that were true," Rayna said. "But you and I both know that the men fall all over her in this town. And why wouldn't they? She's gorgeous, smart, and an engineer. Ugh. Weren't childhood bullies supposed to get what was coming to them as adults? Why does she get this amazing life when she spent our entire childhoods making ours miserable?"

"She'll get her comeuppance," Emma said. "Eventually. Holy shit, why is he sitting with her?"

"Who?" Rayna glanced at Phoebe's table again, a little surprised by the hot jealousy that streaked through her when she saw Stark sit down beside Phoebe. His cousin Jasper sat in the chair on Phoebe's left side, and she gave both men a slow and sexy smile.

"Who's the handsome blond guy?" Emma asked. "Do you know?"

"That's Jasper."

"Stark's cousin that you met on Tuesday?" Emma asked as Rayna let the curtain drop back into place. "You didn't tell me how good looking he is. He wears a suit as well as Stark."

"Yeah, he's hot," Rayna said.

"Maybe it's a Stark thing," Emma mused. "They all have, like, the handsome gene or something."

"Bonus - he's not a complete asshole like his cousin," Rayna said.

"You did mention he was very charming." Emma studied her. "Are you into him?"

"I don't know him that well," Rayna said. "But he's cute and funny, and he was hitting on me at Stark's."

"If he asked you out, would you say yes?" Emma asked.

An image of Stark flickered through Rayna's head, and she had to clamp down on the immediate 'no' that wanted to fly from her lips. Why shouldn't she go out with Jasper if he asked her? She was single, and nothing was stopping her from going out with him.

Nothing at all.

"Rayna?" Emma prompted.

Before she could reply, Zuri and Arianna joined them. Zuri clasped her clipboard to her chest. "We have a serious problem, Rayna."

"What's wrong?" Rayna asked.

"Cheri just dropped out."

"What do you mean she dropped out?"

"She looked at her phone, her face went red, and she said I have to go, and then she left," Zuri said. "We need a new bachelorette."

She stared at Rayna, who said, "Why are you looking at me?"

"Because you're my new bachelorette," Zuri said.

"The fuck I am," Rayna said.

"The fuck you aren't," Zuri said.

"Just go with seven bachelorettes," Rayna said.

"No." Zuri was gripping her clipboard so tightly that it looked like she might crack it in half. "I said there would be eight bachelorettes, and there *will* be eight bachelorettes."

"Zuri, there has to be someone else who can -"

"There isn't," Zuri said. "You're the only single lady."

"You're single!" Rayna said.

"I'm not. I'm dating someone."

"Since when?"

"For almost four months now. She's from... Willington," Zuri said.

"Oh, gross," Arianna said. "Is she, like, super rich or something?"

Zuri ignored her as Rayna said, "Wren! Wren is single!"

She stared desperately at the tiny blonde woman who hovered near the bachelors and surreptitiously eyed Deputy Ian like he was a tasty snack.

"She has a total crush on that deputy guy, right?" Arianna said to Emma. "She looks at him like she wants to ride his face like a pony."

Emma burst into laughter as Zuri said, "I already asked Wren. She can't afford to take someone on a date. It's your rescue, Rayna. You need to take one for the team."

"I'm wearing a t-shirt and jeans," Rayna said. "I didn't do my hair, and I'm not wearing any makeup."

"You never wear makeup, Ray-Ray," Arianna said. She eyed Rayna up and down before reaching out and tugging out Rayna's hair elastic. She sighed dramatically and handed it back to her. "You really need to do something other than a

171

ponytail for your hair. It's, like, permanently indented from the elastic."

She gave her another critical look as Rayna scooped her hair back into a ponytail. "Okay, so I can't do anything about your hair or your clothes, but I can work my makeup magic."

"No time," Zuri said, taking Rayna's arm and tugging her toward the other bachelorettes. "You have a natural beauty, Rayna. Don't worry about it. Now, think of an idea for your date. You have three minutes."

"Zuri, I…"

Her voice died when Zuri gave her a fierce look. "I need you to do this, Rayna. Okay?"

She sighed. "Yeah, okay."

"You look like you're going to throw up," Emma said.

"I might," Rayna admitted. She fidgeted nervously, staring at James as he waited for Zuri to call his name. He stood on the other side of the stage, hidden behind the pulled-back curtains, and he looked just as nervous as Rayna. He was the last bachelor to go on stage, and he nodded distractedly to Wren when she patted his arm a bit timidly and said something Rayna couldn't hear.

"I don't want to do this," she said to Emma for what felt like the thousandth time.

"I know," Emma said patiently, "but I promise it will be fine."

"No one's going to bid on me," Rayna said. "I'll look like an idiot."

"Of course someone will bid on you," Emma said. "Rayna, you're funny and smart and gorgeous."

"I am wearing jeans and a t-shirt and my worse-fitting

bra," Rayna said. "My girls look like they fell off the back of a potato truck."

Emma laughed so hard that it drowned out the sound of Solomon Whittaker's voice as he called out for a final bid for the current bachelorette.

"The back of a potato truck?" Emma said, still wheezing laughter.

Rayna waved her off. "You know what I mean."

"I don't. I really don't," Emma said. "Besides, your boobs look amazing even in that bra. I'd kill for mine to be that perky."

She suddenly paused. "Oh, just a second, I want to see who wins the bid for Cora." She cocked her head, listening intently as Solomon shouted, "And the winning bid goes to Brent Davidson at three hundred dollars. You'll be enjoying dinner at the Windmill followed by indoor rock climbing with the gorgeous and talented Cora."

There was a loud whoop, and Emma grinned. "Oh my God, Brent has had a crush on Cora for months. He comes into the store all the time."

"Is three hundred bucks our highest bid?" Rayna asked.

Zuri appeared out of nowhere, her clipboard still in hand and a pen stuck haphazardly into her long black curls. "Nope. That honour went to Edna Bakersfield. Walter Angleson bid five hundred dollars for a date with her."

"Holy shit," Rayna said.

"Yeah, he got into a bidding war with Ray Franklin over her. I guess they have a pretty big rivalry going on at the assisted living facility they both live in," Zuri said.

Emma laughed. "That's awesome."

"Nix has the highest bachelor bid so far." Zuri consulted her clipboard. "Carrie Wagston paid four fifty for a date with him."

"The lady who owns the Sip and Gulp near Falls Park?" Emma asked.

"That's the one," Zuri said. She paused and then motioned frantically to James, who looked frozen to the floor as Solomon Whitaker called his name.

"Go," Zuri hissed. "James, go!"

Wren gave him a gentle push, and with one last look of desperation at Rayna, James stepped out from behind the curtain and walked onto the stage.

"Oh God, I hope he doesn't throw up," Zuri said as she watched James stop uncertainly next to Solomon.

"He'll be fine," Emma said. "He's just a little shy, that's all."

As Solomon told the guests what their date with James would include, Zuri disappeared down the side stairs, and Rayna glanced into the audience. Or, more accurately, she stared at Stark and Phoebe. After the first half hour of chatting to both Stark and Jasper, Phoebe had clearly chosen her victim, and she'd spent the last hour and a half talking to Stark, that sexy smile permanently in place and her hand grazing his arm and shoulder every few minutes.

Rayna gritted her teeth and told herself to look away. Instead, she continued to watch as Stark bent his head, and Phoebe said something in his ear that made a small smile cross his face.

"I can hear your teeth grinding, you know," Emma said.

Rayna forced her jaw to relax. "No, you can't."

"You're upset because Phoebe has been flirting with Stark all night," Emma said.

"No, I'm not. He's an asshole, and so is she. They'll be the perfect couple," Rayna snapped.

Emma didn't reply, and Rayna sighed. "Sorry, I'm being a dick."

"You're not," Emma said. "Look on the bright side. Phoebe requires a ton of attention. Maybe if Stark starts dating her, he'll be too busy keeping her happy to bug you about selling your place."

"Maybe," Rayna said.

"And the winning bid of two hundred and fifty dollars goes to the lovely emerald-haired Jade! You'll enjoy dinner and a horse-drawn sleigh ride through the Park with James."

"Oh my God," Rayna said as Jade made a soft squeal of excitement before waving at James. "Jade from Brandt Vet Clinic bid on James."

Looking a little dazed, James waved back before walking off the stage toward the table where the other bachelors and bachelorettes had gathered.

"You're up," Emma said.

"Emma, I can't do this. Not with Phoebe Edwards right there in the front goddamn row."

Emma took her by the shoulders and gave her a gentle shake. "Yes, you can. Who the fuck cares about Phoebe? High school was a long time ago, and trust me when I say, you're a million times more gorgeous than her. Go out there, stand tall, and enjoy having a bunch of dudes bid a shitload of money to spend time with you."

"It won't be a bunch or a shitload," Rayna muttered.

"All right, folks, we have one last bachelorette. Now, this was a last-minute change-up," Solomon said, grinning at the crowd, "but I guarantee y'all will be thrilled to see who she is. Let's give a warm welcome to the lovely Rayna Abrams."

"Go, sweetie," Emma said, gently pushing her as the fundraiser guests clapped their hands.

Plastering a bright smile on her face, Rayna walked out onto the stage and stood next to Solomon. He slipped his arm around her and gave her a quick and friendly squeeze. "Hello, Rayna."

"Hi there." Her voice sounded terrified, and she forced herself to stand straight and smile at the crowd. "I can't say thank you enough to all of you for participating in our fundraiser tonight. Little Whiskers Rescue does important work for a lot of innocent animals, and none of it would be possible without your generosity at events like this."

The crowd cheered and clapped as Rayna risked a glance at Stark. He was clapping politely, and Rayna kept the smile on her face with grim force as Phoebe gave her a brittle smile. Phoebe slipped her hand around Stark's bicep and lightly tugged until he bent his head toward her again.

Rayna looked away, scanning the rest of the crowd and hoping fervently that at least one person would bid on her.

"Rayna is offering dinner at the Bronze Blossom and ice skating at the Harmony Falls Sports Complex," Solomon read from a small index card before smiling at the crowd. "Who will start the bid at fifty dollars?"

The silence spun out, and Rayna could feel the red creeping up her neck and into her face. Oh God, she would be forced to stand here in complete silence until the end of time.

Pretty sure the sheer humiliation of the moment will kill you first.

Christ, she hoped so.

"One thousand dollars."

The crowd gasped, and necks craned to stare at the man who'd spoken. Rayna stared dumbly at Jasper, who grinned and winked at her before taking a sip from his wine glass.

"One thousand dollars!" Solomon roared happily. "Thank you, good man! Do I hear eleven hundred?"

Rayna turned to stare at Solomon. Was he crazy? No one else would bid -

"Eleven hundred."

Her jaw dropped, and she stared wide-eyed at Stark. He returned her look calmly as Solomon shouted, "Eleven hundred from Mr. Stark."

Solomon grinned at Jasper. "Do I hear twelve hundred?"

"Two thousand," Jasper said with a glance at Stark.

Rayna grabbed Solomon's arm. Before Solomon could say anything, Stark said, "Twenty-five hundred."

Jasper glared at him over Phoebe's head. Rayna's gaze fell to Phoebe, and she swallowed the hysterical laughter bubbling in her chest at the look of - holy shit, that was jealousy - on Phoebe's face.

What the actual fuck was happening right now?

"Twenty-five hundred!" Solomon shouted. The crowd clapped and cheered, and Rayna turned to stare at Emma, who was giving her a look of pure glee from backstage.

"What do you say, young fella?" Solomon winked at Jasper. "Do you want to make it twenty-six hundred?"

"Three thousand," Jasper said.

"Holy fuck," Rayna said.

Solomon laughed and turned his attention to Stark. "Mr. Stark? Thirty-one hundred?"

Stark glanced at Rayna, his blue eyes burning into hers before he shook his head.

Weird disappointment washed over her as Solomon said, "Three thousand, once, three thousand, twice... the winning bid goes to... what's your name, young fella?"

Jasper's grin widened. "Jasper."

"The winning bid goes to Jasper. Congratulations!" Solomon shouted.

The crowd clapped, and with that useless disappointment still covering her like a thick cloak, Rayna forced a smile and a wave and walked off the stage.

CHAPTER 22

S tark tossed his gym bag over his shoulder before leaving the locker room. His muscles ached, and he was starving, but he didn't regret staying late to get in a workout. Between looking after Molly last week and his work schedule this week, his daily workout had become a thing of the past, and he missed it.

He cracked his neck and checked his phone as he walked out into the main section of the gym. He really needed to… he stopped at the sound of the soft, rhythmic grunting, his gaze swiveling to the lat pulldown machine.

Rayna, wearing just a sports bra and leggings, sat at the machine, making those soft grunts every time she pulled the metal bar down. He stood completely still, barely breathing, as he watched her back muscles flex and contract. Her arms were tight with hard muscles, and her skin had a slight sheen. He studied her waist and the subtle curve of her hips, his cock stiffening against the sweatpants he hadn't bothered to change out of.

She had the exact body type he loved - lean, toned, and athletic. It was obvious that she was a gym rat just like him, and fuck did it turn him on to see her using the gym equipment. God, he really was desperate to get laid if that's what qualified as a turn-on for him now.

Still, he continued to watch her without shame as she finished off her reps before standing and carefully wiping the machine with a towel. He adjusted his cock, hoping his semi wasn't noticeable as Rayna turned toward him.

She let out a small screech and staggered back, raising the towel in her hand like a weapon. "Holy shit! What are you doing here?"

"It's my gym, Ms. Abrams."

Her flushed face turned a little redder. "I meant… what are you doing here now? Hollis said you work out in the mornings."

"Sometimes I switch it up," he said.

"No, you don't," she said, wiping her face with the towel. "Hollis was very clear that you only use the gym in the mornings."

"Is that why you're here now? So you don't have to be here when I am?" He sounded more than a little offended.

She looked away. "No, of course not."

"You're a terrible liar, Ms. Abrams."

"I know."

There was a beat of silence before she said, "Okay, well, it looks like you were leaving, so, uh, have a good night."

"Are you enjoying the gym?" he asked.

She nodded. "I am, thank you. The equipment is the best I've ever used."

More silence as he tried to think of something else to say, something that would continue to convince her he was a nice guy. He wanted to start building in the spring, and if he wanted her property before then, he needed to up his 'nice guy' game.

She was giving him a 'what the fuck' look, and he couldn't

blame her, but he still couldn't think of a damn thing to say. Who the fuck knew it would be so difficult to be nice?

"Ms. Abrams, are you -"

Thank Christ, he was interrupted by the shrill ring of her phone.

"Excuse me," she said and grabbed her phone out of the hoodie draped over her bag.

"Rayna speaking," she said. "Hey, Sheriff, how are you?"

She listened quietly before sighing. "Of course, he is. How badly is the dog injured? Is Louis agreeing to surrender?"

She listened again. "I can come out there, but are you sure you want me to? You know how Louis feels about me. No, it's not a problem. I'm not afraid of him. I'm just in town, but I can be there in about fifteen minutes. Sure. See you soon."

She ended the call and grabbed her hoodie, yanking it on and stuffing her phone into her bag. "I have to go."

He followed her out the door and into the frigid air. "Who is this Louis guy?"

She glanced over her shoulder at him. "What?"

"Louis," he said. "Who is he, and why would the sheriff think you'd be afraid of him?"

She unlocked her car and opened the door. "Just an asshole farmer with too many dogs that he doesn't take care of properly. He," she paused, "isn't my biggest fan and has accused me multiple times of stealing his dogs."

"Seriously?" he said.

"I haven't," she said quickly. "Any of the dogs I've taken from his property, he's willingly surrendered, and I have the paperwork to prove it. But he drinks a lot, and when he's drunk, he conveniently forgets that he surrendered the dogs and occasionally…".

"What?" he asked.

"He's threatened me a few times," she said.

A weird anxiety rocketed through him. "Then why the fuck is the sheriff asking you to come out there?"

She scowled at him. "Because one of his dogs is badly injured, and Louis has agreed to surrender it to the rescue to get vet care."

"So, let the sheriff bring the dog to you," Stark said.

"He has enough on his plate," she said.

"It's dangerous for you to go out there."

"The sheriff will be there," she said. "Nothing's going to happen."

She slid into her SUV, and he immediately jogged to the passenger side and climbed in, tossing his gym bag in the back seat.

"What are you doing?" she said.

"Going with you." He buckled his seatbelt.

"I don't need your help," she said in exasperation. "Get out of my car, Stark."

"Make me," he said.

"Oh my God, not this again," she groaned. She started the vehicle, clicked her seatbelt into place, and gave him a look. "Louis is dumb as a tree stump and mean as a pissed-off alligator. If you say anything that makes him angry, he will not give up the dog. If that happens, I will personally kick your ass, so no matter what he says, don't take the bait. Are we clear?"

"I'll be on my best behaviour, Ms. Abrams," he said, giving her the grin that never failed to charm.

She remained thoroughly not charmed. "Make sure that you are, Stark."

"Thanks for driving out here, Rayna." The sheriff was waiting for them in the front yard of the farmhouse.

"It's not a problem," Rayna said.

The sheriff glanced at Stark, and he held out his hand. "Hi. I'm -"

"Isaac Stark. It's good to meet you officially."

"You as well," Stark said.

Sheriff Gideon Walker was a big man with a calm demeanor. He had a reputation for knowing everything that happened in Harmony Falls. Considering that the sheriff's sister was Stark's real estate agent, he didn't doubt that the sheriff knew he and Rayna were fighting over her property. Still, if he found it strange that Stark was with her, it didn't show on his face.

"The dog is in the smaller barn," the sheriff said. "Looks like a coyote attack, but the wounds are badly infected."

"Did you come out here because of the dog, Sheriff?" Stark asked.

Gideon shook his head. "We're here on another matter, but Lennox saw the dog and convinced Louis to let us call you."

"Sheriff, I've got - oh, hey, Rayna." Lennox materialized out of the darkness, his nose red from the cold and a thick scarf wrapped around his neck. "How are you?"

"I'm good, Lennox. You?"

"Can't complain." He grinned at her. "I have my date with Jasmine on Friday."

"That's great," she said.

"How about you?" he asked. "You set up the date with your big spender yet?"

Rayna glanced at Stark before clearing her throat. "Friday as well."

"Nice," Lennox said. "Anyway, thanks for coming out. Louis is in the barn with the dog and is willing to sign the surrender form."

"Is he drunk?" Rayna asked as the four of them headed across the icy ground toward the barn.

"He's been drinking," the sheriff said, "but he isn't drunk. Not yet."

They entered the barn, and Lennox led them to a stall near the back. A tall, broad shouldered man with weathered skin and wearing a thick wool coat stood outside the stall, a beer can in one meaty hand.

"Well, if it ain't the little rescue bitch," Louis said with a sneer at Rayna.

Stark immediately took Rayna's hand, pulling her closer to him, but before he could tell the man to shut the fuck up, the sheriff gave Louis a hard look. "Knock it off, Louis, or you'll spend the night in a jail cell."

The man's immediate pout would have put a tired toddler to shame. "What the fuck, Sheriff? You can't arrest me for calling someone a bitch."

Gideon just stared at him, and after only a few seconds, Louis looked away. "Whatever. Just take the fucking dog."

Rayna tried to tug her hand free of Stark's, giving him a warning look when he didn't release her. "I need to look at the dog."

Instead of releasing her hand, he started toward the stall, keeping his body between Rayna's and Louis's. They stepped into the stall, and he muttered a curse under his breath, this time letting go of Rayna's hand when she pulled away.

Rayna crouched next to the bloodhound, studying the massive, pus and maggot-infested wound on its right shoulder. She placed a tentative hand on the dog's ribs. He whined but didn't lift his head or make any move to bite her, and she gently scratched around his chin and throat. "It's okay, good boy. We'll get you feeling better soon."

The dog shifted on the ground, and Stark grimaced, covering his mouth and nose with one hand as the smell of rot and infection drifted into the air. He turned to stare at Louis, his body nearly vibrating with anger.

Louis gave him a defensive look. "What the fuck's your problem?"

"My problem is you letting the dog get to this point," Stark snarled. "Why the hell -"

Rayna's hand slipped into his and squeezed so hard, he was pretty sure she cracked a bone. He shut up abruptly and forced himself to look away from the despicable man in front of him, despite his very real urge to grab Louis and slam him into the barn wall until his rage had dissipated.

"You need to sign the surrender form, Louis," Rayna said, her voice calm and even. She reached into her hoodie pocket and pulled out a pen and a piece of paper she'd grabbed from a binder in the SUV's back seat when they arrived at the farm.

Louis's lip curled. "Maybe I've changed my mind about surrendering him. Old Red is one of my best bird dogs."

"Sign the surrender form, Louis," the sheriff said, "or I'll arrest you for animal abuse."

"The fuck?" Louis sputtered, his hand crushing the beer can he held. "It ain't my fault he got bit by a coyote."

"Sign the form," the sheriff repeated calmly.

"Fine, whatever," Louis snarled. "This dumb bitch won't be happy until she takes all of my dogs."

Stark bit the inside of his cheek until the metallic taste of blood dripped onto his tongue. The fucking piece of shit deserved to have his ass kicked, and he hated that he couldn't be the one to do it. He took deep breaths as Rayna handed the pen and paper to Louis. He scribbled his name on it and flung them back at her. "Go on. Take the dog and get the fuck off my property."

Without speaking, Rayna stuffed the paper and pen into her pocket and returned to the dog.

"Here, we'll carry him," Lennox said, glancing at Stark. "He's awfully weak, and I don't think he can walk with his shoulder like that."

Moving carefully, Stark and Lennox picked up the dog. Its whines of pain tore at Stark's chest, and he glanced at Rayna as they carried the dog out of the barn. Her face was pale and grim, and she gently petted the dog's head once they'd placed him in the back of her SUV on a bed of soft blankets.

She closed the back of the SUV and gave the sheriff a thin smile. "Thanks for calling me, Sheriff."

"Thank you for taking the dog," he said. "Let me know if Louis gives you any trouble over it."

"I will." Rayna turned to Stark. "Can you drive?"

He nodded and slid behind the wheel as Rayna climbed into the passenger seat. She was already dialing a number on her phone as he drove down the long driveway toward the main road.

As he headed toward town, Rayna put her phone on speaker and grabbed the surrender form. She scanned it as the phone rang. Expecting to hear Nathan's voice, Stark was surprised when a woman answered.

"Harmony Falls Vet Clinic."

"Hi, Dr. Felton, it's Rayna Abrams."

"Hi, Rayna," the vet said. "How are you?"

"Doing okay, but I have an injured dog. It looks like a coyote attack, but the wound is badly infected. Any chance you could see him tonight?"

The vet hesitated. "I'm on call this evening, but the rescue's bill with the clinic is very high, and it's past due."

"It is," Rayna said, "and I apologize for taking so long to pay it."

"We have an agreement that once the account is a month

overdue, we hold off on assisting the rescue until the bill is paid," Dr. Felton said.

"I know, but I'm hoping you can make an exception this evening. The dog really needs to be seen," Rayna said.

There was another long silence, and Stark's stomach clenched when the vet said, "I'm sorry, Rayna. I can't."

"I understand," Rayna said as defeat washed over her face. "Thank you, Dr. Felton, and I promise I'll have our bill paid off soon."

She ended the call, and Stark said, "You don't want to take him to Nathan?"

Rayna rubbed at her forehead. "He's my preference, actually, but our bill is even higher at Brandt Vet, and I don't want to take advantage of Nathan's generosity toward the rescue."

"I can't believe this other vet won't help the dog," Stark said.

"I understand why she won't," Rayna said. "Running a vet clinic is expensive, and she needs to be paid for her services."

"So, you'll try another vet?" he asked.

"There are three vet clinics in Harmony Falls," she said, "and the rescue uses all of them, but PawPrints Vet clinic isn't on call tonight. The three clinics share the emergency calls so that each clinic has every third month off, and it's their month."

She dialed the number anyway, grimacing when the call went straight to voicemail, and a robotic voice advised them to try the Brandt Vet Clinic or Harmony Falls Vet Clinic if their pet was experiencing a medical emergency.

"Call Nathan," Stark said. "I'll pay for the dog's bill."

"No," she said sharply. "I don't need you to pay the bill."

"You kind of do," he said.

She glared at him. "No, I don't. Nathan will treat the dog

and allow me to add the cost to the rescue's bill. I know he will. I just hate to ask him to do it."

"Then let me pay for the dog's treatment," he said.

She shook her head as her phone rang. "No, thank you. The money coming in from the fundraiser will allow me to pay off the vet bills. Especially since your cousin bid so much for -"

She stopped abruptly, giving him a look he couldn't interpret as the phone stopped ringing, and Nathan's voice said, "Dr. Henshaw speaking."

"Hi, Nathan, it's Rayna," she said. "I have a badly injured bloodhound from Louis Hapson's farm that he's surrendered to the rescue. Looks like a coyote attack, but he's let the wound get infected. It's bad, Nathan. Maggot and pus bad."

"That fucking guy," Nathan said with genuine anger in his voice. "Christ, I hate him."

"Me too," Rayna said. "I hate to ask because I know our bill is high, but -"

"Bring him in," Nathan said. "I'm still at the clinic, and so is Dr. Yale. She's working on a blocked cat, but she's almost finished, and I know she'll stay to assist if I need help."

"Thank you, Nathan," Rayna said. "I appreciate your help."

She ended the call and leaned back in the seat, rubbing again at her forehead. It was only a little after seven, but she looked exhausted. Stark ignored the niggle of worry in his guts as she said, "Head to your office first. I'll drop you at your car before I go to the clinic."

He shook his head. "I'll go to the clinic with you."

"You're not paying the bill," she said, giving him a stubborn look. "I mean it, Stark."

He glared at her, but she didn't back down an inch, and he sighed loudly. "Fine, but I'm still going with you. The sooner we get that dog to the vet, the better."

CHAPTER 23

"This isn't the way to my office," Stark said.

"I'm starving, and so are you. I can hear your stomach growling," Rayna said.

"I'm not sure I can eat after seeing that poor dog," he said.

She nodded. "I get it, but we need to eat. The good news is that the dog is doing better and no longer suffering like he was. He's been given pain meds and fluids, and now that Nathan has cleaned out the worst of the infection, he can start healing."

She pulled into the McDonald's drive-thru. "What do you want?"

He studied the menu board. "I haven't eaten at a McDonald's in years. Do they still have a chicken sandwich?"

She laughed. "Yes. How about I order for you?"

"Sure."

She ordered the food and pulled up to the window. When Stark reached for his wallet, she shook her head and pulled out her debit card. "My treat."

She paid, handed the bags of food to Stark to hold, and stuck the drinks in the drink holders before parking in an empty spot. She took a bag from Stark and opened it, grabbing a few fries and shoving them into her mouth, relishing the salty goodness.

Stark was staring at her, and she shoved more fries into her mouth. "Don't fry shame me."

"I'm not," he said. "I've just never…"

"What?" She unwrapped her cheeseburger and took a big bite.

"Had a woman buy me dinner before."

"Seriously?"

He nodded, and she stared at the container of fries he held. "It's honestly not much of a dinner."

He ate some fries. "They're good fries."

"The best fries," she said. "I don't eat much fast food, but I'd cut a bitch for McDonald's fries."

They ate in silence for a few minutes before he said. "Why are we eating in your car in the parking lot instead of going into the restaurant?"

"Buy a man dinner one time, and he's complaining already," she teased.

He rolled his eyes but didn't look that annoyed by her teasing. She took a drink before saying, "If I go inside to eat, at some point, someone will approach me about a pet they need to rehome or complain about their neighbour's cat who poops in their garden or the dog who won't stop barking, and sometimes I just want to eat my fries in peace."

"How long have you been running the rescue?" he asked.

"Almost four years now," she said.

"Are you a registered charity?" he asked.

"Not yet. I'm working on it with our accountant, but Mack is…"

"What?" Stark asked.

"Dragging his feet on it," Rayna said. "It's a lot of work, and he volunteers his time outside of his regular job, so I get

it, but being able to give people tax receipts for their donations would get us a lot more in donations."

"Why not ask someone else to do it?" Stark said. "Reach
out to some local accounting offices and see if they'd be
willing to donate their time to help you register the charity."

"I can't do that to Mack. He's been with me since I first
started Little Whiskers, and I would be lost without him. I
don't have any spare time to deal with the money side of the
rescue, and without Mack's help, Little Whiskers wouldn't be
what it is today. He keeps the rescue running smoothly on
the financial side of things."

A slight scowl crossed his face. "Do you trust Mack?
Because giving a person that kind of power and not moni-
toring it is dangerous, Ms. Abrams."

She didn't want to be defensive, but she could hear it in
her voice. "I'm aware of the dangers, but I trust Mack implic-
itly, and even if I did monitor it, I'm not sure that would be
very helpful. I'm a plumber, not an accountant."

"Did you always want to be a plumber?"

He changed the topic so quickly that it took Rayna a few
seconds to catch up. "No. I wanted to be a veterinarian."

"Why didn't you?"

She poked at the cheeseburger wrapper before shoving it
into the paper bag. "I looked into it as I was getting closer to
graduating high school, but the schooling was too expensive.
So I went to trade school instead and became a plumber."

"You couldn't get grants or a scholarship?" he asked.

"I applied for a few scholarships, but I didn't get them,"
she said.

"Your parents couldn't help?"

She gave him a look. "Don't pretend you don't know
about my parents, Stark. You've lived here long enough, and
the gossip mill runs very smoothly in Harmony Falls."

"I'm sorry you lost your parents so young," he said.

She could hear genuine sympathy in his voice, and feeling a little off-kilter by it, she blurted out the truth. "I'm not."

He didn't reply, and she said, "I know that makes me sound like a monster, but my parents weren't good people." They were selfish and mean, and I know the disease they suffered from was partially to blame, but it wasn't totally to blame. Even when they were sober, they weren't good people."

"My childhood wasn't as difficult, but I understand selfish and mean parents," he said.

"Yours too, huh?" she said.

"My mother is incredible, and I have a good relationship with her," Stark said. "But my father…"

His face turned cold. "My father has high expectations that can never be met. It didn't stop me from trying, though. Once I graduated from high school, I got my MBA and started working at my father's company when I was twenty."

"Are your parents still together?"

"No, they divorced when I was seventeen," Stark said.

"What does your father do?" Rayna asked.

"He has a gaming company," Stark said.

"A gaming company like yours? He develops video games?"

"Yes," Stark said.

"Oh. But you left and started your own?"

"I did," Stark said. He stared out the windshield at the snow that had started to fall. "Working for my father was… impossible. I had ideas for new games, but he refused even to let me pitch them to him. He said I didn't have the experience or the knowledge."

He shoved his half-eaten sandwich into the bag. "It was a bullshit excuse. I knew as much, if not more, about gaming as he did. My ideas were solid, and he knew it, but he couldn't stand the idea that someone other than him might help the company make a profit. It took me two years to accept that he would never let me develop any of my games. But once I did, I left the company and started my own."

"Holy shit." She stared at him. "You started your own company when you were twenty-two?"

He nodded, and she studied him for a minute before saying, "And now you're a multimillionaire."

"And now I'm a multimillionaire," he echoed.

They sat in silence, the only sound the low hum of the heater and the muted laughter of a group of teens walking behind the SUV.

"How pissed was your dad when your company developed the most popular video game of all time?" Rayna asked.

"Do you game?" he asked in surprise.

"Not at all, but Emma is my best friend, and she's obsessed with your Shadow games and gaming in general. I know a weirdly large amount of information about your company because of Emma."

He grinned, and, holy fuck, there went her hoo-haw, soaking her panties and generally acting like she hadn't seen a dick in years. Why did he have to be so damn hot when he smiled?

She ignored her sudden urge to climb onto Stark's lap and grind her way into an orgasm, dragging her attention back to Stark's words instead of imagining how his lips might feel sucking on her clit. For the first time since she'd met him, there was no tension between them, and she didn't want to do anything to ruin the easy intimacy developing between them. Even if her brain knew it was a mistake to trust Stark.

"So, was he pissed?" she asked.

"He was annoyed," Stark said, that grin widening just a little. "Enough that he's basically ignored me for the last eight years."

"What a dick," she said.

He shrugged, drinking some of his soda before picking at the edge of the straw. "Honestly, I'm happier not having him in my life. Besides, he might not talk to me, but he has no problems sending Jasper to do his bidding whenever he wants or needs something from me."

"He's close with Jasper?" she asked.

"Jasper works at his company. He started working at the company the same year I did."

"Is your father nice to him?"

Stark shook his head. "My father isn't nice to anyone, Ms. Abrams. He uses people until they are no longer useful to them, and then he discards them. Jasper happens to have remained useful to him for longer than most."

"It's weird to picture Jasper working for your dad. He's so friendly and easygoing and funny. Those don't seem like qualities your father would appreciate."

"Jasper isn't who you think he is," Stark said. "You shouldn't have invited him to the fundraiser."

She frowned. "Inviting him to the fundraiser got the rescue three thousand dollars. I'm damn happy I invited him."

"You may think differently after your date on Friday," Stark said.

"Why?" she asked.

"You and Jasper are very different," Stark said.

"Right. Because he's a rich businessman, and I'm just a plumber," she said, trying and failing to hide her immediate annoyance. "This might come as a shock to you, Stark, but some guys don't need a rich lawyer girlfriend who looks like a model with perfect hair and makeup."

He frowned at her. "I didn't say any of that. Don't put words in my mouth, Ms. Abrams."

"You're thinking it," she said.

"I can assure you that I am not," he said icily.

The tension between them had returned, thick and unpleasant and making her stomach churn. Weirdly desperate to return to that easy intimacy, she gave him a teasing smile and said, "Do you know what I think? I think you're jealous of your cousin because he's going out with me on Friday night."

"Hardly," he snapped. "I have never been concerned with who my cousin dates. Besides, I have no interest in dating you, Ms. Abrams. You're not my type."

Christ, every time she was starting to think the guy might be a little bit human, he just had to prove her wrong. Hurt and a little embarrassed, she said, "Oh yeah? Because your dick certainly seemed interested the other night."

His cheeks reddened, and he gave her a look that made her feel about two feet tall. "I can assure you it had nothing to do with you and everything to do with not having sex in a while."

"That's not the flex you think it is," she said.

His nostrils flared, and that muscle in his jaw tick, tick, ticked.

Knowing she shouldn't, but Christ, it was humiliating to see how hard he was working to convince her that he found her repulsive, she said, "If you're not interested, why did you bid on me at the fundraiser?"

He gave her a cool look. "I did it for the rescue, Ms. Abrams. My cousin doesn't like to lose to me, and by bidding against him, I knew it would raise more money. You should be thanking me for that three grand, not my cousin."

She glared at him. "You know, for a millisecond tonight, I was starting to think there might be an actual human under all of that arrogant bullshit."

He pulled out his phone, his thumbs tapping angrily at the screen, and she frowned at him. "Who are you texting?"

"I'm getting an Uber," he said.

"Don't be ridiculous. I'll drive you to your car."

"No, thank you," he said with a smile so cold it made her wet panties freeze.

"Good night, Ms. Abrams." Without waiting for her reply, he opened the door and slid out of the vehicle.

CHAPTER 24

"Fuck me, that hurts!" Rayna grabbed the table's edge and blinked rapidly when her eyes watered.

"Almost done," Arianna said before applying more wax to Rayna's eyebrow and placing a fabric strip over it. She stretched Rayna's skin and gave her a grin. "Ready?"

"No," Rayna grumped, "but do it anyway."

She screeched out another expletive as Arianna ripped away the strip and then showed her the hair on it. "Ray-Ray, you really have to let me do this on a regular basis. You're, like, too young to have old man eyebrows."

Emma snorted laughter from her spot at the end of the table. "Oh God, if Rayna has old man eyebrows, I hate to hear what you think of mine."

"I told you before - you have beautiful brows," Arianna said. "And now Rayna does, too."

She handed Rayna a mirror, and Rayna squinted at her reflection before sighing. "I hate that they look a lot better waxed."

"There's nothing wrong with enhancing your natural

beauty with a bit of waxing and makeup," Arianna said. "Especially when you're going on a date with a hot guy. Are you sure you don't want me to give you a quick makeup lesson?"

"I appreciate the offer, but I have a full schedule tomorrow night with rescue stuff," Rayna said. "I'll do my makeup myself."

"Okay, but there's an art to makeup," Arianna said. "I could try to cancel my plans with Brittany on Friday night and do your makeup before your date."

Just because I don't wear makeup doesn't mean I don't know *how* to apply it, Arianna," Rayna said. "I've worn makeup before."

"I've never seen you in makeup." Arianna sank into a chair. "Okay, I've brought the larger strips like you asked so I can wax your muff, but do you want to wax it right here in front of Emma?"

"Wait, what? You're waxing your lady bits?" Emma said. "Why?"

"Because she's totally letting that tasty snack Jasper all up in her business," Arianna said.

"You're having sex with Jasper?" Emma said loudly and ignored Freddie when he hissed at her from his spot on the counter.

"Yes," Rayna said. "Maybe. Probably. Don't look at me like that, Emmy. I'm allowed to sleep with Jasper if I want to."

"You are," Emma said with a quick look at Arianna, "but is it Jasper you really want to sleep with?"

"Yes. He's hot and seems funny and smart," Rayna said. "I haven't had sex in months. I'm banging him, Emma. I deserve to have an orgasm that doesn't come from a damn toy, and Friday night, I'm getting that orgasm. Hell, I'm getting multiple orgasms."

"Yeah, you are, and you're gonna have a smooth muff when you do it." Arianna held out her fist, and Rayna bumped it. "Drop your pants and hop up on the table, Ray-Ray."

Rayna laughed. "I can wax my own muff, Arianna."

Arianna gave her a skeptical look. "Can you? It's not, like, as easy as it sounds."

"I think I can handle it, but thank you," Rayna said.

"Okay, but make sure you do it tonight or tomorrow night. You don't want to wax the same night as your date. Trust me on this," Arianna said.

Rayna nodded. "I've got it covered, and thank you for letting me use your waxing supplies."

"Of course," Arianna said. She stood and grabbed her jacket from the back of the chair. "If you don't need me to wax your muff, I'm gonna go. I told Oliver I'd stop by the Whiskey Grill for appies with him. Make sure you call me on Saturday and tell me how the sex was with Jasper."

"I most definitely will not," Rayna said.

Arianna pouted at her. "You're no fun, but I love you anyway, Ray-Ray."

"Love you too," Rayna said.

She waited until Arianna had left before saying, "Don't say it, Emma."

"I'm not saying anything," Emma said.

"No, but I know you're thinking it. You think I shouldn't sleep with Jasper because I'm attracted to Stark, but trust me when I say that after last night, I am no longer even remotely attracted to that jerk."

"I'll admit that he was a colossal dick last night, but it's why I'm concerned about your plan to sleep with Jasper," Emma said.

"What do you mean?"

"I'm just wondering if your sudden decision to sleep with Jasper is more of a retaliation against Stark rather than an actual desire to bang Jasper."

"Jasper is sexy and, unlike his cousin, has an actual personality," Rayna said. "I'm sleeping with him because I'm attracted to him."

"Okay, then I fully support your decision," Emma said.

"Good. Now, I need your help deciding what to wear on this date. It needs to be sexy but functional for ice skating," Rayna said.

"Lead me to your closet, girl," Emma said with a smile.

As they left the kitchen and headed upstairs, Rayna ignored the guilty churning of her stomach. She wasn't outright lying to Emma. She did find Jasper attractive, and sleeping with him had nothing to do with Stark.

Girl, please. Jasper might be good looking, but we both know you don't have a lick of attraction to him. Are you really going through with this just because you're pissed that Stark doesn't want to fuck you?

She ignored her inner voice. What did she know anyway?

"You look sad, Isaac."

"Just tired. It was a long week." Stark forced a smile at his mother, wishing he'd listened to his instincts and texted rather than video chatted.

"You can't lie to me, sweet boy."

He rubbed at the back of his neck. "I'm not sad, just... annoyed with myself. I've been a bastard all week because of it. Everyone is avoiding me at work, and I'm pretty sure Hollis is going to either quit or murder me."

His mother laughed. "My money is on murdering. Hollis is a lovely woman but not one to be trifled with."

"I can't blame her. I've been a total ass ever since…"

"Since what?"

"Ever since I was a dick to my neighbour. I fucked up with her a few days ago."

His mother gave him a sympathetic look. "Tell me what happened, sweetheart."

He hesitated, not wanting his mother to know what a dick he'd been, but ultimately who else did he have to talk to? He was thirty-two years old and had no one but his mother to confide in and share with because letting other people see the real him felt too vulnerable.

You shared with Rayna. Even told her about your terrible relationship with your father.

He had, and even though he didn't want to admit it, it felt good to talk to her. She'd listened without judgment, and her admiration over his accomplishments had sent a curious feeling of pride through him. He shouldn't care what she thought of him, but if that was true, why had he spent the last few days acting like an ass to everyone around him because he'd hurt her feelings. And why was he tormented by the knowledge that Rayna would be on a date with Jasper tonight?

"Isaac?"

He sighed and told his mother what had happened. She listened quietly, and when he was finished, she sat silently for another few minutes before saying, "So, was she right?"

"About what?" he asked.

"Are you jealous that she's going out with Jasper?"

"No, of course not," he said.

She sat serenely, waiting for him to crack under the pressure, and he folded less than thirty seconds later.

"Fine, I'm a little jealous, but only because Jasper has convinced her he's a good guy. He's not, Mom."

"Sadly, no, he isn't," his mother said. "But he wears a very convincing mask."

"I'm not a good guy either," he said.

She scowled at him. "One, you have never been the type to jump into a pity pool, and I don't expect you to start now. Two, you *are* a good guy. There is a difference between being horrible and being blunt."

"I went beyond blunt with her," he said, "and now I feel terrible about it, and I don't understand why I feel so goddamn terrible."

"You feel terrible, not because you were blunt, but because you lied to her," his mother said. "You're attracted to her, Isaac. That's plain to see."

"Fine, I'm attracted to her. But I want her property more, and unless I can convince her I'm not the asshole I so often am around her, I'll never get it. Pretending to be nice is a lot harder than it seems."

"Then stop pretending and just be nice," his mother said.

"I don't know how," he said.

Her scowl deepened. "Yes, you do, Isaac. At some point in the last decade, you've convinced yourself that you're an asshole, but, dearest, that simply isn't true. You've put up a shield, and you keep everyone around you at a distance, but it doesn't need to be that way. There are good people out there, people who would care for and love you just as I do if you would let them. I hate seeing you so lonely."

"I'm not lonely." His throat had tightened, and he could barely get the words out.

Her look was loving but firm. "Yes, my boy, you are."

They sat in silence for a few seconds before she said, "I want you to be happy, Isaac. And I think that if you let people in, give them a chance to see the real you, you'll be surprised at the happiness it brings you. We aren't meant to walk alone in life."

When he didn't reply, she said, "Will you try for me, Isaac?"

He cleared the rasp from his throat. "Yes."

"That's my boy." She beamed at him. "I think the first person you should try being yourself with, being the genuinely nice person I know you are under all that gruffness, is Ms. Abrams. Not just because it might help you convince her to sell her property, but because you like each other."

"Like each other? We're not in grade school, Mom," Stark said with a faint grin.

"Thank God," she said. "You were shockingly boring as a child. It wasn't until you became a teen that you got really interesting."

"Mom!"

She laughed. "You're not the only one who can be blunt in this family, sweetheart. Now, I have to run. I'm off to the Marigold for a poker tournament this weekend."

"Have fun. Don't lose all of your money."

She gave him an affronted look. "Need I remind you that I have won seven of the last ten tournaments I participated in?"

"No, you do not," he grinned.

"Good. I love you, my boy."

"I love you too."

He ended the call and smiled at Molly, who had wandered into the kitchen. She chirped at him, rubbing up against his leg, and he gave her a few pets before standing. "I just need to take out the garbage, and then I'll feed you. Go back to your babies, sweetie."

He gave her a gentle nudge in the direction of the bedroom, satisfied when she headed down the hallway toward his room. He grabbed the garbage bag and carried it outside to the bin. Snow was falling steadily, and he glanced at Rayna's house before tossing the bag in the bin.

He turned to go back into the house but froze when he heard the shriek from Rayna's house.

"What the hell?" He paused on the step, listening intently, and when, a few minutes later, he heard another scream, he jogged across his yard toward Rayna's place.

CHAPTER 25

"Oh, this is bad. This is really, really bad." Rayna stared at her pale face in the bathroom mirror.

Don't panic. This is not the time to panic.

"Are you kidding? This is the perfect time to panic!" she said to her reflection.

Cold air blew against her bare legs, but she didn't close the window behind her. She'd started off trying to wax in the upstairs bathroom, but it was too hot and steamy from her shower, and she didn't want to be a sweaty mess by the time she was finished. So, she grabbed the waxing supplies and went to the downstairs half bath, opening the window to keep herself cool. Of course, she was starting to think she should have waxed before she showered, but it was too late now.

She sucked in a deep breath and stared at the wax strip in the sink. Hair and a surprising amount of blood covered it.

"That's just way more blood than I'm comfortable with," she told her reflection.

She reached between her legs, skirting past the fabric strip to touch the bare spot she'd just waxed. The tips of her fingers came away dotted with blood, and her labia burned like fire.

"C'mon, you can do this," she said fiercely. "It's just one strip. You have to rip it off."

She gripped the strip of fabric. Gritting her teeth, she yanked at the strip and screamed again when fresh fire erupted against her labia.

Panting, her eyes watering and her labia begging for mercy, she let go of the strip. It was only halfway off, and she pressed her fist against her mouth to muffle her moans of pain.

Holy fuck. She'd expected it to hurt when she waxed her crotch, but she hadn't expected... this. It felt like she was ripping off a layer of skin.

"Fuck," she muttered before glancing at her phone. Why hadn't she listened to Arianna and not waited until an hour before her date to wax? At this rate, she'd be sitting at the restaurant with a fabric strip of wax clinging to her labia.

She touched the dangling strip of fabric, willing herself to rip off the rest. Her fingers shook, and she gripped the edge of the sink. "Shit. I can't. I can't do it."

"Can't do what?"

She shrieked and whipped toward the open window, grabbing the hairdryer from the counter and raising it over her head like a weapon.

Isaac Stark stared at her through the open window, snowflakes clinging to his dark hair and one thick eyebrow raised. "If you're going to bash my head in with the hairdryer, turn it the other way. It's much more effective."

"What the fuck?" she gasped, her heart knocking against her ribs. "Why are you spying on me?"

"I could hear your screams from my house," he said. "I came over to see if you were being murdered."

She glared at him. "You wish. You know, even if I am

murdered, my will has specific instructions not to sell my property to you."

"Shocking," he said dryly.

"Why the hell didn't you go to the front door like a normal person?" she asked.

"I did. I rang the doorbell three times. Maybe you couldn't hear it over your screaming."

"It's broken," she muttered.

"Is there anything in this house that isn't?" he asked.

"The plumbing works perfectly," she snapped.

What almost looked like a smile flashed across his face. "Why are you screaming?"

"None of your business, creeper," she said. "Go away."

He looked her up and down, and for the first time, she was exceedingly aware of just how naked she was under her very thin, very short, cotton nightgown.

She crossed her arms over her breasts. It was absolutely her imagination that Stark's gaze had lingered on them, but her nipples were stiff from the cold air coming in through the open window. The last thing she wanted was for Stark to think she was attracted to him.

I think he realized you wanted to fuck him when you licked his damn thumb.

"Are you wearing makeup?" Stark asked.

"Yes," she snapped. "Why?"

"I've never seen you wear makeup before. And your hair isn't…"

She touched it self-consciously. She had taken the time to blow dry her hair and use a straightener to smooth out the slight waviness, and she thought it looked good. "Isn't what?"

"In a ponytail," he said.

"I have a date tonight," she said.

"I remember." Stark studied the wax pot on the bathroom

counter and the fabric strips. "All of this screaming is because of a little waxing?"

"Shut up," she said.

"You come across as a lot tougher than that, Ms. Abrams."

"You can talk to me about tough when you've waxed your private parts, Stark," she barked at him.

"Is that blood?" He studied the strip in the sink.

"Can you please leave me to my misery?" she asked.

She went to close the window, and he said, "Did you know you have a fabric strip dangling from your crotch?"

"A gentleman wouldn't mention that." Now, her crotch *and* her face were on fire.

He leaned his arms against the windowsill, the cold and the snow not bothering him at all. "Based on the amount of hair on the strip in the sink, you probably should have trimmed before you waxed."

"Oh, thank you so much for the tip, Mr. Labia Waxing Expert," she snapped.

"I'm not an expert, but apparently, I've waxed more labia than you have. And I haven't had any complaints about the results," he said.

That made her pause. "You're lying."

"Why? Because you think only women are good at waxing? So, now you're a wimp and sexist?"

She glared at him. "I can't imagine a woman would let you near her vagina for waxing or sex, Stark. Not after talking with you for more than five minutes."

"Actually, I do rather well in that department," he said.

"I guess some women think arrogance is sexy," she said.

He just shrugged before glancing at her crotch again. "How long has that wax been there?"

"What does it matter?" she asked.

"Because it'll have hardened, which means you won't be

able to remove it. At least not without ripping off a layer of skin."

She stared at the bloody strip in the sink, her crotch already protesting at the thought of trying to remove the other one.

"You need oil to remove it," he said.

She cursed under her breath. "I don't have any baby oil."

"Olive oil will work," he said.

She glanced at her phone again. "Shit. I'm going to be late."

Without bothering to say thanks, she left the bathroom and hurried to the kitchen. Christ, her crotch hurt.

She hunted through the cupboards, screaming again when Stark said, "Make sure you use a lot of oil."

She whirled around with the olive oil bottle in her hand. "How the hell did you get in my house?"

"Climbed in through the bathroom window," he said like it was perfectly normal for him to climb into her bathroom.

"Why?" she said, her exasperation clear.

"Thought you might need help." He shrugged. "I'm being a good neighbour."

"I do not need help," she said as she poured some olive oil on a paper towel.

"We'll see." He crossed his arms and watched as she stuck her hand under her too-short nightgown and dabbed at the strip stuck to her crotch.

She set the paper towel on the counter and gripped the strip with shaking fingers, giving it a light, experimental tug.

"Fuck!" She blew out a breath, her legs joining in on the shaking. "It still hurts."

"Did you use enough oil?" Stark asked.

She glared at him. "I have no fucking idea. Get that look off your face."

"What look is that?"

209

"The look that says you're enjoying the show."

He grinned, and her burning crotch immediately tingled in response. Christ, now was not the fucking time for her inappropriate lust for her enemy to kick in.

"You need to leave," she said as she glanced at her phone. "Shit, look what time it is. You and your stupid oil idea! I could have maybe, *maybe,* gone on my date with a wax strip stuck to my cooch, but now it's covered in oil and blood and wax and…."

She grabbed the strip and gave it a fierce yank, screaming when fresh, hot pain ripped across her labia, and the strip didn't move an inch.

Her scream didn't wake poor deaf Bea, who was snoring away on her bed in the kitchen, but Stark winced before striding toward her and picking up the oil-laden paper towel. "You definitely didn't use enough oil."

"What are you doing?" She batted his hand away when he reached between her legs.

"I'll remove the strip for you," he said.

"Like hell you will!" she said.

"You have two choices," he said. "Cancel your date with my cousin, who bid a lot of money at the auction to go on this date with you, or let me help you."

"I can reschedule," she said. "He'll understand."

"I'm afraid you don't know my cousin very well," he said. "You reschedule this date, and he'll ask for his 'donation' to be returned."

"He wouldn't," she said.

"He would," Stark said flatly. "You don't know my cousin, Rayna."

It was the first time he'd ever said her first name and her imagination went into overdrive. Would her name sound as good coming out of his mouth when she was on her knees before him and sucking on his cock? It was a question she desperately wanted answered.

Stop it! He's an arrogant asshole doing everything he can to drive you off your land. Remember?

"Make your choice, Ms. Abrams." Stark's voice was indifferent, but that muscle ticked in his jaw, and his eyes had turned the colour of the ocean after a storm.

She swallowed hard. "Fine. You can help me."

OKAY, SO MAYBE STARK WAS TAKING THIS 'BE GENUINELY NICE' idea a little too far, but the look of panic on Rayna's face was very real. Leaving her alone to deal with a stuck piece of wax seemed... rude. Helping her was the gentlemanly thing to do.

Right, it has nothing to do with you taking any excuse to touch her pussy.

It wasn't about that at all. He might be attracted to Rayna, but this was hardly the time to think about how she might look or sound coming all over his fingers.

Oh yeah? Tell your dick that.

He grimaced inwardly, thankful he was wearing jeans that at least somewhat hid his semi. Okay, so getting excited about touching Rayna when it was clear she was only letting him touch her because she was desperate didn't exactly scream good guy, but he would plaster on a poker face and keep his thoughts to himself.

"Stark, are you helping or not?" Rayna gave him an impatient look before staring at the clock again. "It's fine if you've changed your mind, but I -"

"I haven't," he said. "Spread your legs."

Her face bright red, she shifted her feet apart enough for him to slip his hand between her legs. She looked away, staring resolutely at the cabinets. Stark gently swiped the paper towel over the strip and ignored his urge to bury his face in her shiny hair.

She smelled delicious, a combination of vanilla and something flowery, and he studied the curve of her throat and the strands of hair that brushed against her shoulders. They looked silky soft, and he clenched his other hand into a fist to stop from running his fingers over her hair.

"Stark." Rayna's voice was shaky, and he realized he had stopped swiping the paper towel and was holding it against the fabric strip.

"Sorry," he said and set the paper towel on the counter. "Ready?"

"Give me a second." She turned her body to face the counter, gripping the edge of the sink and taking a few deep breaths. "Okay, do it."

"I have to use both hands," he said. "One to pull the strip away, the other to hold the skin taut. Are you good with that?"

"Yes," she said with a touch of impatience. "Just do it, for God's sake."

He stood behind her and slid his arms around her before grasping one of Rayna's firm thighs. Fuck, her skin was so soft. He tugged on her leg, and when she didn't move it, he said, "Open for me, Rayna."

His voice came out too low and too intimate for the situation, but Rayna's body shuddered, and she immediately spread her legs wide.

"Good girl," he said, ignoring the faint moan that escaped her lips.

This does not turn her on, he reminded himself grimly as he slipped both hands between her legs.

He gripped the oily fabric strip with his right hand and pressed his left hand against her labia. Her skin was slick with oil, and his fingers immediately slid across her skin to slip between her lips and press against her clit.

She gasped, her hips bucked against him, and he went from a semi to rock hard in an instant. He gritted his teeth, moving his fingers away from her clit.

"Sorry."

"Th-that's okay." Her voice was breathy and thin.

He tried again, this time managing to pull her skin taut. "On three, all right?"

She nodded, her hands squeezing tight against the sink as he counted down. He pulled the strip off with brisk efficiency. Rayna made a strangled yelp, and her body jerked wildly, her thighs clamping around his hand. He pressed his left hand firmly against her labia to help with the sting as he dropped the strip into the sink with his right.

She sucked in a deep breath, and still keeping one hand against her, he grabbed another piece of paper towel from the roll.

"Turn on the tap," he said.

She turned it on, and he wet the paper towel with warm water. Her thighs were still clamped around his hand, and he said, "Open, Rayna."

She spread her legs, and he used the damp paper towel to wipe away the oil. He pulled it out from under her nightgown, and she studied the dots of blood on it as he tossed it into the sink. "There's not as much blood as I thought there would be."

"The oil helped to stop the skin from tearing," he said.

"Thank you," she said. "I appreciate -"

She gasped, her hips arching again when he slipped his right hand between her legs and ran his fingertips over her pussy.

"Wh-what are you doing?"

"Just checking for any bits of fabric," he said.

"Oh, right, yeah, that's a good… oh, God… idea," she said.

He brushed away the tiny bits of fabric he could feel clinging to her skin and told himself it was an accident when his finger slipped between her pussy lips again to rub against her clit.

Rayna cried out, her hand clamping around his wrist.

Cursing himself for being a pervert, he tried to pull his hand away, but giving him a hot look of need, Rayna pressed his hand against her pussy.

CHAPTER 26

Okay, so Rayna had gone her entire adult life without even a hint of awareness that she was secretly a BDSM enthusiast.

I mean, she had to be. Right? It was the only explanation for why Stark ripping off a stuck piece of wax on her pussy had turned her on.

Open for me, Rayna.

Stark's earlier words echoed in her head and sent a flood of wetness to her pussy. Fuck, if she didn't let go of his hand, he was about to find out just how perverted she was. Instead of releasing him, she held his wrist even tighter, refusing to let go.

He pressed up against her back, and, oh sweet lord, that was his erection against her ass, and she didn't have a hope in hell of stopping herself from grinding against it.

Stark's breath caught in her ear, and she didn't even care that she could hear the amusement in his voice when he said, "You have to let go of my hand if you want me to move it, Ms. Abrams."

"I think there might still be some bits of, um, fabric." Her voice sounded embarrassingly needy.

"Is that right? Would you like me to check again?"

"Yes, please," she said.

His left hand smoothed a path down the outside of her thigh. "You know what I need you to do."

"Open for you," she whispered and shamelessly spread her legs wide.

"That's my good girl," he said.

She moaned when his fingers brushed against her throbbing skin. He explored her pussy with light, gentle sweeps of his fingertips. She squirmed and rubbed against his erection before tugging on his wrist in an attempt to guide his fingers to her aching clit.

His laugh was low and intimate in her ear. "No fabric left."

He brushed against the first spot she'd waxed, and she hissed out a breath at the brief flare of pain.

He kissed her throat. "Sorry, baby. I know it's tender."

"Please," she said.

He stroked her clit. "Is this what you want?"

"Yes," she whispered.

He didn't make her beg. His fingers pressed against her swollen, aching clit and rubbed in firm circles. She cried out, her hips rocking against his hand as pleasure and a deep ache coiled in her belly.

Stark's left arm slid around her waist, and he pressed her back against him, rubbing his dick against her ass as he teased her clit. She let her head fall back against his shoulder, staring blindly at the ceiling while her hips worked hard against his hand.

"No!" she cried out when he moved his fingers away from her clit.

"Shh," he crooned. "I want to know how tight you are."

He pressed against her opening, and she cried out again when he slid his thick finger into her. He added a second one, and she squirmed against him. He kissed her throat again, pumping his fingers lightly back and forth until she moaned and dug her nails into his wrist. "Please!"

Pressing her against his erection, he returned to her clit, rubbing it hard. Hot pleasure blasted through her body, and she bit back her scream as her orgasm burst inside of her in a torrent of heat and light and bliss.

She sagged against Stark, and he held her weight easily, his fingers slowing against her clit before he slid his hand out from under her nightgown.

He kissed her throat again. "Good, baby?"

She nodded, her heart beating wildly in her chest and her lungs battling for air. Stark pressed his cock against her ass, and she rubbed against him, smiling at his low groan.

She turned to face him, both of them jumping when her phone alarm went off with a shrill cry. She snatched it from the counter, shutting it off and staring in horror at the time.

"Oh shit. I have to leave now, or I'll be late for…"

She stared wide-eyed at Stark as the warmth in his gaze disappeared, and he stepped away from her. "Your date with my cousin."

"Stark, I -"

He shook his head and turned away, walking toward the doorway. "Enjoy your date, Ms. Abrams."

"For a restaurant in a dinky little town, the food wasn't half-bad." Jasper smiled at her before sipping his wine.

Irritation threaded through Rayna at Jasper's dismissive

tone. She tried to ignore it, but the entire dinner had been like this - him making passive aggressive jabs at the town she loved.

Despite the fast and efficient service of the Bronze Blossom, the dinner had dragged on, and they still had the damn ice skating to do. She just wanted to go home so she could…

Knock on Stark's door and ask him if he wants to finish what they'd started?

No, of course not. What happened between them was a mistake. A giant glaring one that took every inch of her willpower not to continually analyze, think about, and obsess over during her dinner with Jasper.

Why did you let Stark do that? Hell, you begged him to do it. He's trying to drive you off your property, and you're more than happy to let him stick his fingers up your hooch just because you're a little goddamn horny?

She'd been more than a little horny, and despite how much she hated Stark, she had to admit the guy knew what he was doing when it came to sex. She had never come that quickly with a man before. Especially if it was the first time he'd touched her. But Stark's touch, his voice in her ear, how he took control and -

Rayna, stop it!

She gave herself a mental shake. Now was not the time to rehash her orgasm at the hands of her arch nemesis. She had come so quickly despite the circumstances and the pain of the waxing because it'd been a long time since she'd gotten laid, and Stark was good with his hands. It was a one-time dip into insanity, and she would never allow it to happen again.

"Rayna?"

"I'm sorry." She smiled at Jasper. "What were you saying?"

He eyed her over his wine glass. "I'm really enjoying our date."

"I am too," she lied brightly before finishing off her wine as the server discreetly placed the bill on the table.

Jasper drank the last of his wine as Rayna paid the bill before smiling at him. "Ready to go?"

"Yes," he said.

He helped her into her jacket, and they left the restaurant. Rayna shivered in the cold air, glancing at Jasper's expensive but thin winter coat. He was going to freeze at the ice rink.

She stopped at her battered SUV. Hoping he couldn't hear the lack of interest in her voice, she said, "So, I can give you the address of the Sports Complex, or you can ride with me to the ice rink, and I'll bring you back here to grab your car when we're finished. What would you prefer?"

He smiled at her, and she couldn't deny that he was a handsome man. His dark brown eyes were warm and inviting and didn't radiate one bit of coldness like a certain blue-eyed cousin of his. Unlike his cousin, he was clean shaven, and she studied his mouth, willing herself to be even mildly into the idea of being in his bed. She'd had every intention of having sex with Jasper tonight if he was interested, and her utter lack of attraction to him was baffling. She *should* be into him, so why the hell wasn't she?

Maybe because it's Stark's face you want buried between your thighs?

If her inner voice didn't shut up, Rayna would strangle it.

Jasper took her hand, rubbing his thumb lightly across her knuckles. "To be honest, I'm not really into ice skating."

Relief washed over her. She'd offer to take him for coffee and dessert at Grind My Beans instead. She could fake interest for another hour or so, and then she could go home, have a hot bath, and not think at all about Stark and his surprising ability to make her come.

"That's fine," she said. "How about coffee and dessert?

Grind My Beans downtown has amazing coffee, and they make a delicious coffee cake that's to die for."

Jasper stepped closer and slid one muscular arm around her waist, tugging her up against him. "We could go for coffee, or we could just skip to what we both really want… you in my bed."

He pressed his mouth against hers, his lips gentle and coaxing as he slid his hand into her hair. She returned his kiss, trying but failing to feel anything beyond a weary sort of annoyance.

She pulled back, and Jasper smiled at her before lightly tugging on a tendril of her hair. "What do you say we go back to my hotel? The room is hideous, and the walls are thin, but the bed is comfortable enough."

He leaned in to kiss her again, and she dodged his kiss, untangling herself from his grip. "I think we should have coffee and dessert."

Annoyance flickered across his face before he smoothed it away. "Sure. But can we take my car? Your car looks dirty, and I'm assuming it's covered in animal hair."

"I prefer to take mine," she said, "but Grind My Beans is right on Main Street, so it's easy to find. You can follow me, or I can give you directions."

"Sure," he said before giving her a flirtatious grin. "I doubt anyone in this one-horse town will be surprised to see your car at the hotel later tonight."

"What's that supposed to mean?" she asked as alarm bells clanged in her head.

He shrugged, pulling out a pair of expensive leather gloves and sliding them onto his hands. "They all know how much I paid for you."

"Excuse me?" she said. "Paid for me?"

He waved it off. "Donated to the rescue, same thing."

"No, it is fucking not," she said.

He scowled. "No need to be crude. I hate it when women curse."

"Well, that's too fucking bad," she said. "Because I'm using bad language when someone insinuates that I'm a sex worker."

"Calm down. That isn't what I meant."

"Calm down?" She didn't think it was possible to be angrier, but here they were. "You did not just tell me to calm down."

He took a step back, holding up his hands in a placating manner while giving her a 'what the fuck' look that only enraged her further. "Rayna, come on. What is your problem?"

"My problem is that you're assuming I'll fuck you tonight."

"Of course I am," he said, giving her a bewildered look. "I paid three grand for our date tonight, Rayna."

"No, you *donated* three grand to a fundraiser," she snapped.

"Tomato, tomahto," he said dismissively. "Look, why are we fighting? You're attracted to me, and I paid three thousand dollars to your little rescue. You owe me, Rayna."

"Do you even hear the shit coming out of your mouth?" she asked.

He sighed in exasperation. "You can't honestly believe that I would pay three grand just for dinner and ice skating with you."

"I did because I'm not an asshole."

His lips thinned. "I should have known better than to expect you to be a lady when you plunge toilets for a goddamn living."

"Go fuck yourself," she said before opening her car door and sliding inside.

"Are you kidding me right now?" he said. "You *owe* me, Rayna."

"I don't owe you shit, asshole." She slammed her door, started the car, and flipped Jasper the bird before driving away.

CHAPTER 27

S tark sat back in his office chair and glanced at his office doorway before reaching for his cell phone. He opened the pet camera app and scanned the screen. He'd installed a pet camera in his bedroom last week, and he smiled when he saw Molly nursing her kittens on the bed.

"That's a good girl, sweetie," he murmured and watched for a few more minutes before closing the app.

He glanced at the time. It was a few minutes after noon, and he debated whether to try to work or grab a bite at Nan's Diner. His growling stomach and inability to concentrate all morning decided for him.

He wanted to blame his hunger on his focus issues, but he knew damn well that wasn't the problem. He'd spent all weekend vacillating between lusting after Rayna and jealousy that she'd gone on her date with his cousin instead of staying with him.

He'd paced his house like a lovesick teenager all of Friday night, looking out the den window every hour to see if Rayna had returned home. By eleven, he'd finally admitted to himself that Rayna wasn't ending her date early to come home to him. He'd gone to bed, lying sleepless in the dark with Molly and her kittens and pretending he wasn't waiting to hear the sound of Rayna's car.

He'd fallen asleep still waiting.

He'd hoped that work today would help him forget just how fucking amazing it was to have Rayna come all over his fingers, but no such luck. He didn't know how it was possible, but his lust for her was even more intense despite how many times he'd masturbated this weekend. He couldn't remember the last time he'd been this obsessed with a woman.

You've never been this obsessed over a woman. You need to let it go. It was a one-time thing, and besides, you know as well as I do that Jasper would have gotten her into his bed Friday night. He might be as big of an asshole as you are, but he hides it a fuck of a lot better than you do.

Irritation overtook the lust, and he abruptly stood, yanking on his jacket and heading out of his office. Stark slowed as he approached Lucas's office, debating whether or not to ask him to have lunch with him. For a change, he didn't want to eat lunch alone. Maybe his mother was right. Maybe he needed to start showing people the real Isaac Stark.

He stopped just before Lucas's open door as Lucas's voice drifted into the hallway. "What do you mean he asked for the donation back?"

"He emailed the rescue this morning and demanded his money back." Emma's voice was quiet, and Stark moved closer to the door, straining to hear.

"All three thousand?" Lucas asked.

"Yes."

"But why?"

Emma sighed. "Friday night, when you came to my house after your night out with Connor and Nix, and Rayna was there? That was the night of her date with Jasper. They went for dinner, and after dinner, he didn't want to go ice skating, so she suggested coffee at Grind My Beans. He suggested she go to his hotel room with him instead."

"Bold move," Lucas said.

"Rayna declined, and he got pissed. He said he paid three grand for her, and she owed him sex."

"Motherfucker," Lucas spat, the disgust evident in his voice. "I hope she punched him in the dick."

"She told him to go fuck himself and left. She drove straight to my place, and I've never seen her so upset, Lucas. She was shaking, and she was angry, but it was obvious that what he'd said really upset her, too. It was awful."

Stark stared at his hands. They were balled into tight fists, and he made himself relax, staring at the indents from his nails in his palms. Fucking Jasper. He would kick his cousin's ass for what he'd said and done to Rayna.

"C'mere, baby."

He could hear the squeak of Lucas's office chair as he rolled it back, and Stark took a quick peek into the office. Emma was sitting on Lucas's lap, and he pressed a kiss against her mouth. "I'm sorry Jasper was such a dickhead to Rayna."

"Me too," Emma said. "She stopped at the store this morning in between work calls to tell me about Jasper demanding his donation back, and she…"

"She what?"

"She started crying right there at the store." Emma sounded close to tears herself. "Rayna hardly ever cries, Lucas. But losing that money was a real blow. The rescue owes five grand to Harmony Falls Vet Clinic, and she was planning to use the three thousand toward that. The clinic won't see any of the rescue's animals until the bill is paid off, which leaves her with only two clinics to work with."

"Wait, she returned the money?" Lucas asked.

"She had to," Emma said.

"No, she didn't. He donated it and -"

"Jasper threatened to sue the rescue if she didn't return it," Emma said. "She had Mack e-transfer the money back to him this morning."

"Fuck, that guy is a real piece of work," Lucas said. "I can't believe he's Stark's cousin. Stark can come across as cold, but he's a good guy who would never fuck someone over like that."

"You can't choose your family," Emma said.

"Can Rayna use the money from the other donations to pay the clinic?" Lucas asked.

"She's using the other donations to pay the PawsPrint Vet Clinic bill, part of the Brandt clinic bill, and adding to the Helping Hands program," Emma said.

"Shit," Lucas said.

"She's already talking about doing another fundraiser, but she just looked so… tired and defeated, Lucas. I've never seen her like this before. She's burning the candle at both ends to keep the rescue going, but I don't know how much longer she can keep going."

Stark backed away from Lucas's office, returning to his office and sitting at his desk. He stared at his laptop screen before stabbing a button on his desk phone.

"Yes, Mr. Stark?" Hollis answered on the first ring.

"I know it's your lunch hour, but do you have five minutes?" he asked.

"Of course. I'll be right there." She ended the call and was sitting in his office less than a minute later with a tablet in her hand.

"I want to make a donation to Little Whiskers Rescue," he said.

"Of course. How much?" Hollis swiped a finger across her tablet screen.

"Five thousand," he said, "and I need it to be anonymous. I don't want Ms. Abrams to know I donated."

If Hollis was curious about the secrecy, it didn't show on her face. "That might be difficult. Even if I can contact someone else in the rescue to handle the donation, I doubt that the information wouldn't get back to Rayna."

"I know." He drummed his fingers against his desk, trying to think of how to make it work. "I want the donation to pay the amount the rescue owes to Harmony Falls Vet Clinic."

"You could donate directly to the clinic," Hollis said. "I'll speak with the vet clinic, and we can etransfer the amount owed directly to them. The clinic can let Rayna know it was an anonymous donation. But you know that the rescue isn't yet a registered charity, right? You won't get a receipt for the donation."

"I don't care about that. Do you have time to speak with the vet clinic and make the donation this afternoon?" he asked.

Hollis nodded. "Sure."

"Thank you, Hollis."

"Paid off? The entire bill was paid?" Shock made her knees wobbly, and Rayna sank onto her worn couch beside Bea, absently scratching Bea's stomach when the beagle immediately rolled onto her back.

"That's right. They donated the full amount." The receptionist at Harmony Falls Vet Clinic sounded a little dazed herself.

"Who donated it?" Rayna asked.

"I can't tell you. They were very clear about it being anonymous," the receptionist said.

"Are you serious?"

"I am," she said. "Anyway, Dr. Felton asked me to call and let you know the account has been cleared, and you can book appointments again."

"Okay, well, that's amazing. Thank you."

"You're welcome. Bye, Rayna!"

Rayna set her phone on the couch before staring at Bea. "Bea, it's a frickin' miracle."

The beagle snored loudly, and Rayna laughed before leaning over and kissing the old dog's forehead. "I don't know who paid that bill, but if I did, I'd kiss them, too."

Bea opened one eye, her tail thumping happily against the couch before she farted.

"Oh God," Rayna said, jumping off the couch. "Way to ruin a moment, Bea."

Waving her hand in front of her face, she left the living room and headed down the hallway. Freddie was sitting in the laundry room doorway, and he meowed disapprovingly at her. She nudged his stocky body with her foot. "I know you're pissed because your kittens got adopted, but don't worry, there will be more. Hell, you're lucky Krysta could take Louis Hapson's bloodhound, or you'd be sharing your space with him right now."

Speaking of which, she texted a quick message to Krysta and then folded the laundry she'd left in the dryer while she waited for Krysta's reply. Her phone dinged out a reply, and she scanned the message, grinning at Freddie, who had leaped onto his usual spot on the laundry supplies shelf. "Krysta says Red is doing really well. Eating and resting comfortably."

She reached up to pet Freddie, who growled and gave her a swat. "All right, Mr. Crabby Pants, I'll leave you alone."

She walked upstairs and started the shower. She stripped off her clothes and stepped under the hot water spray, letting the water beat down on her shoulders and back. The heavy weight she'd been carrying since this morning when she'd returned Jasper's donation had disappeared, so why did she still feel so damn tired?

Oh, I don't know. Maybe because you spent your entire weekend barely sleeping and your brain either rehashing the disaster that was your date with Jasper or asking you to knock on Stark's door and beg him to fuck you.

She sighed and washed her hair, trying to keep the thoughts at bay, but they wouldn't be denied. She'd been upset by her disastrous date with Jasper, but by late Saturday morning, she'd been back to obsessing over what had happened with Stark. She'd spent the entire weekend fighting her urge to text him. Hell, to just show up on his doorstep. How pathetic did it make her to be so desperate for sex that she would happily fuck the guy trying to take her house from her?

You could have had sex Friday night with Jasper, and you didn't. So, are you sure you're desperate for sex, or are you desperate for sex with Stark?

She wouldn't think about that. What she would think about is the enormous bullet she dodged by discovering Jasper's true nature before she slept with him. Even thinking about how she'd found him charming and funny made her furious with herself. She was usually a much better judge of character.

Stark might be an asshole, but at least he's upfront about it. Hey... quick thought... you should text him for a booty call.

She muttered a curse and quickly finished her shower, toweling dry and slipping into a cotton nightgown before putting her wet hair in a messy bun on top of her head. She lifted the nightgown and studied her crotch in the full-length mirror before turning to Bea, who had wandered into her bedroom and was stretched out on the floor. "You're too blind to see it, but my cooch looks ridiculous, Bea. She looks like my grandma in a bathing cap."

Bea thumped her tail against the floor in reply. Rayna reached between her legs and touched the two waxed areas. Even just the thought of finishing the wax job made her shudder, and she stared at Bea again. "Nope, not doing it. It'll just have to look weird until the hair grows back. It's not like anyone will be seeing it, so who cares what it looks like, right?

You could ask Stark to wax it. He's done it before, remember?

"Gah!" She stomped to her closet and yanked on her robe, tying it off at the waist before turning to Bea. "C'mon, Bea-Bea. It's time for dinner."

At the word dinner, Bea popped up like a jack-in-the-box, grinning happily and her tail wagging furiously. She followed Rayna down the stairs, her tail whacking against Rayna's leg when she pushed past her.

"You know, sometimes I think you have selective hearing rather than being deaf," she told the dog as she gave her some dry food with a heaping spoonful of wet mixed in. "You never have any trouble hearing when it's time for dinner."

Her tail still wagging wildly, Bea dug into her dinner with relish, crunching the food loudly as Rayna added some canned cat food to Freddie's dish in the laundry room. He sauntered over to the dish, even letting her give him a quick pat as he settled in to eat.

She returned to the kitchen and opened the fridge, studying the contents as she tried to decide what to cook. Her work day hadn't been that busy or challenging, but the lack of sleep over the weekend and the stress of losing the three grand this morning left her feeling exhausted and unmotivated to cook.

She stretched lightly, glancing at her phone on the counter. She really should check her messages and respond to some emails for the rescue.

Eat first, and then you can do some more work.

Good plan. She reached for the bag of salad, pausing when there was a loud knock on the door. Her heart went into overdrive immediately. Maybe it was Stark. Maybe he was here because he couldn't stop thinking about Friday night, either.

She started eagerly toward the door, her footsteps slowing as her common sense kicked in. It wouldn't be Stark. It was always the same when she got a knock on her door. Some random stranger with an animal they no longer wanted and the belief that she had to take it.

Ignoring her disappointment, she opened the front door. There was no one standing on her porch, but a large cardboard box sat on the snowy ground a few feet away from her porch steps.

"Are you kidding me? You couldn't even leave the poor thing on my porch?" She shoved her feet into boots and stepped outside. The cold air immediately brought goosebumps to her skin, and she considered grabbing her jacket to throw over her robe before hurrying down the steps instead. Who knew what was in the box and how injured it might be. The sooner she looked, the better.

She crouched next to the box and peeled back the tape that held it shut. She moved back a little and stretched to open the top flaps, keeping one hand raised in front of her face. She had a feral cat come flying out of a box and attach itself to her face once, and she wasn't going through that again.

No angry, hissing cat came flying out, and she lowered her hand, peering cautiously into the box. "What the hell?"

The box was empty, and she stared in confusion at it

before straightening and studying the darkness. Her skin prickled, and she couldn't shake the feeling of being watched. "Hello? Is there someone there?"

The wind was her only reply, and seriously creeped out, Rayna turned to walk back to the house. She jumped about a foot and nearly fell on her ass when she saw the man standing in front of her porch steps.

"What the fuck, Louis! You scared the shit out of me."

Louis stared at her, his big body weaving slightly and his nostrils flaring like an angry bull's. "I want my dog back, bitch."

CHAPTER 28

Rayna stiffened, her body sending out little alarm bells that made adrenaline spike in her veins. Keeping her voice calm, she said, "You're drunk, Louis. Did you drive here?"

He barked harsh laughter. "Did you hear me? I want Red back. Go get him."

"I don't have him," she said. "He's not with me."

"Bullshit, he ain't," Louis snarled. He produced a flask from his pocket and took a big swallow before shoving it back into his coat. "Give me my dog."

"I'm telling the truth," Rayna said. "Besides, you surrendered him, remember? You signed the paperwork. He isn't your dog anymore, Louis."

"He's my dog!" Louis shouted. "You stole him, and I want him back."

She backed up a few steps when Louis stumbled toward her. "Stop. You're drunk, and you shouldn't be driving. Give me your keys, and I'll call you an Uber. Go home and sleep this off."

"You think you're all fucking that, dontcha, bitch?" Louis

slurred. "Stealing the dogs of hard working, God-fearing people in this town. Well, I ain't gonna stand for it no more. Give me my dog before I have to do something you ain't gonna like."

Cold fear settled in Rayna's stomach. "Don't you fucking threaten me, Louis Hapson."

"It ain't a threat. It's a promise," he growled.

"Get off my property," she said. "I won't ask again."

"Not without my fucking dog," he screamed, his voice echoing in the cold air.

Fuck! She stared at the house, wishing like hell she'd brought her phone out with her instead of leaving it on the counter.

With a heavy grunt, he pushed away from the porch and walked toward her. His body swayed and wobbled, but he still looked dangerous and mean. He was blocking her path to the house, but she was fast on her feet. All she had to do was get past him, and she'd beat him into the house. She'd lock the door and call 911.

More adrenaline surged through her, and she ignored Louis's shout of surprise when she ran toward him. She zigged to the left, triumph rocketing through her when she easily dodged Louis's flailing hand and ran past him.

Fuck you, she thought hysterically as she ran toward the steps. Fucking asshole thought he could -

She screeched out a cry when her feet slipped on some ice, and she went down like a graceless deer. Her left elbow slammed into the hard ground, and she shouted a curse as pain shot up her arm. She rolled to her back, but before she could scramble to her feet, Louis dropped on her like a fucking bowling bowl, straddling her and grinning down at her.

She grunted and shoved at his chest, ignoring the pain in her elbow and arm. "Get the fuck off me, Louis."

"All you had to do was give me my dog, but you just had to be a bitch about it, didn't ya, Rayna?" Louis sneered.

"I said get the fuck off me!" she shouted before punching him in the gut.

His breath hissed out in a startled oof, and she heaved her body upward. Louis shouted in surprise, his body nearly tipping off of hers before he caught his balance and shoved her flat to the ground again. He snarled out a curse and slapped her hard across the face.

"I'm going to kill you, motherfucker!" Rayna screamed, hot anger flashing through her body.

"You stole my fucking dog!" Louis raised his hand again, this time balling it into a fist. Rayna cringed, but the blow never came. A thick arm wrapped around Louis's throat, and he was dragged off her, kicking and sputtering.

She sat up, staring wide-eyed at Stark as he tightened his arm around Louis's neck. His eyes blazing with anger and his face a hard mask, he squeezed tighter. Louis clawed at his arm, his body twisting and his face turning a dark red.

Rayna scrambled to her feet. "Stark, stop!"

He ignored her, squeezing even harder as drool slipped from Louis's mouth, and his hands weakened around Stark's arm.

Rayna yanked on Stark's arm, but it was like trying to bend steel. "Stark, let him go. You'll kill him!"

It was like he didn't hear her, and his arm didn't loosen one bit. Panic rushed through her, and she cupped Stark's face, forcing his gaze to hers. "Isaac, please stop."

He stared at her before his face twisted, and relief washed over her when he released Louis. Leaving Louis gasping and coughing in the snow at his feet, Stark pulled Rayna against him. He wore just a t-shirt and sweatpants, but the cold didn't seem to affect him. He studied her cheek before rubbing his thumb over it. "Are you okay?"

"Yes," she said.

Keeping one arm wrapped around her, he pulled his phone from his pocket and called 911.

Stark leaned against the counter in Rayna's kitchen. He studied Rayna, who sat at the table with a bag of frozen peas pressed against her elbow. Thick silence filled the room, broken only by the sound of Bea's snoring from her bed in the corner.

Rayna glanced at him, her gaze immediately skittering away to land on the table. He didn't blame her. Despite how hard he tried to contain it, the rage inside him was a living, pulsing thing, and he was confident his expression didn't hide how angry he was.

He'd listened silently as Rayna told Sheriff Walker what happened with Louis Hapson, and that terrible rage had only intensified. He welcomed the anger. It was an easier emotion to deal with than the terror that had washed over him when he'd seen Louis on top of Rayna on the ground.

He took a deep breath, his hands clenching into fists. What would have happened to her if he hadn't heard the screaming?

Sheriff Walker returned to the kitchen. He sat in the chair next to Rayna and gave her a reassuring smile. "How are you feeling?"

"Fine," she said. "What did Louis say?"

The sheriff glanced at Stark. "He's pretty drunk, but he wants to press charges against Mr. Stark."

"Are you fucking kidding me?" Rayna said.

"Unfortunately, no," Gideon said. "I'll toss him in a cell for tonight, let him sober up, but you know what Louis is like. I doubt being sober will change his mind."

"He trespassed on my property and attacked me," Rayna said. "Stark was saving my damn life."

"I know," Gideon said. "If you press charges, I can keep him in jail until -"

"When Louis sobers up tomorrow, tell that asshole I won't press charges if he doesn't press charges against Stark," Rayna said.

"What? No," Stark said. "Absolutely not."

She glared at him before turning back to the sheriff. "Tell Louis if he presses charges against Stark, I'll not only press charges for assault, but I'll sue the fucking pants off of him. Tell him I won't stop until I own everything he has, including his goddamn farm."

A slight grin crossed Gideon's face. "I'll pass on the message once he's sober."

"What a fucking shitshow," Rayna muttered before rubbing at her cheek.

Gideon examined her closely. "You sure you don't want to go to the hospital, Rayna?"

"I'm sure," she said. "It's just a bruised elbow."

"And cheek," Gideon said. He sat back in the chair. "I think you should press charges, Rayna. If Mr. Stark hadn't been here, Louis would have really hurt you."

"He's right," Stark said. "You need to press charges."

"No, what I need to do is get that piece of shit off my property," Rayna said wearily. "I appreciate what you're saying, Sheriff, but we both know Louis is a coward. Once he's sober and realizes that I can and will press charges against him, he'll leave Stark alone and slink away like the slime he is."

"I don't care what he says or does to me," Stark said heatedly. "Rayna, the issue is your safety."

"He won't do this again," she said.

"You can't possibly know that," he snapped.

She gave him a look before glancing at the sheriff. "Can we talk about this later?"

"No," Stark said. "We're talking about this now."

Rayna sighed before smiling faintly at Gideon. "Is there anything else you need from me, Sheriff?"

He shook his head. "No. You and Mr. Stark have given your statements to Darryl, and that's all we need. I'll call you tomorrow once Louis is sober and I've talked to him."

"Thank you," she said.

"Goodnight, Rayna." Sheriff Walker nodded to Stark. "Mr. Stark."

"Goodnight, Sheriff." Stark stayed where he was, telling himself repeatedly to keep his cool as Rayna walked the sheriff to the door. She returned and, without looking at him, stuffed the frozen peas back into the freezer.

She tightened the belt on her robe and crossed her arms over her torso before staring at him. "Thank you for helping me."

"You're welcome," he said.

Silence descended, and she gave him an awkward smile. "Okay, well -"

"Why did you open the door?" he asked as that slow pulse of anger beat in his temples.

"What?" She frowned at him.

"Why did you open the door?" he repeated. "You're a woman living alone, and you opened the door to a guy who hates you."

"Did you forget what I said to the sheriff?" Her body had gone stiff. "I didn't know it was Louis."

"That's not the point," he snarled. "You shouldn't be opening the door at all at that time of night."

"Are you victim shaming me?" she asked.

He raked his hands through his hair. "Oh, for God's sake... No, I am not victim shaming you, Ms. Abrams. What

I'm asking is for you to be smarter, to use that damn brain of yours and not open the door when you have no idea who's out there."

"People drop off animals on my doorstep all the time," she said. "It's the middle of winter. Do you expect me just to let them freeze to death in their cardboard boxes?"

"I expect you to use common sense for once and start caring about your safety more than some random animal that is not your responsibility!"

"I run a goddamn rescue!" she shouted. She stalked forward until their bodies nearly touched, glaring up at him. "I do what I do to save animals, not to let them freeze to death in my fucking yard, and just because I have one bad experience doesn't mean -"

"One bad experience?" Holy fuck, her refusal to accept how dangerous it was for her would give him a fucking heart attack. "Rayna, he could have killed you!"

"He didn't," she said. "I'm fine, and I'm not hurt or -"

"You are hurt," he snarled. "Jesus Christ, are you even listening to yourself? It's like you want to be in danger."

"There goes that victim shaming again," she snapped. "That's a real dick move, Stark."

He was pretty sure he was on the verge of a stroke. "I am trying to keep you safe!"

"I don't need you to keep me safe!"

"Well, someone has to because you obviously don't give one fuck about personal safety. You are calling the sheriff's office tomorrow and telling them you've changed your mind and want to press charges against Louis. Do you hear me, Ms. Abrams?"

She barked out angry laughter. "I'm not doing what you tell me to do, Stark."

"It's for your safety," he repeated. "You'll do what I say."

"The fuck I will," she said.

"Oh my God," he said. "Why does everything have to be a goddamn fight with you? Just listen to me for once and -"

He made a muffled sound of surprise when Rayna grabbed the front of his t-shirt and pressed her mouth against his.

CHAPTER 29

Rayna shoved her tongue deep into Stark's mouth, pushing him back against the counter before fisting her hands in his shirt and pulling him even closer. He groaned and angled his mouth over hers, exploring her mouth with hard and angry strokes of his tongue.

His big hands gripped her hips and yanked her lower body flush against his. She gasped at the feel of his erection against her belly and didn't object when Stark opened her robe with two hard tugs.

He pushed it off her shoulders, and she let it drop to the ground. His hot gaze raked over her, and her back arched when he cupped one breast through her nightgown. He ran his thumb over her nipple, kissing her repeatedly as he toyed it into a stiff and aching peak.

He kissed her throat before growling, "Distracting me with your hot little body isn't going to work, Ms. Abrams."

"You sure?" she panted as she stuck her hands up his shirt. "Seems to be working so far."

His free hand cupped her ass, squeezing it tight. "Only because I haven't fucked anyone in a while."

"You're such an asshole," she said before kissing him again.

He broke the kiss, giving her nipple a sharp pinch that sent a wave of hot lust over her. "That may be, but you still want my cock in your tight pussy."

She nipped his throat. "Correction. You're an arrogant asshole."

He pulled her leg around his hip and ground his cock against her pussy. "Be nice, or I won't fuck you."

She gave his throat a harder bite, gasping when he gripped the back of her skull and yanked her head back. "No biting, little minx."

He slid his free hand under her nightgown, grunting in surprise when he gripped her bare ass. "You weren't wearing panties while talking to the sheriff."

"Nice deduction, Sherlock." She licked her way up to his ear, sucking hard on his earlobe.

He squeezed her ass before cupping her breast, and his fingers felt like heaven against her sensitive nipple. "From now on, you wear panties around men who aren't me."

She tugged on his earlobe with her teeth. "Stop telling me what to do. You're not the - oh fuck!"

He'd slipped his hand between her thighs, and she clutched his shoulders, unable to stop the soft moan from slipping out when he roughly rubbed her clit. He kissed her again, sliding his tongue into her mouth as he pushed two fingers into her tight entrance.

She rose on her tiptoes at the invasion, and he sucked lightly on her bottom lip. "Look at how fucking wet you are for me."

"It's not for you," she said. "It's just a general horniness."

"Is that right?" He pumped his fingers in and out of her, rubbing her clit with his thumb and grinning at her loud cry of pleasure.

"Yes," she gasped before slipping her hand inside his sweatpants and pushing past the waistband of his underwear. She gripped his cock, trying to keep her shock at how thick he was off her face, as he made a harsh groan and his hips bucked against her.

"You're just looking for a dick to fuck?" he said. "Is that it?"

"Exactly," she said, her voice turning into a moan when he rubbed his thumb against her clit. "Unfortunately, it's attached to you, but beggars can't be choosers."

His nostrils flared, and she made a soft squeal of surprise when he yanked his hand free before lifting her and setting her on the kitchen table. He pushed between her thighs, pulling her head back and kissing her fiercely. She let go of his dick and shoved his pants and briefs down his legs.

He tried to break the kiss, and she grabbed the back of his head, kissing him roughly as she took his cock in her hand and guided it toward her opening. He moaned and gripped her hips, tilting her slightly as his cock pushed at her entrance.

She released his mouth, staring wild-eyed at him as he paused. "Rayna, are you sure this -"

"Fuck me," she demanded, her need for him a frantic and out-of-control force within her. "Right now, Stark."

"Whatever you want, Ms. Abrams," he said and pushed into her.

She dug her fingers into his shoulders, her eyes nearly popping out of her head at the intense thickness of his cock. "Stark, I -"

"Take it, Ms. Abrams," he growled into her ear as he pushed forward relentlessly. "You wanted it, so be a good girl and take it."

His hot words, or maybe it was how his fingers had slipped between her legs to rub at her clit, sent a surge of wetness to her pussy, smoothing his path and making it easier for him to slide in until his heavy balls pressed against her.

"Oh God," she muttered, her fingers digging into his firm skin. She tried to breathe through the intense burn as her walls stretched around him.

He rubbed lightly at her clit, cupping her hip with his other hand and waiting patiently.

She sucked in a deep breath, loosening her grip on his shoulders. He immediately started moving, sliding in and out of her with shallow thrusts before they quickly turned hard and deep.

She clung to him, rocking her hips against him, taking every stroke of his cock deep into her body. His breathing quickened, and low groans punctuated nearly every exhale. His fingers rubbed hard at her clit, and the pleasure in her belly spread across her body, making her moan with each deep thrust.

"That's right, baby," he panted. "You feel so fucking good around my dick. So tight and warm. I want you to come on my cock. Can you do that for me?"

"Yeah," she moaned. "I want to come."

"I know you do," he said, rubbing her clit in firm circles. "Tell me what you need, baby."

"Harder," she muttered, burying her face in his throat.

He pressed harder on her clit, rubbing and circling it as the pleasure soared in her body.

"Come on my cock, Rayna." His voice was low and rough and so fucking sexy. He caught her clit between his fingers and gave it a firm pinch, and it threw her over the edge. She climaxed with a scream, her body shaking wildly and her pussy clenching around Stark's thick cock.

He groaned her name and grabbed her hips in his big hands, fucking her so hard that the table scraped across the floor. She wrapped her arms around his neck, hanging on tight as he drove in and out of her before his body stiffened, and he shouted hoarsely.

Warmth flooded her pussy, and he made a few more shallow thrusts, his body shaking as much as hers. After about thirty seconds, he eased out of her and took a step back. She lifted her nightgown, and they both stared silently at his cum slowly dripping out of her.

"Fuck," Stark said. "I shouldn't have... that is, I didn't mean to... fuck!"

She hopped off the table, shoving down her nightgown and grabbing her robe from the floor.

"Rayna, I -"

"You should go," she said.

"We should talk about what happened." Stark pulled up his pants.

"Nope," she said as she yanked on her robe and belted it shut. "Absolutely not. What just happened was a..."

She couldn't bring herself to say mistake, even if she could practically see Stark drowning in regret.

"It shouldn't have happened," she said, "and I want you to leave."

"Rayna, we -"

"Please. You need to leave," she said, horrified to realize she was on the verge of tears.

His face grim, Stark nodded and left the kitchen. She waited for the front door to shut before she leaned against the counter, staring at the still sleeping Bea as Stark's cum slid down her thigh.

"Well, fuck," she said.

CHAPTER 30

"So, you seriously haven't spoken to him since you had sex last night?" Emma asked

Her voice cut in and out, and Rayna stepped on the gas, speeding through the stretch of road that always had a poor signal.

"Emma, you still there?"

"Yep," Emma said. "You haven't spoken to Stark?"

"No... well, yes, but not really..."

"What do you mean?"

"I texted him this morning with a brief message that I was on birth control and a copy of my medical records. We're obviously not going to do this again, but I figured it was the right thing to do since we both lost our minds and had sex without a condom."

"What did he say?"

Rayna flicked on her indicator and turned right on the road leading to her house. "He replied with a copy of his medical records."

"That's it?"

"That's it."

"You haven't texted or spoken to him since?" Emma asked.

"No, but it hasn't even been twenty-four hours," Rayna said.

"Sure, but if some guy fucked me on my kitchen table, I'd probably reach out to talk about it," Emma said.

"It was a hate fuck," Rayna said. "I don't think you're supposed to talk after one of those."

There was silence, and Rayna said, "I can hear you judging me, Emmy."

"I am not judging you, honey," Emma said emphatically. "I can see how the adrenaline and the rush of what happened with Louis and then Stark saving you would bring on certain feelings."

"No feelings," Rayna said. "Zero feelings, Emma. This was about a release and nothing more."

"Okay," Emma said. "Are you sure you don't want me to come over tonight to talk more about you being attacked by that fucking asshole Louis and then recovering by banging Stark? I feel like a fifteen minute conversation as you're driving home isn't really covering my best friend duties."

Rayna laughed. "I'm sure. I have a ton of things to catch up on with the rescue, and besides, what else is there to discuss? It was a mistake, and it'll never happen again."

"Okay, but I really wish you would press charges against Louis. What happened last night could easily happen again."

"It won't," Rayna said. "The sheriff called me this morning. Even though Louis agreed not to charge Stark and promised not to go near my property, Sheriff Walker suggested that I get a restraining order against him, which I did. So, if Louis comes anywhere near my place, he'll go to jail."

She could almost hear Emma's concern over the phone. "Rayna, I hate this. If Stark hadn't been there last night…"

"He was, and I'm fine," Rayna said. "It was a scary experience, and I never want to go through it again, but I have zero doubts that Louis will do a repeat performance. He won't, Emma. Listen, I better go. I'm almost home, and you know there's another dead zone coming up. I'll lose the call anyway."

"All right," Emma said. "But we're having lunch together tomorrow, and there will be a serious discussion about you getting a doorbell cam and a better lock for your door. I don't care if I have to pay for it myself. It's happening, Rayna."

Love for Emma rushed over her, and her throat tightened with emotion. "I love you, Emmy."

"I love you, too, Rayna. Text me later."

"I will."

Three minutes later, she pulled up to her property, staring in surprise at the familiar red pickup in her driveway. She parked next to it and climbed out of her vehicle, glancing at the decal on the truck door. The decal was a large black oval with a hammer and screwdriver crisscrossed over the top of the oval, and the words "North Handyman Services" were in bold font across the bottom. She walked toward the house, joining the man standing on her porch.

"Hey, Wallace."

"Hi, Rayna. How are you?"

"Good," she said. She studied Wallace as he turned and rummaged through a reusable bag sitting on one of the porch chairs. Wallace North was in his mid-forties with dark hair and eyes. He had a quiet and calm energy and was the guy most people in Harmony Falls called when they needed something repaired. He was particularly popular with the single ladies, and Rayna could see why. He was nearly twenty years her senior, but she could appreciate a good looking man when she saw one. She studied his ass in his jeans. Especially one with an ass like his.

Sure, but it's not as nice as Stark's ass. His dick probably isn't as big either.

She flushed bright red as Wallace turned to face her. He stared at her red cheeks before saying, "Something wrong?"

"No," she said. "What, uh, are you doing here?"

He pointed to the door. "Installing your new door cam."

"I'm sorry, what?" She stared at the camera installed next to the door.

"Your new door cam," he said before holding out an envelope. "Here are the instructions on downloading the app."

She took it from him numbly, staring at it as Wallace said. "If you unlock your door, I'll install the new door locks next."

She blinked at him. "New door lock?"

"Yes," he said, giving her a puzzled look. "Why do you look so confused?"

"Because I had no idea this was happening," she said. "Who hired you?"

Now, he looked as confused as her. "You didn't know I was coming by this evening?"

"No," she said. "Who asked you to do this?"

"Isaac Stark," Wallace said, glancing over Rayna's head at Stark's house. "Well, more accurately, it was his assistant, but she was calling on his behalf, she said."

He frowned. "I assumed you knew about it, although I guess I should have known better."

"What do you mean?" Rayna asked.

"Stark's assistant was very clear that I was to install both the door cam and the new locks no matter what you said. Stark said you can talk to him if there's a problem."

She sighed in exasperation. "Of course he did, the arrogant son of a bitch."

Wallace raised his eyebrows at her, and she sighed again. "Sorry, it's not... that is... sorry."

"It's fine. So, do you want to unlock the door, and I'll get started?"

"And if I say no?" Rayna said.

He glanced at Stark's house again, and she sighed before unlocking the door. "Yeah, okay. Install the new lock."

Stark wasn't at all surprised to see Rayna standing outside his door when he opened it. Nor was he surprised by the annoyance on her face.

He was surprised by his immediate impulse to pick her up, carry her to his bedroom, and fuck her into the mattress.

"Ms. Abrams," he said. "How can I help you?"

She glared at him before pushing past him into his house. "What the hell, Stark?"

She wore her usual hoodie and leggings combo, but the bulkiness of her hoodie did nothing to help him forget how perfect her breasts were. He'd touched them last night, but why the fuck hadn't he at least sucked on her nipples? Now, he'd never get the chance.

"The door cam and new lock are for your safety," he said.

"*Locks*," she said. "Plural. Wallace installed two locks and a deadbolt on my door."

"Good," he said. "I told him multiple locks were needed."

"You're going overboard," she said.

"No, I am not. Many people have multiple locks on their doors."

"I'm not talking about just the locks. Mary from Safety First Security called me to book a time for their technician to install the new security system," she snapped. "She said, and I quote, 'Mr. Stark wants it installed as soon as possible.'"

"If you're not available for the installation, I'll have Hollis meet the technician at your place for the appointment. Do you have a spare key she can use?"

"One, you are not paying to install a security system at my house, and two, Hollis's job is not to babysit a technician at my house."

"Hollis's job is to do what I ask her to do," he said, "and yes, I am. This is happening, Ms. Abrams."

"Oh my God!" Her face turned crimson. "You are the most arrogant, annoying, stubborn son of a bitch I have ever met."

He grinned. "Thank you."

"For fuck's sake… you are not installing a security system at my house, and that's final."

She started to push past him, and he slapped his hand against the wall, using his arm to prevent her from leaving. She whirled to face him, her back against the wall and annoyance on her face. "Move, Stark."

Instead of moving, he placed his other hand on the wall, penning her in as he said, "The security system is not an option."

"You can't tell me what to do!" she said.

His gaze dropped to her mouth. Christ, what he wouldn't give to kiss her again. Just being close to her had him hard as a rock, or maybe it was her sheer outrage with him. He couldn't deny that riling her up was a huge turn on for him.

He told himself not to, then moved in close anyway, letting his erection brush against her belly. "You didn't have a problem with me telling you what to do last night, Ms. Abrams."

She swallowed hard, her pretty brown eyes landing on his mouth. "I don't know what you're talking about."

Fuck, he had to touch her. He *had* to.

He traced his thumb across her bottom lip, his cock

straining at his zipper when her mouth opened, and undeniable desire blazed in her eyes.

Still holding her gaze, he reached for the zipper of her hoodie, pulling it down slowly until he had a view of her perfect breasts. She wore a thin t-shirt beneath the hoodie and no bra, and he traced the hard bud of her nipple through the soft material.

"I told you to come on my cock, and what did you do?" He lightly pinched her nipple before sliding his hand down her flat stomach and slipping it under her leggings.

He traced the waistband of her panties. "Answer me, Ms. Abrams."

"I came on your cock." Rayna's voice was a low moan.

"That's right, you did." He slid his fingers under her panties. "Open for me."

She parted her legs, and he cupped her pussy. "That's my good girl."

She moaned and grabbed his arms, staring at him as he made light circles against her pussy. His fingers brushed against the bare spots from the waxing, and she gasped, her hips arching into him.

He bent his head and kissed the curve of her jaw. "Do you want me to touch your clit, baby?"

"Yes," she whispered, her hands digging into his arms.

"Ask me," he said.

Instead of asking, she kissed him, her tongue pushing past the barrier of his lips. His lust spiked at her familiar taste, and he pressed his body against hers, returning her kiss hungrily as he rubbed her clit in slow circles.

When they broke apart, they were both panting, his cock was a hot length of steel, and he had two fingers deep in her pussy. She squeezed around his fingers as she stared wide-eyed at him, her mouth swollen and red and her nipples hard against her t-shirt.

He had told himself repeatedly all day that he could never fuck Rayna again, but standing here now with his cock practically begging to be buried in her hot body and the look of need on Rayna's face made every good intention fly out the window.

He pulled his hand out of Rayna's pants, ignoring her cry of dismay, and took her hand, tugging her down the hallway toward his bedroom.

"Stark…"

He stopped, measuring the sudden trepidation on her face as she looked past him toward his bedroom door. He turned abruptly and led her to the living room instead, instinctively knowing that taking her to his bedroom was too much for her.

He pulled her to a stop in front of the couch before stripping off her hoodie and then his shirt. She stared greedily at his naked chest, one hand reaching out to touch the light layer of hair on his chest.

He unbuttoned his jeans, pausing when Rayna said, "Stark, what are we…"

He reached for her t-shirt, holding the hem of it as he said, "I'm about to sit on the couch, and you're going to ride me until you come on my cock. Do you have a problem with that, Ms. Abrams?"

She stared silently at him before raising her arms above her head. With a satisfied grin, he pulled her shirt over her head.

CHAPTER 31

S tark tossed Rayna's t-shirt to the floor and cupped her breasts. She arched into his touch, and he kissed her again, teased her nipples until they were stiff peaks. When he reached for her leggings, she helped him push them and her panties down her legs, kicking them and her boots and socks off impatiently as he removed the rest of his clothes.

He fucking loved how greedily she eyed his dick, and he made a show of stroking it a few times before sitting on the couch and patting his lap. "Come here, Rayna."

She straddled him eagerly, and he reached between her legs, rubbing her clit again before sliding two fingers into her. She ground herself against his fingers and huffed in frustration. "I want your cock."

"Just making sure you're ready for me," he said.

He gave her clit one final stroke before cupping her waist and helping her lift up. She gripped his cock, guiding it to her wet entrance. He hissed out a breath when he breeched her, his entire body shuddering as he buried himself into her hot, silky core.

She settled on his lap, her knees pressing against his hips

and her hands gripping his shoulders. Before she could start moving, he cupped her breasts and bent his head, sucking one stiff nipple into his mouth.

She cried out, her back arching and her nails digging into his skin. He sucked hard on the taut peak, curving his tongue around it as she made sweet little moans that set his nerve endings ablaze.

He switched to her other nipple, teasing it until she threaded her hands in his hair and yanked his head back. She kissed him hard, her tongue invading his mouth with a desperate need that he couldn't get enough of.

They broke apart with a gasp, and she stared wild-eyed at him before bracing her hands on his chest and riding him with short, hard thrusts.

"Slow, baby," he said, cupping her hips and forcing her to stop.

"No!" She glared at him, and he grinned before giving her ass a light slap.

"Yes. Ride me slow."

Her scowl deepened, but she did what she asked, switching to long, slow thrusts. He leaned back, watching her pussy take every inch of his dick as she kept that same steady pace.

"Good girl," he groaned, teasing her nipples again with his fingers. Her head fell back, and he could hardly hang onto his self-control when she made a spiraling, twisting motion with every downward thrust.

"Fuck," he moaned, reaching between her legs to rub her clit.

She made a cooing sound of delight and moved faster, her tight body bouncing on his cock as she worked hard to find her pleasure. Her body was starting to tighten around him, and he stopped rubbing her clit, ignoring her cry of dismay.

She shoved her hand between her legs, and he grabbed

both her wrists, yanking her hands to her side and holding them there. "No, baby."

"Please!" she said. "I was so close!"

"I know," he said. "And as soon as you agree to have the security system installed, I'll let you come."

She hissed at him like an angry cat, baring her teeth at him. "You can't blackmail me while we're fucking."

He grinned, releasing her hands and sliding his hand between her thighs again. He rubbed her clit hard, and she ground her little pussy against him, squeezing his cock so hard he almost came right then and there.

He gritted his teeth, fighting the urge to fill her tight pussy with his cum. She was close again, and he stopped touching her, grinning at the frustrated squeak she made before he grabbed her wrists again.

"Stark, no!"

"Shh, baby," he said, making a gentle rocking motion with his hips. She met the gentle motion eagerly, but he could see the frustration building on her face. "Say yes to the security system, and then you can come on my cock."

She squeezed her inner muscles around him, gasping when he gave her a sharp slap to the ass before gripping her wrists again. "Behave, Rayna."

She bit her bottom lip, her cheeks flushed, and her body rocking against his before her pretty brown eyes stared directly at him. "Isaac, please, let me come."

Fuck! Just hearing her say his name nearly made him blow his load. He clenched his jaw, making a few hard and out-of-control thrusts deep into her wet pussy. She moaned happily as she took each stroke of his cock like the good girl she was.

He clawed back his self-control, forcing his hips to stop and ignoring her pout. "Don't stop!"

"You know what I want, Rayna," he said, giving her a few

shallow pumps of his hips. "Say it, baby, and I'll let you come."

She chewed on her bottom lip before snapping, "Fine! I'll do the security system."

He wrapped his arm around her waist, holding her tight as he drove in and out of her pussy. She moaned, her hands clenching onto his shoulders again. He stared at her perfect breasts bouncing wildly as he fucked her, holding onto his self-control by a precarious thread.

"I hate you," she moaned, even as her hot little body took every inch of him.

"Your pussy doesn't seem to hate me," he panted, driving up into her before reaching between her legs and rubbing her clit.

"Ohhhh," she moaned, her hips immediately switching to a rocking motion. Suddenly on the verge of his climax, the tight slick grip of her pussy too much for his iron control, he rubbed her clit faster, groaning her name when she immediately cried out and came hard around him. Her pussy tightened exquisitely around his throbbing cock, and he made one final thrust before the pleasure overtook him.

He held her quivering body tight against him, his hips bucking as he came deep inside her pussy. She collapsed against him, her head landing with a thunk against his chest even as her pussy continued to milk him, pulling his seed into her body.

He rubbed her back with long, slow strokes, his breath roaring in and out of his lungs. He was starting to soften, but when she tried to climb off his lap, he cupped her ass, holding her still. "Don't move, Rayna."

She hesitated before relaxing against him again, burying her face in his neck. Her nipples were still hard pearls against his chest, and her body shook lightly. He rubbed her back again as they both caught their breath.

"It was a dick move not to let me come until I agreed to the security thing," she said, her voice muffled by his skin.

He grinned at the ceiling. "Yeah, I know."

"It's not, like, a legally binding contract or anything," she said.

He laughed. "No, it isn't. But if you don't allow it to be installed, the next time we fuck, it'll be full-on orgasm denial. And I won't budge on letting you come no matter how much you beg."

She sat up. "There is no 'next time we fuck', Stark. There shouldn't have even been a this time. I came over here to yell at you, not fuck you."

"You have to admit, this was a hell of a lot more enjoyable," he said.

"It was fine," she said.

He squeezed her ass, not the least bit annoyed by her blatant lie. "Do I need to remind you how many times you begged me to come, Ms. Abrams?"

She flushed, her gaze skittering away from his. "Begging is a strong word. I asked politely a few times."

He laughed so hard that her entire body jiggled on top of him. She poked him in the chest, but her back arched when he cupped her breasts and rubbed his thumb over her nipples. "Stop that."

"I could stop," he said, leaning forward to kiss along her collarbone, "or you could join me in the shower, and I'll give you the chance to ask me politely to come again."

Her hands gripped the back of his head, but instead of pulling him away, she pushed his mouth toward her nipple. He sucked it into a hard point again, her soft moans and cries urging him on.

He muttered a curse when her phone rang, and she tugged him off her nipple. "Ignore it."

"I can't." She climbed off his lap and snagged her phone from her hoodie pocket. "Rayna speaking."

He had a blanket draped over the sofa arm, and she wrapped it around her naked body. Damn shame that was. He sat back on the couch as Rayna frowned.

"Wait, they're what?" Rayna asked.

She listened and then said, "Okay, well, we don't usually take small animals. How often is he sneezing? Can you put them in another room with the door closed for now? I know of someone who might be able to foster them. I can talk to them tomorrow, and … no. No, you absolutely cannot put them outside. No, not even if you cover their cage with a blanket. They will freeze to death, Ginny. Yes, they will. No, you can't…"

Rayna hit mute on her phone and snapped, "For fuck's sake! Why are people so fucking awful!" before taking a deep breath and unmuting the call. Her voice calm and pleasant, she said, "Ginny, I'll be there in twenty minutes. Do not put them outside, all right? Good. I'll see you soon."

She ended the call and started dressing. He grabbed his clothes. "What's going on?"

"Ginny Mayler's oldest brought home two guinea pigs, and her youngest is sneezing and stuffed up. She's freaking out, thinks they'll put him into anaphylactic shock or something and wants to put them outside."

He buttoned and zipped his jeans. "Can't the older kid just take them back to where they got them?"

"Apparently not." She yanked her t-shirt over her head. "She took them from some kid at school whose father threatened to kill them if he didn't get rid of them."

"But you're a cat and dog rescue," he said.

"Technically, yes, but we take in small animals like guinea pigs and bunnies in emergencies."

She shoved her feet into her boots as he pulled his shirt

over his head and followed her toward the door. She paused in the hallway. "What are you doing?"

"Going with you," he said.

"No," she said.

Hurt washed over him, and he was immediately annoyed by both the feeling and the fact that she could see her rejection hurt him.

"I'm just picking up guinea pigs. It's nothing dangerous," she said.

"Right," he said. Christ, he sounded like a pouting little kid.

Her face softened. "Ginny is best friends with Seo-Jun. If you come with me to pick up the guinea pigs, Ginny will tell Seo-Jun she saw you with me, and Seo-Jun is -"

"The biggest gossip in Harmony Falls. Yeah, I know," he said.

They stared silently at each other for a few seconds before she said, "I have to go."

"I know," he said, still sounding like a petulant toddler. "Good night, Ms. Abrams."

Her lips pressed into a thin line, and for a second, he thought he saw hurt flash across *her* face before she gave him an annoyed look. "Good night, Stark."

CHAPTER 32

Stark wasn't expecting to see the sheriff's SUV in Rayna's driveway when he arrived home Wednesday night. Nor did he expect his immediate rush of panic. He climbed out of his car and practically ran across the front yard and up Rayna's porch steps.

He knocked hard on the door, his stomach churning. Had that asshole Louis shown up on Rayna's property again? Had he hurt her? He knocked again, nearly bruising his knuckles with the force.

"C'mon," he muttered. "Answer the fucking door, baby."

He was about to knock a third time when the door opened. He stared at Sheriff Walker, his stomach dropping all the way to the fucking ground. "Where is she? Did he hurt her? Did he -"

"She's fine," the sheriff said. "I'm not here on business."

He shouldered past the sheriff, needing to see Rayna for himself. "Rayna, where are... holy shit."

He stared in disbelief at the giant dog sitting in the hall-way. His tail wagging madly, the dog stood and took a few steps forward before the sheriff said, "Tank, sit."

The dog sat obediently, but his tail wagged even harder when Bea wandered into the hallway. The two dogs touched noses, and Bea licked Tank's nose. Tank's tail smacked against the wall, and Gideon sighed. "Do not put a hole in the wall with your tail, Tank."

"This is your dog?" Stark asked.

"Yes," Gideon said. "He's a Great Dane, he weighs about a buck seventy-five, and he eats ten cups of food a day."

Stark grinned. "I guess you get asked those questions a lot."

"You have no idea," Gideon said with a laugh.

Stark walked toward the fawn coloured Dane, holding his hand out for Tank to sniff before scratching his throat and behind his ears. The dog chuffed happily and stood before leaning hard against Stark. He braced his feet before he could get knocked into the wall. "Whoa, big guy."

"Sorry, he's a leaner," Gideon said.

Bea whined happily before sitting on Stark's feet. He leaned down to pet the old beagle and got a giant dog tongue slurping across his face for his efforts.

"Tank, c'mon, buddy," Gideon said with a sigh. "No licking the guests."

Stark straightened and wiped the drool from his cheek as Gideon said, "Rayna and Grace are in the living room."

Stark followed Gideon into the living room, Tank and Bea both competing to see who could knock him off his feet first. Although he didn't doubt the sheriff's assurance that Rayna was fine, he didn't truly relax until he saw Rayna in the room with a curvy, dark-haired woman.

They were both crouched in front of a long white metal cage, and he could hear weird squeaks and whistles coming from the cage. He nudged Bea off his feet and joined the two women.

"So, this one is Nadia, and this one is Penny." Rayna

pointed first to a tricoloured guinea pig and then a pure white one. "I've held them a few times, and they're skittish but not bitey. You'll need to pick up some more supplies for them - hay and pellets, and some fresh veggies - which, as a foster, you can submit the receipt for reimbursement."

The dark-haired woman shrugged. "I don't need reimbursement."

"Okay, but we won't be able to give you a donation-in-kind receipt," Rayna said. "Not until I finish setting up Little Whiskers as a registered charity. Sorry, Grace."

"No worries," Grace said. "I'm just glad that Tank doesn't see them as a snack."

Rayna laughed. "Me too. Although, when you told me way back when that you'd foster a guinea pig, I bet you didn't expect me to actually make you keep that promise."

Grace grinned at her. "Maybe not, but I'm happy to help and -"

She stopped, glancing behind her as she noticed Stark for the first time. She stood gracefully and held out her hand. "Hello, I'm Grace Larken."

"Isaac Stark." He shook her hand as Rayna stood.

"What, uh... what are you doing here?" Rayna asked.

"I saw the sheriff's vehicle and thought Louis was giving you trouble again," Stark said.

"He won't," Rayna said. "I'm perfectly safe."

"You'll be safe once the security system is in place," Stark said. "Did you call them today?"

"Yes. They're coming on Monday."

"Not until Monday?" He hated the idea of her being without the security system for that long.

"That was their first availability," she said. "Anyway, everything's fine, as you can see, so thanks for checking in, but -"

"These are the guinea pigs, huh?" He turned to Grace. "And she's convinced you to foster them?"

"Rayna can be very persuasive," Grace said with a smile. "In all honesty, I'm glad I can do something to help. I'm allergic to cats so I can't foster them, and Tank in the house is more than enough dog."

At the sound of his name, Tank woofed softly and joined them, leaning against Grace so she could scratch around his ears.

"Speaking of which, how are you feeling?" Rayna asked Grace. "I put Freddie in the laundry room and did a quick dust and vacuum of the downstairs before you arrived, but I didn't do a deep clean or anything. Mostly because the cat hair is what helps keep this place standing."

Grace laughed and stroked Tank's ears. "So far, I'm feeling fine. I took some allergy meds before we came over, and as long as I'm not actively petting a cat or in the same room with them, I can avoid a hospital visit."

"You're sure?" Gideon joined them and slid his arm around Grace's waist, squeezing her hip gently.

Stark had the sudden inane urge to do the same to Rayna and immediately shoved his hands into his pockets to stop himself.

"Positive," Grace said. "Unless you're trying to get out of buying us dinner like you promised? Because I've been looking forward to Chinese food all day, and I have the delivery app queued up and ready to go on my phone."

Gideon chuckled before pressing a kiss against her mouth. "Decide what you want and order the food. I need to do a quick phone check-in with Ian."

"All right." Grace watched Gideon leave the room before grabbing her phone and scrolling across the screen. She smiled at Rayna and Stark. "I was thinking we could do some family-style dishes. That should be more than enough for the four of us."

An awkward silence hit the room, and Grace made a face. "Uh oh, I just put my foot in my mouth, didn't I?"

"No," Stark said quickly. "But I should go. I have a... thing."

He started across the room, moving more slowly than usual, refusing to admit to himself that he wanted Rayna to ask him to stay for dinner. Why would she? They hated each other, and people who hated one another did not go on double dates, even if the date was just ordering in dinner.

"Stark," Rayna said.

He turned, hoping his desire to stay wasn't written all over his face like some childish love-struck fool.

Rayna glanced at Grace before she said, "You should cancel your... thing and stay for dinner."

He couldn't stop the grin from crossing his face. "Consider it cancelled."

"THERE'S AN AWARDS CEREMONY FOR VIDEO GAMES." GIDEON took a drink of beer before arching an eyebrow at Stark. "Seriously?"

Stark laughed, leaning back in the kitchen chair and reaching down to scratch the top of Bea's head, who was sitting at his feet. "Completely serious."

"Have you won any?" Grace asked.

"A few," Stark said.

"More than a few," Rayna said. "Emma told me your Shadow Game series has won multiple awards."

"That's impressive," Grace said.

"I have an amazing team of developers and designers," Stark said. "The awards are because of them."

Rayna took a sip of her beer. She often told Stark he was arrogant, but for someone with his arrogance, he sure was modest about his work accomplishments and quick to praise his team.

"I know Lucas loves his job and has nothing but good things to say about it," Grace said.

"You know Lucas?" Stark asked.

"We do," Grace said. "He's best friends with Connor, and Connor is dating my best friend, Kira."

"Small world," Stark said.

"Small town," Rayna corrected.

He grinned at her, and her hand was actually inching across the small space between them to rest on his thigh before her common sense returned. They weren't dating, for God's sake. Unease trickled through her, and she quickly finished off her beer before standing and gathering the empty food boxes.

Gideon stood and cleared the dishes from the table, and she smiled at him. "Thanks, Gideon."

Tank nosed his way in between them, and she petted the giant dog. "Does anyone want coffee?"

"Normally, I would be all over that, but my eyes are starting to water, and my nose is tickling a bit," Grace said. "I think my allergy meds are wearing off."

She stood, smiling at Rayna and Stark. "This was a lot of fun. We should do it again, but maybe at our place next time? I love cats, but they just don't love me."

"Oh, um…" Rayna glanced at Stark. Shit, Grace thought they were dating.

Of course she does. You invited Stark to stay for dinner. The two of you haven't fought once tonight, and if you think for one minute that you're doing a bang-up job of hiding how attractive you think he is, I have a bridge to sell you. You're acting like you're dating. Why wouldn't she think you are?

Her stomach dropped. She and Stark *were* acting like a couple tonight. From sharing the story of rescuing the stray dog from the barbwire fence to finishing each other's sentences more than once. What was she doing? Tonight was a mistake. Just because they had fucked twice didn't mean a goddamn thing. Stark was only being nice to her because he wanted her house, and thinking he was starting to feel something for her was dangerous.

No more dangerous than how you've caught feelings for him.

She nearly dropped the dish she held. She hated Stark. He was an arrogant ass trying to bully her out of her home and - shit! She realized she'd been staring at Grace for close to a minute without saying anything, and the air was thick with awkwardness.

Get your shit together, Abrams!

"We'd love to," Stark suddenly said. "Just let us know when."

"Perfect," Grace said before standing. "Thanks again for the fun evening."

Her stomach still churning, Rayna stayed quiet as Stark and Gideon carried the guinea pig cage to his SUV before Gideon loaded Tank into the back. She smiled and waved at Grace and Gideon, then disappeared into the kitchen like the giant chicken she was as Stark closed and locked the door.

She gripped the sink, staring out the window into the cold darkness. Despite knowing that Stark was only trying to get on her good side to buy her house, she was still tempted to ask him to fuck her again, and how pathetic was that?

She took a deep breath as Stark joined her in the kitchen and turned to face him. He smiled at her, his face relaxed and open, and leaned against the counter beside her. "That was fun."

"It was," she said.

"Thanks for inviting me to stay."

She nodded, her throat suddenly too tight to speak. Christ, she needed to remember that she was literally sleeping with the enemy, and it couldn't continue, no matter how good the sex was between them.

She stiffened when Stark reached out and hooked a finger in her belt loop. He tugged her toward him, giving her a slow, inviting smile. He bent to kiss her, and she shook her head before backing away.

"What's wrong?" he asked.

She folded her arms over her torso, studying Bea, who had fallen asleep in her bed in the corner. "I don't... we shouldn't be having sex. We hate each other, remember?"

His lips thinned, and she was stunned by the hurt that covered his face.

"Stark, I -"

"You're right," he said. "Good night, Ms. Abrams."

He stalked toward the front door, and she hurried after him. "Stark, I'm sorry. I didn't mean to hurt your feelings."

He opened the door with a derisive snort. "Trust me, Ms. Abrams, it would take a lot more than a rejection from you to hurt my feelings. The sex wasn't *that* good between us."

"You can't help being a dick even when someone is apologizing, can you?" she snapped.

Stark stepped out into the cold and slammed the door shut behind him.

CHAPTER 33

Rayna opened the door of Stark Entertainment and stepped inside. The reception desk was empty, and she stood awkwardly next to it as a burst of laughter came from somewhere inside the bullpen.

Rayna, just go! You're so pathetic right now. You know that, right?

Her insides squirmed as her gaze landed on Stark's open office door. She wasn't here in the hopes of catching a glimpse of him. The fact that she hadn't seen Stark once in the last six days didn't bother her in the least. It was what she wanted.

She definitely hadn't spent the last six days obsessing over their last conversation or the hurt on his face or how, despite her new compulsive habit of checking out her windows every hour to see if she could catch a glimpse of him coming or going, even a single sighting of him had eluded her.

As the minutes passed with no sign of Aditi, she looked for a bell or something to ring. More laughter drifted down from upstairs, and she chewed indecisively at her lip as her gaze turned to Stark's office again.

Leave before you embarrass yourself.

Shit. What was she doing? Her inner voice was right. She was being ridiculous. She turned to leave, grimacing when a voice said, "Rayna?"

She turned back, smiling at Hollis. "Hi, Hollis. How are you?"

"Fine, thank you." Hollis glanced at the empty reception desk.

"Um, I'm not sure where Aditi is," Rayna said.

"She had to leave early for a doctor's appointment," Hollis said. "Is there something I can help you with?"

"Um, yeah, uh, I just wanted to check in to see if it was all right if I used the gym right now," Rayna said.

"Why wouldn't it be?" Hollis asked.

"Well, I normally come by later at night when there aren't any employees using it, but it's, um, only four thirty, so I imagine employees will be using it now, and I didn't know if that would be a problem."

She sounded incredibly lame, even to herself, and she forced a smile at Hollis as her cheeks flushed.

"It isn't a problem," Hollis said. "You're welcome to use the gym at whatever time you'd like."

"Right, okay. Well, thank you for confirming that," Rayna said.

"Sure," Hollis said.

Her gaze slipping to Stark's office door again, Rayna said, "So, I'm gonna go and... work out now."

"Enjoy," Hollis said, one perfect eyebrow raising slightly.

"Thanks." Feeling absolutely ridiculous, Rayna turned to leave as the front door opened, and a blast of cold air washed over her. Her cheeks went hot and then ice cold as she stared at the two people standing behind her.

Her hand tucked securely around Stark's arm, Phoebe

Edward's smile turned condescending. "Hello, Rayna. This is a surprise."

As pointless and inappropriate betrayal pumped through her body, Rayna stared at Stark. His look of indifference morphed into concern, and his brow creased. Before he could speak, Rayna said to Phoebe, "What are you doing here?"

Phoebe's patronizing smile turned sickly sweet. "Isaac and I had coffee, and now he's giving me an office tour. I think the better question is, what are *you* doing here? Is there a toilet backed up somewhere?"

Hot jealousy poured over Rayna, and that feeling of betrayal intensified until she thought her head might pop right off. Phoebe's use of Stark's first name kept clanging in Rayna's head. Were they fucking? Is that why she was so comfortable with calling him Isaac? Had he spent the last week in Phoebe's bed instead of Rayna's?

Anger swallowed the jealousy and betrayal. Anger over her pointless emotional response and that Stark could so easily go from fucking her to fucking Phoebe - a shallow, spiteful woman who had spent the last decade taking every opportunity to belittle and mock Rayna.

Her stomach a tight knot, Rayna gave Phoebe a brittle smile. "Always nice to see you, Phoebe."

She pushed past them and out into the cold air, walking briskly toward her vehicle. She grabbed her gym bag from the front seat, slammed the door shut so hard that rust from the door drifted to the snow, and stalked toward the gym. She would work off her rage in the gym and not think once about Isaac fucking Stark.

HOLLIS KNOCKED ON STARK'S OPEN DOOR. "SORRY TO interrupt, Mr. Stark, but your five o'clock call is on the line."

"Thank you, Hollis." Stark stood and walked around his desk, staring pointedly at Phoebe, who stood reluctantly. "Have a good evening, Ms. Edwards."

She slipped her hand around his arm again, giving it a warm squeeze. "Isaac, I've asked you to call me Phoebe. Why don't we have dinner tonight? I'm happy to stick around until your call is over. Have you tried the carbonara at the Whiskey Grill? It's the best you'll ever taste, I promise."

"Thank you, but I have plans for this evening," Stark said.

"This weekend, then," Phoebe said. "I'm free Saturday night."

"No, thank you," Stark said.

Her lips thinned, and her smile turned stiff. "Right then. Good night, Isaac."

"Good night, Ms. Edwards."

She followed Hollis out of his office, and he returned to his chair, sinking into the soft leather before rubbing his forehead and closing his eyes. When he sensed Hollis's presence a few minutes later, he said, "I'm giving you a goddamn raise, Hollis."

He opened his eyes just in time to see a rare smile cross Hollis's face.

"All these years of working together, and I didn't realize mind reading was one of your talents," he said. "Or could you just feel my 'get her out of my office' vibes through your office wall?"

Another smile flitted across her face. "Something like that. Faking a five pm phone appointment is barely worthy of a raise, but I'll notify the payroll department of my increase in pay."

He laughed despite the tension headache that lurked at the base of his skull. "You're worth every penny."

"I know," she said before glancing at her watch. "Are you heading out for the day?"

"I am. Have a good night, Hollis."

"You as well, Mr. Stark."

She returned to her office, and Stark stared at his laptop for a few seconds before closing it abruptly. Throughout the entire torturous half hour that Phoebe had been in his office, his mind kept returning to the look on Rayna's face when he'd walked in with Phoebe.

His stomach clenched, and he stared moodily out the window. What did he care if Rayna was upset? He wasn't dating Phoebe and had no intention of dating her, but he didn't have to share that with Rayna. She'd made it clear last week that he was nothing more than a dick for her to use.

Is that why you've spent the last week avoiding her like she's a rabid mongoose?

He stood, grabbed his jacket and gym bag, and then headed outside to the parking lot. He wasn't avoiding her. It had been a busy week at work, and maybe he'd spent every evening alone at home, but that wasn't anything new for him. It was what introverts did.

They sat alone in their bedroom, working or playing video games with nothing but a cat and her three kittens for company. Just because he'd had a surprisingly good time with Rayna, Gideon, and Grace didn't mean anything. He liked his privacy and his space, and that weird aching loneliness he felt more and more often was just a bizarre blip.

He unlocked his car, pausing with his hand on the door handle, when he saw Rayna's SUV in the parking lot. He locked his car and walked toward the gym. He'd worked out that morning and absolutely didn't need another workout tonight, but that didn't stop him from opening the door and stepping inside.

"Hey, boss!" Rupert was running on a treadmill, and he gave Stark a brief wave.

Stark nodded to him before staring at Rayna, who was using the rowing machine. She stared resolutely at the wall, even though he was in her line of sight. Ear buds in her ears, her cheeks red, and her forehead gleaming with perspiration, she kept a steady rhythm on the machine. He headed toward the men's locker room and changed into his workout clothes.

He returned to the central area of the gym and was immediately smacked in the face with a healthy dose of jealousy. His movements jerky, he stalked to the closest treadmill and started a brisk warm-up walk.

Rayna and Rupert were both standing by the free weights on the other side of the gym. Stark was too far away to hear what Rupert was saying, but he couldn't miss the appreciative looks Rupert kept giving Rayna's body.

Stark gave Rayna a stiff nod when she glanced at him. With an inscrutable look on her face, she turned back to Rupert. Stark's jealousy skyrocketed when Rayna smiled warmly at Rupert before laughing at something he said. When she touched him, just a brief brush of her hand against his chest, Stark's hot jealousy turned into a fiery inferno.

His stomach was a flaming ball of lead, and he told himself to go the fuck home instead of torturing himself watching Rayna flirt with Rupert. Instead, he upped the speed and the incline on the treadmill and stared grimly ahead.

CHAPTER 34

I gnoring every instinct screaming at him that this was a mistake, Stark knocked on Rayna's door. He'd been at the goddamn gym for nearly an hour, punishing his muscles into another needless workout just because he couldn't stand the thought of leaving Rayna and Rupert alone. They had finished their workout, and even though Stark had watched Rayna leave in her car, his tension had been sky high the entire drive home.

He'd had no idea what he would have done if Rayna's SUV hadn't been in her driveway or, worse, if Rupert's car had been there. Thankfully, it was only Rayna's SUV in her driveway.

He was too worked up to eat dinner, but he had a hot shower and then fed Molly. Even his now nightly habit of bringing the three kittens onto the bed and cuddling them hadn't eased his irritation. He kept seeing Rayna flirting with Rupert, the images in his mind driving him crazy, until here he was, knocking on her door, full of jealousy and bad intentions.

The wind was ice cold, and he waited impatiently for only

a minute or so before knocking again and shoving his hands into his jacket pockets.

The door opened, and Rayna, her wet hair tucked behind her ears and - *fucking hell* - wearing nothing but a long t-shirt, said, "You don't have to pound on the door. I have a working doorbell now, thanks to you."

He pushed past her, the jealousy and anger and lust a swirling mass in his belly.

"Come on in," she said with an exaggerated eye roll before closing the door and locking it.

They stared silently at each other in the narrow hallway before Rayna finally said, "What do you want? I was just about to go to bed."

He folded his arms across his chest and scowled at her. "I gave you a pass to my gym to work out, Ms. Abrams."

"I'm aware," she said, giving him a 'why are you acting so dumb' look that only inflamed him more.

"Are you sure? Since you spent the entire evening flirting with my employee instead of working out, maybe I should take back the gym pass."

Her eyes widened, and his scowl deepened when she started laughing. "You're taking away the gym pass because you're jealous I made a new friend at the gym?"

"You want him to be more than a friend, and I am not jealous of your *flirting*," he snarled.

"I wasn't flirting," she said.

"Bullshit."

She paused before grinning. "Yeah, you're right. I was flirting. Rupert's cute."

"You are not allowed to flirt with my employees," he snapped.

She laughed again. "Says who?"

"He's too young for you," he said, as what suspiciously sounded a little like desperation coloured his voice.

"He told me he's twenty-four," she said. "Stop acting like I'm robbing the cradle."

"Ms. Abrams, I forbid you to flirt with my employees."

"Oh, you forbid me now." She crowded in close, and his cock turned to stone when her breasts brushed against him. She stood on her tiptoes and curled her hand around the back of his neck, lightly tugging until he bent his head and his mouth was only inches from hers. "What will you do to me if I keep flirting with your employees?"

"Rayna," he groaned. In an instant, his jealousy became an uncontrollable burn for her. Christ, he wanted to kiss her. *Needed* to kiss her.

"Will you spank me, Stark?"

His breath shuddered out of him as the last of his control eroded. He grabbed her hips, yanking her fully against him and grinding his dick against her. "If you want me to."

Her right hand squeezed the back of his neck as her left hand fisted in his shirt. "There are a lot of things I want you to do to me."

"Like what? Be specific," he said.

Her tongue darted out to wet her lower lip, and he tracked the movement like a predator. She rubbed her lower body against him, and he hissed out a breath at the pressure against his aching cock.

"Kiss me," she said.

He dropped his mouth onto hers, his hands tightening on her hips as she opened her mouth and invited him in. They kissed greedily, their tongues twisting and turning. He slid his hands under her shirt to cup her ass, grunting in surprise when he felt her warm, naked skin.

He pulled back, studying Rayna's kiss-swollen lips. "You're not wearing panties."

Her grin was saucy. "You said I only had to wear under-wear around men who *weren't* you."

"Fuck, you're killing me, woman," he said before squeezing her ass.

She kissed him again, not objecting when he slid his hands to her thighs and lifted her. She wrapped her legs around his waist, rubbing her pussy against his denim clad erection. She gasped, her hips moving shamelessly faster, and he gripped her ass again. "Does that feel good, baby?"

"Yes," she said, still rocking against his cock, "but unless you want me to come all over the front of your jeans, we need to get you naked."

"Yes," he muttered, trailing kisses down the soft skin of her throat. "I definitely want to be naked with you."

He carried her toward the living room, stopping when she tugged lightly on his hair. "Take me upstairs."

He hesitated, and she gave him a lightly mocking smile. "Unless it's too much for you to carry me? You are thirty-two, after all. Maybe I should call Rupert and ask - ouch!"

She gave him an outraged look. "You spanked me!"

He headed toward the stairs. "Be a good girl, and I won't do it again."

She nipped his throat hard. He hissed out a breath and slapped her ass again before climbing the stairs.

"First door on the right," she said.

He walked into her bedroom. Freddie was lying on the bed, and he made a disgruntled meow before jumping down and strutting out of the room. Stark set Rayna down beside the bed, and she immediately began to strip off his clothes. He tossed his shirt aside as she unbuttoned his jeans and shoved them and his briefs down his legs. They got caught on his boots, and he muttered a curse as Rayna laughed.

She tugged and pulled on him, shuffling him around until he was in front of the bed before giving him a hard shove in the chest. He fell back on the bed, and she pulled off each of his boots and then quickly removed the rest of his clothes.

She eyed his cock with a shameless hunger that made precum drip from the head. He fisted his cock, stroking it slowly as Rayna yanked her shirt over her head and dropped it on the floor.

"Fuck," he said with a low groan.

She grinned and cupped one perfect breast, toying with the already taut nipple before slipping her hand between her legs. She rubbed lightly and showed him her soaked fingers.

His mouth watered, and he was suddenly desperate to taste her. Before he could invite her to sit on his face, she said, "Move to the middle of the bed."

He did what she asked, stuffing a pillow under his head when she hopped onto the bed and then straddled him backwards.

"Fuck me," he said as she spread her legs, and he had the perfect view of her incredible ass and tight pussy.

"That's the idea," she said before reaching between her legs and gripping his cock. She lowered herself down onto his cock, making soft gasps and moans as she slowly took him into her body.

"So fucking gorgeous," he moaned as her little pussy took him inch by torturous inch. When she was stuffed full of him, she stared at him over her shoulder, her face flushed and her eyes bright with desire.

"Okay, baby?" he asked.

She took a deep breath. "Yeah, I just need a minute."

He rubbed and stroked her ass, his breath catching when she leaned forward and braced her hands on his shins. She moved up and down, and he couldn't stop his moan as he watched his cock slide in and out of her pussy.

"Fuck, baby, you feel so good on my dick," he said.

She moved faster, her pussy squeezing his cock, her ass grinding against him with every downward thrust. His hips rocked up to meet each of her thrusts as his breath quickened and pleasure radiated through his body.

He gripped her hips and pumped into her, needing to move harder and faster. She tore his hands from her hips and lifted herself off him. He groaned when his dick slipped out of her pussy, and he stared at her soaking wet hole, harsh need rocketing through him, before reaching for her hips again.

"No," she said and pushed his hands away.

"Baby, I need to be in you," he groaned.

"I know," she said, "but you'll be a good boy and not move while I fuck you, or neither of us get an orgasm tonight."

He muttered a curse but held perfectly still as she lowered herself onto his dick again. He gripped the sheets in tight fists, his eyes glued to her pussy, and praying for mercy as she rode him excruciatingly slow.

"Rayna," he gritted out. "Faster."

She peeked over her shoulder at him. "Admit you were jealous of my new friendship with Rupert, and I will."

"Don't say his name while you're fucking me," he said.

She squeezed around him, then leaned forward and tilted her hips so that he slipped out of her again. He let loose with another curse before glaring at her. "Rayna!"

"Admit it," she said.

"Fine. I was jealous," he ground out, "but you shouldn't have been flirting with him in front of me."

Her little pussy swallowed his dick again, and he was in heaven. "So, you're allowed to flirt with other women, but I can't flirt with other men?"

"What are you talking about? Fuck, baby, move faster."

She kept the same slow pace of fucking him. "Phoebe Edwards. You were on a goddamn date with her today."

"I wasn't," he said.

She glared at him over her shoulder, her dark brown eyes

bright with jealousy before she pulled off him again. "Liars don't get pussy, Stark."

Oh, Jesus, she would be the fucking death of him. "I'm not lying. She ambushed me in the coffee shop."

She stared at him, her hot little pussy only inches from his dick, and he said, "I swear, baby."

Thank fucking Christ, she settled onto his dick again, her pussy squeezing him tight as she rode him a little faster. "You invited her back to the office."

"She invited herself," he panted, his hands tightening in the sheets. "Baby, can I touch you? Please, I need to touch you."

"Yes, you may," she said.

He grabbed her ass, squeezing and kneading the firm flesh as she took him deep. "She wants to fuck you, Stark."

Before he could reply, she rode him hard and fast, bouncing on his dick, the hot glide of her pussy making his eyes roll back in his head and his body arch.

"You're not allowed to fuck her," she said.

He didn't reply, his entire focus narrowed to the slick grip of Rayna's pussy on his dick. Christ, he was so fucking close. Just a few more strokes and -

"Fuck!" The word exploded out of his mouth as Rayna leaned forward, and he slipped out of her again. "Rayna!"

Her giggle was both adorable and evil as hell. "Yes, Stark?"

"Give me your pussy," he said.

"Promise me you won't fuck Phoebe, and you can have my pussy," she said.

He blinked at her. Why the fuck were they talking about Phoebe? "I'm not attracted to her."

"Promise me you won't fuck her," Rayna said before sliding him back into her pussy.

He squeezed her ass, desperate for her to move. "Fuck me, baby."

She stared at him over her shoulder. "Promise me, Isaac, and then I'll fuck you."

"I promise I won't fuck her," he said quickly. "Please, Rayna, I need you."

Her beautiful face broke out into a smile. "That's my good boy."

She rewarded his obedience by fucking him hard and fast. He moaned her name, holding her hips and staring at her perfect body before he suddenly sat up and hooked his arm around her waist.

He kissed the back of her shoulder, his hands cupping her breasts. "Baby, turn around to face me."

She arched into his touch, her breath releasing in a soft moan when he pulled lightly on her nipples. "You don't like the reverse cowgirl?"

He kissed her throat. "I like it, but I want to see your face when you come."

She stared at him before suddenly kissing him hard. He sucked on her tongue, cupping her breasts and rubbing his thumbs over her nipples as she dug her nails into his thighs. When they broke apart, he rubbed her flat stomach. "Will you turn around for me?"

She nodded, and he laid on his back again, watching as she turned and straddled him before guiding his cock into her pussy. They both moaned as she sank onto him, and he rubbed her thighs. "Come here, baby."

She leaned over him, propping herself up on her hands and gasping his name when he cupped her breasts and sucked hard on one nipple. He teased both nipples with hard sucks and nips before sliding his hand between her thighs and rubbing her clit.

She moaned his name, grinding her body against his fingers, as her head fell back. He gave her clit a light pinch and kissed between her breasts. "Fuck me, Rayna."

"Yes, Isaac," she breathed, bracing her hands on his chest. He held her hip in a loose grip with his left hand, keeping his right hand between her thighs and rubbing her clit as she rode him hard and fast.

"Oh, oh, oh," she panted, her fingers digging into his chest. "Oh fuck, I'm close."

"Me too," he gritted out, his hips rising and falling with every thrust of Rayna's hips. "Faster, baby."

She did what he asked, her hips working furiously and her beautiful breasts bouncing.

"Oh God, Isaac, ohhhh…" Her breath rushed out of her as her body tensed and her pussy clamped down around his dick. He rubbed her clit hard as she cried his name again, and her body shook wildly.

"Fuuuck," he groaned, pumping himself into her clenching pussy over and over again until the pleasure consumed him. He yanked her down against him, holding her tight as her pussy milked every drop of seed from his willing body.

She relaxed against him, her face buried in his throat as his body shook lightly beneath hers. He sucked in a breath, closing his eyes and threading his fingers through Rayna's damp hair as their bodies came down from the high.

Nearly five minutes passed before he said, "I don't want you to date Rupert."

She sat up and slid off him, sitting naked on the bed beside him as a grin crossed her face. "Lucas told me you have a no personal talk rule with your employees. You should reconsider that."

"Why?"

"Because then you'd know that Rupert isn't single."

He ignored his immediate relief. "He has a girlfriend?"

"A boyfriend," she said.

"He was checking out your body," Stark said.

She shrugged. "Maybe he's bi. Either way, he's not single."

"How do you know?"

"Because pretty shortly into my flirting with him at the gym, he told me all about his boyfriend," she said.

He sat up and gave her a mock scowl. "You could have told me that earlier."

"I could have," she said with a soft giggle. "But I was enjoying your jealousy a little too much."

God, he loved how blunt she was. "You were jealous, too."

She shrugged before sliding off the bed and snagging her t-shirt off the floor. She slipped into it. "Phoebe was my childhood bully. Hell, she's still a bully, and she doesn't deserve anything as nice as riding your magnificent dick."

"Magnificent, huh?" he said with a grin.

"Oh God, now your ego is going to trap you in my bedroom."

He laughed, and there were a few seconds of awkward silence before she glanced at the doorway. "So, this was a lot of fun, but you should probably go before we ruin it with a fight or something."

It took him a minute to realize the hurt he felt was because he wanted to stay. He wanted to sleep in Rayna's bed with her soft body against his and wake up to her gorgeous face.

He shoved those dangerous thoughts out of his head before they could take root. He planted an easygoing grin on his face and slid out of her bed. "Good point."

He dressed quickly and patted Bea when he walked out of Rayna's bedroom to find the beagle sitting at the top of the stairs. They walked silently down the stairs, and he studied the security system control panel on the wall beside the door.

"Installation went smoothly?" he asked.

"Yes," she said before hesitating. "Thank you for doing

that. I appreciate it, but I also think I should pay you back for it. If you're willing to do a payment plan, then I could -"

"No," he said. "Consider it a gift."

She chewed on her bottom lip but then nodded. "All right. Thank you."

"You're welcome." He opened the front door, glancing at the control panel again. Despite knowing Rayna didn't need the reminder, he said, "Don't forget to set the alarm."

"I won't," she said. "Good night, Stark."

"Good night, Rayna."

CHAPTER 35

S tark glanced out the den window before pulling up
Rayna's name in his messages. He hesitated, staring at
the warm light spilling from her windows. It was Friday
night, and he hadn't seen or talked to Rayna since Tuesday
night.

Hell, this was the first time he'd seen her vehicle in the
driveway since Wednesday morning. It didn't seem to matter
how often he checked to see if she was home, her house
stayed dark, and her driveway remained empty. If it weren't
for the fresh tire tracks in the snow leading out of her
driveway every morning, he would have assumed she hadn't
been home at all.

Worry gnawed at his insides. Was she avoiding him
again? And if so, why?

*Oh, I don't know. Maybe because you're not friends. She knows
you want her house. Why should she have anything to do with you
beyond scratching an occasional itch?*

His inner voice was right, but it didn't stop him from
sending a text to Rayna.

STARK

Hey. I'm a little worried about one of Molly's babies. Its eye is a bit squinty. Can you come over and take a look at it?

He stared out the den window again as if he might actually see Rayna responding to his text. When five minutes passed, and there was no reply, he made himself return to the kitchen. He hadn't eaten yet, but any appetite he'd felt earlier had disappeared with Rayna's lack of response to his text.

It's been five minutes, asshole. Chill out. Besides, what will you do if she does come over? There's nothing wrong with that baby's eye, and you know it. You're straight up lying because you're that desperate to be laid.

So what if he was a little desperate? Could you blame him? He and Rayna had insane chemistry, and their no-strings-attached sex was precisely what he liked.

It used to be.

He ignored his inner voice and opened the fridge to study its meager contents. He wasn't much of a cook and often ordered in, but even that didn't appeal to him at the moment. His phone buzzed, and he yanked it out of his pocket, scanning the screen eagerly.

RAYNA

Sure. Give me five minutes.

He managed not to fist pump the air in triumph but couldn't stop the grin from breaking out on his face. He quickly brushed his teeth before changing into one of his tighter t-shirts that highlighted his dedication to exercise. He caught a glimpse of himself in the mirror as his doorbell rang, and he was slightly embarrassed by the little boy's look of eagerness on his face.

Telling himself to rein it the fuck in, he opened the front door. "Hey, come in."

It was bitterly cold tonight, and Rayna wore a thick winter jacket with the hood up. She removed her boots and pushed the hood back, and his smile faded.

"What's wrong?"

She unzipped her jacket, shrugged it off, and hung it on the coat tree. "Nothing's wrong."

"Something's wrong," he said. "You look exhausted and worried."

"Aren't you the charmer," she said, but it wasn't accompanied by her usual eye roll, as if she didn't even have the energy to be annoyed.

She pushed past him, and he followed her to his bedroom, worry eating at his stomach. She'd obviously just gotten out of the shower. Her wet hair was in a messy bun, and she wasn't wearing a bra under her t-shirt. But his usual erection at even the thought of Rayna braless wasn't happening, his lust buried under a thick layer of concern. What had happened the last few days?

A sudden thought struck him as they entered his bedroom. "Is it Louis?"

She paused by the bed as Molly hopped out of the plastic container with a happy chirp. "What?"

"Are you upset because of Louis? Did he do something or say something? Did he show up on your property again?"

"No," she said. "He hasn't been around since I took out the restraining order on him."

She petted Molly, giving her a few chin scratches. "Hi, sweet girl. You're looking so good."

Molly rubbed up against her as Rayna studied the babies. "Which one has the squinty eye?"

"Oh, uh, the grey tabby," he lied.

She scooped up the baby, a soft smile crossing her face as she glanced down at Molly. "They're getting so big. Good job, Mama."

"She's a great mom," Stark said.

"She is," Rayna said as she carefully examined the baby's face.

He tried to keep his face neutral as she gently ran her finger over the baby's head. "Which eye was it?"

"The right," he said.

She brought the baby up to her face, holding it closer to the light and doing another careful examination. "It looks fine to me now." She flipped the baby over and checked his bottom. "He's a boy." She studied his face a third time. "His eye isn't red, there isn't any discharge, and he isn't squinting now."

"Oh, okay, well, that's good, then," he said.

She nodded and put the baby back before taking the other two out and giving them a quick look over. "Both boys and they're looking great."

She petted all three a final time before giving Molly a few more pets. "If you want to name the babies, feel free. Just let me know what their names are so we can add them to the foster database."

"Sure," he said. "Will you tell me what's wrong?"

"It's all good," she said. "But I do have a busy night, so I need to get back to my place."

He caught her arm as she walked past him and drew her closer before sliding his arm around her waist. "Please tell me what's wrong, Rayna."

She sighed. "Honestly, there isn't anything wrong. I've just had a crazy few days."

"What's going on?" he asked.

"Wednesday afternoon, Deputy Ian did a welfare check on an elderly woman. The neighbours hadn't seen her in a couple of days, and her dogs were barking nonstop."

"Uh oh," Stark said.

"She's okay," Rayna said. "Well, she fell and broke her hip, but she's in the hospital and doing well. However, when Ian went into the house, he discovered she had a lot of dogs."

"How many?" Stark asked.

"Twenty-seven," she said.

"Holy shit."

"Yeah. They're all Shih-tzu crosses, and all of them have matted fur and overgrown nails, and a bunch of them have eye infections. The house smelled terrible." Rayna shuddered in his arms. "Urine and feces were ankle deep on the floor."

"That's awful," he said.

"It really is," she said. "The poor woman was honestly trying her best with the dogs, but she got overwhelmed, and it devolved into a hoarding problem."

He rubbed her lower back as she sighed. "For the last few days, I've been working on getting the dogs examined by a vet, having the more severely matted ones groomed, and trying to find a place for them to go. The woman has agreed to surrender all of the dogs, but Little Whiskers doesn't have the financial capacity or the number of fosters needed to help all of them."

"Where are they now?" he asked.

"Still at the house," she said, her face twisting. "I feel terrible about that, but we don't have anywhere else for them to go currently. Myself and other volunteers go to the house every few hours to take them outside and check on them, but it's still a pretty awful environment for them."

She hesitated before resting her forehead on his chest. He continued to rub her back, and they stood in silence, the only sound in the room the rasp of Molly's tongue as she groomed her babies.

When Rayna slid her arms around his waist and let her whole body lean against him, warmth flooded his chest. He hated that she'd had such a terrible few days but loved that she was seeking comfort from him.

Her voice muffled, Rayna said, "Between my regular job, the normal rescue stuff I take care of, and trying to help these dogs, it's been a really long fucking week."

"What can I do to help?" he asked. "I could keep a couple of the dogs here if that helps."

She lifted her head to smile at him. "I appreciate the offer, but I've found a rescue that's willing to take all of the dogs."

"That's great," he said.

"It is, but the rescue is in New York, which means I need to find a way to get the dogs to them," she said. "Between myself and two other volunteers, we can drive all of the dogs to New Cassel this weekend, but getting them from New Cassel to New York isn't as easy. I've already talked to my boss and am taking vacation days on Monday and Tuesday, but my driver volunteers only have Sunday to help, and that isn't enough time to drive all of the dogs to New York and return home."

She leaned her head against his chest again, and he kneaded the back of her neck. She made a soft groan of relief. "That feels good. Thank you."

"You're welcome."

"Sorry to dump all of this on you," she said.

"It's fine."

Her stomach growled loudly, and she grimaced.

"When did you eat last?" he asked.

"I had some toast for breakfast." She pushed away from him, and he was surprised by his intense desire to pull her back into his arms immediately.

"I need to go." She glanced at her watch. "I have a few different people in the rescue community that I can contact who might be able to help arrange a dog transport train to New York. But it's a huge coordination effort, and the rescue in New York wants them there by Tuesday at the latest. Otherwise, they won't be able to help."

"Why not?" he asked.

She rubbed her forehead, another look of weariness crossing her face. "I have no idea, and I didn't ask. I lucked out that they'll even take the dogs, and I don't want to do anything to annoy them."

She turned to leave, and he caught her hand. "I haven't eaten dinner either. Why don't you relax on the couch, and I'll order us something?"

"That's okay," she said. "I'll grab some cereal at home."

He frowned. "That isn't enough, Rayna."

She just shrugged, and he said, "You have to eat."

"I know," she said, with another glance at her watch, "but I also really need to get this dog train thing sorted out, and I don't have time to sit and wait for food to arrive. I'm not trying to be rude, I swear, but I just… I have a lot to do."

"All right," he said. "We'll go to your house. I'll order the food, and you can work while we wait for it to arrive."

"I don't have time to," she hesitated, soft pink rising in her cheeks, "socialize tonight."

"I know," he said. "I have some work to do as well."

She chewed at her bottom lip as he waited with more anxiety than he should have felt for her to say yes. His need to spend time with her tonight, even if they weren't having sex, had become a bright flame impossible to ignore.

"Okay," she said before giving him a faint smile. "It'll be nice to have some company while I beg strangers for help."

"Let's go then," he said and held out his hand.

She stared at it for a moment before sliding her hand into his. Still holding hands, they left his bedroom.

"DON'T YOU DARE QUIT ON ME, YOU BASTARD." RAYNA LIFTED her laptop and smacked the bottom of it with her hand.

Instead of stopping, the laptop's whirring and groaning sounds grew steadily louder.

"No, no, no," she chanted before whacking it again. The screen flickered rapidly and then turned black, accompanied by a rapid popping sound, and the smell of fried electrical circuits drifted out of it.

"Are you fucking kidding me?" Rayna dropped her dead laptop on the table, blinking back the hot tears. She rarely cried, but the frustration and exhaustion had her emotions on edge.

"What's wrong?" Stark walked into the kitchen, tucking his phone into his pocket as his nose wrinkled. "Why does something smell like it's burning?"

"My stupid laptop just died." Rayna bit the inside of her cheek, willing herself not to cry.

"I'm not surprised," Stark said, examining the laptop. "This thing looks older than me."

Rayna stared at Bea, who was asleep on her bed in the kitchen. Her frustration was overwhelming. A tear escaped, and she quickly brushed it away, but it wasn't fast enough to hide from Stark.

"Shit," Stark said, crouching in front of her. He wiped away the second tear sliding down her cheek with his thumb. "Baby, don't cry."

"I'm not crying," Rayna said. "My eyes are aggressively watering."

He laughed and sat in a chair before pulling her into his lap. "Come here."

She sat in his lap and put her arms around his shoulders before burying her face in his throat. She took a few deep breaths as Stark rubbed her back with his big, warm hand. He'd been unbelievably sweet to her all evening, ordering in from her favourite restaurant, cleaning up after they ate, and even feeding Bea and letting her out into the backyard a few times.

Bea had spent more time alone this week than she should have, and she'd spent most of the evening sitting on Stark's feet every time he stopped moving and whining for him to pet her. He'd been patient and gentle with her, giving her lots of attention while Rayna worked to find transport.

Speaking of which… she made herself sit up. As much as she wanted to sit in Stark's lap all night - forget that, what she really wanted was to take him to her bed - she couldn't use orgasms as a procrastination tool. Not when she had twenty-seven dogs waiting for her to save them.

Are you sure we couldn't just get one from him? It's a great stress buster, right?

She sighed inwardly, wishing she could give in to what she wanted, but she was rapidly running out of time to get the dogs to New York. And with her laptop dead, that left her with just her phone to make arrangements and holy shit, that was about to be a right pain in her ass.

She tried to slide off Stark's lap, staring at him when he tightened his hold around her waist. "I have to get back to work. I'm still waiting to hear back from three different people about possibly transporting from New Cassel to New York, and I haven't gotten a solid yes from a single person, which means -"

"I've arranged to get the dogs from New Cassel to New York on Sunday afternoon," he said.

She stared at him. "I'm sorry, what?"

He kissed her upper chest. "I've booked a private plane to fly the dogs to New York. We need to have them at the airport in New Cassel by eleven am on Sunday morning."

Her jaw dropped. "You booked a private plane?"

He nodded. "Yes. Sorry it took so long to get it done. Andrew wasn't replying to my texts."

"I… who's Andrew?" She sounded like a rhino had knocked her over.

"He owns the company I use to charter private flights," Stark said. "The office is closed for the night, so I texted him directly. He was at dinner with his family, so it took him a while to get back to me. But the flight is booked and confirmed, so you can go ahead and contact the New York rescue."

She stared silently at him, and when he leaned forward and pressed a gentle kiss on her chest again, she said, "Isaac, you seriously booked a private plane?"

"I did," he said.

"They're not going to let you bring twenty-seven dogs onto a private plane," she said.

"Baby, I'm rich. They let me do whatever the fuck I want," he laughed.

"I can't… I mean, that's amazing, but there's no way the rescue can afford a private plane to fly these dogs," she said.

"The rescue isn't paying for it. I am," he said.

"Isaac, that is so incredibly generous of you, but I can't -"

"You can and you will," he said firmly. "I want to do this, Rayna. It's my gift to you."

"I think I'm kind of terrible at graciously accepting gifts," she said.

He laughed and squeezed her hip. "You're welcome?"

Confident she was about to start crying again, Rayna hugged Stark hard. "Thank you, Isaac. Truly. This is the nicest thing anyone's ever done for me, and I don't know how I'll return the favour, but I -"

"It's a gift," he said. "You aren't supposed to return the favour."

She cupped his face and kissed him, slipping her tongue into his mouth when his lips parted. He pulled back and grinned at her. "Unless you want me to carry you to your bedroom like a caveman, you need to stop kissing me like that and call the New York rescue."

She pressed another quick kiss against his lips before sliding off his lap and grabbing her phone. Stark leaned down to pet Bea, who had woken up and left her bed to sit on his feet again.

She watched him stroke Bea's ears with infinite gentleness as the old dog panted happily. Warmth bloomed in her chest, and she clutched her phone tightly. She was feeling something for Stark that she had no right to feel, and she quickly left the kitchen before Stark saw those emotions on her face.

She stared at herself in the mirror in the hallway before taking a deep breath and blowing it out in a hard rush.

"It's fine," she muttered to her reflection. "Everything's fine. You're just feeling overwhelmed by and grateful for Stark's generosity."

Her face didn't look like it believed her, but she took another deep breath and said softly, "You are not falling in love with Isaac Stark."

CHAPTER 36

"Isaac?"

"One second." Stark was texting on his phone when Rayna joined him in the living room. He was sitting on her lumpy couch, with Bea practically sleeping in his lap. Dog hair covered his pants, as well as a healthy amount of Bea drool.

Freddie twined around Rayna's ankles, and she bent to pet him, grimacing when he gave her a bite for her effort. "C'mon, Freddie, don't be a dick. This is why you're never getting adopted."

"He's a foster?" Stark stuck his phone into his pocket before petting Bea. "I thought he was your cat."

"No, he's a foster," she said as Freddie glared at both of them before stalking out of the room with his tail swishing. "But he has trust issues and likes to bite, so it's not easy to find the right home for him. He was adopted out once, but she brought him back after only a few days."

"Because he bit her?"

"Yes, and because he stalked and terrorized her niece who

was visiting. He kept pouncing on the poor kid every time she even looked at him."

Stark laughed, and Rayna couldn't help but grin even though she said, "It's not funny."

"It's kind of funny," Stark said.

"Yes, well, I'm holding out hope that there is the perfect home for him out there, but it'll need to be one without kids."

"Everything arranged with the New York rescue?" Stark gave Bea a gentle push to get her off his lap before standing. She snorted her displeasure but stretched out in the warm spot he'd left behind, her soft snores starting up almost immediately.

"Yes," she said. "They'll have volunteers at the airport waiting for us when we arrive."

"That's great." He stood awkwardly in the middle of the room for a moment before glancing at his watch. "It's getting late. I should probably go so you can get some sleep."

Rayna slipped her arms around his waist when he started past her. She pressed a kiss against his mouth. "Don't leave."

"You're tired."

"Not that tired." She kissed her way up his throat before licking the curve of his ear.

He hesitated, and feeling a little desperate, she kissed him again, licking and nibbling at his lips until he parted them. She slipped her tongue into his mouth and slid her hands up his shirt. She traced the hard muscles of his stomach before rubbing her thumb over one flat nipple.

He groaned into her mouth, his hands sliding around her to cup her ass and squeeze tight. His erection pressed against her stomach, and she rubbed against it before nipping at his jaw. "Bedroom now, Isaac."

"Yes, Rayna," he said with a cute grin.

Leaving Bea sleeping on the couch, they went to her bedroom. Rayna pulled impatiently at Stark's shirt the moment they were in the room. He lifted his arms, and she peeled it off him. She stared appreciatively at his upper chest before tracing his six-pack with her fingertips.

They kissed each other with greedy need as she unbuttoned his pants, and he cupped her ass again, kneading it firmly. He groaned into her mouth when she slid her hand inside his briefs and gripped his cock. His head fell back, and his fingers dug into her ass. She rubbed his dick with long, slow strokes, delighted by the low moans and gasps he made.

She kissed his throat again, soft lingering ones against his warm skin. Warmth and desire bloomed in her belly, and while it was as intense as it always was, it felt different... sweeter.

It took her a moment to realize why it felt so different. It was the first time she was taking Isaac to bed without being irritated or, hell, downright furious with him. She paused in kissing his throat. This wasn't a hate fuck with her enemy. This was...

No. Stop it. You are not falling in love with him, Rayna. This is about thanking him for everything he did for you tonight. So get on those fucking knees and suck his dick until he can't think straight. The man deserves the best blowjob of his life.

"Baby?" Isaac's hand cupped the back of her skull, tugging lightly until she looked up at him. "You okay?"

She nodded, refusing to acknowledge that Isaac calling her 'baby' suddenly somehow felt more intimate. It didn't mean anything. He called her baby when they were hate fucking.

True, but you thinking of him as Isaac instead of Stark is a new thing, isn't it?

She groaned inwardly as Isaac - *goddammit, Stark!* - gave her a look of concern. "We can stop if you're not into it anymore."

She pushed every single confusing feeling deep down,

refusing to let them into the light. Now was not the time to analyze what the fuck was happening in her brain.

She gave him a teasing smile and rubbed her thumb over the head of his cock. He moaned, and her grin widened. "Not a chance, Stark. I want your gorgeous dick in my mouth, and you're not allowed to leave until it happens. Lose the pants."

She stepped back and stripped off her clothes as Stark finished undressing. When she stood naked before him, he looked her up and down, and she loved the hot lust that covered his features.

They kissed again, his warm hand cupping her breast and teasing her nipple into an aching hardness. She started to kneel in front of him and twitched in surprise when he hauled her to her feet and backed her toward the bed.

"What - oh shit!" She squealed when he lifted her abruptly and tossed her onto the bed. She stared wide eyed at him as he gazed hungrily at her pussy.

"Hey," she sat up, "lie on your back and -"

"No," he said before pushing her to her back again and leaning over and kissing just above her navel. "Open for me, Rayna."

"Isaac," she gripped his head and made him look at her, "I want to go down on you."

"Later," he said. "I need to taste your pussy."

"I'm into that, but I want to make tonight about you," she said.

He shook free of her grip, squeezing one thigh with his hand. "Not this time. Open for me."

"Okay, here's the thing... I'm still only partially waxed."

"I'm aware," he said.

"Right, but it's one thing to have you touching me or fucking me while my pussy looks like a half-bald cat, but another to have you face to face with it. Forgetting it looks like a hot mess, I'm thinking of your poor tongue and the work he'll have to do just to find my clit. There's a real can't see the forest because of the trees situation happening down there."

He laughed so hard that the bed shook. She sat up again, cupping his face and giving him an earnest look. "I promise you can go down on me another time, okay? I'll wax tomorrow and -"

"Oh God," he said, "you and your horrifying inability to wield a wax strip are not going anywhere near my pussy."

"Your pussy?"

"Yes, mine," he said unapologetically. "I won't allow you to torture her again, not when I'm perfectly capable of waxing her."

Now, it was her turn to laugh. "You're going to wax my muff?"

"I am," he said. "But not tonight. Tonight, I'm going to eat your pussy until you come on my face."

"Isaac," she said.

He pressed her onto her back again and dipped his head, sucking one nipple into his hot mouth. She arched, her hands clutching at his head as he teased both nipples with soft sucks and licks until she couldn't remember what they were even arguing about. He kissed along the underside of one breast before giving it a light nip.

"Open for me, baby."

She spread her legs, and he smiled with satisfaction before kissing down her body, stopping to trace her navel with his tongue and nibble at each hip before settling on his stomach between her legs.

He studied her pussy, and self-doubt crept in. "Isaac, I don't think -"

"You don't need to think, baby. Not tonight. Just let me make you feel so fucking good."

His low rasp, or maybe it was the slick glide of his tongue

over her wet pussy lips, made any further protest die a quick death. She grabbed the sheets in tight fists as Isaac licked the two waxed spots. She gasped at the sensation, and he smiled up at her before rubbing his beard against the sensitive skin on her inner thighs, then used his thumbs to spread her pussy apart. Cool air washed over her throbbing clit, but it was immediately replaced by the soft wetness of Isaac's tongue.

She moaned loudly, her hips arching as Isaac licked her clit with flat strokes of his tongue.

"Oh God," she gasped.

"Such a pretty clit," he said before licking it again. "You taste so good, baby."

"Fuck," she muttered, her body twitching and jerking when Isaac investigated her entrance with his tongue. "Isaac, please."

He made a low chuckle and returned to her clit, licking and sucking until she was nearly mindless with pleasure, her hips rising and falling and her breath coming in short, harsh pants.

When he stopped, she immediately gripped his head, trying hard to press his face back into her pussy. "Don't stop!"

He kissed her thigh, his beard tickling and teasing. "Shh, baby, we have all night."

"Please," she pleaded, her body throbbing for the release she needed. "I can't... I need this. Please, Isaac."

He studied her, and she could have cried with relief when he said, "You have had a hard day."

"Very hard. Teasing me when I'm so stressed out isn't nice, right? So, you should probably be nice and make me come right now," she said.

He laughed, and she cried out when he slid one thick

finger into her aching pussy. "We both know I'm not nice, Rayna."

"You are. You're sooo nice. Everyone in the Falls talks about how nice you are," she babbled frantically.

He laughed again as he added a second finger and fucked her with his fingers. "You're adorable when you want to come."

"Isaac."

She would lose her fucking mind if she didn't come. She tried to push her hand past his head, and he growled before knocking her hand away. "Stop that, baby."

The throbbing and need were more than she could stand. "Please," she moaned. "Make me come, Isaac."

He kissed her thigh again before, sweet merciful Christ, licking her throbbing clit. His fingers still fucking her, he sucked hard on her clit, and she shrieked, her back bowing as her orgasm hurtled through her. She held his head, grinding her pussy against his mouth and fingers as the pleasure flowed through her entire body.

She finally collapsed against the bed, her hands falling limply to her sides. Stark gave her clit a final soft kiss before he sat up and wiped his face on the sheet. He knelt between her legs, patting her thighs. "Wider, baby."

She let her legs fall open wide, staring hazily at him as he guided his cock to her entrance. Before she could offer to blow him, he was sliding into her, his thick cock filling and stretching her in all the right ways.

"Ohhh," she moaned, gripping his arms when he propped himself up on his hands above her.

He kissed one diamond-hard nipple. "Okay?"

She nodded, shifting slightly and making them both gasp at the sensation.

"So tight," he groaned before making two hard thrusts. "I need to fuck you hard, baby. Are you good with that?"

"Yes." She squeezed his arms. "I can take whatever you give me, Isaac."

He moaned, and without another word, he thrust into her, fucking her hard, his powerful body moving fast and smooth above hers as she watched the desire and need flood his face. He stared at her breasts, and she cupped them, playing with her nipples and making him drive into her at a nearly frantic pace. The bedsprings squeaked loudly as the headboard banged against the wall, and she urged him on with soft cries.

He cried her name when she traced his chest and lightly pinched one flat nipple, his head falling back and his hips working furiously. He made one final thrust, his body going still as he said her name over and over, and hot warmth filled her pussy. She squeezed around him, making his body shudder wildly. When he finally collapsed against her body, she wrapped her limbs around him, kissing his shoulder repeatedly as he buried his face in her throat.

He rolled off her with a soft groan, tugging at her until she curled up on her side against him. She flung her thigh over his, pressing a kiss against his chest. "You okay?"

"Yeah," he said. "Other than coming so hard, my balls may be permanently empty."

She laughed. "I don't think that's a thing."

"I hope not," he said. "I want kids."

He paused for a beat. "How about you?"

"Yes," she said. "At least two. I hated being an only kid."

"Me too," he said.

Rayna tried to sit up, but Isaac's arm tightened around her. She kissed his chest. "I need to clean up before the ocean of cum you left in me turns the wet spot into an untenable situation."

He laughed and released her. She used the bathroom and couldn't deny the surge of happiness she felt when she returned to the bed and Isaac was still in it. She'd half-expected he would be dressed and on his way out the door.

She climbed into bed and curled up against him, slinging her arm around his waist and resting her head on his chest. He stroked her back, and they lay silently. She yawned and snuggled in closer. After the stress of the last few days and her epic orgasm, she was so tired she could no longer even try to stay awake.

"Rayna?" Isaac's voice was low.

"Hmm?"

"Should I go?"

She tightened her grip on him even as her body drifted closer to sleep. "I want you to stay. Will you?"

His body relaxed against hers, and he kissed her forehead. "Yes. I'll stay."

CHAPTER 37

S tark groaned, blinking blearily as the shrill ring of the phone permeated the room. He was the little spoon to Rayna's big spoon, and he patted her hand resting against his stomach. "Baby, your phone is ringing."

"Not mine," she mumbled before turning away from him and burying her head under the covers. He groaned and leaned out of the bed, snagging his pants from the floor and fumbling his phone out of his pocket.

He squinted at the screen and sighed loudly before hitting the answer button and collapsing on his back on the bed. "What?"

"Hello to you, too," Jasper said.

Anger washed over Stark just hearing his cousin's voice. He hadn't spoken to or seen Jasper since his cousin's disastrous date with Rayna. He rubbed a hand over his jaw. "It's seven o'clock on a Saturday morning. What the fuck do you want?"

Rayna rolled over at his tone, giving him a worried look. He shook his head, rubbing her smooth thigh as Jasper said, "It's your father."

"What about him?"

"I told you - he wants to meet with you," Jasper said. "In person. He's willing to come to Harmony Falls this week."

"And I told *you* that I won't meet with him. If my father wants to talk to me, he can call the office and book a phone meeting."

"You're being an asshole about this, Isaac."

"You're one to talk," Stark snapped.

"What's that supposed to mean?" Jasper asked.

"You know exactly what I'm talking about," Stark said. "You think I wouldn't find out what you did to her?"

"I didn't do jackshit to that bitch," Jasper said. "Whatever she told you is a fucking lie."

Stark glanced at Rayna. She sat up, the worry on her face returning.

Another surge of anger washed over him, deep enough to make him wish he could throttle Jasper through the phone. "Lose my fucking number, Jasper."

He ended the call before Jasper could reply, and Rayna immediately said, "I'm sorry."

He scrubbed his hand through his hair. "You didn't do anything wrong."

"You're fighting with your cousin because of me," she said.

He leaned over and pressed a hard kiss against her mouth. "I'm fighting with my cousin because of what he *did* to you. Big difference."

"How do you know what happened?"

He hesitated. "I overheard Emma telling Lucas about it at the office."

"Oh." She chewed at her bottom lip. "Isaac, I don't want you to destroy a family relationship because of me. It's no big deal and -"

"It is a big deal," he said fiercely. "What he said and what

312

he did to you was wrong, Rayna, and I don't care if he's my fucking cousin. I don't want someone like that in my life. Okay?"

"Okay," she said.

He sighed. "Shit. Sorry. I didn't mean to yell."

"I know." She studied him carefully. "It was you who paid off the rescue's bill to Harmony Falls Vet Clinic after Jasper demanded his donation be returned."

He looked away. "I don't know what you're talking about."

She cupped his face and turned him to face her, giving him a quick kiss before resting her forehead against his. "Thank you, Isaac."

He rubbed her quilt-covered thigh. "Sorry to wake you so early."

"It's fine," she said. "I have to be at the house of horrors at eight thirty to check on the dogs anyway."

She leaned back and took his hand. "Do you want to talk about it?"

"About what?" he asked.

"About why you don't want to meet with your father."

He swallowed hard, his stomach churning acid until he tasted bile in the back of his throat. "Not really."

"Okay," she said, raising his hand to her mouth and kissing his knuckles. "But I'm happy to listen if you change your mind."

He opened his mouth to say there was nothing to talk about and instead said, "He wants to meet with me and just expects me to do it, like he hasn't ignored me for the last fucking eight years."

She scooted closer, her warm, firm body pressing against his as she took his hand. "Do you know why he wants to meet?"

"No, and I don't care. He'll want something from me, and I'm not interested in giving it to him, no matter what it is."

"What if it's your forgiveness he wants?" she asked.

"What do you mean?"

"What if he wants to say sorry for how he treated you?"

He laughed bitterly. "My father does not say sorry. Ever."

"People change," she said. "Eight years is a long time."

He thought it over, Rayna sitting quietly next to him as she let him work it out in his head. Finally, he shook his head. "No, that isn't it, Rayna. You don't know him like I do. Feeling remorse or guilt for something he's done is impossible for him. He's a narcissistic sociopath who is incapable of loving anyone, including me and my mother."

She squeezed his hand before resting her head against his shoulder. "I'm sorry, Isaac."

"I can't meet with him," he said, hating the slight waver in his voice. "I'll talk to him on the phone, but to see him, after everything he put my mom and me through… I just can't. When I told him I was starting my own company, do you know what he said to me?"

"What?" she asked gently.

"He told me that I would fail. That I was a stupid, naive idiot who didn't have a clue about running a business or how to succeed. He said if I left, he'd disown me as a son because it would be too embarrassing to have people know I was his son when I failed."

"Wow. I hate him," she said.

He studied her, his voice hoarse when he said, "Me too."

She kissed him, resting her forehead against his again. "It's okay that you do, honey."

"Is it?" he asked.

She nodded. "Yes. Take it from someone who has a lot of parental trauma - your feelings are valid and absolutely normal. Why did you move to Harmony Falls? Was it to get away from your father?"

"No, it was easy enough to avoid him in New Cassel once

I was an adult. I spent a few summers in Harmony Falls as a kid. My maternal grandparents had a cabin here, and my mother would send me to live with them during summer holidays."

He stared off into space. "It was one of the best times of my life. I missed my mother, but not being around my father, not listening to him tell me how every single thing I did was wrong... it was a fucking relief. I could be myself here. I could *breathe* here."

"I'm glad, honey," she said.

"Will you tell me about your parents?" he asked.

She hesitated. "I didn't bring them up to make this about me. I just wanted you to know that I understand and support you."

"I know," he said. "I'd still like you to tell me about them."

She sighed. "There isn't much to say. They were both raging alcoholics. My mother was mostly sober when I was in elementary school, but by the time I started high school, she was as addicted as my father. Neither of them could keep a job, and we spent most of my childhood being kicked out of rental after rental on the south side."

He squeezed her hand as Freddie jumped up on the bed and sat at the end of it, staring at them with his bright green eyes.

"There were plenty of times when I went hungry because they spent their money on booze instead of food."

He could feel useless anger filling him up and could hear it in his voice when he said, "Were they abusive?"

"Not physically or emotionally, but they were neglectful. I was six when they first left me alone to drink at the bars."

"Jesus Christ," he said, "why didn't anyone call Child Protective Services on them?"

"When I was younger, they were better at covering their alcoholism and acting normal around other adults. Eventually, however, their luck ran out. We'd been homeless off and on all growing up, but we'd always managed to at least stay in gross motels until my father and mother could earn enough money to rent another place. At least, that was the case until my last year of high school. The alcohol had a pretty strong hold over both of them at that point, and neither was capable of holding down a job. We got evicted from our rental, and there wasn't enough money for a motel. We had to live in the car."

"I'm so sorry, baby," he said.

"It was bad," she said. "I couldn't shower or wash my clothes, and we had barely any food. My dad worked part-time at a convenience store, but he and my mom used most of the money to buy more booze."

She studied their clasped hands. "I never found out who called Child Protective Services, but I suspect it was the guidance counselor, Mrs. Wilding."

"Why do you think it was her?" he asked.

"She was kind to me." She laughed a little bitterly. "That's understating it. She used to bring an extra lunch for me to school every day, and sometimes I'd find an envelope with twenty dollars in my locker that I'm pretty sure was from her. After they took me away from my parents, she…"

He rubbed his thumb soothingly on her hand. "She what?"

"I turned eighteen only a week after Child Protective Services took me, which meant I aged out of the foster system. So, I could either try my luck with the homeless shelter in Harmony Falls or live with my parents in their car again."

He put his arm around her and tucked her up against him. "That's not much of a choice."

"I decided the homeless shelter was the better option, but as soon as Emma's parents found out what was happening, they insisted I stay with them."

He kissed her forehead, and she snuggled in closer, resting one hand on his chest. "It was unbelievably kind of them, and I appreciated it so much, but they had a pretty small house, and I was basically sleeping on Emma's bedroom floor. I didn't care. It was way better than anything I'd had in a long time, but I worried that it would affect my friendship with Emma. She was - *is* - my best friend, and the thought of losing her..."

She swallowed hard, the bright shine of tears in her eyes, and he tugged her toward him. "Sit in my lap, baby."

She did what he asked with zero protest, resting her head on his chest as he rubbed her back with long, slow strokes.

"Mrs. Wilding came to Emma's house two days after they took me in. She offered to let me stay with her. She was widowed young, and her kids were grown, and she said I would be doing her a favour, that she was lonely living by herself. She had an extra bedroom I could use, and she wouldn't kick me out after graduation. I could stay with her for as long as I needed."

She sat up, a soft smile on her face as she stared at him. "She told me I would have to get used to the pets, though. She had four dogs and five cats, and she was forever finding stray animals to care for, she said."

He laughed. "So, that's why you went into the animal rescue business."

"It definitely played a part," Rayna said. "I had always loved animals and knew I wanted to be a vet from a pretty young age. I'd desperately wanted a pet as a kid but obviously never had one. My parents could barely afford to feed me. Mrs. Wilding's numerous pets made the idea of living with her more enticing, not less."

She toyed with his chest hair, her fingers moving restlessly against his skin. "I moved in with Mrs. Wilding, and I stayed with her after I graduated high school and went to trade school. I didn't move out until I got my first job. Who I am and what I have today are because of Mrs. Wilding. I owe her so much, and I will never be able to thank her enough."

"She sounds like an incredible person," he said.

"She is. She moved to Willington a few years ago. Her daughter married someone from Willington, and she'd just had a baby. Mrs. Wilding wanted to be closer to her and her grandchild."

"How often do you see her?" he asked.

"We have a monthly dinner," Rayna said. She looked around the room, her eyes going hazy with memories. "She was nearly as proud as I was when I bought this place. She bought a bottle of champagne, and on the day I took possession, she, Emma, and I drank champagne from plastic cups in the living room. It was one of the happiest days of my life."

She lapsed into silence, and they sat quietly. The only sound in the room was the soft rasp of his hand sliding up and down her back. She blinked rapidly, her gaze clearing before she smiled at him. "Anyway, now you know the sad details of my childhood, which I'm sure doesn't at all make you find me pathetic."

His hands slid to frame her face, his gaze true and steady. "It makes me believe you're one of the strongest people I know, Rayna Abrams."

"Isaac," she whispered.

He bent his head and kissed her, a gentle brush of his mouth against hers. She moaned and leaned into him, her body going soft against his, her tongue already seeking entrance inside his mouth. Before they could deepen the kiss, her phone alarm went off, a harsh bray that made them both jump.

She sighed before smiling at him. "Sorry, I need to go to the house of horrors to feed the dogs."

She slid out of the bed, giving him a look of surprise when he said, "I'll go with you."

"Trust me, you don't want to do that," she said. "The smell is horrendous. Also, I have, like, two hundred errands to run for the rescue today."

"I don't care," he said. "I'm going with you, Rayna."

Her smile turned warm and soft. "Thank you, Isaac."

CHAPTER 38

"Bea, I swear to God, if you don't stop farting in the kitchen, I'm banishing you from it for good." Stark glared at the beagle.

If her wagging tail was any indication, Bea didn't seem all that concerned by his threat. Or, more likely, she couldn't hear it. She let out another long braaaap before sitting and staring hopefully at him.

Waving his hand in front of his face to dispel the smell, Stark said, "You don't get a treat for farting, Bea."

She whined, and he sighed before opening the treat jar and taking out a treat. Bea's tail thumped happily, and Stark said, "To your bed, Bea."

She immediately jumped up and ran to her bed, moving pretty spryly for her age. He gave her the treat. "Funny how your hearing becomes remarkably better when there's a treat involved."

His phone buzzed, and he checked his text before heading toward the front door. Hollis had shown up earlier than expected. He opened the door, smiling at Hollis, who stood on Rayna's porch with a bag in one gloved hand. "Hi, Hollis. Come in."

"Hello, Mr. Stark." She joined him in the hallway, and he shut the door behind her.

She handed him the bag, and he said, "Thank you, Hollis. I appreciate you working on a Saturday. I thought I would have time myself, but the day's gotten away from me."

After he and Rayna had finished feeding the dogs, they'd gone to the gym for a workout before running the errands for the rescue.

"You're welcome," she said.

Although she had to have found it odd that he was in Rayna's house, she didn't mention it or ask any questions. He also knew she wouldn't say a word to anyone about him being here. Her refusal to speculate or participate in gossip was another quality he appreciated about his assistant.

Freddie walked into the hallway, his tail held high and the usual suspicious look on his face. To Stark's surprise, Hollis immediately crouched and held out her hand, making a soft clicking noise with her tongue. "Hi, kitty."

"He bites," Stark said quickly as Freddie stalked toward Hollis, no doubt thrilled at the chance to meet a new victim.

Freddie sniffed Hollis's fingers, and Stark's mouth dropped when he made a soft meow before rubbing against her hand. Hollis smiled and petted his body, her hand stroking his fluffy tail. "Oh, aren't you the cutest boy? Yes, you are."

"Holy shit," Stark said when with another meow, Freddie jumped into Hollis's arms. She straightened, holding him against her chest as Freddie butted his forehead against her chin.

"I wouldn't let him that close to your face," Stark warned. "Seriously, he bites."

"No, you don't, baby," Hollis cooed to Freddie. "A big handsome boy like you would never be a bad boy and bite, would you?"

A low rumbling filled the hallway, and it took Stark a minute to place it. Freddie was... purring?

"Oh, you are just the sweetest boy," Hollis said, her voice a soft, sweet pitch Stark had never even imagined she was capable of. "Don't listen to him saying you're a bad boy. You aren't. No, you are not, my big, handsome boy."

Freddie's purrs grew even louder, and he kneaded and headbutted Hollis repeatedly as Stark continued to stare at them. Had he fallen into some alternate universe? It was the only explanation for both Hollis and Freddie's behaviour.

"Isaac? I thought you were meeting me upstairs. I've been naked for nearly fifteen minutes, and my cooch is severely disappointed she's not being pounded by your lovely thick cock."

Rayna's hand slapped him hard on the ass, making him jump, and a high-pitched squeak escaped his lips.

Fuck. *Double fuck.*

Hollis's gaze landed on his. One perfect eyebrow rose a quarter of an inch, and her mouth twitched ever so slightly before her face returned to normal.

"Isaac?"

Please don't be naked. Please don't be naked.

He whirled around, ready to keep Rayna shoved behind his back if she was, in fact, naked. To his relief, she wore a long t-shirt, and while he had no doubt she was naked underneath it, at least she wasn't going full Monty in the hallway.

"Hey! What's wrong?" Rayna smiled at him. "Why haven't you come upstairs?"

"Um..."

She cocked her head. "Is that? Is Freddie purring?"

She peered around his broad body, and her face turned an astonishingly bright shade of red. "Well, shit."

She sighed, and he gave her major props for bravery when she straightened her shoulders and stepped around him. "Hello, Hollis."

"Hello, Rayna."

"I suppose it's too much to hope that you didn't hear what I said."

A rare smile crossed Hollis's face. "Would you like me to lie? Because I can if it'll make you feel better."

"Shit," Rayna said again before she stared at Freddie. "Wait, are you... is that Freddie?"

Stark couldn't help but laugh at the dumbfounded look that Rayna gave the cat in Hollis's arms. "Yes, that's Freddie."

"I don't believe it," she said. "Why hasn't he tried to bite off her face?"

"I don't know," Stark said as Hollis frowned at both of them.

"He's a sweet boy," she said.

"He's a demon," Rayna said.

Hollis's scowl deepened. "You shouldn't say mean things about your cat."

"Oh, he's not my cat," Rayna said. "He's a foster."

She glanced at Stark, her eyes lighting up with excitement before she turned back to Hollis. "He's available for adoption if you're interested. You can fill out an application on our website, and one of our volunteers will contact you to chat about Freddie."

"I can't believe no one has adopted this very handsome boy," Hollis said before rubbing her cheek against Freddie's. Rayna tensed. Hell, Stark did, too, but Freddie just purred loudly before licking her face.

"He shouldn't be in a home with kids, though. He stalks

and attacks them, so if you have children or are planning on having kids, Freddie isn't the right cat to adopt," Rayna said.

"That's okay, baby boy," Hollis said in that same sweet, coddling voice as she stroked gentle fingers over the scars on Freddie's face. "I don't like kids either. They're the worst."

Stark and Rayna watched in silence for at least another three minutes as Hollis and Freddie fell deeper in love. When she finally set him on the floor, brushing the cat fur from her jacket, Freddie made a sorrowful sounding meow before rubbing against Hollis's leg.

"Don't cry, baby boy. We'll see each other again soon," Hollis said.

She cleared her throat and gave Stark and Rayna a polite smile. "Rayna, nice to see you again. Mr. Stark, I'll see you on Monday."

"Thank you again, Hollis," Stark said.

She nodded, and with one last look at Freddie, she left, closing the door gently behind her. Freddie made another of those sad little meows, and Rayna bent to pet him.

"It's okay, buddy. She'll be - ouch! Goddammit, Freddie! Stop biting me."

Stark couldn't help but laugh as Freddie growled at Rayna before stalking past both of them with his tail flicking rapidly.

"Sorry about the whole pound me with your cock thing," Rayna said.

"It's fine."

"Is it?" she asked with worry in her voice.

He wrapped an arm around her and pulled her close. "Yes. Hollis won't say a word to anyone. I wouldn't have had her come to your house if she were a gossip. I'll admit, I didn't anticipate you asking to have your pretty pussy pounded in front of her, but that's the risk I take by being so good at fucking."

She snorted and pinched his butt before her brows creased. "Wait, why did you ask Hollis to come here?"

He held out the bag. "I needed her to buy something for me. I meant to do it myself but ran out of time."

"What is it?" she asked.

"Open it and find out," he said.

She took the bag from him, carrying it into the kitchen and setting it on the table before reaching inside. She brought out the laptop in its box, staring blankly at it. "A computer? Why did you need Hollis to buy you a laptop today?"

He grinned at her. "It's not for me. It's for you."

"What?" She stared at him in shock. "What do you mean it's for me?"

"Your laptop died, remember?" he said.

"I know, but..."

"What?" he asked.

"You've already done so much with paying off the vet clinic bill and hiring a freaking private plane tomorrow that -"

"I want to do this," he said, taking the laptop from her hands and setting it back on the table. He pulled her up against him. "You can't do your rescue work without a laptop, Rayna."

"I know, but I can look for a second-hand one when we return from New York."

"Now you don't have to," he said.

"Isaac, I..."

He nuzzled her throat. "I wouldn't do this if I didn't want to, all right?"

She nodded, and he pressed a kiss against her collarbone. She hugged him tight. "Thank you, Isaac."

"You're welcome, baby." He reached down and squeezed

her ass through her t-shirt. "Now, why don't we go upstairs, and I'll do something incredibly sexy to you."

"Why do I suspect your sexy and my sexy means something very different?" She stared down at her crotch. "Oh God, you're going to wax my muff."

He laughed and squeezed her ass again. "Yes, baby, I am."

"That is not sexy," she said sadly.

"If you're a good girl for your waxing, I'll make sure shower time afterward is ridiculously sexy," he said.

"You have yourself a deal, Mr. Stark."

RAYNA STARED AT THE DOZENS OF PET CARRIERS IN THE MAIN cabin of the very posh, very expensive looking private plane. A few of the dogs inside the carriers were whining or barking, but a surprising amount of them were lounging contently inside their carrier, gnawing happily on their chew stick.

"I can't believe they let us load the plane with twenty-seven dogs," she said in a hushed voice.

Stark grinned at her. "I told you, when you're rich, they let you do what you want."

"Apparently," she said before peering out the window of the plane. A flight attendant was waiting for them when they arrived at the plane, but the pilot and copilot hadn't arrived yet.

She studied the gray and cloudy skies. "I hope the weather holds out."

"It will," Stark said confidently. "There's supposed to be a big storm hitting New Cassel, but that won't happen until tomorrow morning. We'll be landed and back home in Harmony Falls by tonight."

The flight attendant joined them. "Mr. Stark, would you like something to drink?"

"Just water, thank you, Henry," Stark said.

"And yourself, Ms. Abrams?"

"Water is great. Thank you," she said.

"Of course. We'll also be serving snacks during the flight. A cheese and cracker plate with cheeses imported from France."

"Looking forward to it. Thank you, Henry," Stark said.

The man retreated to the back of the cabin, where a small kitchen was located, complete with better quality appliances than Rayna had in her kitchen.

"I've never had French cheese before," she whispered.

Stark bent and pressed a lingering kiss against her mouth. "You'll love it."

Someone cleared their throat behind them, and they turned to see a woman and a man, both wearing pilot uniforms, standing in front of the cockpit. The man nodded to Stark before slipping inside the cockpit, but the woman stayed where she was, her green eyes assessing Stark coolly.

Stark's body stiff, he said, "Captain Malek, nice of you to finally join us."

Rayna gasped, her eyes flying wide as the woman's gaze turned frosty. "Stark. There's a line, and you're grazing it."

They stared each other down. Rayna immediately had visions of her, Stark, and twenty-seven dogs being left on the tarmac. She was trying her best not to hyperventilate when a smile cracked the pilot's face. Stark began to chuckle, and Rayna watched in astonishment as he and the pilot embraced.

"It's good to see you again, Amanda," Stark said.

"You as well," she said.

Stark put his hand against Rayna's lower back and

ushered her forward. "Rayna Abrams, meet Captain Amanda Malek. She's an old friend from high school."

"It's nice to meet you, Captain," Rayna said.

"Please, call me Amanda." She peered past Stark, staring at the carriers. "So, you're a dog guy now, Stark? Because I heard a rumour that you have cats living at your house."

"You need to stop texting with my mother, Amanda," Stark said, but Rayna could hear the amusement in his voice.

"How else am I supposed to keep tabs on you?" she asked.

He rolled his eyes, and she grinned before glancing at her watch. "All right, let's get these dogs to New York."

She joined the copilot in the cockpit, and Stark and Rayna took their seats. She buckled her seat belt and placed the bottle of water Henry handed to her in the cup holder. Her nerves were singing high soprano, and she listened carefully as Henry went over the safety instructions. He finished and took his seat at the front of the plane as the engines began to power up. She stared out the window, anticipation and nerves swirling in her belly.

"You okay?" Stark took her hand and squeezed it gently.

"Yes." She fidgeted in her seat before blurting, "This is my first plane ride."

He blinked at her. "Seriously?"

"Yes. I'm, um, a little nervous."

"There's nothing to be nervous about," he said. "Amanda is a top-notch pilot." He paused. "You've really never been on a plane before?"

"You and I live very different lives," she said with a shrug. "I've never even left the state. I've always wanted to go to Paris, but any money I save up inevitably gets used for the rescue."

She paused. "That doesn't bother me. I hope it doesn't sound like I'm resentful because I'm not. The rescue means a lot to me."

"I know," he said. "You don't sound resentful. But you do deserve a vacation."

"Right?" she said with a grin. "Like, sooo deserve one. Someday, I'll do it. I'll go to Paris and sit at a fancy cafe's outdoor patio, drinking coffee and eating delicious pastries while I people watch."

She smiled at him, her breath catching in her throat when Stark leaned in and pressed a gentle kiss against her mouth. "That sounds perfect, Rayna."

CHAPTER 39

Rayna slid behind the wheel of her SUV as Stark climbed into the passenger side. She started the vehicle, turning the heat to high and rubbing her hands together to warm them.

"You okay?" Stark asked.

She grinned at him. "Am I okay? We rescued twenty-seven dogs today, and I had my first plane ride. I'm fantastic!"

He laughed. "That's true, but the return flight had a lot of turbulence. That can be scary if you haven't taken a lot of flights before."

"I was a little nervous but not terrified or anything. I appreciate you letting me hold your hand the entire time, though," Rayna said with a small smile, trying to ignore the warmth she felt from his concern.

He doesn't mean it. He's being this way because he wants your house.

She stared out the windshield at the gray sky. She needed to remember that fact, needed to *believe* it, but it was increasingly difficult. Isaac made it difficult with his sweetness.

She nearly snorted out loud. Who would have thought she'd ever describe Isaac Stark as sweet?

How long will you keep doing this, Rayna? There isn't a future for the two of you. You're already halfway to being in love with the guy trying to take your house from you. Do you know how stupid you're being?

She ignored her inner voice. Not that it wasn't making good points, but now wasn't the time. It'd been a long and stressful day, and she still had to make the drive from New Cassel to Harmony Falls.

Will you invite Isaac to stay the night? Let him sleep in your bed again?

"Rayna?"

"Yeah?"

"What's wrong?" Stark's hand covered hers, and when he linked their fingers together, she had to bite down on her inner cheek to stop herself from blurting out that she might be falling in love with him.

"Nothing," she said. "Just lost in my thoughts for a minute."

He studied her, and she looked away, thankful when the ring of his phone broke the thick silence. He checked his phone. "It's my mom. She's video calling me."

"I can leave the car and give you some privacy." Rayna reached for the door handle, but Stark squeezed her hand and shook his head.

"It's fine." He hit the answer button, and a silver-haired woman with pretty blue eyes smiled at him.

"Hi, Mom."

"Hello, darling boy. How are you?"

"Good. How are you? Is something wrong?"

"Nothing's wrong. What are you up to today?"

"Uh, not much," Stark hedged, glancing at Rayna. "Just usual boring weekend stuff. Running a few errands."

"Boring weekend stuff," his mother repeated. "That sounds delightful."

Stark sighed. "You know I'm here."

His mother laughed. "Darling, of course I know you're here."

"You need to stop texting with Amanda."

"Never. You know I adore her. Now, I assume you're still at the airport? Amanda said you'd just landed."

"I am," Stark said.

"Perfect. Dinner is in an hour, and with traffic, you'll make it just in time."

"Mom, I can't stop in for a visit this trip," Stark said with another glance at Rayna.

"Of course you can," his mother said.

"I'm not alone," Stark said. "But I'll drive up next weekend and spend all of Sunday with you."

"Doesn't work for me, darling. Next weekend I'm going skiing. And I know you're not alone. You have your neighbour, Rayna, with you."

"I do, so -"

"Although Amanda seemed to be under the impression she was your girlfriend," his mother carried on relentlessly. "She told me she saw you kissing her."

"Oh my God," Stark said as his cheeks went red. "Mom, gossiping with Amanda is not -"

"It's not gossip if it's true," his mother said cheerfully.

"She's not my girlfriend," Stark said.

"Well, I would love to meet the girl you're currently kissing."

"*Mom*," Stark said.

"Did you or did you not kiss her on the plane, Isaac?"

Stark sighed in defeat. "Yes, I kissed her."

"Then, until you introduce me to her, my nickname stands. If you don't want me referring to her as 'the girl my son is currently kissing' to everyone at poker night, you'd better bring her for dinner."

Rayna clapped her hand over her mouth to hold back her laughter. Any exhaustion or desire to be home had disappeared, and she was dying to meet Stark's mother.

Rayna could almost see the flash of inspiration on Stark's face when he said, "We really need to get home. Rayna has an elderly beagle who can't be left alone for that long, and I have Molly and the babies, so -"

"Did you forget that Emma said she would check on both Bea and Molly and the babies? We have time for dinner," Rayna said in an 'I'm so sweet, sugar wouldn't melt in my mouth' voice.

Stark gave her a 'what the fuck' look that made her clap her hand over her mouth to muffle another laugh.

"Perfect," his mother said triumphantly. "We'll see you soon, Isaac."

She ended the call before Stark could reply, and Rayna immediately burst into giggles. "Oh my God, the look on your face right now."

He shook his head, a smile toying at his lips. "I didn't expect this day to end with you and my mother teaming up on me."

"Poor Isaac," she said with a sarcastic pout.

He laughed and leaned over to kiss her pout away. "Are you sure you want to have dinner with her, Rayna? I appreciate you being accommodating, but Mom will understand if I tell her we're heading straight home."

"Are you kidding me? Your mom seems like a total hoot. I'm dying to meet her," she said.

"She's nothing like me," he warned. "She's nice."

The lightness in his voice had disappeared abruptly, and there was a vulnerability in his gaze that tore at her heart.

She cupped his face in her hands, smoothing his beard with her thumbs as she stared gravely at him. "You're nice, Isaac. No, scratch that... you're more than just nice. You're kind and generous, and you are one of the best people I know. Don't ever doubt that."

"Thank you," he said, his voice a little choked and emotional.

She brushed her mouth against his. "You're welcome. Now, take me to meet your mother."

———

"ARE YOU SURE YOU HAD ENOUGH TO EAT, RAYNA?" ISAAC'S mother handed her a cup of tea and then sat next to her on the couch.

"I did. It was delicious. Thank you so much, Mrs. Stark."

"Oh, darling, I told you, you must call me Angela," she said, settling into the sofa and smiling at Stark, who sat in an armchair across from them.

Rayna really didn't know what to expect when she parked in the driveway of Angela's mid-century modern home, located on the edge of downtown New Cassel. She had a sudden and unexpected bout of nerves as Isaac guided her into the house, his big hand on her lower back, but his mother was right there with a warm smile and hugs for both of them.

She had immediately felt at ease, and dinner had been a delicious chicken stew accompanied by homemade biscuits. She was fascinated by Isaac's close relationship with his mother and loved how kind and respectful they were to each other. They were fond of teasing each other, and Rayna had laughed more than once at their antics.

Angela had a knack for asking questions that didn't feel

nosy or intrusive, and Rayna found herself sharing more than she normally would with someone she'd just met. But Angela's friendly warmth made it easy to share.

"You have a beautiful home, Angela." Rayna sipped her tea as she studied the room. They had left the dining room for the comfort of the cozy family room. "I love your decorating style."

"Oh, you are so sweet," Angela said happily. "I am enjoying you so much more than the previous girlfriends Isaac has introduced me to."

"*Mom,*" Isaac said.

"Sorry, your lady friend who you are currently kissing," Angela said with a wicked grin, making Isaac sigh loudly.

Rayna couldn't help but laugh, and Angela smiled at her. "I'm serious, though, Rayna. The fact that you're actually interested in me and not just eyeing up every piece of art in my house and wondering how much you can sell it for when I kick the bucket is a relief."

"Mom," Isaac said. "Lilith was an art dealer. That's why she showed so much interest in your artwork."

"Oh, my sweet summer child," Angela said with a soft smile before turning to Rayna. "Isaac likes to think the best of people. It's one of his best qualities, and I do love that about him, but it can occasionally get him into trouble. Like with little Ms. - I love your artwork, remind me again how old you are, Mrs. Stark - Lilith."

"She was not waiting for you to die, Mom," Isaac said.

Angela stared at him with a raised eyebrow, and Isaac made a noise of defeat. "She wanted me to convince you to move into assisted living and give the artwork to me so she could sell it immediately."

Rayna's jaw dropped, but Angela burst into laughter. "I knew it!"

"In my defense," Isaac said to Rayna, "I broke up with her as soon as she said that."

"I was only fifty-five and in the middle of a resurgence of my bang everything that moves era that I so enjoyed in my early forties," Angela said. "I would never have agreed to move into an assisted living facility. The women outnumber the men in those places by a significant margin, and I'm only into men."

"Oh my God," Isaac said, his face turning red. "You're sharing too much, Mom."

"Am I sharing too much with you, Rayna?" Angela asked.

"Not with her, with *me*," Isaac said.

Rayna laughed again as Angela winked at Isaac. "Sorry, sweetheart."

A sudden gust of wind rattled the windows. With a frown, Isaac stood and crossed to the closest window, pulling up the heavy wooden blind that covered it. "Shit."

"What's wrong, dearest?" Angela asked.

"The storm hit early," he said.

Rayna and Angela joined him at the window, and Rayna stared in disbelief at Angela's small backyard. "Holy crap. How long has it been snowing?"

"At least a couple of hours," Isaac said as another blast of wind swayed the large pine tree at the back of the yard. "We need to go, Mom. I have a feeling it'll only get worse."

"Maybe you should stay in New Cassel for the evening," Angela said. "The roads will already be terrible, and it scares me to death to think of the two of you driving all the way to Harmony Falls in this."

Isaac glanced at Rayna. "We could stay at my place. It's only about a fifteen minute drive from here."

Rayna nodded. "I'd prefer that to driving home in this."

"Perfect," Angela said with a relieved smile. "I'll pack up a few breakfast items for you before you go. I'm quite certain you don't have any fresh food at the house and with how terrible this storm is, I don't want you going out at all if I can help it."

"Thanks, Mom," Isaac said.

Angela reached up to pat his cheek gently. "You're welcome, my boy."

CHAPTER 40

"Did you talk to Emma?" Stark finished putting the last of the food in the fridge.

Rayna joined him in the kitchen and tucked her phone into her pocket. "I did. It was perfect timing, actually. She and Lucas were just finishing checking on Molly and the babies, and she said she'd take Bea back to her house for the night."

"Okay," he said.

"Molly is fine," Rayna said. "She was all over Lucas while Emma fed her and scooped her litter box. They spent about half an hour with her and the babies."

"Okay, good," Stark said.

"Why are you acting like you already know this?" Rayna asked.

"I'm not. How would I know that?" He cleared his throat and refused to meet her gaze.

"Spill it, Stark," she said, giving him a light poke in the stomach.

His cheeks hot, he said, "I installed a pet camera in the

bedroom so I can check on Molly and the babies when I'm not there. I checked on her when we first got here and saw Emma and Lucas with her."

He waited for her to tease him, but she gave him a sweet smile. "That's adorable. I love that you did that."

His embarrassment faded, and he leaned against the counter. "Are you hungry? Mom also sent some 'midnight snacks,' as she called them."

Rayna laughed. "I'm not hungry, but are we allowed to have midnight snacks if it's only nine o'clock?"

"Maybe not." He pulled her against him, resting his hands on her hips. It was a little ridiculous how difficult it had been not to touch her while they were at his mom's house. He'd come close to resting his hand on her leg during dinner more than once. Hell, twice, he'd almost leaned down to kiss her. When they'd moved to the family room, he'd deliberately chosen the armchair. His ability to resist touching her had worn away to non-existent by that point, and he didn't want to give his mother the wrong idea that he and Rayna were dating.

Too late for that, buddy.

Rayna traced light circles on his chest. "Where'd you go just now?"

"Just in my head," he said. "I feel bad that I got us stuck here in a snowstorm."

She studied the kitchen, which featured high-end appliances, modern teak cabinets, and sleek marble countertops. "Oh yes, because it's such an inconvenience to be trapped in your giant luxury penthouse. Remind me again, how many showerheads do you have in your shower?"

"Multiple," he said before squeezing her ass. "Interested in trying it out with me?"

She leaned forward and kissed a slow path up his neck. "I thought you'd never ask."

His cock already beginning to stiffen, Stark led her to his bedroom. Rayna studied the king size bed and the French doors leading to the balcony. She crossed the room to stare outside. "I bet when there isn't a blizzard, the view of the city is incredible."

"It is," he said, standing behind her and wrapping his arms around her waist. He kissed her neck as they stood silently and watched the snow fall as the wind howled. The sound would have been a lonely, desolate one if he hadn't had Rayna in his arms, weathering the storm with him.

Rayna made a startled 'eep' when the building noticeably swayed. She grabbed onto his arms, staring wide-eyed at him. "Shit. Did you feel that?"

"Yes," he said. "The building sways in high winds."

"Oh, I don't like that. I don't like that at all," she said.

He kissed the tip of her nose. "Trust me, we'd have more to worry about if the building didn't sway."

"I'll take your word for it." Her hands tightened on his arms when the building swayed again.

"I think," he kissed her jaw, "the best idea is to get you into the shower and occupy you with other things, so you don't notice the building swaying."

"Is that right?" she said as he led her into the primary bathroom. He turned on the multiple showerheads, adjusting the water until it was the perfect temperature. When he turned back to face Rayna, a groan escaped his lips. She was completely naked, her clothes in a heap on the floor, and a wicked smile on her face.

"Something wrong, Isaac?"

"No, baby," he said hoarsely, his hands already yanking his t-shirt over his head. "Everything is perfect."

He stripped off the rest of his clothes in record time. Rayna's smug smile at the sight of his already erect cock made him grin. "Come here, gorgeous."

She stepped into the shower with him, sighing happily when she stood under the showerheads and let the hot water beat down her back. "Oh God, this feels so good."

"Hmm," he agreed, his hands already reaching for her perfect breasts. He cupped them gently, kneading and squeezing them as they kissed. She gasped into his mouth when he lightly pinched her nipples before gripping his cock and giving it some long firm strokes that made his eyes roll back in his damn head.

"Isaac?" She pressed a kiss against his wet chest.

"Yeah? Fuck… don't stop, baby. That feels so good."

She smiled but didn't give him what he wanted. "I'm still noticing the swaying building."

"Is that right?" He smoothed her hair back from her face, his thumb tracing her bottom lip. "I guess I haven't distracted you enough."

"Maybe there's something else we can try?" Her tongue flicked out to lick her bottom lip before she glanced at his cock.

More blood rushed to his cock, turning it painfully hard. He nuzzled her neck again, licking away a few drops of water. "Well, I was going to eat your sweet pussy, but I think I have a better idea."

He led her toward the built-in bench as she made a little whine of disappointment. "No, I like that idea. I *love* that idea, Isaac."

"I'm sure you do, but I think it's time you show me what a good girl you are, baby."

He pushed her into a sitting position on the bench and stood in front of her. She was at eye level with his cock, and the disappointment on her face was immediately replaced with a hot lust that made precum drip from his cock.

He gripped the back of her skull with his left hand and

the base of his dick with his right. "Would you like a taste, good girl?"

"Yes," she said eagerly.

He pressed lightly on her head, urging her forward. Her little pink tongue slicked across the head of his cock, cleaning away the drops of precum that clung to it. He hissed out a breath as she stared up at him, her dark eyes filled with a wanton, hungry need that made him ache to shove his cock straight down her throat.

Instead, calling on a willpower he didn't know he had, he smoothed her hair back from her face again and said, "Suck."

She didn't hesitate, her hot, wet mouth sliding down his cock and sucking until her cheeks hollowed. He cried out when she drew back, and her tongue teased the sensitive spot beneath his crown.

"Fuck, Rayna!" he groaned. "Oh, fucking hell, baby."

She slid him into her mouth, and her loud moan sent a vibration of pleasure through his dick right to his balls. He made a hoarse cry, his hips jutting forward in an eager attempt to lodge his cock down her throat. She responded with more enthusiastic sucking, her hand squeezing and twisting lightly at the base of his dick as she bobbed her head back and forth.

Desperate for more, he fucked her mouth in a hard rhythm, his gaze locked onto hers as she kept her mouth open wide and took everything he gave her.

"So fucking beautiful," he crooned. "Can you take more for me? I need you to take more. Relax your throat, let me in, baby."

Her nostrils flared as she struggled for breath, but he could see her trying to swallow more of him. The hot friction around his throbbing cock sent fresh pleasure rocketing through him. He drove deep into her mouth, gasping out a moan when he slipped down her throat, and it clenched around his aching, weeping cock.

"Fuck!" For a moment, he was nearly past the point of no return, and despite how good the suction of her hot mouth felt, he yanked himself out from between her lips, clamping his hand down on the base of his dick.

"Isaac, no!" She tried to reach for him, her lips red and swollen, her gaze frantic with desire.

His chest heaving for air, he yanked her to her feet and spun her around before bending her over.

"Open for me," he growled into the steamy air.

She immediately spread her legs wide, crying out when he cupped her pussy. He toyed with the small patch of pubic hair he'd left at the top of her mound when he'd waxed her before running his fingers over her smooth lips and then rubbing her clit. She moaned at the contact, her body shuddering against his. She was hot and slick and ready for him, and with another low growl, he slammed his cock into her velvet heat. She rocked forward, her hands slapping against the shower wall to brace herself.

He grabbed her hips. "Wider, baby."

She slid her legs farther apart until he could see her muscles strain from the effort. He wound one hand into her hair, tugging her head back as he slid out in a slow, smooth motion and then drove back in.

"Isaac!" Her pussy gripped him tight as he fucked her roughly. The shower echoed with the sounds of his groans, her breathy cries, and their slapping skin. Every snap of his hips sent a moan hurtling from her lips, and when he shifted her slightly and drove in again, a feral cry erupted from her throat.

He grinned savagely and drilled into her, the head of his cock pressing against her g-spot with every wild thrust. Her breath stuttered, her body tensed, and her core fluttered around his cock before squeezing him so tightly that it pulled a sound that was half-plea, half-curse from him.

Her body shook wildly, her pussy clamping down around him again, and he was done. With a guttural roar, he sank into her a final time and held still, groaning at the sheer intoxicating pleasure of his release. He pumped lightly back and forth, smoothing his hand over her ass before finally pulling out.

Rayna went to close her trembling legs, and he slapped her lightly on the ass. "Stay open, baby."

She peered at him over her shoulder as he held her thighs apart and watched with satisfaction as his cum dripped from her opening.

"Isaac?"

"So fucking pretty," he said to her. "Do you have any idea how much I like seeing you full of my cum?"

"Oh my God," she moaned, her cheeks darkening to an even deeper red. "Isaac, you shouldn't say stuff like that to me."

"Why not?" He reached between her legs, catching some of his cum and rubbing it into her pussy lips before lightly rubbing her clit. "It's the truth. Your little pussy looks so pretty when it's dripping with my cum."

Her soft moan made him grin, and he pulled her straight before turning her to face him. He slid his hand between her legs, his fingers circling her clit again.

"Isaac, I can't have another one," she gasped. "That last one nearly knocked me unconscious."

He leaned down to suck on her bottom lip, refusing to stop touching her clit even when she tugged at his wrist. "You will have another one for me, baby or else I'll put you on your knees and make you suck me until I'm hard again."

She swallowed compulsively. "That's not really a threat for me."

He grinned at her, his fingers still relentlessly circling. "Be my good girl and show me again how pretty you are when you come, Rayna."

Her arms circled his shoulders, and she pressed her wet body against his. "If you insist, Isaac."

CHAPTER 41

"Rayna?"

"Hmm?" She closed the book she'd taken from the bookshelf and glanced up from where she was tucked under a soft and cozy blanket on the large sectional. She frowned at the look on Isaac's face. "What's wrong?"

"Nothing's wrong." He sat down beside her, uncovering her feet and placing them in his lap.

He rubbed them, and she moaned with pleasure, snuggling deeper into the sectional. "That feels amazing."

He laughed. "Should I be insulted that the 'I'm rubbing your feet' moans sound very similar to the 'I'm fucking your pussy' moans?"

She wiggled her toes at him. "There are subtle differences."

Still rubbing her feet, he said, "The travel advisory from last night and this morning has been lifted. We can head back to Harmony Falls."

It was impossible to ignore the disappointment coursing through her. She'd only been at Isaac's penthouse for roughly sixteen hours, but it had been one of the best sixteen hours she could remember in a very long time.

She'd fallen asleep in Isaac's arms and slept until nearly nine. After a slow and very thorough round of lovemaking, instead of doing some work as she expected, Isaac had made them brunch while she took a bath in his soaker tub.

He'd given her one of his t-shirts to wear and put her clothes in the washing machine before instructing her to relax on the couch while he cleaned up the brunch dishes. She'd never felt so spoiled or taken care of, and she had even given herself permission not to check rescue texts and emails compulsively.

"I don't have to work tomorrow," she said hesitantly. "Maybe we could stay another day?"

His face showed genuine disappointment. "I have an in-person meeting tomorrow at the office that I can't miss."

"Okay," she said. "Just let me get dressed, and we'll go."

He pulled her into his lap when she threw back the blanket. He gave her a sweet kiss that weirdly made her want to cry. "I really enjoyed being here with you, Rayna."

"I did too," she said. "Thank you, Isaac."

He nodded and, that disappointment still on his face, released her when she tugged at his hands. She grabbed her clothes from the dryer and changed in his bedroom, telling herself not to be so damn upset. Staying another day here with Isaac would be a mistake. It would lead her to feel things she had no right to feel.

This again? You're already in love with him. When will you stop soaking in that pool of denial you're currently in?

Arranging her face into a cheerful smile, she headed back to the foyer, where Isaac waited for her. "Okay, I'm ready to go if you are."

Isaac opened the closet but then turned to her without taking out their jackets. "Maybe I could reschedule -"

The elevator at the far end of the foyer dinged, and the doors slid open. Isaac turned to stone beside her, a combination of anger and fear settling on his face. On instinct, she grabbed his hand, squeezing it reassuringly as she studied the man who strode out of the elevator.

He was Isaac's father. She didn't need an introduction to know that. His blue eyes, jawline, and walk were eerie echoes of Isaac. He stopped in front of them, peeling off his leather gloves as he studied Rayna, found her wanting, and turned his gaze to his son.

"Hello, Isaac."

"What are you doing here, Dad?" Isaac's hand squeezed hers until her fingers went numb.

"I've been asking you to meet with me for weeks," his father said. "Since you've been ignoring me, you've left me no choice but to show up unannounced."

"How do you know the elevator code? I've never…". Isaac's face twisted. "Fucking Jasper gave it to you."

His father's nostrils flared. "Language, Isaac."

"How did you know I was in town?" Isaac ignored his father's rebuke.

"Your mother told me."

"Oh, that is some bullshit right here," Isaac snarled. "Tell me the fucking truth."

"Christ, you get worked up so easily," his father said. "Calm down and -"

"Tell me!"

"Your doorman has my number. I asked him to text me the next time you were in town."

Isaac rolled his eyes. "You bribed the goddamn doorman."

"As I said, you left me no choice."

Isaac stayed silent, and while his grip had loosened, Rayna could practically feel the anger radiating off him. She smoothed her thumb over his as his father stared at her again.

He held out his hand. "Alexander Stark. And you are?"

"Rayna Abrams."

She refused to shake his hand, and after a few seconds, he dropped it and looked her up and down. "You don't look like my son's usual type."

"Get the hell out of my house," Isaac growled, half-pulling Rayna behind him.

She placed a hand on his back, rubbing in soothing circles as his father said, "I'm not leaving until you speak with me."

Isaac barked harsh laughter. "Your days of telling me what to do are finished."

"You owe me!" his father snapped. "You quit the company and became my competition out of spite. You owe me the decency to listen to what I have to say, Isaac. I am still your goddamn father."

"I don't owe you shit," Isaac said. "I won't let you gaslight or manipulate me anymore. Leave."

"I'm not leaving until you listen to what I have to say," Alexander said.

"Fine. We'll leave." Isaac started toward the elevator, pulling Rayna with him.

"I'm going to lose the company," his father said.

Isaac stopped so suddenly that Rayna bumped into him. She stepped back, trying not to wince when Isaac's hand tightened painfully on hers again. He turned to face Alexander. "You're losing the company?"

Alexander's face was a dark red. "Yes, and I want to speak with you about it." His gaze landed on Rayna. "In private."

Isaac put his arm around her waist, one big hand cupping her hip. "Anything you say to me, you can say in front of her."

"I won't talk about my business in front of your latest… fling, Isaac."

"Then we don't talk at all." He started for the elevator again.

"Fine," his father snapped.

There was a thick and heavy silence that made Rayna want to find the nearest exit. Instead, she took Isaac's hand and said, "Why don't the three of us go to the kitchen, and I'll make us coffee while you and your father speak."

Isaac put his mouth to his ear, his voice low for only her to hear. "Don't leave me alone with him."

She cupped his face, rubbing her thumb across his cheekbone and smiling reassuringly at him. "I won't, honey."

"Listen to your fling," Alexander said. "Talking to me is -"

"Her name is Rayna!" Isaac snarled. "Call her my fling again, and I'll toss you in that goddamn elevator and never speak to you again."

Alexander held up his hands. "Okay, okay."

"Apologize to her," Isaac growled, his hand tightening on Rayna's hip.

"I apologize for my rudeness, Rayna," Alexander said stiffly.

She nodded, and with Isaac still holding her hand like she was his lifeline, the three of them walked to the kitchen.

STARK GRABBED THE MILK AND THE SUGAR AS RAYNA MADE the coffee. The thick silence was as oppressive as a Georgia heat wave, and he was so nauseous that he wasn't sure he could take a single sip of coffee without immediately throwing up.

His father striding into his penthouse like he owned the damn place had sent his head into a tailspin. He'd immediately felt small and insignificant, his brain overwhelmed by the rush of adrenaline, the urge to flee, and that small voice in his head that reminded him he wasn't smart enough, creative enough, or good enough for his father.

He probably would have completely spiraled if it hadn't been for Rayna. Her small but comforting presence had kept him grounded. He hadn't even been embarrassed by his plea for her to stay with him. Her reassurance that she wouldn't leave had helped center him and remind him that he wasn't alone. She was right there with him and wasn't going anywhere.

Rayna placed the steaming hot coffee mugs on the table before sinking into the chair next to him. He took her hand again, holding it tightly as they watched his father add milk to his coffee and take a sip.

"How is your mother doing?" he asked.

Stark grimaced. "This isn't a social call, and you don't get to talk about her ever. Just tell me what's going on with the company."

Alexander's nostrils flared in annoyance, but his tone was civil when he said, "The company's in a bit of a downturn, currently."

"Currently? Your company has been failing steadily for months," Stark said.

His father's lips pressed together in a thin line. "At this moment, I don't have enough cash flow to cover our monthly expenses, including payroll and the building rent."

He arched an eyebrow at him. "So, cover it yourself. You have plenty of liquid cash."

"I have bankrolled the company for the last year and a half," Alexander said. "My personal funds are no longer enough to keep the company functional."

"Year and a half... are you fucking kidding me right now?" Stark said.

"Obviously, I am not," his father said grimly. "If I don't

find an investor in the next few days, Stark Gaming will fold. Which is why I'm here."

Rayna jumped when Stark barked harsh laughter. "You want me to invest in the company?"

"I do," Alexander said.

"No," Stark said. "Find someone else."

"Don't you think I've tried? Believe me, I have exhausted every possible avenue when it comes to investors, Isaac. You are the company's last chance."

He leaned forward when Stark didn't say anything, his fingers tapping out a nervous beat on the table. "The company is solid. You know it is. We've just had a few missteps in the last couple of years."

"A few?" Stark said. "The last six games you've released have failed dismally. Why should I invest in your company when it's failing?"

His father took a deep breath. "Five months ago, we hired a new developer. A kid named Jaxon Miller. He's good, Isaac. Really good. The game he's developing right now will turn the market on its head. I promise you. We're releasing it in three months. All I need is enough of an investment from you to keep the company afloat until its release. You will get your money back. I promise you."

Stark rolled his eyes. "The developers Jasper hires don't know shit about gaming. Why the fuck you ever let Jasper take charge of the company is beyond me. He's useless and -"

"I hired this developer, not Jasper! And the reason Jasper is with the company is because you abandoned me," his father snapped. "I couldn't run the company on my own, and you knew it, but you still left. What did you expect me to do when you walked away?"

He didn't want to feel guilty, *shouldn't* have felt guilty, but he could feel it creeping in anyway, like a rank smell in the house that you couldn't get rid of no matter how often you cleaned.

"He didn't abandon you!"

Stark stared in surprise at Rayna as she leaned forward, her face full of fury. "Isaac left because you refused to see how talented he is. Even if the games he produced weren't number one in the gaming community, you know goddamn well how amazing he is. It's the reason you drove him away. Instead of being proud of him, of supporting him and his incredible talent, you couldn't stand the idea that your son was better than you because you're a terrible fucking father. Even now, when you're asking him for help, you have to try to cut him down because that's what people like you do. You make yourself feel big by making others feel small. What an absolute dumpster sack of rancid donkey meat you are."

His father's mouth gaped open, a look of stunned surprise on his face. Hot warmth flooded Stark's chest. Rayna's utter lack of fear in standing up to his father and her fierce defense of Stark filled him with pride, joy, and... love.

He stared at Rayna, his pulse skipping wildly, and the knowledge that he loved her an all-consuming drumbeat in his brain.

"You... you can't speak to me that way," his father said.

"Why? Because I'm a woman or because I'm telling you the truth?" Rayna asked.

"Isaac," his father gave him a look, "control her, please."

Laughter bubbled out of Stark's chest as Rayna snorted. "Control me? Christ, no wonder Angela dumped your sorry ass."

His father's face turned an alarming shade of red. He pushed back his chair and stood, his hands clenched into fists at his side. "I've said what I came here to say, and the rest is up to you. Just remember that Stark Gaming employs people with families, people who need their jobs and would be screwed if the company folds. These are good people who don't deserve the actions of what your selfishness would create."

He paused in the kitchen doorway. "Call me if you decide to care about someone other than yourself for once."

Stark didn't reply, and his father left the kitchen. Rayna waited until they heard the elevator doors close before turning to him. "You are not responsible for taking care of his employees, honey. Don't believe that, okay?"

"I know," he said.

"I can't believe he even said that," Rayna said angrily. "Is there no low he won't stoop to?"

"Obviously not," Stark said.

She stood and paced angrily back and forth. "I know you said your dad was an asshole, but my God, Isaac, that's honestly just sugarcoating it. I hate him. I'm sorry. I know he's your dad, but I seriously hate him."

He stood and pulled her into his arms, kissing her until her body melted against his. She clung to his hips, giving him a dazed look when he finally pulled back. "Wow."

"Thank you," he said hoarsely. "Thank you for staying with me and for standing up for me. You... you were incredible, Rayna."

She hugged him hard, her beautiful face warm and full of kindness. "Isaac, I meant every word I said, and I will always be your biggest cheerleader and supporter. I mean that."

He swallowed hard, giving in to his overwhelming urge to tell her that he loved her. "Rayna, I -"

Her phone rang, and she grimaced before pulling it out of her pocket. "Shit, it's Reba, my medical coordinator. She only calls if there's something wrong. I have to take this."

"Okay," he said.

She bit her lip indecisively as her phone rang again. "What were you going to say?"

"Nothing that can't wait," he said.

CHAPTER 42

"I'm being ridiculous, Bea."

The beagle stared at her, tail thumping happily before rolling to her side on the couch for a belly rub.

Rayna rubbed Bea's belly, combing her fingers through the dog's short, coarse hair. "We've been apart less than five hours, and I miss him like crazy. But I don't think he's in the mood for company. I can't text him to come over, right?"

Bea cracked open one eye, and Rayna said hastily, "Not for sex. I'm worried about him. His father was such a dick to him, and I don't know if Isaac would prefer to be left alone or if he wants company, you know? I want to support him, but it's not like we're dating."

Bea's eyes closed, and she made a contented sigh before shifting so that Rayna could scratch along her ribcage. Rayna rested her head on the back of the couch and stared at the ceiling.

The drive home to Harmony Falls had been quiet and a little tense. Reba had been calling about a foster dog who had eaten some chocolate and been taken to Harmony Falls Vet Clinic, and the foster was freaking out. Rayna's guilt over not being at the clinic to support the foster and Isaac's obvious stress over his father's visit meant neither of them was in the mood to talk.

She dropped Isaac at his house before heading to the vet clinic. Thankfully, the dog would make a full recovery, and Rayna had spent some time with the foster before driving to Emma's house to pick up Bea.

Emma had been working at the store, but Rayna let herself in using her key and texted Emma that she'd grabbed Bea before she drove home. Isaac's car hadn't been in the driveway when she'd returned home. Feeling tense and uneasy, she'd busied herself with setting up her new laptop, her ears straining to hear the sound of Isaac's car. Despite actively listening, she didn't hear him return home and only realized he was back when she'd finally peeked out one of the windows facing his house.

"It's just a bit of light stalking," she told Bea. "Nothing to be concerned about. I'm not being weird about him."

Bea snorted and let out a loud fart. Rayna immediately jumped up and made her escape to the kitchen. Freddie sat on the counter, and he growled lightly at her before jumping down and stalking out of the room.

She opened her text to Stark's name, her thumbs hovering over the keyboard. She should text him, right? She didn't have to invite him over, but it wouldn't hurt to check on him. It was something a casual sex partner would do, right?

The doorbell app chimed, and she opened the camera. Her pulse skyrocketed, and undeniable happiness washed over her when she saw Isaac standing on the porch. She shoved her phone into her pocket, nearly ran to the front door, and yanked it open.

"Hi!" She sounded like a teenage girl greeting her prom date.

"Hey." Isaac held up a large paper bag with 'Nan's Diner' stamped on it. "Have you eaten dinner yet?"

"I haven't," she said. "Come inside before you freeze to death."

He joined her in the hallway, and she took the bag of food. He took off his jacket and boots and followed her into the kitchen. He studied the open laptop. "Sorry, are you busy? I should have texted first to see if you wanted company."

"I just finished setting up my laptop, and I'm glad you're here," she said.

"Yeah?" Isaac's uncertain smile was kind of adorable.

"Yeah," she said. "In fact, I was about to text you."

The uncertainty in his face fled, and he leaned down to kiss her. "Of course you were. I'm great."

She laughed and gave him a gentle poke in the stomach before opening the bag of food.

"I got two orders of the lasagna. Hopefully, you don't hate Nan's lasagna."

"One, everything Nan cooks at the diner is delicious, and two, who could hate pasta? I work out so much because of my love of pasta," Rayna said.

He pressed a kiss against her neck. "Samesies."

She laughed again before nudging him toward the silverware drawer. "You set the table, and I'll open a bottle of wine. Sound good?"

He pulled her close, giving her another sweet kiss before breaking into a smile. "Sounds perfect."

"DO YOU WANT TO TALK ABOUT YOUR DAD?" RAYNA ASKED.

A small smile crossed Isaac's face, and he pushed his

empty plate away before sipping at his wine. "I love how blunt you are."

"That's good because it's an integral part of my personality," she said with a grin. "I didn't bring it up over dinner because I didn't want to ruin our appetites, but I am happy to listen if you need to talk."

He ran his finger around the rim of his wine glass, studying the liquid. "I haven't decided if I'll give him the money."

"It's okay if you don't. You know that right?" she said.

"I do," he said, "but I appreciate you saying it."

She sipped at her wine as Isaac continued to stare at his glass. "But he's right in that a lot of good people will lose their jobs if I don't help."

She stayed quiet but reached for his hand, linking their fingers together as he gave her a brief smile. "But his fuck-up isn't my responsibility, is it?"

"No," she said. "It's not."

"I don't want other people to suffer because of his bull-headedness and stupidity, but I don't want to deal with him again," he said. "Investing in his company means being a part of his life, and I don't want that. I know that makes me selfish, but -"

"It doesn't," she said. "Setting boundaries doesn't make you selfish, Isaac. Besides, you have no idea if investing in his company will do anything beyond keeping them afloat for another three months."

"I looked into this Jaxon Miller guy," Isaac said. "Turns out, he's a rising star in the gaming community. He was working for a small gaming company in New Cassel before he joined Dad's company. They released a few games he developed that did well enough to win them some awards. I talked to Lucas about him, and he said he met him at a conference about six months ago. He impressed Lucas, and

Lucas tried to get him to send in a resume to Stark Entertainment, but the kid declined."

"So, what your father said was true," Rayna said. "He could be the key to turning their company around."

"Possibly," Isaac said.

Rayna squeezed his hand. "Could you help your father's company without investing?"

"What do you mean?"

"If you don't care about getting the money back, you could give him the money as a gift instead of an investment," Rayna said. "You'd help his employees without being sucked back into your father's orbit."

Isaac stared silently at her, and she blushed before standing and clearing the dinner dishes off the table. "Sorry, that's a stupid idea. Obviously, you would want your money back. I really shouldn't give financial advice of any kind. I still can't even get my damn accountant to meet with me to go over the rescue finances and - oh!"

Isaac had moved silently behind her, his big hands cupping her hips and turning her to face him. Before she could say anything, he kissed her hard on the mouth, stealing her breath and skyrocketing her pulse.

He pulled back and grinned at her. "You're fucking brilliant, Rayna Abrams."

"I... thank you?"

He laughed and hugged her hard before picking her up. She wrapped her legs around his waist as he nuzzled her neck. "I want you to sit on my face."

"Right here?" She stared at Bea, who was sleeping on her bed. "I don't think I can do that in front of Bea. She can be kind of judgy sometimes."

He laughed again before carrying her out of the kitchen. "I was thinking we'd go to the bedroom, but it's good to know you're an exhibitionist."

"What? I've just proved that I'm the opposite of an exhibitionist," she said.

He grinned wickedly at her and started up the stairs, his hands squeezing and kneading her ass. "All I really care about is whether you're agreeable to sitting on my face."

"Agreeable? It's all I've been thinking about for weeks," she said.

"Naughty girl," he said as he carried her into the bedroom.

"And you love it," she said.

He nipped at her collarbone. "Yes, Ms. Abrams, I do."

CHAPTER 43

"A gift?"

Stark could hear the harsh surprise in his father's voice. He shut his office door and put his phone on speaker, placing it on his desk as he sat down.

"What do you mean a gift?" Alexander's surprise had been replaced by suspicion.

"I'm not investing in your company, but I will give the money to you, free and clear. No expectation for you to pay it back," Stark said.

A heavy silence filled the air before his father said, "What's the catch?"

"Two catches, actually," Stark said. "The first one is that this is it for us. I give you the money, and you stay out of my life for good."

"And the second?"

"You fire Jasper."

"I can't fire Jasper," his father sputtered. "He's my CEO, for God's sake."

"Those are my terms for getting the money," Stark said calmly.

"Isaac, be reasonable," Alexander said. "I can't fire Jasper. He's family."

"Family? That's the reason you're keeping him on?" Stark said. "You let me leave without a single protest, but you can't fire Jasper even when he's destroyed your company."

"He hasn't destroyed it," his father said. "A few bad decisions don't mean -"

"You're in this mess because of him," Stark said. "Refusing to acknowledge it doesn't mean it isn't true."

"Son, I get that you've always been jealous of Jasper, but stooping to this level of pettiness isn't you."

"How would you know? You don't know anything about me," Isaac said. "But for the record, I'm not asking you to fire Jasper because of jealousy. I'm only doing this to help you and your company."

That wasn't entirely true, but Stark didn't feel any guilt. His father could either accept his terms or not, and after this, Stark would never have to deal with him or his cousin again.

His father sighed deeply. "Fine. I'll fire Jasper. But you should know that this lack of commitment to your family is deeply disturbing to me."

Stark laughed hard and with genuine amusement. "That's fucking rich coming from the man who whined about firing the man destroying his company but didn't balk at giving up a relationship with his son for money."

"You're forcing me to do that," his father snapped. "You're the one deciding to end our relationship, Isaac, not me."

"You're right," Stark said. "And it's a decision I will never regret. I'll transfer the money as soon as I have proof that Jasper no longer works for the company. Goodbye, Dad."

He ended the call, a giddy excitement bubbling up inside of him. He expected to feel guilt, maybe even a little remorse at the death of his relationship with his father, but there was just that giddiness and a feeling of freedom.

There was a knock on his door before Lucas opened it and stuck his head in. "Hey, do you have a minute to… whoa, you okay?"

"Why?" Stark asked.

"You look weird," Lucas said before grimacing. "Shit, that was rude. Sorry."

A large grin crossed Stark's face. "I just got my cousin fired because the son of a bitch thought he could mess with my woman."

Lucas blinked at him. "Yeah, I'm gonna need the whole story on that."

Stark motioned for him to come in before reaching into the bottom drawer of his desk and bringing out a bottle of whiskey and two glasses. "Only if you have a celebratory drink with me."

Lucas closed the door. "You don't have to ask me twice."

It took nearly twenty minutes for Stark to tell Lucas what he'd done. He'd even given Lucas the Cliff's Notes version of how bad his relationship with his father was and how happy he was to have him out of his life for good.

Now, sitting in the silence of his office, he thought he would have instant regret over sharing so much personal information with a coworker. To his surprise, he didn't have any regrets. It felt good to share with Lucas.

"God, I am thrilled that fucker Jasper got what was coming to him," Lucas said.

"You don't think insisting my father fire him was over the top?" Stark asked.

"Oh, it was totally over the top," Lucas said with a laugh. "Which is what makes it so great. Fuck that guy."

"Fuck that guy," Stark echoed, raising his glass.

Lucas raised his, and they both drank.

Despite his lack of regrets, a bit of insecurity raised its

ugly head, and Stark couldn't help but say, "Sorry to share so much personal shit."

Lucas shook his head. "No apology necessary. I'm glad you shared. Not to sound like a cheesy Lifetime movie, but I'd like to be friends if you're interested."

"I'd like that," Stark said with a grin.

"Good, because our ladies are best friends, and we're about to spend a whole shitload of time together," Lucas laughed. "When did you and Rayna start dating? Because Em hasn't said a word to me about it."

"It's not exactly official," Stark said. "I haven't told Rayna how I feel yet. But I will tonight."

Lucas leaned forward, holding out his glass. "To finding the one you love."

Stark clinked his glass against Lucas's. "To finding the one you love."

STARK RANG RAYNA'S DOORBELL, SMILING AT HER WHEN SHE opened the door. "Hey there."

"Hi!" Her look of happiness at seeing him on her porch made him feel good. "Come inside."

He stepped into the warmth, shutting the door behind him as Rayna said, "Have you eaten? I'm making dinner. It's chocked full of vegetables and disgustingly healthy. Want to join me?"

He laughed. "I'd love to."

"Good, you can chop the vegetables," she said.

Five minutes later, he stood at her kitchen counter, facing a chopping board and a truly epic pile of raw vegetables.

"You weren't kidding about the vegetables," he said.

"I know, right? I'm not really that great of a cook, but this is an easy recipe, and I make it a lot." Rayna studied Bea, who sat at Stark's feet, staring eagerly at him. "You'll need to give her a piece of every vegetable you cut. If you don't, she'll whine until your ears bleed."

"Good to know," he said before cutting off a slice of carrot and tossing it to Bea.

She caught it with a snap of her jaws, crunching it happily.

"How was your day?" he asked.

"Good. Busy at work, and then I did a few rescue related things afterward. Yours?"

"I spoke with my father today," he said.

She stopped cutting the chicken and turned to face him. "How did it go?"

"I took your advice and gave the money to him as a gift," he said.

"How do you feel about that?" she asked.

He loved the concern on her face and that she was worried about him.

"It was the right decision," he said. "But I did have some conditions."

"What do you mean?" Rayna added the chicken to the hot pan on the stove.

"I'll give him the money as a gift, but he has to stay out of my life forever and fire Jasper."

She paused in stirring the chicken, the sizzle and pop growing louder as she stared at him before suddenly smiling. "I'm so proud of you, Isaac."

Warmth washed over him, and any lingering doubt he felt over his conversation with his father dropped away. "You are?"

"Yes," she said before turning the heat down under the pan of chicken and nudging her way past Bea. She slid her arms around his waist. "You're helping the employees at your father's company *and* setting boundaries. Your father is toxic and doesn't deserve to have you in his life."

"Thank you, baby." He pressed a kiss against her lips.

She squeezed his waist before giving him a hesitant look. "Hey, um, you wanted your dad to fire Jasper because he's trashing the company, right?"

"Mostly," he said.

"Isaac," she chewed at her bottom lip, "I don't -"

He stopped her with another kiss before resting his forehead against hers. "He deserves everything he's got coming to him, baby."

"Comeuppance," she said.

He arched an eyebrow at her, and she reddened slightly. "Emma says terrible people get their comeuppance eventually, and she was right."

He kissed her again before she returned to the stove to continue cooking the chicken. They worked in silence for a few minutes. He glanced at Rayna, love and an almost euphoric contentment rushing through him. He would tell her he loved her over dinner, tell her how much she meant to him and that he couldn't live without her.

He dropped a piece of cauliflower into Bea's open mouth, grinning at the excited way she chewed it. Stupid little daydreams were already running through his head... he and Rayna marrying, tearing down their houses and building the home of their dreams for them and their children. He'd have a kennel built on the third property, he decided. A large and heated kennel with all the latest technology that would allow Rayna to save even more dogs. She would love that.

"Can you pass me the oven mitts?" Rayna pointed to a pair of oven mitts sitting on the counter.

He grabbed them and handed them to her, then studied the backsplash. It was a truly horrendous beige and gold colour with orange and yellow flowers stamped on every third tile. The overwhelming eighties of it rivaled the pink, sparkling roses wallpaper in his house.

"This backsplash is something else," he said.

She laughed. "It's retro."

"That's one way of describing it," he said.

"Says the guy with the glittery pink wallpaper," she teased.

"Watch it, or I'll ask them to keep some of it when they tear the house down and have them install it in the new house." He gave Bea another piece of carrot before realizing Rayna wasn't laughing.

He looked over at her, his stomach tensing at the look on her face. "What's wrong?"

"Nothing," she said, turning off the stove and dumping the chicken into a glass dish.

"Something is wrong," he said. "Tell me what it is."

She shrugged. "I'd just forgotten what this was between us."

"What's that supposed to mean?" he asked.

She gave him a fleeting smile. "You're being nice to me because you want my property."

A tidal wave of hurt nearly drowned him. He dropped the knife on the counter and stepped back, putting even more space between himself and Rayna.

"You think what's happening between us is because I want your property?"

"Yes," she said.

"Why the fuck do you believe that?"

She gave him a bewildered look. "Because, Isaac, we have nothing in common except fantastic sex. I am not your type at all. You date lawyers and doctors who wear makeup, have an actual fashion sense, and aren't covered in a layer of dog and cat hair. I know that I will never be someone you actually want to date, okay? I just let myself be swept up in…"

She released her breath in a heavy sigh. "It doesn't matter. I know what you want from me, and it isn't a relationship."

"So, that's who you think I am? A shallow asshole who's sleeping with you to get your property."

She frowned and started toward him, stopping when he held up his hand. "Don't, Rayna."

Anger settled over her features. "Are you seriously doing the wounded bird act with me right now? Do you or do you not want my property, Isaac?"

"You know I do," he spat. "But that's not the point. The point is -"

"That's exactly the point," she said. "You want to buy my property. I am not selling it to you. That won't change no matter how amazing the sex is between us or how nice you are to me."

Stark stared silently at Rayna, his chest so tight he could barely breathe. The whole time he was falling in love with her, she thought he was just using her. She didn't believe anything he'd said to her was real, and the weight of that knowledge nearly crushed him.

"Isaac," Rayna started toward him with confusion and what almost looked like hurt on her face, "sit down and -"

"Don't, "he repeated, backing toward the doorway. "It isn't only about your property for me."

She bit at her bottom lip, looking like she was about to cry. "Isn't it? Because you just talked about tearing down my house, Isaac."

"Because I want…"

He trailed off, his surety that Rayna was the one for him lying in tatters at his feet. How could he be in love with someone who couldn't see him for who he really was?

Now, a tear did slip down her cheek. "You want this house gone because it's stopping you from getting what you want. You can't see how much it means to me, how hard I worked to make it mine."

"That isn't true," he said.

"Isn't it?" she said softly.

Harsh despair replaced the anger and the hurt. His shoulders slumped, and he took a deep breath and swallowed the golf ball that had suddenly lodged itself in his throat.

"No," he said hoarsely, "but it doesn't matter anymore. You're right. You're not my type, and whatever this was between us is now over."

Hot fury replaced the hurt on her face. "Of course it is. Because what Isaac Stark wants, Isaac Stark gets. Right?"

"Precisely," he snapped, his anger suddenly as hot as her own. "My involvement with you was a mistake, Ms. Abrams. It won't happen again."

As fast as it appeared, her rage disappeared, leaving behind a sick hurt that nearly destroyed him despite his anger with her.

"I want you to leave," she said, her voice dull and void of emotion. "Leave and don't ever speak to me again, Stark."

"Happy to," he bit out. His stomach churning, he grabbed his jacket and stalked out of her house, slamming the door behind him.

CHAPTER 44

"I'm worried about you, honey." Emma pushed Bea to the side and sat beside Rayna on the couch, sliding her arm around Rayna's shoulders.

"I'm fine," she said.

"Oh, that is some bullshit right there," Emma said. "It's a Tuesday afternoon, and you called in sick to work. You *never* call in sick."

"I'm taking a mental health day," Rayna said. "Also, you know you don't have to sit here with me, right? I'm sure you have a ton of stuff to do at the store."

"I'm not going anywhere," Emma said. "You've been a mess since you and Stark broke up, and you need my support right now."

"We didn't break up. We'd have to be dating to break up," Rayna said.

"Right, but Lucas said -"

"That Stark was going to tell me how he felt," Rayna said tiredly. "Yeah, I remember. But instead, he talked about tearing down my house. I appreciate you telling me what

Lucas said, Em, but he obviously misunderstood what Stark meant."

"Maybe," Emma said doubtfully.

Rayna wiped at the hot tears sliding down her cheek. "I miss him so much, which is ridiculous, but I…"

"You're in love with him," Emma said softly.

Rayna started to cry in earnest before burying her face in Emma's shoulder. "I am, and I am so goddamn stupid, Em."

"No, you're not." Emma kissed the top of her head, rocking her lightly back and forth. "Have you seen him at all in the last week?"

"No," Rayna said, sitting up and scrubbing the tears from her face. "I'm doing everything in my power to avoid him. I leave the house and basically run to my vehicle without looking at his place, and I haven't gone for coffee once at Grind My Beans, not even if I think there's zero chance he'll be there. Lucas returned the gym pass to Hollis for me, right?"

"He did," Emma said.

"Thank you," Rayna said. "I couldn't risk going there myself."

Emma sighed. "Honey, spending the rest of your life trying to avoid Stark isn't going to work. You know that, right? Forgetting how small Harmony Falls is, he's your next-door neighbour. You'll see him eventually."

"I know," Rayna said, "but for now, I just need some space and time."

She glanced at her phone when it rang, her brow creasing when she saw the number. "Why is the bank calling me?"

She hit the answer button. "Rayna Abrams speaking."

"Hello, Ms. Abrams. This is Carla at the Harmony Falls First Bank. I'm calling regarding some overdue payments for Little Whiskers Rescue."

"Oh, um, right. That's typically handled by my accountant, Mack Roberts. I can give you his number if you -"

"We have Mr. Roberts's contact information and have been trying to reach him for quite some time now," Carla said. "He hasn't returned our calls."

"Okay, well, I can speak with him and have him make any payments that are due asap," Rayna said.

"Unfortunately, the rescue's outstanding debt is significant, and with no payments to your credit cards or line of credit being made for the last three months, we have no choice but to send the debts to collections."

"Whoa, wait...just... what do you mean no payments for three months, and credit cards and line of credit? Little Whiskers only has one credit card and no line of credit," Rayna said as unease drifted into her belly.

There was a moment of silence that only worsened Rayna's anxiety before Carla said, "Ms. Abrams, in the last year, Little Whiskers has opened two credit cards and a line of credit."

"No, that's not possible," she said. "I didn't authorize that."

There was some keyboard clicking before Carla said, "Mr. Roberts opened two more credit card accounts and a line of credit. According to our records, he has the signing authority on the account to do so."

"How much does the rescue owe?" Rayna said through lips that felt like they'd been shot up with Novocaine.

"The total debt incurred by the rescue is one hundred and fifty-three thousand dollars and seventy-two cents," Carla said.

"Oh my God." Rayna immediately felt like she'd been hit by a sledgehammer. "I... are you sure? There has to be some mistake."

"What's wrong?" Emma mouthed.

Rayna swallowed the bile rising in her throat as Carla

said, "Ms. Abrams, I think it might be best if you come into the bank. Can you meet with me today?"

"I can be there in fifteen minutes," Rayna said.

"Perfect. See you soon."

Rayna ended the call and stared at Emma, her body beginning to shake. This couldn't be happening. It had to be a mistake.

"Rayna, honey, what's wrong?" Emma asked.

Her fingers trembling, Rayna called Mack. The nausea intensified in her stomach when she heard the robotic, 'The number you are calling is no longer in service.'

"Rayna, talk to me," Emma said.

"Em… it's bad," Rayna said. "It's really fucking bad."

"THE BANK SAID MACK CAN'T BE CHARGED WITH FRAUD? Seriously?" Lucas sank into the kitchen chair, absentmindedly petting Bea when she sat on his feet. Lucas had come over as soon as he'd finished work, bringing all three of them dinner from Nan's Diner, but Rayna wasn't able to eat a single bite.

"No, because…." Emma glanced at Rayna, who stood by the sink, staring out the window.

She tried to smile at Emma, but it was hard to smile when her entire world had come crashing down on her.

"Because I'm a fucking idiot," she told Lucas before sitting in the chair beside him.

"No, you're not," Emma said immediately.

"I gave Mack total control over the finances of the rescue, and I never bothered to check what he was doing with said finances," Rayna said. "I basically gave him carte blanche, and now the rescue is fucked."

"You had a lot on your plate, honey," Emma said.

Rayna barked harsh laughter. "It's no excuse, Em."

"There has to be something we can do," Lucas said.

"The bank has agreed to hold off on sending the rescue to collections if I can pay off at least fifty percent of the debt owed in the next fourteen days," Rayna said.

"Okay, that's a start," Lucas said. "People in this town love you, Rayna. We'll throw a big fundraiser to raise the cash needed."

"People aren't going to donate because of my stupidity," Rayna said.

"You're not stupid," Emma said firmly. "You trusted someone who took advantage of that."

"They won't care about the reason," Lucas said. "You do so much for the community, and you provide a valuable service. People will be happy to donate."

"Even if I could raise seventy-five thousand in two weeks, I still have to pay off the other seventy-five grand. I can't keep the rescue running under that kind of debt. There's just no way we would get enough regular donations to help the animals and make monthly debt payments."

"Fuck," Lucas said. "Any chance we can find Mack and force him to pay the money back?"

"He's gone," Rayna said dully. "Emma and I went to his apartment after we left the bank, and the building manager said he had moved out last week. His cell number is no longer in service. It doesn't matter anyway. Even if I could find him, I have no way of making him repay any of the money. What he did wasn't illegal, remember?"

"If we can prove that what he spent the money on wasn't for the rescue, then maybe we could, I don't know, sue him or something," Lucas said.

"I have no money to pay for a lawyer," Rayna said.

"There must be something we can do," Lucas repeated.

"There is," Rayna said as dread settled in her stomach. "I can sell my property to Isaac Stark."

"No," Emma said. "We'll come up with a different solution."

"There isn't one," Rayna said. "You know I'm right, Em. Stark was willing to pay eight hundred grand for my property. I doubt he'll pay that now, but I can offer the property to him for five hundred. That will give me enough money to pay off what I owe on the house and the rescue's debt and leave me with enough cash to keep the rescue operational."

Emma took her hand, squeezing it tightly. "Honey, you love this place, and you worked so hard to buy it."

She shrugged, blinking back the hot tears with effort. "I do, but I have no choice, Em. The rescue is more important than a house. Besides, we both know this damn place is falling apart around me. Even if this hadn't happened, fixing up the house was always a bit of a pipe dream."

"Oh, Rayna." Now, Emma looked like she was going to cry, and she took Lucas's hand when he held it out to her. "I think you should take some time to think on this before -"

"I don't have that luxury," Rayna said. "If I want to save the rescue, this is my only option."

Tears slid down Emma's cheeks, and Rayna gave her a faint smile. "Don't cry, Em. It'll be okay."

Emma shook her head before reaching out and hugging Rayna. "Stop comforting me. I'm supposed to be comforting you."

Rayna buried her face in Emma's shoulder. "I love you, Emmy."

"I love you too, honey."

CHAPTER 45

"You look terrible, dearest," his mother said. Even his phone's small screen couldn't hide the worry on her face. "Please talk to her."

"I told you during our last call that I won't discuss Ms. Abrams anymore," Stark said.

He winced inwardly at the harshness of his tone, waiting for his mother's deserved anger.

Instead of scolding him, Angela gave him a sympathetic look. "I know you miss her, my boy. Talk to her. What happened between you can be fixed."

"No, it can't," he snapped. "She doesn't trust me. She doesn't believe that I care about her and thinks I'm only being nice to her so I can get her damn house."

"To be fair, that was your original motive," Angela said.

He scowled at her. "You're not helping, and I said I don't want to talk about this anymore."

"I know you're angry, sweetheart, and I understand why you are, but is holding on to that anger worth losing her?" his mother asked.

"I'm not angry," Stark said. "Ms. Abrams did me a favour,

actually. She reminded me of what happens when you're weak, when you let your feelings dictate your actions. It was a valuable lesson and one I won't forget."

"Isaac, being kind is not a weakness, and if you just speak with Rayna again, tell her how you feel about her. I'm sure she would -"

"No, I have nothing to say to her."

His mother looked at him with exasperation. "Isaac, I love you, but you're doing that thing you do."

"I don't know what you mean," he said stiffly.

"Yes, you do," she said. "You're hurting, but you refuse to feel that hurt. Instead, you're shoving it deep and pretending everything is fine."

"I'm not," he said.

"You are, my boy," she said. "You have to allow yourself to feel your emotions. You need to acknowledge that you love Rayna, and she hurt you."

"It won't change the situation," he said.

"It might," she said. "Pretending you don't need anyone - don't need her - isn't healthy. As much as you think you can just shut off your feelings and your love for someone when they hurt you, it doesn't work that way."

"I don't do that," he insisted.

"You do, my love," she said softly.

His mother's look of love brought all those emotions he had suppressed dangerously close to the surface again. Instead of allowing them to be free, he said, "I have to go, Mom. I love you."

He ended the video call before she could reply, staring blankly at his computer screen as his stomach churned and his head throbbed. He refused to admit how hellish the last week had been, instead throwing himself into work every day and spending his evenings alone in his house.

Well, not entirely alone. Molly and her babies were still

with him, and snuggling with Molly and playing with the kittens every evening was the only bright spot of each day. He had fully intended to make the rescue take them back, but it wasn't just his reluctance to speak to Rayna about it that stopped him. At some point in the last few weeks, imagining a life without Molly and her babies in his home was impossible.

As impossible as a life without Rayna?

He shut that thought down immediately. In the last week, he'd let his anger over what Rayna had said grow thick and strong. The anger was easier to handle than the hurt. If he stayed angry with her, he wouldn't think about how much he missed her, how much he loved her.

He glanced up at the knock on his door, studying Lucas when he opened it and stuck his head into his office.

"What's up?" Stark asked.

"Do you have a minute to talk?" Lucas asked.

"If it's work related, then yes. If it's personal, no, I don't."

Lucas hesitated, and Stark gave him a cold look. "Is what I said confusing you, Lucas?"

"No." Lucas walked away without another word, and Stark shoved that pang of regret straight down with every other pesky emotion he absolutely didn't need to feel. He'd gone this long without friends and was perfectly fine. He didn't need them now.

His phone rang, and he glanced at the screen before frowning. Why was his real estate agent calling him?

He pressed the answer button. "Ms. Walker, how can I help you today?"

"Hello, Mr. Stark." Kira's voice had an undercurrent of excitement. "Is this a bad time, or do you have a few minutes to speak with me?"

"I have time," he said.

"Great!" Kira chirped. "I have some news that I think will make you very happy."

"What's that?" he asked, his head throbbing harder at the cheeriness in her tone.

"Rayna Abrams contacted me this morning. She's agreed to sell her property if you're still interested."

His jaw dropped, and he sat back in his chair, staring in stunned silence at his desk.

After about a minute, Kira said, "Mr. Stark? Are you still there?"

"Yes," he said. "I'm sorry, did you say Rayna Abrams has agreed to sell her property?"

"She has," Kira said. "Honestly, I am as surprised as you."

"Did she say why?" he rasped.

"She didn't," Kira said before hesitating. "Should I have asked?"

"No," he said.

"Okay." Kira cleared her throat. "She's asking five hundred thousand for the property. As you know, the property is only worth three hundred, but agreeing to the five hundred would certainly speed up the process and -"

"No," he said. "Offer her three fifty and make it clear that's as high as I'm willing to go. I will not negotiate."

There was silence on the other end of the phone before Kira said, "All right. I'll speak with Rayna and let you know if she accepts your offer."

"Thank you." He ended the call and scrolled to Rayna's name, his fingers hovering over the keyboard before he muttered a curse and set his phone on his desk. He had no idea why Rayna was suddenly selling her property, but did it matter? Knowing the reason why wouldn't change the outcome.

He sat back in his chair, waiting for that feeling of satisfaction of finally getting what he wanted. It didn't happen.

Instead, there was only curiosity, shock, and a liberal amount of guilt.

Three hundred and fifty thousand was a more than generous offer for her property, so why did he feel so shitty about it?

"Rayna? Where are you?" Emma called as the front door slammed shut.

"In the laundry room," Rayna shouted.

She opened up the garbage bag, dumping the litter from Freddie's litter box into it and carrying the empty litter box to the deep sink beside the ancient washer. She ran hot water and soap into the box before scrubbing it as Freddie sat on the shelf next to the laundry soap and watched.

"Hey." Emma joined her, moving over when Bea squeezed into the small room as well.

"Hi, Em."

"You didn't return my call last night or today," Emma said.

"I'm sorry." Rayna rinsed the box, added more soap and hot water, and scrubbed it again. "I went to bed early last night, and work was insane today, but I should have called you."

"What happened when you sent Stark the offer yesterday?" Emma asked. "Is he buying your house?"

Rayna rinsed the litter box a final time and grabbed an old dishtowel to dry it. "He is. Kira will have the papers for me to sign on Monday."

"That's great. Well, not great," Emma said, "but at least you can save the rescue now."

Rayna didn't reply, instead bending to set the litter box down and pouring more litter into it before squeezing past Emma and Bea and heading toward the kitchen.

"Rayna?" Emma followed her. "Please talk to me."

She washed and dried her hands in the sink and then grabbed two beers from the fridge. She opened one and handed it to Emma, then sat at the table and motioned for Emma to sit down.

Rayna opened her beer and drank a few big swallows before smiling at Emma. "Stark agreed to buy the property, but he'll only give me three fifty for it."

"Shit," Emma said. "You can't negotiate?"

She shook her head, staring at Bea as the old beagle climbed into her bed in the corner. "No. Kira said that would be his only offer and that I could take it or leave it. So, I took it."

"But that isn't enough money," Emma said.

"It isn't, but it's enough money to pay off what I owe on the house and the fifty percent the bank is asking for," Rayna said.

"You could list it on the market," Emma said. "Find another buyer who will pay more."

"Honestly, I'm lucky to get three fifty from Stark. No one else will pay more than three hundred for it. Hell, they'd probably offer less after seeing the house. Plus, Stark is willing to close in fourteen days. He'll just be tearing the house down, so he doesn't need an inspection or anything like that."

"Oh, honey," Emma said. "I'm so sorry."

Rayna picked at the label on her beer bottle. "It's a fair offer, and I knew it was a long shot that he would agree to the five hundred. I hoped he would, but..."

She drew in a shaky breath. "At least he's still willing to buy it, right?"

"Okay," Emma gave her a determined look, "I'll talk to Zuri first thing in the morning, and we'll brainstorm some fundraiser ideas. You'll still owe, what… fifty-eight grand on the rescue debt? We can -"

Rayna took her hand. "Em, stop."

"What?" Emma said. "We can do this, Rayna."

"No, honey, we can't. Our biggest fundraiser, the bachelor/bachelorette night, only raised thirteen thousand dollars, including the three grand from Jasper. We'll never be able to raise nearly sixty grand."

"Okay, but even if we raise ten grand, that can go toward the debt and -"

"It's not enough," Rayna said gently. "The only way I could keep the rescue going is if I completely paid off the debt immediately."

Emma leaned back in her chair. "What happens now?"

Rayna took another deep breath. "I've been in contact with three rescues in neighbouring counties. They've agreed to absorb Little Whisker's fosters into their rescues. I've already spoken with Zuri, Reba, and the cat and dog foster coordinators. I'll send out a bulk email to our fosters tonight informing them that the rescue is dissolving and that the foster coordinator will be in touch with them regarding the placement of their foster animal with one of the new rescues. We'll give them the option to adopt their foster animal free of charge, and I'm hoping that a good number of them will take that option. I don't want to overload the other rescues if I can help it."

"And then what?" Emma said.

"What do you mean?" Rayna asked.

"You close down the rescue, you place all the animals, and you move out of the house you love, and then what?"

Rayna drank some more beer. "Tomorrow, I'll look for a place to rent on the south side that will allow me to keep Bea and Freddie. I'll start packing up my stuff this weekend."

"I don't want you living on the south side," Emma said.

Rayna smiled faintly. "You and me both. That's bringing up way too many childhood trauma memories, but with the monthly payments on the remaining balance of the rescue's debt, I can't afford anywhere else. I hate to ask, but is there any chance the three of us can stay with you temporarily? I doubt I'll be able to get a place in the next two weeks."

"Of course, you can. You can stay as long as you need," Emma said.

"Thanks, Em. I'll rent a storage unit this weekend so that you won't have all of my crap at your house as well. Hey, do you think Lucas and some of his friends would be willing to load and unload some of my furniture if I found a truck to borrow?"

"Yes," Emma said, giving her a troubled look. "Rayna, I'm so sorry."

Rayna shoved down her sorrow, forcing herself to smile at Emma again. "It's all right, Emmy. I have no one to blame but myself."

CHAPTER 46

"Hey, don't bite your brother's ear." Stark gently separated the three kittens, lifting the biter and pressing a kiss against his spotted belly. "You don't even have any teeth yet, so what's with the biting? You're going to be a troublemaker."

Molly walked into the bedroom and jumped on the bed, rubbing up against Stark before stretching out on the bed beside him. The three kittens wobbled over to her immediately, lining up at her belly like cowboys at a bar. Molly chirped and purred to them, grooming them as they settled down to nurse, their purrs mixing with hers as they kneaded at her belly.

"Did you enjoy your break from the babies?" he asked, scratching under her chin. "Never thought I'd spend my Sunday night babysitting kittens so their mama can have a little alone time."

Molly purred even louder, and he bent to kiss her forehead. "You're my little sweetheart, aren't you?"

He leaned back against the headboard, one hand still lightly stroking Molly as she fed the babies. Tomorrow, Kira would send the paperwork to Rayna, and in ten days, her property would be his.

He had no idea why Rayna had agreed to the three-fifty or why she wanted such a quick closing date, and he told himself he didn't care. He'd gotten what he wanted, and that was all that mattered. He was happy.

No, scratch that.

He was fucking *delighted* to have all three properties finally, and he couldn't care less what Rayna Abrams did with the rest of her life.

Oh yeah? Then why did you feel so guilty when you saw Rayna loading up her crappy SUV with boxes not even an hour ago?

He could feel a muscle ticking in his jaw. He should never have gone into the fucking den. Should never have looked out the goddamn window. Seeing Rayna carrying box after box to her SUV made him feel sick to his stomach, but he hadn't been able to look away. She was obviously packing up her things, and it didn't matter how many times he told himself he didn't feel bad, the nausea in his stomach told a different story.

He'd watched her from behind the blinds like a damn stalker until she'd finished loading the boxes, climbed into her SUV, and drove away. His stomach clenched at the memory of how sad and defeated she'd looked.

Of course she looks sad. You took her fucking home from her, asshole.

He hadn't. She came to him with the offer.

And you fucking lowballed her.

No, he didn't. He'd given her a very generous offer, more than she would have gotten from anyone else.

Whatever helps you sleep at night, buddy.

Christ, if he clenched his jaw any harder, his goddamn teeth would crack.

He petted Molly repeatedly until some of the tension left

his body. When his phone rang, he stared at the unfamiliar number and considered not answering it before reaching for it.

"Stark speaking."

"Hello, Mr. Stark. My name is Gianna. I'm the cat foster coordinator for Little Whiskers."

"What can I do for you?" he asked.

"As you know, the rescue is closing down, and we're reaching out to each foster to make arrangements to have their foster animal transferred out of their care."

He sat up straight, his spine rigid and a vein pulsing to life in his forehead. "What? The rescue is closing?"

"Yes," she said. "There was an email from Rayna sent to the fosters on Thursday night. Did you not receive it?"

"Uh, I don't think so," he said. He'd gotten the email. He'd deleted it without opening it as soon as he'd seen Rayna's name.

"Oh shoot," Gianna said. "I assumed you'd seen the email. I apologize for sharing the news so abruptly."

"Why is the rescue closing?" He stood and paced his bedroom.

"Unfortunately, I don't know the details of why it's closing," Gianna said. "We have three rescues who are taking over the care of the Little Whiskers foster animals. Our database says you currently have one cat named Molly and her three kittens. Is that correct?"

"Yes," he said.

"Perfect. Would you be willing to transport them to their new foster, or do I need to arrange for a volunteer driver?"

"New foster?" he asked. "A new foster for Molly?"

"Yes," she said patiently. "Another rescue will take Molly and her babies in."

"No," he said. "That is not fucking happening."

The silence on the other end was deafening, and he took a deep breath. "I apologize."

"Right," she said, her tone now on the frosty side. "We are offering fosters the chance to adopt their foster animals free of charge. Am I to assume you would like to adopt Molly?"

"Yes," he said. "I'll adopt her."

"Perfect. I'll have an adoption contract sent to you in the next forty-eight hours. Please sign and return the document to us via email as soon as possible. Now, are you willing to keep the babies with Molly until they're weaned? Once they're weaned, we'll send them to a different rescue. If you want them moved immediately, we'll need to send Molly to the other rescue temporarily until her babies are weaned, and then you can take her back."

"I'm adopting the babies as well," he said.

More silence before she said, "I'm sorry?"

"I'm adopting Molly *and* her babies," he said.

"All three of the babies?" Gianna asked.

"Yes," he said. "Send me adoption contracts for Molly and the three babies."

"Okay," she said, sounding a little dazed. "We'll do that. Thank you, Mr. Stark. Have a good evening."

He ended the call and stared at Molly for three seconds before jogging from the bedroom to the den. He stared out the window, muttering a curse when Rayna's driveway was empty. He called her, pacing the den in large strides, snarling out another curse when it went straight to voicemail.

"Ms. Abrams, call me immediately," he snapped before shoving his phone into his pocket.

What the fuck was going on?

STARK STARED OUT HIS OFFICE WINDOW, SCANNING THE parking lot as his entire body nearly vibrated with anxiety and impatience. Where the fuck was Lucas?

He cursed himself for about the fiftieth time. He'd called and texted Rayna multiple times, but she hadn't read his texts or returned his calls. His plan to stare out the den window until Rayna returned so he could talk to her in her damn driveway, if necessary, had failed miserably.

He hadn't slept well all week, and the lack of sleep had finally caught up to him. He'd fallen asleep in the chair in the den, waking up early this morning to a kink in his neck and Molly standing on his chest.

He'd immediately checked out the window. Rayna's driveway was empty, although he could see fresh tire tracks in the snow, and he'd cursed so loudly that Molly had run from the den.

He rubbed at the kink in his neck as he craned to see the far end of the parking lot. Where the fuck was Lucas?

"Isaac!"

He spun around, staring in disbelief at Hollis, who was standing in his office. "Did you just call me Isaac?"

"Yes," she said. "Because you aren't responding to the seventeen Mr. Starks that I practically shouted at you."

He rubbed harder at his neck. "Sorry. I didn't... what's wrong?"

"Nothing is wrong," she said. "It's time for our usual Monday morning meeting."

He glanced at his watch. "Shit, sorry. Um... right. Do you know why Lucas isn't in the office yet?"

"He's here," Hollis said. "He was upstairs the last I saw him, but that was five minutes ago."

"Fuck," Stark snapped before heading toward the door. He brushed past Hollis. "Can we meet later? I have to talk to Lucas."

"Sure," she said.

He stepped into the hallway, his anxiety cranking up a notch when he saw Lucas walking into his office at the far end of the hallway. "Lucas!"

He nearly ran down the hallway, barging into Lucas's office without knocking. Holding a cup of coffee in one hand, Lucas arched an eyebrow at him as he sat in the chair behind his desk. "Hey. What's up?"

"We need to talk," Stark said. He shut the door and sat in the chair across from Lucas's desk. "Why is Rayna closing the rescue?"

Lucas's face shuttered closed immediately. "That isn't my story to share."

"A volunteer called me about moving Molly and her babies and said the rescue is closing. Rayna won't return my calls," Stark said.

Lucas sipped at his coffee, and Stark glared at him. "Tell me, or you're fired, Lucas."

Lucas laughed hard, and Stark flushed. "Okay, sorry, you won't be fired. But something is obviously wrong. Rayna sold me her property, and she's shutting down the rescue. I'm worried about her. Tell me what's going on."

"No," Lucas said. "If Rayna isn't returning your calls, then obviously, she doesn't want you in her business."

Feeling like his heart might explode from unfamiliar panic, Stark said, "I love her, Lucas."

Lucas paused with his cup of coffee near his mouth. "What?"

"I love Rayna. I fucked up, okay? I know I fucked up, and I did that thing I always do, which is push people away when they hurt me. I shouldn't have done that, and I regret it immensely, but I am also freaking the fuck out that something terrible has happened to the woman I love. But because I fucked up so bad, she won't talk to me, and I don't blame her for that, but Lucas, I am losing my mind with worry for her. Please tell me what's happening," Stark said.

"Holy shit. I think that's the most you've ever said to me at once," Lucas said. "And all of it was personal as fuck."

Stark stared at him, his chest tight and that panic still fluttering in his stomach.

"You really do love her, don't you?" Lucas said.

"Lucas, I am about five seconds away from taking a wrench to the gym shower and then demanding Sneaky Leaks send Rayna to fix it so that she can't keep avoiding me."

A grin crossed Lucas's face. "She'd probably get here and throw that wrench at your head."

"Probably," Stark agreed. "I'm still going to do it, though."

He stood, and Lucas shook his head. "Holy shit, sit down. I'll tell you what happened, so leave the gym showers alone. They're innocent."

He couldn't even manage a chuckle at Lucas's joke. Not when every fiber of his being was worried for Rayna.

He returned to his seat, giving Lucas an expectant look. Lucas sighed and said, "So, it turns out that the rescue's accountant, Mack, is a dirtbag piece of shit..."

CHAPTER 47

"Hey, kid." Doug sat next to her in the staff room at the Sneaky Leaks office.

Rayna forced herself to smile at him, to pretend everything was fine even though she had just lost her house, her rescue, and the man she loved. "Hi, Doug. What's up?"

"You look like shit," he said bluntly.

She made a face at him. "Keep talking that way, and I'll put in an HR complaint, Douglas."

He didn't laugh at her joke like he usually did. His face solemn, he put a warm hand on her forearm and squeezed. "Judy told me what happened, kiddo. I'm real sorry about the rescue and the house. I know how much both meant to you."

Oh great, now she was going to freaking cry in front of her boss. Could this day get any worse?

Her eyes watering like crazy, she blinked hard and looked away. "Thanks, Doug." Her throat tight, she said, "I signed the papers for the sale of the house and dropped them at the real estate agency before I started work this morning. That was... hard."

He gave her a sympathetic look. "You find Mack yet?"

"I didn't tell anyone in the rescue what Mack did. How do you know about it?" she asked sharply.

"Judy overheard a few people talking about it at the coffee shop this morning."

She sighed. "God, this fucking town. Nothing ever stays a secret, does it?"

"It sure doesn't." Doug squeezed her arm again. "Go home, kiddo. In fact, take the week off."

She shook her head. "I just took some vacation."

"You've got plenty left over," he said.

"I do, but that's not the point," she said. "I have two calls this afternoon and a full schedule this week."

"We've got it covered," he said. "Ranjit will cover your jobs today, and Judy and I will figure out the rest of the week."

"Doug, I can't do that to you," she said. "It isn't fair and -"

Doug shook his head. "I'm the boss, not you. Go home, take care of yourself, and call me when you're moving out your furniture. I'll bring my truck and our two oldest to help."

Now she did start to cry, the hot tears sliding down her cheeks in a heavy torrent she couldn't stop. Doug reached into his pocket and pulled out a worn but clean handkerchief. He handed it to her. "Wipe your face, kiddo, you're leaking a bit."

She took it from him with a small smile, scrubbing her face dry as Doug stood. "Go home, Rayna. That's a direct order, and you have to do what I say because I'm your damn boss."

She smiled again, reaching out to snag his hand and give it a tight squeeze. "Thank you, Doug."

"You're welcome, kid."

RAYNA COLLAPSED ON THE COUCH WITH A SOFT SIGH. BEA WAS snoring away on the far end, and she petted the beagle as she stared at the empty bookshelf on the far wall. She'd just finished packing everything on it, and a wave of depression overtook her as she stared at the boxes.

She didn't want to give in to her sorrow or her regret, but holy fuck, the temptation to just climb into a hot bath and cry her eyes out was overwhelming. She rested her head on the back of the couch, rubbing at her temples.

"Crying in the bathtub won't help, right, Bea?"

Bea snorted softly, her tail making quiet thumps against the couch before she started snoring again. Rayna stared at the ceiling, telling herself not to cry as her throat burned and the ache in her chest threatened to drown her in grief.

She'd come home from work and immediately started packing, knowing that if she even took a moment, like she was doing now, to allow herself to think about how badly she'd fucked up, she would be a useless puddle of grief and regret.

So, why the fuck are you just sitting here? Thinking about how you've lost everything you love isn't going to get shit done.

That was very true, but her sudden exhaustion kept her ass firmly on the couch as tears leaked down her cheeks again. She'd told herself repeatedly that if she kept her head down and worked her ass off, maybe even found a second job, she could have the rescue's debt paid off and start over in a few years. She could help animals again, and, yeah, maybe she wouldn't have a house that was all hers, but did it matter? It hurt like fuck, and losing her home made her feel like a fucking failure, but ultimately, what mattered was helping the animals. And she could start helping them a hell of a lot sooner if she put money toward starting up the rescue again rather than saving for a down payment on a house.

She scrubbed at her face and stared at the ceiling again.

The other rescues had agreed to take all of the animals from Little Whiskers into care, and she had a solid plan for how she would fix this screw up and start over. So, why was she so fucking sad? Why did it feel like she was suffocating under a grief so deep that she'd never find her way to happiness again?

Because you know that you will never be truly happy again? Not without Isaac.

Another harsh wave of bleak depression washed over her. She fished her phone out of the pocket of her hoodie, her thumbs hovering over the keyboard. She had blocked Isaac's number, not because she thought he would try to contact her, but so that it would stop her from texting or calling him.

She'd been so angry with him that night… no, that wasn't being honest with herself. She'd been so *hurt* by his casual talk of tearing down her house. She'd convinced herself that Isaac now understood how much the house meant to her, that he couldn't still possibly want her property. Not when they were…

Falling in love?

She took in a shuddering breath. Did Isaac love her? She'd hurt him terribly on Tuesday evening, she had seen it on his face, but his ability to so casually toss her from his life, to so quickly and cruelly announce that she was nothing but a mistake to him, had cut her to the damn bone.

You still love him.

She barked harsh laughter, making Bea snort herself awake, yawn, and give her a bleary look of disapproval before closing her eyes again.

"I do still love him, Bea. Even after everything that's happened, even after he tears this damn house down and builds a new one in its place, I'll still love him. How's that for ridiculous?"

Bea's reply was a low snore, and Rayna scratched Bea's

throat before saying, "What will I do when he finds someone else? When he falls in love and gets married and has babies?"

The chime of her doorbell app was her only answer. She brought up the video feed, hoping like hell it wasn't someone trying to drop off an animal. No doubt, everyone in town knew the rescue was closing and the reason why, but she wouldn't put it past people to still drop off animals at her doorstep. It was -

"Oh my God." Her breath caught in her throat, and she sat up straight, staring wildly at the screen. "What is he doing here?"

She stood, taking only a few steps toward the door before stopping and biting at her bottom lip. She couldn't answer the door. She would say something ridiculous like "I love you" if she answered the damn door.

She jumped about a foot when Isaac knocked hard on the door, and his voice, muffled but clear, said, "Rayna, I know you're in there. I stopped at Sneaky Leaks, and they told me you were home."

Feeling way too panicky, she pressed the microphone button and said, "I'm not home."

Isaac raised an eyebrow and stared directly into the doorbell camera. "Your car is in the driveway."

She slapped herself on the forehead before saying, "I'm out with Emma. She drove."

"No, you're not," he said.

She crept down the hallway toward the front door. She stared indecisively at the door handle before studying Isaac on her phone screen. God, he looked so good.

You should let him inside. He probably just wants one last hate fuck. Nothing wrong with that, right? We need one last time with him, one last chance to remember how he tastes, how he kisses, how he fucks... please, Rayna.

She reached for the door handle before pausing. What

was she doing? She didn't know why Isaac was here, but it wasn't to fuck her. And it certainly wasn't to tell her he loved her.

"Rayna, open the door."

It was so hard to resist him, but she said, "It's not a good time."

"We need to talk about the house sale," he said.

Her stomach clenched. "I signed the papers. You can talk to Kira - she has them."

"I know you did." He held up a brown envelope before sliding the papers out of it. "I stopped at Kira's office and asked her to give them to me."

Shock made her stagger toward the door when, with a determined look on his face, Isaac held up the papers and tore them in half.

CHAPTER 48

Rayna fumbled with the two locks and the deadbolt before yanking the door open. "Isaac, what are you doing?"

He immediately pushed his way into the house, the look on his face suggesting he thought she might slam the door in his face if he didn't move quickly.

"What did you do?" She grabbed the torn papers from him, a panicky part of her wondering if they would still be valid if she taped them together. She nearly ran into the kitchen, setting the papers on the table and grabbing some tape from the drawer.

"Rayna, stop, baby," Isaac said as she pushed the ripped pieces of paper together. He gently tugged the tape dispenser from her hand. "I'm not buying your house."

Despair crashed over her, and she sank into a kitchen chair, burying her face in her hands for a few seconds before taking a deep breath. She was fucked if Isaac didn't buy her house. She had to change his mind. She'd get on her knees and beg if she had to.

Without looking at him, she said, "Three twenty-five."

"What?" he said.

"I'll sell it to you for three twenty-five," she said.

"No. That isn't -"

She made herself meet his gaze. "Three hundred. I'll sell you the house for three hundred."

Despite her best effort, she was crying again for a record third time today. "You have to buy the house. Please, Isaac."

He crouched in front of her, his hand cupping her face, his thumb swiping at the tears. "Shit. Don't cry, baby. God, I am fucking this up *again*."

Before she could stop him, he scooped her out of her chair and sat in it, pulling her into his lap and wrapping his arms around her. He kissed her upper chest. His lips were cold, and he smelled like snow and pine trees.

"I'm so sorry, baby. So fucking sorry," he said.

"Please don't back out on the house sale," she said. "I know you're angry with me, but you want the property, I know you do, and -"

"I want *you*," he said.

For one crazy moment, she wondered if maybe she could offer him sex in return for buying the house. Before she could blurt out that insane statement, Isaac said, "Our fight was my fault, and I'm so sorry I hurt you, Rayna."

She stared wide-eyed at him, barely registering how his thumbs were busy wiping away the tears from her cheeks again.

"I'm sorry," he repeated. "When people hurt me, I push them away because being vulnerable is hard for me. You're one of only a few people who I've ever truly been myself with, and when I thought that you didn't see the real me, that you thought that I was only being nice to you because I wanted your property, it hurt me."

"I'm so sorry," she said.

He shook his head quickly. "No, it's... I know why you

thought that, and part of the reason I was upset and angry is because, deep down, I knew it had started that way. I was only nice to you because I thought it would get me what I wanted. Then I got to know you and realized how incredible you were, and I felt so fucking guilty. I know this doesn't make it right, but I regret it intensely, Rayna. I'm an asshole, but I'm working hard not to be one and to be a genuinely good person."

She cupped his face. "You *are* a genuinely good person, Isaac. Everything you've done for me and the rescue... it was stupid of me to pretend that it was only because you wanted something from me. In my heart, I knew that it wasn't that, but I... I guess I felt a little vulnerable myself."

"You're incredible, and I love you," Isaac said.

"You love me," she whispered, her body going still with shock.

"Yes," he said.

Her body trembling, her mind racing, Rayna said, "I love you, too."

The tenseness left his shoulders, and he gave her a relieved smile. "Thank fucking Christ."

"Please buy my house," she said.

He kissed her instead of answering. She returned his kiss eagerly, sliding her tongue into his mouth, his familiar taste almost making her cry again. She'd missed him so damn much in the last week, and suddenly the only thing that mattered to her was getting him into her bed. She needed to be with him again, craving that connection she had only with him.

"Come upstairs." She tried to slide off his lap, but he shook his head and tightened his arms around her.

"We need to talk, Rayna."

"I know, and we will," she said. "I need you, Isaac."

"I need you too, baby," he said, but instead of releasing

her, he studied the boxes sitting on the kitchen table. "I know what Mack did."

Embarrassment rocketed through her, but she wasn't surprised. The entire damn town probably knew at this point. Straightening her spine, she said, "Then you know why it's so important I sell the house. I fucked up, Isaac, and this is the only way to fix it."

"You didn't fuck up," he said fiercely. "Mack is the bad guy, Rayna."

She sighed, hating that Isaac knew how stupid she'd been. "You were right about it being a mistake to give Mack the control I did with the finances. I should never have done that. This is my fault. I am so stupid."

"No, you aren't," he said. "You trusted someone you believed was a friend, and he betrayed that trust, baby. You are far from stupid."

She smiled at him. "Thank you for saying that."

"I mean every word of it," he said. "On Tuesday night, when I talked about tearing the house down, I -"

"I overreacted," Rayna said. "I'm sorry."

He kissed her throat. "You don't need to apologize for anything. But let me say this, okay?"

She nodded, and he smoothed her hair back from her face before tracing his fingertip over a hole in her leggings. "I realized that day how much I loved you, and I was picturing a life with you. When I talked about tearing the house down, it was because I was thinking about the house we would build together. But obviously, that wasn't clear to you because I hadn't said a word to you about how I felt. I got caught up in the moment, I think."

"You want to build a house with me?"

"I want to build a life with you," he said.

She pressed her lips together, trying hard to stave off the tears. "Shit, I'm going to cry again."

"That's okay," he said.

She sniffed loudly. "I *never* cry, Isaac."

"That's fine. I can be the crier in our relationship."

She couldn't help but giggle at the solemnity of his face, and he grinned at her. "I love you, baby."

"I love you too," she said.

"What I said about us being a mistake wasn't true. I was hurt and upset, but I shouldn't have said that, and I'm sorry."

"It's okay," she said, resting her forehead against his. "I'm sorry that my insecurities reared their ugly heads. We're very different, and I'm worried that eventually, you'll grow to hate me for it."

"I won't," he said. "I love everything about you, Rayna Abrams." He placed his hand against her heart. "From your incredible kind heart to," he touched her leggings, "your complete inability to wear a pair of pants that doesn't have holes. I love it all, and yes, while we are different, we're the same when it comes to what counts the most."

"What's that?" she said softly.

"How much we love and respect each other," he said. "You are the most amazing woman I know, Rayna Abrams, and nothing would make me happier than to spend the rest of my life with you."

"Holy shit. Did you just ask me to marry you?"

He cocked his head. "Huh, I guess I did."

She stared wide-eyed at him, and he grinned. "Too soon to be talking marriage?"

"I… actually, no, I don't think so," she said.

Maybe she was acting completely insane, but nothing had ever felt more right to her than marrying Isaac Stark.

"Good. I'll buy you a ring tomorrow," he said.

Her head spinning, Rayna said, "Not to be a total downer, but I really would prefer if you bought my house instead. I'm not sure how much you know about what Mack did, but -"

"I know everything," he said. "I hadn't read your email, so I didn't know the rescue was closing until I got a call about sending Molly and the babies to a different rescue. When I couldn't get you to respond to my calls or texts, I -"

She grimaced. "I blocked your number. I'm sorry, but I did it because I didn't trust I wouldn't text you, and I was pretty sure you hated me."

He hugged her close. "It's okay. I was an asshole, and you should have blocked me for my behaviour. Anyway, I stalked Lucas at the office this morning and then threatened to fire him when he wouldn't tell me what was going on."

She laughed. "Are you serious?"

"Yes," he said. "When that didn't work, I told him I had fucked up and that I loved you, and that convinced him to tell me what happened. He told me how much debt Mack racked up and that you needed to pay it off quickly."

"If you know all of that, why did you rip up the papers I signed?" Rayna asked.

"Because you don't need to sell your house to pay off the rescue's debt," Isaac said. "I'll pay what is owed to the bank."

"No," she said immediately, pushing free of his lap before pacing the kitchen. "You are not paying the debt I owe because of my mistake, Isaac."

He stood and caught her hand, pulling her to a stop before pushing her against the counter and caging her in. He kissed up her throat before nuzzling along her jaw. "Please let me do this, baby."

"It's too much money," she said.

He leaned back, sliding his arms around her waist. "Rayna, I am a multimillionaire."

"I'm aware," she said. "But I'm not taking advantage of that or making you feel obligated to help."

"Baby, listen to me." He stared directly at her. "I am doing this because I love you and because what you do is incredible and so important. I have seen first-hand the difference you make in the lives of these animals and how often you help the less fortunate in this community care for their pets. Losing the rescue would be a massive blow to Harmony Falls. They need you, and I am in a position to help you help them. I am doing this for those reasons and not because I feel any obligation to help. I *want* to help you, baby. Let me."

"You're making it very difficult to say no," she said.

"Then don't," he grinned.

"Could we consider it a loan?" she asked. "If you buy the house for three-fifty, then I'll only have about fifty-eight grand left to pay. I could pay that back to you with interest in five years or so if I'm careful with my money and find a cheap place on the south side."

"One, it will be a cold day in hell before I let you live on the south side," Isaac said. "And two, paying off the rescue's debt is my wedding gift to you. We're getting married, remember? There's no way in hell you're living anywhere but right here with me."

"You really want to marry me?" she asked.

"I really do," he said.

She grinned at him. "Everyone will think we're crazy."

"Probably," he said. "I don't care. Do you?"

"No," she said.

He squeezed her gently. "Do you want to renovate the house before or after we get married?"

"You hate this house, Isaac," she said.

"I don't hate it," he said. "But I would very much like to have a shower that fits the both of us, a kitchen that doesn't look like the eighties threw up all over it, and a front door that can't be kicked in by a miniature donkey with a grudge."

Rayna laughed so hard that it woke up Bea in the living room. She wandered into the kitchen, sniffing the air and her tail wagging happily when she smelled Isaac's scent. She squeezed between them and sat on Isaac's feet, staring blindly up with a happy grin on her face.

"Hi, Bea," Isaac said before bending and giving her a few gentle pets. "I've missed you, sweetheart."

Rayna cupped Isaac's face, making him look at her. "You would be okay with living in this house with me?"

"Yes," he said. "I want you to be happy, baby. That's all that matters to me."

She hugged him hard, her heart overflowing with joy and a love so deep she felt nearly faint from it. "I love you so much, Isaac."

"I love you too," he said.

She leaned back so she could see his face. "I think we should tear the house down and build a new one."

He blinked at her. "Baby, no. You love this house."

"I do," she said, "but with everything that happened, I realized that as much as I love the house, it isn't the building that matters. What matters is how it made me feel to buy the property, to accomplish something I never thought possible, you know? So, tearing down the house doesn't feel like a defeat. It feels right to start fresh with you. This house did what it was meant to do - it gave me a sense of security and a feeling of home. Now, I'm ready to move on."

Isaac kissed her. "I just want you to be happy, Rayna."

"I know, and I want you to be happy. So, let's build a house together."

"Yeah?" The hopeful look on his face was adorable.

"Yeah," she said.

He hugged her tight. "Thank God. This house is way too small for all of us."

"All of us?" she said.

"We need the extra room for Molly and her babies."

"What?"

"Didn't I tell you? I'm officially adopting Molly and the boys," he said.

"All three of them?"

He nodded. "Yes. They're my babies, Rayna. If you're marrying me, I come with four cats. There is no negotiating on this."

She laughed. "I wouldn't dream of trying to convince you otherwise. I guess we're a four cat family now. Well," she glanced at Freddie, who walked into the kitchen with impeccable timing, "make that five."

"Pretty sure Freddie will be living with Hollis before the month is up," Isaac said with a grin.

She took a deep breath. "Isaac, are you sure - really sure - that you want to pay the rescue's debt? Because -"

"Ms. Abrams, if you ask me one more time if I'm sure about paying off the rescue's debt, I will take you upstairs and do very naughty things to you."

"How naughty? Be specific," she said.

He leaned down and whispered into her ear. Heat immediately pooled in her core, and she licked her lips before giving him a wicked grin. "Are you sure you want to pay off the rescue's debt?"

With a delicious growl, he picked her up and carried her toward the stairs. "You, Ms. Abrams, are trouble with a capital T."

She kissed him, then smiled sweetly at him. "I love you, Isaac."

"I love you, Rayna."

Keep reading for an excerpt from Wicked Harmony (Harmony Falls, Book Seven), coming soon!

WICKED HARMONY EXCERPT

(BOOK SEVEN, HARMONY FALLS)

"You really don't have to come inside to help." Nola smiled at Nix as he unlocked Crimson Tattoo's front door. "It's just a few scrapes."

"Your elbow is still bleeding." Nix pointed to the fresh blood that had bloomed through the tissue she held against it. "And you're unsteady on your feet. I don't want you falling again."

Because you're drunk, Nola! Because you indulged in the sin of alcohol. You're a wicked, wicked girl!

"I've had too much to drink," she informed Nix before clapping her hand over her mouth. Why was she admitting her sin to him?

A small grin crossed his face. "Yes, you have."

He guided her across the tattoo shop with a big hand at the small of her back. Her pulse immediately went haywire at even that innocent touch.

Or maybe it was because Nix was about to be in her bedroom.

Not your bedroom. Your apartment, Nola. Get your mind out of the gutter. Just because Nix is about to see your bed doesn't mean anything will happen.

Probably not, but she still had butterflies crashing and careening through her belly at the thought of Nix being near her bed. Already, her nipples were hardening, and her core was starting to throb with a familiar heavy ache.

She grimaced inwardly. Abraham had been right about her. She was a sexual deviant. What kind of woman became aroused just because a man touched her lower back? Or because in a few moments, he would be close enough to her bed that she could theoretically push him onto it, straddle his big body and –

Nola!

She realized with a jolt that Nix was steering her not toward the back of the shop but to his tattoo station. He stopped in front of the bed and patted it. "Sit down."

She ignored the pointless disappointment swooping in. Nothing would have happened even if Nix had gone upstairs to her bedroom – *apartment*. Nothing at all.

The tattoo bed was raised to its highest position. She was too drunk even to attempt to hop onto it, but before she could ask Nix to lower it, those big hands gripped her hips. He lifted her in an easy, smooth motion and set her on the bed.

She stared wide-eyed at him, her pulse immediately going haywire again. "Thank you. I was much too drunk to climb up there. I would have fallen on my face."

Another small smile that warmed her faster than the alcohol had. "You're welcome. Stay here, okay? Don't try to get off the bed."

"I won't," she said as he walked toward the back of the shop. "I'm too drunk! I would fall."

Nix disappeared into the bathroom and returned with

the first aid kit. He sat it on the bed beside her and rummaged through it as she said, "I had two margaritas, and Wren and I did three shots. Three! They were blue. I liked the margaritas, but I didn't like the shots. They tasted funny. I don't even know what they were. Did I tell you they were blue?"

"You did," he said as he tore open an antiseptic pad. "This will sting."

He tugged away the tissue and examined her elbow. Her skin was torn and raw but no longer bleeding freely. Nix wiped her elbow with the antiseptic pad, and she hissed out a breath at the stinging pain.

She instinctively tried to pull away, but Nix gripped her forearm and held her still as he wiped the scrape again. He made a soothing sound under his breath as she hissed out another breath.

"Almost done, little dove," he murmured.

Another flush of heat invaded her body, and the pain dimmed as she stared at Nix's tattooed hands. They were big and rough looking, but he was infinitely gentle as he used another antiseptic wipe to clean the scrape near her wrist and the one on the palm of her hand.

"I think we should bandage your elbow, but the other ones are okay as is," he said.

"All right."

Her pulse was still skittering along at a pace that was too fast, and she tried to ignore the growing ache in her pelvis as Nix taped a small white bandage to her elbow. He smoothed down the final piece of tape before smiling at her. "There. All better."

"I'm sorry," she said.

He frowned. "For what?"

"For going out to a bar and getting drunk, and then you had to come to my rescue," she said.

His scowl deepened. "One, you are allowed to get drunk, and two, I'm thankful I was there to rescue you."

The warmth washing over her now had nothing to do with the alcohol. She was sure of it. She leaned forward, giggling when she nearly fell off the bed and had to brace her hands on Nix's broad chest.

He cupped her arms lightly. "You okay?"

"I'm wonderful," she said. She tilted her head, studying Nix intently, her gaze lingering on his mouth. "You're so nice."

He didn't reply, and her gaze flickered to his gorgeous blue eyes. "You're so nice and so… pretty."

Her entire body aching with need for Nix, she slid her hands around the back of his neck and pressed her lips against his.

ABOUT THE AUTHOR

Elizabeth Kelly was born and raised in Ontario, Canada. She moved west as a teenager and now lives in Alberta with her husband and a menagerie of pets. She firmly believes that a person can survive solely on sushi and coffee, and only her husband's mad cooking skills prevents her from proving that theory.

For more information about Elizabeth, check out her website at

www.elizabethkelly.ca

- facebook.com/EKellyBooks
- instagram.com/elizabethkelly_author
- amazon.com/Elizabeth-Kelly/e/B00EOHZ0MS
- bookbub.com/authors/elizabeth-kelly
- bsky.app/profile/elizabethkelly.bsky.social
- threads.net/@elizabethkelly_author

ALSO BY ELIZABETH KELLY

Tempted Series

Tempted

Twice Tempted

Forever Tempted

Breathless

Tempted Trilogy (Books 1-3)

Red Moon Series

Red Moon

Red Moon Rising

Dark Moon

Alpha Moon

Pale Moon

The Recruit Series

The Recruit (Book One)

The Recruit (Book Two)

The Recruit (Book Three)

The Recruit (Book Four)

The Recruit (Book Five)

The Recruit (Book Six)

The Shifters Series

Willow and the Wolf (Book One)

Ava and the Bear (Book Two)

Katarina and the Bird (Book Three)

Porter's Mate (Book Four)

Bria and the Tiger (Book Five)

Rosalie Undone (Book Six)

The Dragon's Mate (Book Seven)

Rise of the Jaguar (Book Eight)

The Assassin and the Bear (Book Nine)

Elora and the Crow (Book Ten)

The Draax Series

Reign (Book One)

Rule (Book Two)

Rebel (Book Three)

Surrender (Book Four)

Survive (Book Five)

Salvation (Book Six)

Harmony Falls Series

Sweet Harmony (Book One)

Perfect Harmony (Book Two)

Forbidden Harmony (Book Three)

Redeeming Harmony (Book Four)

Absolute Harmony (Novella)

Beautiful Harmony (Book Five)

Reckless Harmony (Book Six)

Seasoned Romance Series

Bet Your Heart on Me (Book One)

Take a Chance on Me (Book Two)

Place Your Trust in Me (Book Three)

Individual Books

The Necessary Engagement

Amelia's Touch

The Rancher's Daughter

Healing Gabriel

The Contract

A Home for Lily

Saving Charlotte

Shameless

The Fairy Tales Collection

Broken

An Unlikely Seduction

Holiday Romance

The Christmas Wife

The Christmas Rescue

The Christmas Nanny

The Christmas Boss

Sordid Games